W9-CLP-425

The Avalon Chanter

A JEAN FAIRBAIRN/ALASDAIR CAMERON MYSTERY

THE AVALON CHANTER

LILLIAN STEWART CARL

FIVE STAR
A part of Gale, Cengage Learning

Detroit • New York • San Francisco • New Haven, Conn • Waterville, Maine • London

GALE
CENGAGE Learning

Five Star™ Publishing, a part of Cengage Learning, Inc.

This novel is a work of fiction. Names, characters, places, and incidents are either the product of the author's imagination, or, if real, used fictitiously.

LIBRARY OF CONGRESS CATALOGING-IN-PUBLICATION DATA

Carl, Lillian Stewart.
The Avalon Chanter / Lillian Stewart Carl.
pages cm
"A Jean Fairbairn/Alasdair Cameron mystery."
ISBN-13: 978-1-4328-2804-2 (hardcover)
ISBN-10: 1-4328-2804-5 (hardcover)
1. Murder—Investigation—Fiction. I. Title.
PS3603.A7523A95 2014
813'.6—dc23
2013031784

First Edition. First Printing: January 2014
Find us on Facebook– https://www.facebook.com/FiveStarCengage
Visit our website– http://www.gale.cengage.com/fivestar/
Contact Five Star™ Publishing at FiveStar@cengage.com

Printed in Mexico
1 2 3 4 5 6 7 18 17 16 15 14

For all the Scottish musicians who have enriched my life, starting—but not ending—with Brian McNeill, John Taylor, and Ed Miller.

"Do you play with a band?"

"I play with Gallowglass from time to time."

"They're good," Jean temporized . . .

—*The Secret Portrait,* book one of the Fairbairn/Cameron series.

Chapter One

Jean Fairbairn gazed past the edge of the map, at the gray-green hills gliding anonymously outside the car window. "Dang! I wanted to get there by the time she opens the grave!"

Her husband favored her with a glance from his keen blue eyes. "Professor Lauder and her chantry chapel, eh? What's she on about this time?"

"She hasn't said. I mean, the purpose of a press release is to tease and promote, not answer ques—What do you mean, *this time*? Are you thinking of that old court case?"

"The woman was on trial for murder."

"Well, yeah. Big scandal and all that, but she was acquitted. Even an old cop like you—former cop, not old, I mean—even a meticulous guardian of truth, justice, and the British way like you has to cut her some slack. It happened twenty years ago and she's been a model citizen ever since."

Alasdair slowed the car. His hint of a frown, Jean estimated, commented on their location, not their conversation.

"As for the chantry chapel and the mysterious tomb," she went on, "I think I know where Lauder's going, considering her earlier work and who her mother is. Or was, poor thing. *You* know how much I love a reality–mythology smackdown."

"That I do," he said with a sigh. "I'm wishing we knew where we were going just now." He peered over the weathered stone wall hemming in the strip of blacktop that passed for a road. The hills weren't so much rolling as twitching, with sudden screes and narrow gullies sprouting bristly shrubs, lumpy grass, and the occasional sheep. And the ruins of farms long gone.

Britain was one of the most thickly populated countries in the world, and yet there were areas you'd swear hadn't seen a human being since Eric Bloodaxe was a pup. "When I called Miranda I told her we were taking the scenic route," Jean rationalized. "Country roads, Roman and Dark Age sites, Flodden Field and the flower of Scotland a' wede awa'—I'll do some sort of 'Legends of the Scottish Borders' article for *Great Scot* if the chapel, grave, thing, turns out to be a bust."

"*If* it's a no-go? Not *when* it's a no-go?" He sped up again.

"Oh ye of little faith in the follies of an archaeologist on the trail of the next big discovery. You don't get funding opening the grave of some nameless peasant."

All he replied was, "Next time we're hiring a car with GPS. Or bringing along a guide."

"I could try again with the GPS on one of our phones, but . . ." Pulling out her handheld supplemental brain, Jean switched it on, saw that it was still registering a lack of contact with its own kind, and switched it off again. "Well, we can actually see the sun today, and since it's going down behind us, we're heading east. If we keep going, we'll either meet the main highway or tip over into the North Sea. Then we'll know where we are."

Alasdair muttered something about English roads—or perhaps about England, period.

"We're only a few miles into Northumbria, a long way north of Hadrian's Wall. It's barely England. You can stow the rampant lion of Scotland in the trunk of the car. The boot of the car."

Stopping at a crossroad, Alasdair considered both directions, said "Right!", and turned left.

Jean folded the map—no, not that way. She tried again. Not that way either. "GPS," she said, half to herself. "Global Positioning System. How about Green Pastures Strange? That has a Biblical sound to it."

"Gratuitous Passenger Speech," stated Alasdair.

"Yes, dear," she replied. Funny how his remark provoked an indulgent smile, not resentment. They were settling into married bliss, a little give, a little take, a trim of the sails here, a solid push-back there. They'd learned from their first marriages. They were determined to have learned from them.

Jean forced the map into a bulging rectangle, tossed it into the back seat, and once again inspected the hills outside the window. They were smoothing out, calming down. There lay an inhabited farm, and beyond it, rising from the horizon, the massive rotating blades of several wind turbines. In the tender light of the April afternoon they looked like alien spaceships.

"Well then. Ancroft. Civilization of a sort." Alasdair slowed to a decorous crawl through the photogenic village, but not slow enough for Jean to fully appreciate the church, part house of worship, part fortress.

"Historical physics," she wrote aloud. "Two independent entities can't occupy the same territory at the same time. Roman, Celt, Briton, and Pict, Angle, Saxon, and Dane, Scotsman and Englishman, sometimes fighting with, sometimes against each other. Dark and bloody ground, the Borders, like all borders, physical or metaphorical. Like the borderlands of perception where ghosts walk."

"Yes, dear," Alasdair said with an indulgent smile of his own.

Between a break in the hills glinted the sea. The road traced a tight curve, like a thread of interlace design on the Lindisfarne Gospels, and came to a stop at the wide tarmac of the A1. Traffic sped by, seeming almost as alien as the wind farm.

Jean winced as Alasdair swung into a right turn, across traffic—over a year in the UK and her instincts still defaulted to the American side of the road. Then she widened her eyes to watch for signs. Within moments she spotted one indicating the village of Beal and the causeway crossing to Lindisfarne, the Holy Island itself. Waiting cars were backed up almost to the highway.

"Here's me," said Alasdair as they drove on by, "worried about catching the tide. If it's low enough for driving the causeway to Lindisfarne, it's too low for the ferry crossing to Farnaby Island."

"Oh. You can tell I was born and raised a long way away from anything having tides. That never occurred to me."

"I'm hoping a Plan B's occurred to you. If the ferry's not this side of the crossing, there's no point our calling for it. We'll be sleeping the night on the mainland, and going across with Michael and Rebecca tomorrow."

"Dang," Jean said again. "First we miss the grand opening—not that your average dig is run with military precision—and now we might miss Hugh playing tonight."

"We're always hearing Hugh playing. The walls between our flat and his aren't so thick as all that."

"You know what I mean. Hugh in session with the students at the Gallowglass School, since he's this week's artist-in-residence. A shame Gallowglass the group never could get going again after the accident. You remember Hugh talking about that, how their van slid off the road in a snowstorm, crashed into a gully, and injured them all. Wat Lauder never really recovered, and their comeback was a bust."

"Losing him's what drove the last nail into their coffin. Intending no pun."

"Poor Maggie Lauder, losing her father, and her mother so ill. I hope she's found what she thinks she's found at the chapel, although I doubt if it's actually there to be found . . . Oh! There's the sign. Farnaby Island. Ferry."

Alasdair guided the car onto a strip of part blacktop, part gravel. It jounced over a railroad crossing and between several high shrubs to emerge in a parking area pitted with mud puddles. Six or eight vehicles sat there, no two pointed quite the same direction. Jean had eyes only for the small ferry just pulling into the dock. "Yes! Plan A is officially under way."

Wasting no words on the obvious, Alasdair parked the car, leaped out, opened the boot and extracted their bags. They were heading for the ferry, their suitcases jolting behind them, by the time it scraped against the pier's weedy stones.

Above the smooth lower flanks of the boat, a metal panel walled off a flat deck like a mini-aircraft carrier's. As the rumble of the engine changed tones, the rusty metal sheet creaked, gaped, and then with a mighty squeal and clang unfolded onto the dock.

You could only bring a vehicle to Farnaby Island with special permission. Jean had been anticipating stepping off a curb or two and not looking either way, let alone both, an indulgence that would be suicidal in Edinburgh.

But no one brought any vehicles away from Farnaby, either—not one rolled off the ferry. Several men and women surged over the now almost-horizontal metal panel, up the dock, and into the parking lot. Jean detected not a smile among them, even at finding their paths clear to happy hour at the closest pub. The sea was calm, only small waves tripping and falling onto the beach beyond the pier, so they couldn't be seasick. Or not all of them could be seasick, although one or two might have a stomach as delicate as that of Jean's friend and professional partner at *Great Scot,* Miranda Capaldi, who would get queasy in a hot tub.

Every one of the tight-lipped departing passengers held some sort of electronic slave—a smartphone, a laptop, a tablet. One man whose prison pallor, colorless hair, and sagging physique indicated long years of hunching over electronic slaves used his iPad to photograph Lindisfarne and its shadow, Farnaby. Jean sensed her brethren and sistren from the fourth estate.

So did Alasdair. "Your lot," he said from the corner of his mouth.

"Yep." She homed in on the photo-taking man, the only one standing still. "How did the opening of the tomb in the chantry chapel go? Any big revelations or no more than another medieval nobleperson?"

"Ah, Loony Lauder and her dog and pony show, with no dogs and no ponies. No worms, come to that."

"The grave was empty?"

"Who's to know? She cancelled the entire do. Instead, she sat us all down in the church and tried to buy us off with tea, scones, and a lecture on some Dark Age cavalry bloke. Dead loss, save for the scones." His blunt fingertips tapped the screen. "This lot, in church? Surprised we weren't struck by lightning."

"Some Dark Age cavalry bloke? As in, Arthur, King of the Britons? You know, Camelot. Lancelot. Guinevere. Not that any of them actually existed, although according to Professor Lauder's mother . . ."

"Jean!" Alasdair called. "The ferry's away!"

"Farnaby," said the reporter. "Loony Lauder. Better you than me, luv. Much better." He strolled toward the parked cars, so focused on his tablet Jean figured he only knew she was female from her voice.

She hustled on down to the dock, telling herself the man must work for a tabloid. He was probably texting the office in a plea not for hazard but for boredom pay—no dead body and any living ones having nothing to do with celebrities such as, say, Princess Kate, as many Americans called her. But if not for the honorary "Duchess of Cambridge," her name would be Princess William, counterintuitive as that sounded. A princess by marriage.

Past a battered, out-of-style phone booth—a direct connection to ferry HQ on the island, Jean suspected—and a garishly red life preserver like a huge cherry, well, Life Saver, and she reached the end of the metal gangplank. Alasdair left their bags standing on the deck of the boat and stepped back to seize her elbow and steady her up the slope of the surface.

"Thanks," she said, the final sibilant concealed by the squeal of the rising gangplank.

Chapter Two

The gangplank thudded home. Engines roared. A tall muscular young man wearing the universal uniform of T-shirt, jacket, and jeans leaped from empty dock to deserted deck. He coiled the mooring ropes, then stepped forward, hand extended. "That'll be five pound each."

Alasdair reached into his pocket before Jean could bring her mini-backpack around. "Locals ride for free, do they?" he asked.

"We've got us a subsidy from Westminster, being the only public access to the island." The man crammed the bills into a pocket, adding with a grin so broad every white tooth gleamed with good humor, "Never you mind, Jock, you'll get your five quid worth of scenery."

Alasdair's neutral expression crackled with frost. So close to the Border, and he was already hearing Scots jokes.

An older, rather shrunken version of the young man emerged from a superstructure that appeared to be bridge, crew quarters, and passenger waiting room all in one. With his jacket and peaked cap, to say nothing of the gray stubble on the lower half of his weather-beaten face, he had to be both captain and father.

"Mind your manners, lad," he said, and to Jean and Alasdair, "I'm Clyde Eccleston. This here's my boy, Lance. His sense of humor's a bit over the top."

"Lance" was short for Lancelot, Jean assumed, an appropriate name for someone probably born and bred in sight of Bamburgh Castle.

Lance's crest fell, if only slightly. "Sorry. No offense."

"None taken," lied Alasdair, and, thawing, "I'm Alasdair Cameron."

"Jean Fairbairn. We were supposed to attend Professor Lauder's press conference and . . ." She stopped before she said, *dog and pony show,* although in academia dogs and ponies were likely to perform amazing tricks. "Well, I hear she called it off."

"She opened the grave and found nothing?" asked Alasdair.

"No," Eccleston Senior replied before Jean could. "She cancelled the do before it started. No reason I could see, but then, wasn't my party, was it? I'm only ever carting folk back and forth, music students, twitchers after counting their birds, wildfowlers after shooting them, divers, even the odd tourist, though never so many as go out to Lindisfarne."

"I've been to Lindisfarne a couple of times, but never to Farnaby." She didn't add that if Maggie Lauder's hypothesis held up, Clyde and Lance could see a surge in business. Although what Jean often saw were metaphorical castles in the air crashing down, undermined by reality. She'd been responsible for more than a little undermining herself.

Sidling back toward his command center, Clyde added over his shoulder, "The Lauder clan's good folk, never mind being newcomers to Farnaby. Wat and Elaine came in as newlyweds, fifty years ago. Maggie was born here, bonniest lass you've ever seen, and now—forty if she's a day."

"That clock keeps right on ticking," Jean murmured.

"They've all gone traveling, mind you, but they've always come back. Somewhat peculiar, the womenfolk are, poking about things all dead and gone. But the music's good, and who isn't peculiar, in their own way?"

Jean grinned at that and glanced at Alasdair, who shrugged agreement. Clyde seemed happy to cut Maggie Lauder slack. The reporter in the car park and his colleagues would not.

The boat lurched, hitting the slow swell of the sea. Simultaneously Alasdair and Jean spun toward and down onto a bench beside the railing. Lance, unsurprisingly much more sure of foot, ambled away across the expanse of deck. His tanned face and blue eyes beneath a mane of flaxen hair made him look like a throwback to his Viking forebears. All he needed was a horned helmet and berserker's sword.

"The Ecclestons have likely lived on Farnaby for generations," Alasdair said.

"No surprise Clyde called the Lauders newcomers."

"Newcomers or not, they've all had fine careers, by the sounds of it."

Lance avoided a rusty, muddy puddle only to step in proof that the ferry also transported cows and sheep. Alasdair's eyes crinkled in mingled sympathy and entertainment.

"Oh yeah," Jean said. "Wat and Gallowglass, Elaine and her literary studies, and now Maggie, digging all over the UK. She was part of the team at the recent Winchester Cathedral excavation, for example, and has worked off and on at Vindolanda on Hadrian's Wall. She's worked on digs in other countries, too."

"Ambitious, is she?"

"Ambitious and smart—she's worked hard to get a good academic reputation to complement the model citizen bit."

"You've met her, then."

"At the odd conference, where we talked about forensics, historiography, archaeology—research stuff, not our own backgrounds. Which is understandable. I may have an academic scandal in my past, but a murder trial is another order of magnitude. She was accused of killing her boyfriend, wasn't she?"

"Bagging the unfaithful lover's a traditional sport. The tabloid lot will have another go at her now. Cancelling her press conference will not be improving their temper."

"No, it won't," agreed Jean. "She's shot herself in the foot. In the column inches. Peculiar, like Clyde said."

"Scholars can be a bit peculiar," Alasdair said with a thin smile—*just teasing.* "Has she ever been married?"

"Only to her work, so far as I know, hence the good academic reputation."

"You can be having the one with the other, surely."

"Not necessarily." Jean's first husband had magnanimously allowed her to get her doctorate because the university would pay her more if she had "Ph.D." behind her name. "Who *did* kill Maggie's boyfriend, way back when? Or is it a cold case?"

"Now, now, earlier the day you were after letting bygones be bygones."

"I'm curious. As well as peculiar."

This time he didn't stop with a thin smile but unleashed a full grin. "I'm thinking a chap was eventually sent down for the crime—bagging the rival's a tradition as well—but it all played out in Cambridge, mind you, where Maggie attended university, nowhere near my patch in Inverness. I was no more than a constable, then. An ambitious one."

"Ah, a man in uniform," Jean said with an exaggerated sigh. "Smart in both meanings of the word."

Lance strolled back by, whistling the old folk tune "Maggie Lauder." *Wha wadna be in love wi' bonnie Maggie Lauder?*

Funny how he brought a sarcastic tone to a simple whistle. But then, Jean knew the words. *For I'm a piper to my trade; My name is Rob the Ranter: The lasses loup as they were daft, When I blaw up my chanter* . . . It said something about her louping, or leaping, brain cells that she always read a double meaning into the story of Maggie, dancing madly as the piper plied his chanter—the clarinet-like part of the bagpipes on which the tune was actually played. The business end, so to speak.

"I'm sure the poor woman's heard every possible joke about

her name," she told Alasdair. "A shame her parents couldn't resist. Wat wasn't even a piper, but played the fiddle and guitar like Hugh. I wasn't really familiar with Gallowglass until last year . . ." She let the sentence die away, remembering the circumstances under which she'd gotten to know Gallowglass.

"You've made up for lost time." Alasdair no doubt visualized the length of her trad-music playlist. "Her mum's an academic as well? Your lot again?"

Jean had been a history professor a lot longer than she'd been a journalist. "Elaine was an academic, yes, before she—I hate to say, lost her mind. You don't lose your mind the way you misplace an umbrella. Succumbed to dementia. Miranda says Maggie came back to Farnaby to care first for her father and then for her mother."

"Pity. Still, Maggie looks to have made a discovery. A grand coincidence, that. Or is it?"

Alasdair's tone was so freighted with skepticism Jean elbowed him lightly in the ribs, in companionship rather than criticism. She might be a detective by marriage, but skepticism was a characteristic of both their former lives. "Spoken like a cop."

Alasdair nodded acknowledgment.

"The guy I talked to said she tried to buy the reporters off with a lecture on King Arthur. No surprise there, not with her mother's work on Guinevere and her own on the Anglo-Saxon invasions."

"He'd rather have had her open Arthur's grave, I reckon. A skeleton in armor, holding a sign reading, 'Merlin was here.' If that's where you're thinking she's going."

"Don't laugh. Elaine's not the only scholar to maintain Merlin actually existed. So yeah, I think that's where she's going. There's no better way to get the British press and academia both to sit up and take notice than produce some relic of Arthur. You remember all the hysteria in ninety-eight, over an inscription from Cornwall with the close-but-no-cigar name of Artognou."

"No, I'm not remembering that at all. At the time I was right distracted by more contemporary matters."

"Well, yeah, you were."

"As for Professor Lauder's motives," Alasdair counseled, "and what's gone wrong with her plans, we'll be learning in due course."

"But speculating without evidence is one of my favorite hobbies, right up there with jumping to conclusions."

"That it is."

Not that she had any evidence to speculate with right now. Had Maggie gone out on an inferential limb, only to find some source that snapped it off at the last minute? She could have saved more face—and less media criticism—by opening an empty grave than by turning uncooperative.

Waves dashed against the sides of the boat and a fine spray of sea water flecked Jean's glasses. Through them she saw Lindisfarne seeming to rise and fall on the horizon, a low green land spiked at one end with the rooftops of the village, the broken arches of the medieval priory, and the small but pronounced protuberance of the castle.

Farnaby Priory was the stepsister of the famous monastery on Lindisfarne, first established by the Irish Saint Aidan and Anglo-Saxon King Oswald in the seventh century. Farnaby had been a nunnery, women only, rather than a mixed house in Celtic fashion like the one at nearby Coldingham, ruled by an abbess. But that sort of equality and siblinghood had been stamped out by the Roman church early on, even before Viking sails appeared on the horizon and Viking warriors stamped out more than religious custom. By the time William the Conqueror's Norman knights moved into the area in the eleventh century, little was left of the original priories.

Beyond Lindisfarne, the smaller and yet taller profile of Farnaby materialized from sun-shimmer on the sea, little more than a mirage, a floating island momentarily tethered near the shore of Northumbria. If not for the low rays of the westering sun picking out a rocky headland above a frill of white breakers, it would be invisible.

Like mythic Avalon, Jean thought, where grieving queens carried the mortally wounded Arthur—Wat had been mortally wounded when he came home to Farnaby . . .

An electronic deedle broke into Jean's reverie. A ringtone, but not hers or Alasdair's.

At the far railing, Lance pulled a cell phone from his pocket. "I'm working now, I can't . . . Yeh, last run of the day . . . Likely so, aye, not much else doing of an evening . . . I'll buy my own pints, thanks just the same . . . See you there, then . . . Must run, bye." He stabbed at the phone and jammed it into his pocket with a scowl of frustration.

Hmm, Jean thought. What red-blooded young Brit would reject a mate's offer of a pint?

The breeze was salt-fresh, slightly fishy, slightly oily, and chilly enough that Jean huddled both into her coat and closer to Alasdair. "There's a cabin," he said, nodding toward the superstructure.

"Yeah, and I bet the diesel fumes are even worse in there. I'll make do with the open air, thanks."

White gulls spiraled overhead, their harsh cries mingling with the softer, more poignant ones of oystercatchers—Jean looked around to see several black-and-white birds skimming the waves, probably heading toward the nearest beach, bed, and board. She glanced at her watch. "Two minutes shy of six."

"Going on for tea time, then."

"No wonder I'm getting hungry. Our B and B doesn't do dinner. I bet the pub is open, though."

"I'm hoping they're properly provisioned. Musicians and reporters, they all march on their stomachs."

So do ferrymen, Jean thought, eyeing Lance's stiff back as he stood with arms braced on the railing. "With the press conference and the concert at the music school Saturday night, the village is probably jumping."

The boat bucked and wallowed and Jean fell silent, not because her stomach shimmied rather than marched, but because Lance was right about getting five pounds' worth of scenery.

Behind the boat the sun melted ever nearer to the green horizon. To their right Bamburgh Castle rose from its crag, appearing more movie set than stones and mortar. But it was no set, no castle in the air. Fortifications had risen from that hillock for two thousand years and more. No surprise some traditions named it as the home of Lancelot, knight of the Round Table and Guinevere's adulterous lover.

Bamburgh. The music school on Farnaby. Weapons and musical instruments, both very early inventions of mankind. So was adultery, but that could only have been invented—or recognized—after the creation of marriage.

Alasdair cocked his head to the side, eyeing the castle not as a tourist but as the head of Scotland's Protect and Survive. She wasn't sure what his English opposite number would be, not quite English Heritage—they were into conservation more than security, whereas P and S had their priorities the other way around. That's why they'd hired a retired policeman to run their show. "Is English Heritage in charge of Farnaby Priory? I mean, they're in charge of Lindisfarne Priory, right? What if Maggie didn't fill out some sort of form or get whatever permission she needed to open a tomb?"

"The priory's listed as privately owned, likely by Maggie herself. Still, it's a listed building, so she's needing permissions before digging, aye. Not getting them seems right careless for someone with that good academic reputation." Alasdair's head swiveled, following the course of a smallish boat cutting across the path of the ferry, the glassy sea churned to froth in its wake.

Farnaby Island had resolved itself from the glare and now appeared as a long, tapering wedge of charcoal-gray rock topped with green fields. The small boat throttled back and disappeared around the headland. Seabirds blossomed from the cliff face like feathered fireworks, squawking and flapping. Some skimmed past the ferry, others spiraled upward past a small tower that could be anything from a Roman signal station to a World War II gun emplacement.

Right now Jean pondered the boat. Simple physics told her that a sleek, aerodynamic number like that would be fast. Knowledge of the world told her that one painted dark blue and marked with an insignia belonged to the authorities. "Police boat?"

Lance hulked over them, briskly coiling a rope. "That's P.C. Crawford from Bamburgh village. Must've been in a right hurry to come straight across instead of round by the road and then the ferry."

"Likely he knew he'd missed the ferry," suggested Alasdair, "being a local lad and all, and his business couldn't wait till tomorrow."

"Not much call for police on Farnaby," Lance said half to himself. His features didn't quite crease into a frown, but the frown was imminent in its tightened lines. He added, "Loony Lauder," as though that explained everything, and headed for the gangway.

Funny, even the local people called Maggie loony. What was she up to? "Curiouser and curiouser," Jean murmured to Alasdair, who nodded in agreement.

Chapter Three

The ferry followed the police boat around the headland and into a bay that was little more than a shallow scoop lined with one curving street and its assorted buildings. Farnaby St. Mary.

Like the ancient settlers of Bamburgh building their fortress on a defensive promontory, the seventh-century founders of Farnaby Priory had chosen their ground wisely, setting their thatched huts into the concave south face of the island where they would be protected by rising land on the north and east. Not that Jean's searching eye could see the priory from the harbor. It must be concealed by the village, its broken walls not as tall as those on Lindisfarne.

The police boat disappeared into a relatively modern harbor, passing between slab-sided concrete and boulder breakwaters that looked like the jaws of a huge pair of pliers. By standing up, Jean could see the tops of several other boats tucked away inside, of the fishing and sailing variety. Two bright red kayaks rested atop the breakwater amid odds and ends of ropes, nets, boxes, and mysterious items her landlubber eyes couldn't identify.

The ferry angled straight for the beach, slowed, and with a bump that caused Jean to sit back down again, Alasdair's hand on her arm, came to a halt against a concrete ramp. The gangplank screeched and landed with a thud. Lance galloped down it and threw a coil of rope over a waiting post.

"So what do the villagers do if they need to get off the island while the tide is out?" Jean asked.

"Take a small boat to the back side of Lindisfarne or some other place along the coast," answered Alasdair. "And you could be landing a small boat on one of its beaches even at low tide."

"Ah." Mysterious were the ways of sea-going peoples. Jean and Alasdair gathered up their things and, with a wave at Clyde in his command center, regained terra firma. She threw a thank-you at Lance as they passed.

He made no response. He knotted the rope so slowly his movements seemed almost sensual, his fingertips gliding over the nylon coils. Jean followed the direction of his gaze to see an elderly Land Rover coming to a halt at the top of the ramp. From it stepped a young woman. On her slender, graceful body, the muddy wellie boots, mud-splashed camouflage pants, and mud-spattered denim jacket looked like Paris couture. What had probably started the day as a sleek chin-length haircut was now a russet tousle. She stood, legs apart, hands on her hips, head thrown back, her delicate features turned toward a point far beyond the island.

Jean glanced around and saw nothing more than the sun continuing to sink, as the sun tended to do late in the afternoon. It touched a layer of clouds, spilling a wash of pink and peach over them. "Now there's a five-pound view."

Alasdair abandoned his scrutiny of the young woman, glanced at the clouds as though inspecting them for Claude Monet's signature, said, "Aye, lovely that," and, "Who's the girl?"

"Not a clue. If she's waiting for us, we're about to find out."

Yep. The—well, let him call her a girl; she could hardly be older than twenty—the vision looked down at them. The words of a song of Wat Lauder's era came to Jean, about roses in a garden bowing and asking a young woman's pardon. But no. This young woman's blooming complexion was dusted with gray, the lush pink lips were braced tautly, and the startlingly blue eyes were hooded with caution.

Her polite smile touched only her lips. In a thankfully mild variation of the adenoidal screech young women used for voices these days, she asked, "Ms. Fairbairn? Mr. Cameron? Ms. Capaldi called and said you were running late."

Good thing Jean had confessed to Miranda, who captained the *Great Scot* ship, that they'd wandered off-schedule. "Guilty as charged," she replied, and then winced, telling her unruly subconscious to get off the matter of Maggie's scandal, already.

The smile acknowledged no double meanings. "I'm Tara Hogg. I'll run you to your B and B."

"Professor Lauder's graduate student?" Jean hazarded. "Research assistant?"

"Her daughter."

Daughter? Maggie Lauder had a daughter? Jean's glance at Alasdair noted the scrunch of his calculating eye. So much for tiptoeing around Maggie's past. Tara was the right age to date from the episode of the murdered boyfriend. Lover, rather. But for a last name she bore the screamingly inappropriate—to her appearance, not the locale—Hogg.

Maggie's daughter, blood-related to the peculiar Lauder clan. No wonder she watched the sinking sun signal the end of a stressful day.

A movement in the corner of Jean's eye resolved itself into Clyde stepping down the gangplank of the ferry and regarding his son, who still lingered over the knotted rope, with a look of something between impatience and disgust. Not that Lance saw him. He was still focused on Tara. It was hardly the first time a strapping young warrior had been reduced to jelly by a beautiful woman.

Jean managed to shape her smile of amusement into one that mirrored Tara's courtesy. "Thank you. We were hoping to go straight out to the priory and the excavation."

"Sorry," said Tara, "but there's a problem with that."

By this time Jean was almost dancing with curiosity—not least because she detected an American accent in the young woman's voice. Beside her, Alasdair's alert stance mimicked that of a cat at a mouse hole. He asked, "A problem with the excavation, or with us seeing it?"

"We could give you a tour tomorrow. It's almost sunset . . ."

"Sunset's at half-past seven. It's hardly half-past six."

"Mags wants me to bring P.C. Crawford out."

Alasdair went inexorably on, "Miss Capaldi wouldn't have bothered making our excuses if Professor Lauder weren't expecting us for the entire weekend, as distinct from the day-trippers who came only for the press conference."

Tara opened her mouth and shut it again. She turned away, presenting them with her shoulder.

An American accent, definitely. Had Maggie given Tara up for adoption, way back when? And now . . . Jean almost felt sorry for her. Still, she bumped Alasdair's chest with her own shoulder: *Thanks.* His bland expression was mitigated by the merest lift of a brow-end and the slightest tuck of a mouth-corner: *Once a cop, always a cop.*

The cop on active duty emerged from the enclosure of the harbor, duly wearing a lime-yellow reflective jacket over his uniform and a billed cap with a checkerboard band. Tara beckoned and took a couple of steps toward him.

So did Alasdair, extending his hand in the tall, lanky man's direction. "Alasdair Cameron. Detective Chief Inspector, Northern Constabulary, retired. Currently head of Protect and Survive, Edinburgh. My wife, Jean Fairbairn of *Great Scot.*"

"Ah." Crawford stopped dead. His narrow, nearly ascetic face, polished red by the wind from the North Sea, reminded Jean of someone, but she couldn't think of whom. He shook Alasdair's hand as cautiously as though he expected to find a buzzer concealed in the palm. "P.C. Edwin Crawford. Bamburgh. Sir."

"Now then, Constable." Alasdair might be four inches shorter and more or less the same age, but he was definitely In Charge. "What is it about this problem with the grave that's requiring the police? Can I be of assistance, in either of my capacities?"

Crawford said, "Ah."

"She's a reporter," murmured Tara, ducking her head toward Jean.

"I do history and travel articles, not . . ." Go ahead, say it, she told herself. ". . . scandals and gossip. I'm a former history professor myself, a colleague of Professor Lauder's."

Crawford's features seemed to narrow even further, like the gap between a closing door and its frame.

"Your luggage," Tara said, her voice positively deflated. "You need to take it to the B and B."

"No problem." Jean turned toward the father-and-son team of Ecclestons, who had stopped even pretending to work and were watching the scene before them like spectators at a rugby match. Flipping her backpack around, she reached inside. "Lance, could you please take our bags to the Angler's Rest B and B? They told me it's a few steps from the ferry terminal. It doesn't look like anything in Farnaby St. Mary is more than a few steps from the ferry terminal."

Lance blinked like someone suddenly waked up. "Angler's Rest?"

"That's The Angle's Rest," Clyde said. "Angles, Saxons, that lot. The Angles landed here, set themselves up a beachhead, way back when."

"Oh," said Jean. Well, she supposed people fished here, too. No matter. She held out a five-pound note. "For your trouble."

"Ta." Lance's stroll up the ramp was too stiff to be casual. He accepted the bill and seized the handles of the two small suitcases. "The B and B's just along here."

"Thank you," Alasdair told him.

Lance took advantage of his proximity to Tara to lean in close. "Proper little bitch, aren't you now?"

Well, Jean thought, that was hardly a sweet nothing.

"Stuff it where the sun don't shine," Tara hissed back.

Alasdair, at his most expressionless, opened the back door of the Land Rover and Jean climbed in before the parade passed her by.

With an unintelligible mutter under her breath, Tara plucked a smartphone from her pocket. She swiftly keyed in a text as she slipped behind the wheel, no doubt warning Maggie about the two stubbornly inquisitive, if hardly unexpected, new arrivals.

Crawford removed his hat and claimed the front passenger seat—riding shotgun, an American would say. His face was so utterly blank, Jean was impressed. Very few people could do a great stone face as effectively as Alasdair could. Unless Crawford's blank face indicated no one home behind it. That might explain why a man who had to be over forty still served as the constable in a small seaside community. Although, to be fair, he might be content where he was, with no ambitions to move up the ladder. Unlike Alasdair, who'd climbed the ladder so quickly he came down with a nosebleed.

She shoved a couple of electronic umbilical cords and a muddy trowel out of her way. The nylon of the seat was spattered with mud, but every now and then you had to sacrifice your clothes for a story. She was glancing around to see what was piled in the back of the vehicle—more digging implements, folders of computer printouts, a bin holding mud-caked items of the pottery shard type—when Alasdair clambered into the other side.

Surreptitiously Jean offered him the flat of her hand. *We're in!*

Kudos to the team! Instead of returning a high five, though, Alasdair shot her a stern look. She retracted her hand and tried a sheepish shrug instead. No, he didn't like pulling rank, not when his purpose for doing so was still undefined.

Tara fired up the engine and took off, flinging Jean against the seat back.

Chapter Four

Reddish stone, gray stone, and lumpy white pebbledash facades whizzed by the window. A pub, *The Queen's Arms* written in Gothic script on its signboard. A cobblestoned alley. A Co-op grocery store, where a woman with a shopping bag stepped off the curb, then stepped quickly back as they sped past. A tea room. The smell of baking bread and frying potatoes filtered into the musty interior of the Land Rover and Jean's stomach emitted a forlorn growl.

Then they were screeching around a hairpin turn, climbing a hill behind the village. Jean grabbed for the handle above the window. The back of Crawford's head, covered with the brown stubble of a military-style cut, held perfectly steady.

A strain of pipe music, bravado in sound waves, rose and fell. A kilted man with hair so black it glistened even in the diffused light played a set of Great Highland bagpipes in front of a long, low building. Two teenagers held chanters to their lips and presumably followed along.

The village church was a small beige-walled and tile-roofed structure not much bigger than the vicar's house next door, and displayed no more than a stub for a steeple. Both probably dated to mid-Victorian times, but seemed downright modern compared to . . .

Yes. Beyond a cemetery surrounded by a low stone wall lay Farnaby Priory. When the vehicle skidded to a stop, Jean was ready. She flung open her door, leaped out, and tried to check out as much as possible before any fecal matter started hitting any fans.

Like Lindisfarne, the surviving ruins of Farnaby Priory had been built in the early Middle Ages of red and silvery gray sandstone, now sculpted by time and weather into flowing patterns that seemed more Art Nouveau than Norman French. Unlike Lindisfarne, Farnaby's remains were far from dramatic. A rectangle of roofless walls marked the church, one of them barely tall enough to retain a row of round-headed windows behind a columned arcade. What had once been the cloister was filled by a walled garden, gravel paths laid out between scraggly beds dotted with flowers and thick with weeds such as thistles and stinging nettles. A couple of rabbits raced across a shaggy plot of grass and into the shrubbery.

The other buildings—refectory, prioress's hall, kitchens, dormitory—were marked by little more than the footings of the original walls. Several archaeological test trenches cut across grassy areas and over walls, their slumping sides softened by opportunistic plants. Maggie Lauder's focus had moved on.

Alasdair stepped up beside her and Jean pointed to the one roof still intact, its mossy slates peeking over the windowed wall. "There's the chapel."

"I was thinking chapels were generally on the east. That's on the north."

"Depends on the lay of the land and the whims of the builders. Maggie's trying to prove the chapel has at least an Anglo-Saxon substructure. If she's trying to make an Arthurian connection, then she's hoping the chapel dates back even further, to the original Celtic priory. It might. The records don't have nearly as much about Farnaby as they do about Lindisfarne."

"Are the records saying anything at all?"

"There are legends of an early prioress with magical powers, but I bet those are typical Celtic saint stories. All we know for sure is that the chapel isn't a Lady Chapel—why should it be, the whole priory is dedicated to St. Mary—but a chantry chapel. A chapel endowed by somebody wealthy in honor of a dead relative or comrade or even himself, including funds to pay a cantarist, a priest, to man it."

"A cantarist? Like the cantor in a Jewish service?"

"Yep. The root's from the Latin for 'sing', *cantare* or something like that, although I guess chantry priests didn't always sing or chant. The point was to offer prayers to decrease the time the honored person's soul spent in purgatory, and to keep on offering the prayers forever. Forever arrived at the Reformation, though. I guess purgatory is pretty crowded these days."

With eerie cries, several oystercatchers spiraled down into the nearby cemetery and settled into a circle on the grass. Next to them rose a monument in polished granite, so new the emblem of a fiddle and bow was still sharply incised, as were the dates beneath. *Walter "Wat" Lauder.* He had barely achieved his allotted three score years and ten.

The other half of the monument displayed a carved scroll, the words *Elaine Peveril Lauder,* and a birth date two years before Wat's. The blank patch of granite yet to be engraved reminded Jean of an open grave.

"Jean," Alasdair said. "We're away."

She looked around to see Tara and Crawford walking toward the priory. A human figure sat on a broken column drum in the shadow of the tallest wall. A tentative shadow, the sun now filtered by cloud and casting not the golden light of early evening but a thin gilded gleam.

Loony Lauder herself. Stepping lively, Jean and Alasdair caught up with the others at the gap in the wall that marked the church's western door.

Maggie sat in the attitude of Rodin's famous statue *The*

Thinker, back curved, elbows braced on thighs, chin set on fist. Her boots, camouflage pants, and jacket resembled Tara's. Her body, more abundant in hips and chest, did not. Neither did her face when she looked up.

Jean deleted her memory of precise features. The pale and puffy face before her resembled that of a corpse pulled from deep water. Maggie's blue eyes, which had once sparkled with intellectual inquiry, now seemed reclusive and dull. Her brown hair, which had once been cut in a short, professional style, was now long, purplish-red, and tied in a straggling bun atop her head.

Mid-life crisis, Jean told herself. Go figure. She and Alasdair had each endured a mid-life crisis and ended up with each other. The jury was still out on what Maggie would end up with.

"Thank you for coming, Edwin. Ms. Fairbairn, good to see you again. I assume this is Mr. Cameron?" Maggie's voice originated in her diaphragm rather than in her sinus cavities like Tara's, but still it squealed with tension.

Murmurs of greeting and handshakes passed back and forth. "Sorry to get here so late," Jean went on. "We got lost—er, took the scenic route—were delayed—I hear Miranda rang."

"Quite so." Maggie looked past the red-tiled and gray-slated roofs of the village, more than a few of them sporting small satellite dishes. She looked past the little tower atop the cliff over the sea to the smeared streak of the mainland and the much larger towers of Bamburgh. Tara crossed her arms and looked down at her boots. Crawford didn't look at anything at all, but stood at parade rest, waiting.

Alasdair inhaled, exhaled, inhaled, and when no one else did, spoke. "I'm hearing things did not exactly go to plan the day."

"Not half. The reporters are no doubt savaging me in their respective media. I'm an easy target."

"I've been there myself, sort of," Jean said, partly trying to establish a sisterhood, partly distancing herself from her ink-stained brethren.

If Maggie heard her, she didn't reply. Groaning audibly, she stood up, squared her shoulders, and raised her chin, leading Jean's eye upward, but then, most other women, let alone men, were taller than she was. *Ready, aim* . . . "When the balloon goes up," Maggie stated, "anything the media's said today will be insignificant. They'll run mad."

After a long moment, Alasdair asked, "Aye?"

"This morning I had a quick peek into the tomb, the better to stage the reveal, sort out the lighting and such. I don't like surprises. I've never been proved more justified in that sentiment."

A bagpipe lament, borne on a gust of wind, swelled, faded, and left a lingering resonance among the broken arches. Several black birds, crows or ravens, stirred uneasily atop the walls. One of Gallowglass's greatest hits, Jean remembered, was "The Ravens of Avalon."

"Well, there's nothing for it. Come along." Maggie strode toward a round-headed door tucked into the inside corner of the church and disappeared through it. Glancing almost belligerently over her shoulder at the others, Tara followed. Crawford paced along a step behind.

Alasdair gestured Jean on ahead. She took one step out of the wind into the shadowed stillness of the chapel and stopped dead. She'd expected it to be dank and cold. But the air of the tiny room, no larger than her and Alasdair's living room in Edinburgh, froze her bones. It was so thick with the scents of mud and decay that she gagged. In that moment she felt not a pricking of her thumbs, but a prickle of the back of her neck. Her ghostly early-warning system. Her paranormal detector.

From behind, Alasdair's hands grasped her upper arms. He

felt it, too. *Steady on.*

Then the spine-tingle evaporated. The atmosphere in the room lightened to merely chill with an elusive hint of damp rot. Jean patted Alasdair's hand—*I'm okay*—and he released her. His voice murmured so quietly in her ear she had to cock her head back and up to hear it. "What, or rather who, was that?"

"We'll be finding out in due course," she whispered back.

"Yes, dear."

The others were picking their way around two fresh test trenches, black gashes cut through uneven flagstones, toward the largest window in the room. The bits of broken tracery lining the opening looked like thorns against the darkening eastern sky. Jean and Alasdair took up their places beside Crawford even as Tara hung back.

Maggie lifted an industrial-sized flashlight, large as a policeman's truncheon, and trained its beam of light toward a flat box of excavation tools and a rectangular pit at the front of a low dais—access to a small vault. The last resting place of the person to whom the chapel had presumably been dedicated, set into the floor before the now-vanished altar. The pieces of the slab that had once covered the tomb now leaned against the wall behind Tara. Surely Maggie hadn't broken it—that would have been archaeological heresy.

Maggie knelt at the edge of the hole as though in prayer. Her light illuminated a bright blue plastic tarpaulin about eight inches down. Grasping one corner, she jerked it up and back.

The body was almost a skeleton, but not quite.

In the slightly shaky beam of light—Maggie's hand must be trembling—bone, cloth, skin, strands of hair, all were a dismal brackish brown. The corpse looked more like a child's effort at modeling a human body in clay than the real thing.

Alasdair emitted a long sigh. Jean didn't breathe at all. The chill that oozed down her back had nothing to do with temperature. Mortal clay, she thought. Feet of clay. Although the miasma emanating from the hole wasn't that of clay. Mildew, mold, muck . . .

That's why Maggie had cancelled the press conference at the last minute. That's why she'd waited until the tide ebbed and sealed off the island before presenting the genuine, non-stage-managed reveal.

The arch of the skull resembled an obscene egg. The eye sockets, filled with mud, stared sightlessly upward. The jaw gaped open, revealing brown teeth and two gold fillings that glinted in the light.

Not medieval, then.

The arms were folded across the waist, the arm bones sinking into the body cavity, a few finger bones scattered alongside the arches of the hips. Worms. Rats, maybe. Or no more than gravity.

The feet were still encased in rubber Wellington boots, one turned upright, the other slumping to the side.

Mid to late twentieth century.

Somewhere water dripped. A sheep bawled. The accumulated steam of four breaths formed wraiths in the air. The body did not breathe, the eyes did not blink, the jaw did not move. No invisible tongue gave voice to—what? Fear? Surprise? Had the vacant eyes seen death coming, or had they been closed suddenly, without warning?

Had they closed at all, Jean wondered, or had he—she—been dumped into the tomb with eyes still open, watching as the stone slab closed off the ceiling, the light from the window, the birds flying freely beyond?

Someone had to say it. She obliged, her voice seeming shrill in the deadened air. "Do you have any idea who it is?"

The light-beam steadied. Maggie slumped back on her

haunches. When she spoke her words were directed to the ravaged face in the tomb. “I think it may be my father.”

Chapter Five

Jean glanced so quickly back through the door, toward the cemetery and Wat Lauder's grave, her neck cricked. "Say what?"

"It's a long story. One I've always thought was nothing but . . ." Maggie's voice ran down and dissipated into the gathering darkness.

Gossip? Hearsay? Myth?

Tara's crossed arms tightened. Her boots were now turned pigeon-toed. *It's not my fault.*

Crawford leaned forward, his hatchet nose pointed downward.

Alasdair stared at him, blue eyes gleaming in the light. Jean knew only too well the strength of that stare, like a laser burning a hole not in your retina but in your awareness. Sure enough, the constable looked around, cleared his throat, and said, "Time I was ringing Berwick and asking for back-up."

"I'm thinking that's the best plan, aye," Alasdair told him.

Crawford pulled a phone from his pocket and headed for the door. By the time he disappeared into the main sanctuary, he was speaking, his voice oddly deep for one coming from such a stork-like neck. ". . . Farnaby Island . . . unexplained death . . . no, no, not recent . . . coroner, inquest . . ."

Alasdair took the flashlight from Maggie's hand and gave it to Jean, then pulled the woman to her feet. She didn't seem to notice but kept staring into the grave.

"Did you break the slab covering the tomb?" Jean asked. Not

that the condition of the slab mattered now, but Maggie's face was ashen, glistening with cold sweat—she looked as though she was about to faint and topple into the grave alongside its inhabitant. Inhabitants, plural.

"It was cracked. It's been cracked long as I can remember. My mum tried to mend it with a dab of concrete, but that had broken away. When I pried up the one end, it broke. I took photos, measurements beforehand. I don't have the resources of a well-funded expedition—no laser scans, no fiber-optic cameras for the grave itself."

"Is there an inscription on the stone?"

Now Alasdair went down on one knee, shining the flashlight into the tomb. The sepulcher. Maggie craned over his shoulder.

"An inscription?" repeated Tara. "Not really, no. A few carvings Granny, Elaine, interpreted as horsemen. Mags tried computer-enhancing a rubbing, but there's not much of anything to enhance."

Horsemen? Evidence for Maggie's theory about some Dark Age cavalry bloke? Jean remembered only too well another grave inscription, one that had been enhanced by human imagination. Alasdair had to be thinking of that, too.

He said, "Professor Lauder, you're telling us this is a man's body."

Okay, then, he wasn't having flashbacks to that particular inscription. He'd always been better at single-tasking. Jean stepped closer and peered over his other shoulder. Tara made no move to join them—if anything, she shrank farther back. Was she helping with the excavation because of her relationship with Maggie, not because she had any particular interest in archaeology? So far as Jean knew, the girl could be anything from a fashion model to a business administrator.

"Heavy brow ridges," said Maggie. "Narrow pelvis. A man—in my professional opinion, at the least."

Maggie had a professional opinion. Jean couldn't tell what was bone, what was shadow, what was mud or decay or some ghastly, slimy mixture of both. The moving light created optical illusions and then dispelled them.

"Berwick's on the way," Crawford's voice said behind them.

"Very good," Alasdair replied.

"They're sending a boat. Not worth a helicopter, D.C.I. Webber reckons, but still, D.I. Grinsell's coming himself, not just sending a sergeant."

"Detective Inspector Grinsell?" Alasdair passed the flashlight off to Jean so quickly she had to grab its weight with both hands before it thudded down onto the, ah, evidence. He rose to his feet and turned around. "George Grinsell? Was he with the Cumbria Constabulary some years ago?"

"I'm thinking he was, aye."

Great. Alasdair's tone wasn't exactly filled with delight at meeting an old colleague. It shouldn't matter—he wouldn't have jurisdiction over an unexplained death back home, never mind here, but if he had previous track with this particular detective . . . Jean peered up into his shadowed face and saw nothing. As usual, he played his cards so close to his chest they snagged on his buttons.

A cold hand fell on hers and she jerked.

"Sorry." Maggie directed the beam of light away from the body, around the sides of the grave.

Jean swallowed her heart back into her chest, took a deep breath—and was sorry she had, the burial smelled like the worst case of bad breath ever—and followed the track of the little searchlight.

The body sprawled atop a layer of mud and rubble clods. Below them she glimpsed a more-or-less horizontal, deep gray surface, decorated by small punch marks. "A lead coffin? Wow, those are rare."

"Meaning the original burial is that of someone of high rank of the Romano-British period. The lid of the coffin's a bit crushed—it's right thin lead, considering." Maggie knelt back down, Jean at her side. The stone beneath her shins radiated damp and cold.

The rectangular cavity of the tomb was lined with flat stones turned on edge rather than by a mortared wall. Jean was reminded of an ancient cist burial or the chamber in a prehistoric passage tomb. "Which saint does the chapel commemorate?"

"Saint Genevieve," Maggie replied.

"Saint Genevieve? She's French. The chapel must date only to the Norman rebuilding after all."

"Or earlier. Chantry chapels were quite the thing in France in the ninth century, and King Athelstan established more than a few in England in the tenth."

"Considering the number of people who died in his wars with the Celts and the Vikings, I'm not surprised."

"Perhaps this one was rededicated, then or by the Normans," suggested Maggie. "Given a new name as well as a new building."

"It's possible."

"Out with the old, in with the new. Genevieve's feast day is January third."

"Is it now?" asked Alasdair.

Jean didn't add that January third was their wedding anniversary. They had yet to have an anniversary. "So who do you think was buried here, anyway?"

"That's another long story."

"Yeah. That's the one I came to hear. Professor Lauder . . ."

"For heaven's sakes, call me Maggie."

"Maggie." Yes, there was something very intimate about this moment, the two of them kneeling side by side over a dead body. A lost soul. Perhaps the mouth gaped open in prayer for release from purgatory. Perhaps it claimed its own identity. Perhaps it was caught in a nightmare, screaming and screaming and making no sound.

Alasdair sank down on Jean's other side, his wry glance saying as clearly as words, *once an academic, always an academic.* "What's that?"

"What's what?"

He retrieved the flashlight and focused it steadily on the body's left side. "Either he's got a third arm, one laid straight by his side, or that's some sort of stick."

A presence at Jean's shoulder was either Tara or Crawford leaning in for a better look.

Ignoring them, she squinted, trying to resolve the shape. A baton. A wand. A long, thin, black, pitted and scabby tubular shape with a flat flared end.

"It's a chanter," said Maggie. "Made of wood, likely African blackwood. I saw it earlier. That's why . . ."

"You're thinking the body is your father?" Alasdair asked when she didn't finish her sentence. "You've got a name for him, then?"

Maggie didn't reply. There could be no short reply to that non sequitur. And Alasdair wasn't in a position to interrogate her.

For I'm a piper to my trade, Jean thought, managing at the last second not to vocalize the words. *My name is Rob the Ranter: The lasses loup as they were daft, When I blaw up my chanter.*

If Maggie thought the man was her father, that implied her mother had done some out-of-wedlock louping. And raised more questions than it answered, number one of which was, why the hell had the man, any man, ended up in this old tomb?

Someone cleared his throat. Oh, Crawford. He'd perfected the butler's discreet *ahem.* "I'll mind the scene till Berwick arrives. Best you be taking Maggie home, Tara. A nice cuppa, that'll turn the trick."

"Like a cup of tea is going to fix anything?" Tara seized her mother's shoulders and pulled her upward. "Come on, Mags. It's past supper time. Granny'll be wondering where we are. If she remembers we exist."

Maggie's eyes released the sight of the grave with an almost audible pop. They gazed from face to half-obscured face, toward the roof and the far wall with its row of narrow windows, through the larger window overhead, its broken ribs fading as the light failed. "Your Granny," she said. "Mum. Elaine Lauder that was." And she began to laugh, a quiet chuckle building toward hysteria.

"Mags!" Tara gave her a little shake.

With a hiccup, Maggie caught herself. "Off we go, then." Side by side the two women walked away.

Jean stood up, and only then realized how cold her legs had become, the chill oozing up from the ancient stone. Sometimes, she thought, pilgrims desperate for redemption crawled on their knees toward a sacred site.

She tottered off after Tara and Maggie, then paused while Alasdair passed the flashlight over to Crawford. Passed the torch, both literally and figuratively.

When he joined her all he said was, "Mind those trenches."

Even with dark-adapted eyes, falling into one of those trenches was an ever-present risk—you wouldn't break your neck, but you'd damage more than your dignity. Minding the trenches, they left the chapel and the ruined church. Outside a cold sea breeze was scented delectably with peat smoke and cooking food. Back there at the edge of the grave Jean would have thought she'd never eat again, but no. Her appetite couldn't be defeated for long. She indulged in a quick fantasy of scones or chips or something else fattening and comforting.

Her pace steadied.

The sun had dipped below the horizon, but its light lingered on the clouds that were rising up the sky from the west, coloring them pink and gold and peach. In the east the evening star rose in turn. J. R. R. Tolkien's Sam Gamgee had seen a star above the mirk of Mordor and realized beauty and peace still existed beyond the shadows of Middle-earth. Or of the real Earth.

"You've got to admire Maggie for holding it together long enough to talk to the reporters," Jean told Alasdair. "That couldn't have been long after she discovered the body."

"We have only her word for when she discovered the body."

"Well yes, but—Tara was there, too. Wasn't she? We had to bully her into taking us to the scene."

Unsurprisingly, Alasdair committed himself to nothing.

Maggie and Tara stopped by the Land Rover, Tara looking back at Jean and Alasdair. "I'll run you into the village as soon as I've got Mags squared away."

"Thank you," Alasdair replied. "We'll walk. It's not so far."

"You think? You could walk to the far end of the island in half an hour. Whatever, the B and B's just this side of the pub, on the corner of Cuddy's Close."

"Thanks."

Instead of climbing into the car themselves, mother and daughter walked on down the narrow blacktop road, past the cemetery, past the darkened church. Jean and Alasdair followed a discreet dozen paces behind. Enough light was left for her to read the sign with its simple Church of England cross-in-a-circle logo: The Parish Church of St. Hilda.

Tara steered Maggie along the low stone wall surrounding the manse, the vicar's house between the church and the music school, through a wrought-iron gate and up the garden path.

"I guess Farnaby's church doesn't rate a full-time vicar

anymore," said Jean.

Alasdair replied, "Nothing like the Lauders living above the shop."

The manse's Gothic Revival details seemed overwrought compared with the simplicity of the other buildings in the village. Light shone from the windows, defining their pointed arches, and from the ceiling of a porch whose support posts were decorated with scalloped trim. In other parts of England the protuberance of the porch would be hung with vines. This one sported a couple of shovels leaning against a post and a wicker basket holding what looked like scraps of stone. What an American would call the front yard was filled with more unkempt garden beds. A large wheelbarrow rusted away beneath a hillock of weeds, and the water in a birdbath was slimed with algae.

The door opened. A stooped, scrawny woman peered out. Her white hair was set in the bangs and flipped ends of the sixties and a knitted shawl in a subtle shade of purple draped her shoulders. "Maggie? Where were you?"

"I was over at the priory, Mum, as usual." Maggie's voice carried the forced cheerfulness usually applied to a fretful child.

Elaine's voice sounded thin and tentative. "Is your father there? He's late for his, his—the meal. Tea."

After what Jean could only call a pregnant pause, Maggie replied, "He's not coming tonight, Mum."

"Oh. Pity." The pallid face turned toward Tara. "How do you do. I don't believe we've been introduced."

"Tara Hogg," the young woman told Elaine. "Nice to meet you."

Jean's stroll slowed to a dawdle. She tried to reconcile this haggard woman with the elegant studio portrait on the back of Elaine Lauder's controversial *The Matter of Britannia,* a book that had thrown a few scholarly planets out of their orbits at its publication. She tried to reconcile this woman with Maggie, for that matter, to no avail.

A woman about Tara's age drew Elaine back into the house. From her smock with its glint of a name tag and the tidy binding of her red hair, Jean deduced she served as a nurse or home health aide.

Maggie and Tara stepped over the threshold and the door shut with a solid thunk, cutting off the sound of a clock striking.

"What a shame," Jean told Alasdair. "According to the date on that gravestone, Elaine's seventy-five. These days that's not much past middle-aged."

"That's as may be, but it's not making you and me teenagers. Time we were feeding ourselves and settling in for the night." Alasdair's large, strong hand on the small of her back urged her on.

One last backwards glance showed her the sign on the garden gate that she'd missed when they'd sped past earlier. *Gow House.* Wat must have named his home for Neil Gow, the legendary fiddler.

The school building was the newest one on the road, by a century at least, built in the uninspired style of the nineteen-eighties that seemed to Jean's eye to be no style at all. Its sign read *Gallowglass School of Traditional Music.* What sort of traditional music wasn't specified, but then, the school was located in Northumbria, home of multiple mixed and matched traditions. Gallowglass had made its reputation adding new world beats to old British songs, in a genre Jean thought of as Country Eastern. A shame the school was no longer open year-round, but Wat's injuries and subsequent death had deprived it of a permanent artist-in-residence.

There, too, windows gleamed. Through them came the sound of fiddles, an accomplished one carrying the tune, a bouncy jig, several others squeaking along behind. The leader had to be Hugh Munro, punctilious as usual about training up the younger generation in the way in which it should go. They'd either catch up with him at the B&B or at the pub.

In a silence less companionable than mutually puzzled, Jean and Alasdair walked around the hairpin turn and onto the main street of Farnaby St. Mary. Gulls squawked overhead, sounding a little like the student violins. Somewhere in the darkness beyond the pebbled beach the sea murmured, and the horizon rose and fell gently in the last glimmer of daylight.

They could keep on going, Jean thought. It wasn't their case. They had no battles to fight here, other than academic interest in the chapel and the constant gnawing of curiosity. But short of commandeering one of the kayaks on the breakwater and heading for Lindisfarne, where the causeway was open, they were stranded.

The sign reading *The Queen's Arms* creaked in the wind. According to a small sign high on the pub's side wall, the cobblestoned alleyway running alongside was named Cuddy's Close. Cuddy, also known as Cuthbert, Lindisfarne's other saint. Supposedly his body was still intact in its shrine in Durham Cathedral.

They could safely assume, Jean told herself, that the body in St. Genevieve's chantry chapel was not that of Cuthbert. That was about all they could assume.

The reddish-gray walls of the house on the corner indicated that it, like so many other buildings in Farnaby St. Mary, had been built with stones robbed from the priory. Its front window displayed a placard reading, *Angle's Rest B&B. Four stars.* "Here we are," Alasdair said, and opened the door for Jean.

Chapter Six

"Hello?" Alasdair called.

"There you are!" A pleasantly upholstered woman popped out of a side door into the hallway, bringing with her a scent of baking bread that made Jean go weak in the knees. "Lance turned up with your cases ever so long ago, I thought you'd changed your minds and moved into the students' hostel down the way."

"We were delayed," Jean evaded, and went on to introduce herself and her spousal unit.

The woman's handshake was brisk, firm, and slightly floury. "Oh, sorry." She wiped her hands on the front of her apron, succeeding only in rearranging the dusting of flour already there. "Penelope Fleming. Pen, that is. We've got no need for ancient Greek names here on Farnaby. Your room's just up the stairs here."

She led the way, giving Jean a good look at her back, from chestnut-brown pincurls to a capacious purple sweatsuit to fuzzy pink bunny slippers. "Hugh Munro's in the single room down the hall here, and the Campbell-Reids will be in the double on the ground floor when they arrive tomorrow. It's all ready for them, save adjusting the cot for the size of the child."

"She's almost ten months old," said Jean. "She can pull herself up but isn't walking yet."

"Oh, a lovely little lass, I'm sure."

With a long way to go before she found herself forty and facing a mid-life crisis.

A sitting area at the top of the stairs had room for two easy chairs, a table piled with magazines, and a padded window seat. On it lay a lump of fur striped in gray and black—which opened one golden eye, considered the newcomers, flicked a whisker in disdain, and closed the eye again.

"You're not allergic to cats, are you?" Pen asked. "I'll bring Hildy downstairs if so."

"No, no," Jean assured her. "We have one of our own back in Edinburgh."

"Edinburgh's a brilliant town, isn't it? The theaters, the restaurants—you'll be thinking you've come to the ends of the earth here." Pen threw open a door. Her smile beamed not only from her lips but from her plump cheeks, and her hazel eyes, nested in equally upturned wrinkles, were framed by oversized glasses. "Here you are. No matter where you go, there you are, eh?"

Smiling in return, Jean looked around the room. Soft colors, floral fabrics, landscape photos. Windows on both the right- and left-hand walls. A wide bed, chairs and a table with a tea set. A subtle odor of fresh potpourri. A U-turn brought her to a sparkling clean bathroom and a closet where their suitcases sat ready on racks. What would Pen have had to do to rate five stars? Gild the water faucets? "It's perfect. Thank you. Just one thing."

"What can I be doing for you, Miss Fairbairn?"

"Jean, please." She leaned closer to the picture hanging next to the bathroom door, a close-up of the tower atop the headland. In the tenuous spring light of the photo—light much like today's—the massive stones of the bailey wall surrounding a small roofless keep seemed brutal, laid down by giants in some antediluvian era. "What's this tower? Is it a fort?"

"Oh, aye, mostly dating to Tudor days, like the fortlet on

Lindisfarne that's now Lindisfarne Castle. Though Elaine went poking about there once upon a time and thinks the foundations are those of a watchtower dating to the Viking raids."

"I can see the priories on Farnaby and Lindisfarne setting up an early-warning system."

Alasdair stepped up to take a look. "This one's not been renovated into a mansion, though."

"No, and more's the pity," Pen replied. "The Castle is lovely now, isn't it?"

"Yes, it is," said Jean.

"Elaine and Wat were going on about a similar job on Merlin's Tower."

"Merlin's Tower?"

Pen shrugged. "Elaine's thinking the name's no older than Victorian times. Any road, she and Wat were planning to renovate the tower after he retired. Even had an architect in from Alnwick. The place is habitable, but only just. Music, though, it's like the priesthood, you never truly retire." Pen's slight frown segued into a firm smile that rejected images of Wat taken before his time and ailing Elaine. "Is there anything else?"

"Can we have ourselves a meal in the pub next door?" Alasdair asked.

"Oh my, yes—James has all the basics—James, he's my husband, call us the Trumps of Farnaby St. Mary, real estate moguls, right?"

"Right." Judging by his grin, even Alasdair was charmed. "Cheers."

They should bottle this woman and spray her over various government assemblies, not to mention ranting talking heads. She was not only infectiously good-natured, she now backed away toward the door without demanding further conversation. "Breakfast is at eight unless you'd rather have it earlier. There's a bit of a menu just there on the desk. Ta ta for now." And the door shut.

Jean glanced not at the list of foods on the menu but at the name at its top. "Not only did I say Angler's Rest to Lance, when I first booked the place I read it as Angel's Rest. You're always seeing 'angel' for 'angle' and vice versa."

"You and your proofreader's eye." Alasdair opened his suitcase.

"Angles. Saxons. Jutes. And later on, Vikings and Danes. Some people called them pirates, but they saw themselves as bold explorers, opening up new lands, never mind people were already living there. Kind of like Attila and his Huns."

"Eh?"

"Saint Genevieve supposedly saved Paris from Attila the Hun in the fifth century. That was a time of barbarian invasions into the old Roman Empire, the era of a historical King Arthur . . . Well, Maggie's got to have more going for herself than a connection that slender, I don't care how ambitious she is."

"Eh?" Alasdair repeated, a little louder.

Jean started pulling items from her suitcase, beginning with her tablet computer. "Earlier you were wondering if it was a coincidence Maggie moved back to Farnaby to help her parents and still managed to make a brilliant discovery."

"Oh aye, coincidences happen, but it's her finding a grave worth presenting a press conference, in her own garden or so nearly as makes no difference, that's making me itch."

"You and me both. Farnaby isn't the end of the Earth, Pen to the contrary, but Maggie still might feel as though her career's been put on hold here."

"There you are, motivation for—well, I'm not suggesting she's salted the dig, just that she's making a mountain from a molehill."

"So far she hasn't presented any evidence one way or the

other. All she's discovered is a dead body, and she sure didn't plant that."

"No, that she did not. Consider her timing reporting the body, though."

Jean spread her toiletries out on the bathroom counter, marveling that this bathroom had a counter, unlike many. She could only assume that Brits were capable of making their hygiene and beauty aids levitate beside the sink.

Her image in the mirror made her grab for her hairbrush—the wind had caused her naturally surly auburn locks to become openly hostile. "No surprise she'd put off calling Crawford," she said toward the other room, "until access to Farnaby was closed. She's lucky she's in a place she could keep outsiders away and the situation under control. Not that you and I aren't outsiders, but we got here after the other reporters had left—that was a serendipitous shortcut making a long delay, wasn't it?"

"We're owning to good credentials, to say nothing of Miranda's good word."

"Miranda's magic tongue could open the gates of Fort Knox, no doubt about it."

"Still," Alasdair replied, "Maggie could not be keeping the truth under wraps forever."

"Couldn't she? She could have replaced the slab on the tomb and gone on her way. Especially if Tara wasn't there this morning helping her out and she had no witnesses. The hue and cry from the double-crossed media would die out eventually. Loony Lauder . . . *Hmm.*" Jean walked out into the room. Alasdair had turned off all the lights except for a dim bedside lamp and now peered out of the right-hand window.

The view swept down to the harbor and out to sea. Crawford's small boat bobbed up and down next to a fishing boat, but Jean saw no sign of any other official forces staging a landing.

"Too soon," he told her, and went on, "If Tara's Maggie's daughter, she's not making a reliable witness, one way or the other."

"We'll have to take their word for it."

"You'll have noticed the American accent, still quite strong."

"Not like Rebecca's, with more serial numbers filed off all the time. My accent's going that way, too, I bet. It's a braw, bricht, nicht . . ."

"You've got a ways to go," Alasdair told her. "With Tara calling Maggie 'Mags,' not 'Mum' or the like, I'm guessing she was adopted at birth and they've only lately been reunited. Not to mention Hogg being a fine Borders name."

"It's a fine Texas name, too. Maybe she went to her father's family, presuming her father is the dead lover, but that's not a given."

"Not a bit of it."

"So if the body is Maggie's biological father, then Elaine maybe potted a lover, too. You said yourself, bagging the unfaithful lover is a traditional sport. Or bagging the rival—the death might be Wat's doing."

"No obvious gunshot wounds. Cannot tell whether the man was bagged at all." Alasdair had an annoying and yet endearing habit of taking her metaphors literally. "We've got no reason as yet to assume it's a murder."

"I don't see any way it could be a death by misadventure. What? The guy crawled in there playing hide and seek and pulled the slab closed?" Jean shuddered, sensing a crushing wave of claustrophobia. "Or a robbery. What robber would go to such effort to hide his victim?"

"Come to that, we've got no 'we' at all. It's Grinsell's case, for better or worse."

The acid trickling suddenly through his tone caused Jean to dart a sharp look at his face. His great stone face. "Alasdair, who's George Grinsell? And I don't mean a D.I. from Berwick or Cumbria or wherever. I mean . . ."

". . . What's he to me? Nothing personally. We've met is all. But there was a right old stramash some years ago with him following a female suspect across the border into Scotland and harassing her once he caught her up, even though Lothian and Borders Police was on the scene and in charge of the situation."

"There's another fine old tradition for you, a border leaking all sorts of people back and forth and squabbles over territorial imperative."

"Aye, but the days of the Border Reivers and their ilk are long gone. We're now living the days of bureaucracy and political correctness."

"Which can certainly be carried to extremes, though I gather that's not the case with Grinsell."

"He's having none of that nonsense, no. He made some statements at the time of the border dispute that had folk in both England and Scotland calling for his resignation, if not his head on a pike above Carlisle Castle. Sounds as though he's merely been moved sideways, from the Cumbrian Constabulary to the Northumbria Police."

"Let's hope he's mellowed a bit."

Alasdair sighed. "It's none of our affair, lass."

"Yeah, right. I've heard that one before." Shaking her head, Jean crossed the room and checked the view from the opposite window. This one overlooked the ruined priory, which now, in the cloud-shrouded twilight, seemed no more than charcoal sketches upon shadow. A ghostly fluorescence moved through the grounds. She extended one tendril of her sixth sense and *listened,* but detected nothing, no hint of the spirit or soul or discorporate presence she and Alasdair had sensed there earlier.

What she saw was Crawford, his jacket reflecting the lights of the village and the backspatter of his own—well, he had Maggie's—flashlight. Its beam swept across the window-wall and the gaping maw of the chapel door. He had strong nerves, to stay out there alone. But then, not everyone was as given to populating the darkness with phantoms as Jean. Crawford didn't strike Jean as being the imaginative sort, let alone one of the rare people cursed by an allergy to ghosts.

An even less decipherable shape walked toward him, up the road from the direction of the church. Jean hoped it was Tara or Maggie or the red-haired nurse consoling the constable on duty with a cup of tea and a sandwich. By leaning into the window bay, she could see the almost invisible shape of the church and the lights of Gow House, puny against the swallowing night.

Alasdair picked up her backpack from the bed and handed it to her. "There's a pint in the pub with my name on it, and a plate of food with yours."

"Oh yeah. But speaking of Miranda, I need to call her before the news people get on the scent. I can see them all turning around and speeding back to the ferry slip."

"The tide will be coming back in and going out again before dawn tomorrow. The island's well closed till noon or so."

"Whenever, this time Maggie won't be able to buy them off with a lecture on Arthur or Genevieve or anyone except Rob the Ranter."

"Who?"

"The chanter in the grave made me think of the line from 'Maggie Lauder,' the one about Rob the Ranter. We don't have any other ID for the dead man."

Alasdair said, "Just because the chap was buried with a chanter does not mean he was a piper."

"Yeah, but wasn't the chanter why Maggie suspected she knew who it was?"

"That's her inference, aye, though we're compounding her guess with ours."

"An experienced guess," Jean told him.

He shrugged with his eyebrows rather than his shoulders. "Best you be making your calls whilst you're vertical."

"Assuming my phone didn't go belly-up hours ago." Great, it only now occurred to her that while they were hardly at the edge of the world here—they'd been farther from civilization on Skye last New Year's—they might be off the grid. Lance had cell phone reception on the ferry, but he lived here and no doubt had his phone set up accordingly. Jean dived into her bag. The phone was buried at the very bottom, as always.

Yes. She had a minimal collection of bars. She tapped Miranda's name.

CHAPTER SEVEN

"Miranda Capaldi here," said her friend and colleague's smoky voice. "I'm out and about, who knows where or why. Leave a message and I'll make my way to you in due course."

Jean left a message. "It's probably best if you call me back, because it hasn't hit the media yet—I know you're media yourself, but unless you've developed ESP—let's just say Maggie cancelled the news conference for a very good reason and Alasdair and I are—well no, we're not exactly on the case, but we're here. Bye."

"I'm sure she'll be finding that very informative," said Alasdair from the desk, where he was now perusing the breakfast menu.

"We speak the same language," Jean returned, and tapped "Campbell-Reid."

This time she hit a home run. "Hello, Jean," said Rebecca's voice. "How are things on Farnaby?"

"Funny you should ask." Jean gave her friend a rundown of events, edited for running time and discretion, concluding, "It's not like the case in Edinburgh in February. There we had a possible ID right from the start."

"I wish I could say I was gobsmacked by it all, but knowing how you and Alasdair attract this sort of thing . . ." After a moment of silence, Rebecca went on, "I understand Maggie trying to reinvent herself, but by now I reckon she's wishing she'd left well alone."

"I bet she is. But that leads me to a not unrelated question. You're more in touch with British academic circles than I am. Have you ever heard Maggie called Loony Lauder?"

Alasdair, now standing by the door, mouthed, "Does that matter?"

"You're always saying we don't know what matters and what doesn't," Jean mouthed back.

In her ear Rebecca said, "No, not Maggie, but it seems to me 'Loony Lauder' was going around about Elaine several years ago."

"Elaine?"

"*The Matter of Britannia* alone earned her a few cat-calls. Then she told an interviewer she was basing the sequel on psychic revelations about Farnaby Priory. Rather like Bligh Bond at Glastonbury, who said he was getting messages through automatic writing from one of the old monks. But no matter. Not now. When word went round about her dementia, everyone who'd called her loony, even about *Britannia,* crawled away red-faced."

"Well yes, I should think so. Except . . ."

". . . Except I'm more than occasionally picking up images, vibes, stray emotions from the past, and I'm not demented. Nor you and Alasdair and your ghosts."

"Exactly. Dementia is too easy an answer."

Alasdair mimed pouring a drink down his throat, followed by eating motions.

"Well," Jean said with a *down boy* gesture, "I'll let you go. You're going to love the Angle's Rest, by the way."

"Good! Michael and I will pack the baby and the bagpipes and be seeing you tomorrow afternoon, then."

"Safe journey." Jean switched off and let Alasdair usher her out the door.

She opened her mouth to fill him in, then saw Hildy the

tabby cat still ensconced on the window seat. Now, however, she sat upright, ears perked forward, tail twitching, nose pressed to the window, which from this angle was little more than a mirror. "What is she looking at?"

"What are cats ever looking at?" Alasdair found a light switch and pressed it.

The sitting area plunged into shadow rather than complete darkness, but even as they zeroed in on the window seat the illusion of the mirror cleared. Peering past the cat, Jean remembered the old wives' tale that if you looked between a cat's ears you'd see a ghost. Funny about old wives' tales, how many of them had some basis in reality.

Although what she saw now was nothing paranormal, just a large, blond, very much alive Lance Eccleston stamping down the alley outside the four-foot-tall garden wall. "That's not who I saw walking up to the priory," she said.

"That's Crawford at the priory," said Alasdair beside her, his breath misting the glass.

Hildy looked up at him, then at Jean, and made a hasty retreat first to the floor and then down the stairs.

"Yeah, I know. You can see his jacket reflecting the light. A little while ago he was shining the flashlight on that wall of windows and now it looks like he's sitting on the bench in the cloisters. But also a little while ago I saw someone walking up the road toward him, not in anything reflective and without a flashlight."

"Good way to go falling into a trench, with no torch. How'd you know it wasn't Lance, in the dark and all?"

"Not as large. I thought it was Tara or the redhead from Gow House."

"No good judging size in the darkness," Alasdair stated.

"Yeah, well . . ." Jean's stomach grumbled. "Come on. Let's stop stalling around and get some food."

She allowed Alasdair his roll of the eyes, which he pretended to hide as he turned the light back on. He followed her down the stairs, out the door onto the street, and across Cuddy's Close.

The signboard fixed to the front of The Queen's Arms sported a generic crown, not a portrait of either of the Elizabeths or even Mary, Queen of Scots. Considering the nearby priory, the eponymous queen could be Mary, Queen of Heaven. Or the queen of a chess set. Right now Jean didn't care. The door of the pub stood open, allowing a bright streak of light to fall invitingly across the pavement, and windows shone behind baskets filled with wind-buffeted flowers. Voices and the clink of glassware echoed from inside.

Within minutes she and Alasdair had introduced themselves to James Fleming behind the bar, obtained alcoholic beverages, ordered meals, and found a bench in a corner as quiet as a pub was likely to provide.

Jean sipped cautiously at her Lindisfarne mead, sweet but potent honey wine, and decided that if bees drank this, she was signing up for the hive. Taking a good swallow, she assessed her surroundings.

If she hadn't already known James was Pen's husband, she would have thought he was her chubby, cheery, and mustachioed male twin. In fact, the pub seemed to be the male principle to the B&B's female, perfumed with potatoes instead of potpourri, equipped with all the traditional comforts but on the shabby rather than the sparkling side.

The clientele seemed similarly easygoing, probably because they hadn't yet heard the news from the priory—although a couple of heads were bent together in sotto voce speculation about something. Maybe they were discussing football scores or the spring bird count.

Jean recognized two faces. Lance fidgeted on a stool not far from the beer taps, gazing balefully at Tara, who occupied a tiny table across the room. She already had one empty pint glass in front of her and was starting in on another, to the accompaniment of what looked like a shepherd's pie. She must have fled here instead of eating her tea at home, assuming she called Gow House home.

Jean turned her eye to her husband, who drank deeply of his dark ale. She could trace its path from his throat to his stomach and through his nervous system not by a slackening in his expression—he never slacked—but by a mellowing. His features, like his body, were economical, compact, reserved. Even his hair was cut short and plain, resembling amber waves of grain touched by frost. Only his eyes revealed what nuclear fires burned behind the lead shielding of his manner. Or, rather, she knew what his eyes revealed because she'd learned the hard way how to read them and their freezes and thaws.

She would never have believed that a year after her divorce she'd remarry, going from twenty years in purgatory to this state of grace. Alasdair would never have believed that years after the bitter disillusion of his first marriage, he would now find himself with another wife who—well, Jean wasn't perpendicular to reality, she simply had her own slant on it.

Maggie had never married after the tragedy of her youth. Was she lonely? Was she self-sufficient?

What about Crawford? Was there a Mrs. Crawford over in Bamburgh, covering a dinner plate and tucking it away? Were there smaller Crawfords needing help with their homework?

Jean thought of Crawford sitting in the darkened cloister—the word that was the root of "claustrophobia." A cloistered nun or monk might feel closed-in, never mind soaring hymns and transcendental ceremonies. A monk or nun on Farnaby, or Lindisfarne, or distant Iona, might feel particularly enclosed, looking out at a wide horizon but having no way of crossing it. And yet a remote island was at the same time part of the world and not part of the world, a portal between planes of being.

How did Maggie feel? She hadn't chosen Farnaby. Was she trapped by love and duty, watching her horizons creep closer and closer and her ambitions molder away? What about Tara, breaking out of Gow House as fast as she could tonight?

Alasdair turned his blue eyes, now warm as a summer sky, toward her. "Tuppence for your thoughts, lass."

"Isn't the expression, 'a penny for your thoughts'?"

"Yours are aye worth double."

"I'll remind you of that the next time they leap from A to G and you want me to map out B, C, D, E, and F."

He toasted her with his glass.

Raising hers in turn, first toward him and then to her lips, Jean filled him in on what Rebecca had said—automatic writing, different sorts of sixth senses, lingering sensory waves from the past or parallel universes or something. What if Elaine had been communing in some fashion with the spirit Jean and Alasdair themselves sensed in the priory?

"In my experience," said Alasdair, "the dead are not shy about appearing. Communicating? No."

"I've only encountered one that even seemed to be aware of my presence." Jean let that memory fade into the vivid here-and-now. "What I'm wondering is why that reporter from wherever he was from—not from one of the sober papers or magazines, I bet, not with that haircut—anyway, why did he call Maggie 'Loony Lauder'?"

"Heard someone here on Farnaby saying it, most likely Lance Eccleston on the ferry."

"Yeah, that works."

"Loony Lauder? I'm agreeing with you that either Maggie or Elaine, or the both of them, are the pivot points here, but . . ."

His caution dangled unfinished as James Fleming set plates

of fish and chips and mushy peas on the table, the rising steam redolent with mouth-watering scents. "Would you prefer tomato sauce, Ms. Fairbairn?" he asked, plunking down a bottle of malt vinegar.

"Oh no, thank you—the American ketchup habit is one I've managed to moderate."

James grinned beneath his whisk-broom of a moustache. "Ah, good. There's some places offer tomato sauce to kill the taste of poor-quality ingredients. Not here. That there haddock is fresh off the boat and the potatoes from the ground. Enjoy!"

Jean didn't have to be told twice. She applied a sprinkling of vinegar and dug in, leaving Alasdair to throw a "cheers" at James's retreating back. The crunchy batter, the sweet, flaky fish, the mealy potatoes with their sharp malt dressing, the slightly peppery mushy peas had barely dulled the edge of her appetite when another familiar face appeared in the doorway.

Hugh Munro carried his guitar case and his fiddle case, proving Jean's often-made point that he'd rather play music than eat. His rosy, bearded face beneath its halo of silver hair, that of a cherub surprised by middle age, turned toward Jean and Alasdair. "You're here, then."

"Aye, that we are," Alasdair told him.

"How's wee Dougie getting on back in Edinburgh? The cattery's all right for him, is it then?"

If he'd been spending the weekend in his flat next door, Hugh would have offered to look after Dougie.

"He's likely dining with his own sushi chef, considering the cost of his upkeep." Alasdair had long ago accepted that Dougie and Jean came as a package. The little cat was her feline significant other, not that Alasdair didn't have his feline moments. Declining further commentary on the economics of pet care, he said, "Have a seat, Hugh."

"For the moment, thanks. Almost time for the Friday night

session." Hugh pulled around a chair from another table and sat down.

"Are you playing with some of the students tonight?"

"Not just now. I've worn them down the day. No, there's an Irish lass stopping here, name of Neeve McCarthy, has a voice like an angel."

Jean's crunch on a particularly succulent bit of batter muffled the name. "Did you say Nieve? Spanish for 'snow'?"

Alasdair's lips, glistening with grease, spread into a smile. "I'm thinking it's N-i-a-m-h, pronounced 'Neeve,' one reason I did not do well with the Gaelic as a child. It's never spelled as it's said."

"Niamh McCarthy, a good Scots-Irish name," Hugh repeated, and added cryptically, "We have the Spanish influence here as well. Ah, here's the lass now." Gathering up his instruments, he rose again and headed for an empty corner of the room.

"Good," Alasdair said. "Not only music, but we're not obliged to be telling him what's happened just yet . . . Oh. Well now."

The nurse from Gow House walked in the door, now clothed in civilian garb, a sweater, jeans, and boots. Released from its bindings, her hair cascaded over her shoulders and down her back, a reddish-gold—"ginger" in the UK—silk curtain framing an oval face carved as delicately as a cameo. Every eye in the place turned toward her, Jean noted, except Lance's, which kept a bead on Tara, even as a blank-faced Tara settled back to enjoy the show.

Jean spared a thought for Maggie, shouldering the care of her mother as well as, now, the care of a cold case.

Hugh fingered an introduction. Niamh began to sing "Foggy Dew."

No. Her voice wasn't that of an angel. Nothing was celestial about that vibrato like a serrated edge. The chills that trickled down Jean's spine weren't unlike those warning of the paranormal.

A song about the Irish Easter Uprising might not be the most diplomatic of choices here in England. But still, every other voice in the pub fell silent. Not one glass clinked. Niamh seemed to be an ancient priestess, chanting an anthem of war, and grief, and lost love . . .

Clyde Eccleston strode through the door, shouting, "A police boat's come in to the harbor. Chap in charge is saying we've got us a murder up the priory."

"Well done, Grinsell," said Alasdair. "A right fast turnout."

Tara pushed back from her table so quickly it crashed to the floor.

Chapter Eight

Hugh's fingers fell across the guitar strings, stilling them. His eyes flashed over the tops of his glasses. Niamh stopped in mid-phrase, a wave of scarlet flooded her cheeks, and she darted a sharp glance first at Tara, then at Lance.

"Sorry, James." Tara scrabbled on the floor collecting shards of glass. Fortunately, Jean saw, only one of her pint glasses had broken.

"You've cut yourself." Lance stepped forward, reaching for her hand.

"I'm okay, it's nothing," Tara snapped. Lurching to her feet, she tucked her hand behind her back.

Niamh seized it and pressed a napkin to it. "The cut's not so deep. A plaster'll do the trick, soon as the bleeding's stopped."

"Thanks," Tara said over her shoulder, but Niamh's eyes were fixed on Lance.

Lance made an abrupt about-face and joined the general rush out the door.

"There's an interesting romantic triangle," Jean murmured as she and Alasdair extricated themselves from behind their table.

He considered James advancing toward the two young women, a first-aid kit in hand. "Eh?"

"Never mind," Jean told him with a smile.

Hugh caught up with them at the door. "Anything you're wanting to be telling me?"

Jean wanted to return, *It's not our fault.* But Hugh knew that.

Alasdair said, "Maggie Lauder's discovered a body in the priory. Not the one she was meaning to discover."

"This one's twentieth-century," Jean added, and blinked at the sudden darkness outside.

It was rush hour in Cuddy's Close. Perhaps fifteen people jostled between the walls of the pub and the B&B's garden, then up a set of steps to the priory, now illuminated by swooping flashlight beams like strobe lights at a rock concert. Here came Pen along the close, her own flashlight in hand, her bunny slippers replaced by lime-green fluorescent running shoes. She asked of the air, "What's happening?"

James came up behind Jean and Alasdair. "Clyde's saying there's been a murder at the priory."

"Is that why Edwin Crawford's been moping about the place? Lad could have had himself a cuppa and minded the scene from our window." Pen surged forward.

"Kudos to the lad for minding the scene on the scene," muttered Alasdair.

"So it wasn't Pen I saw walking up to him," Jean replied, and was swept up in the stampede.

She lost Hugh but hung onto Alasdair. They found themselves in the blacktop parking area and dived for cover next to the Land Rover, still parked where Tara had left it.

Living bodies lined the strip of blue-and-white police tape now strung from column base to column base across the front of the priory. Alasdair swept a critical gaze past the perimeter, to where voices echoed, lights waggled, and shadows shot up the walls and across the grounds. He'd have had the scene organized quick-smart, if he'd had to wade in with a cattle prod.

A slight figure blocked the chapel doorway, his spread legs indicating he expected the coveralled figures of the crime-scene team to pass deferentially beneath them. "Grinsell?" she asked.

"Oh, aye. Same attitude, more's the pity. Ah. There go the arms as well."

Grinsell braced his arms on his hips. Every time someone tried to enter or leave the chapel, he grudgingly pivoted aside, like a rusty turnstile. There was Crawford—no, Jean corrected herself, the male shape a head taller than Grinsell wore a suit beneath his reflective coat, not a uniform. Whoever he was, Grinsell favored him with an even slower pivot and a dismissive gesture as well.

A scrape of footsteps made her jerk around. Niamh hurried along the road toward Gow House. The front door opened and Maggie stepped out onto the porch. Onto the stage. She stood motionless as the younger woman brushed by her and vanished into the house. If either of them spoke, Maggie asking Tara's whereabouts, for example, Jean didn't hear.

"Poor Maggie, getting reacquainted with police procedure," she told Alasdair.

"It's no crime finding a body. You and me, we'd be banged up good and proper if it were so. Concealing the discovery, now, for how long and why . . ."

"That's the issue," Jean finished for him.

Steps on her other side almost gave her whiplash. But the rounded male figure, light shimmering on his bald head, was Hugh Munro, now accompanied by a stocky, black-haired man wearing a kilt. Where had she seen . . . Oh, yes. He was the piper who'd been conducting a class on the doorstep of the music school.

"There you are." Hugh paused to catch his breath. "I've just come across Hector here, setting out for the hostel and amazed to find the polis have landed."

"Almost missed the whole thing," said Hector's mild voice from the darkness. "I thought Farnaby was going to be the boondocks, you know, quiet as the grave. I guess not."

Jean choked back a gurgle—quiet as the grave, yeah, right—and introduced herself and Alasdair, adding, "It sounds like you're from the same part of the world I am."

"Santa Fe, New Mexico," he said. "Hector Cruz, piper."

"He's the school's other artist-in-residence the week," Hugh added. "A McCrimmon on his mother's side. The Scots, they got around."

" 'The Rovin' Dies Hard.' " Hector offered the name of Hugh's classic song with its chorus about Fortune dealing the Scots the wildest of cards.

Jean connected with the extended hand of Hugh's "Spanish influence," as he'd joked in the pub when she misheard Niamh's name. Then she passed his hand over to Alasdair, who shook politely, even as he craned past Hector's broad shoulder toward the chapel. He'd never gotten the hang of being a gawper, a looky-loo, rather than an investigating officer.

The wind had stilled, and an almost transparent mist veiled the priory—the accumulated breaths of the spectators, Jean assumed, although the air seemed to be thickening behind her as well as before her. If it weren't for the flaring and retreating beams of light, the bare ruined choir would be invisible.

She stepped closer to Alasdair. Her arm brushed the cold, damp metal of the Land Rover and a chill rippled up her spine—whoa—that chill was paranormal as well as natural . . . No. The ghost, the spirit was no more than a hint, and quickly gone.

An inhabited body pushed its way through the watchers, accompanied by a reflective jacket. A nasal, acid voice announced, "I'm in charge here. I'm wanting a car. No good going about shanks's mare and falling into every pothole—typical villagers, lazy sods can't be bothered maintaining the roads."

An indignant murmur percolated through the gathered islanders.

"We're wanting an incident room as well," the voice went on.

"There's an empty shop along the main street," replied a familiar, much warmer voice. "I'll fetch the key."

The beam of a flashlight targeted James's rotund figure and held him fast. "Who are you?"

"James Fleming. I own the pub."

"Nice work, that. Spend loads of time straining beer through that moustache. Fetch the key then, give it to my sergeant here, there's a good chap."

The flashlight waved right, waved left, and bagged the quartet by the car. Jean flinched as the bright light hung in her face, blinding her.

But the light wasn't focused on her. "Well, stuff that for a game of soldiers. Alasdair Cameron. And here's me hoping the local plod's, Crawley, Crawford—hoping he's hallucinating saying you're here. But it's not enough we've got prats of our own, is it? Scotland's sending theirs to interfere."

"Hullo, George," Alasdair said evenly, but Jean sensed his body go even colder than the car.

"Who's your entourage, then?"

"Hugh Munro and Hector Cruz from the music school. My wife, Jean Fairbairn."

Again the light dazzled her eyes. "One of those, are you, girl? Too pleased with yourself to take your husband's name?"

She wouldn't have detailed the whys and wherefores of her name choices to a much more affable person, never mind this man. Following Alasdair's example, she offered a terse, "Hello."

People milled about, going from priory to village to the road and back. Jean was vaguely aware of twin dots of lime-green carrying Pen back to her post at the B&B, and of Hugh seizing the arm of Hector's windbreaker and pulling him away into the surrounding darkness. She was much more aware of Grinsell.

A car came up the road, lurched into a pothole, and after a

brief spin of its wheels lurched out again. Its headlights caught the man like an insect in amber. He stood about the same height as Alasdair, but was more slightly built, bar the protrusion of a small pot belly. Thinning reddish hair, a sour slit of a mouth, the sly sideways cant of his eyes close together in a long face, a sharp chin—he resembled a fox, Jean thought, and she didn't mean foxy as in attractive.

Handsome is as handsome does. At five-foot-eight, Alasdair was hardly on the tall side, but he stood with his usual quiet reserve, at ease if also poised, having no need to prove his manhood or anything else.

The headlights went out. Grinsell again assumed the power position, legs spread, shoulders braced beneath the weight of their chips. "What's your business here, Inspector? Oh, excuse me. *Chief* Inspector."

"My wife is here writing a magazine article on Farnaby Priory. I'm having myself a bit of a busman's holiday. Nowadays I'm head of Protect and Survive in Edinburgh."

"Edinburgh?" The word was a sneer in Grinsell's whine. "So you've taken on some namby-pamby job with the greenies. Made the Northern Constabulary too hot to hold you, eh, playing the knight in shining armor?"

Yes, Alasdair had once made a very painful decision to do the right thing. Jean tightened her lips over her teeth and clasped her hands behind her back so tightly the bones squeaked. *Don't let him know his words have any effect on you.*

The tall man in the suit and reflective jacket loomed up beside them. "Sir, I've had the lads set up the incident room in the vacant shop."

"You have, have you?" Scenting new prey, Grinsell spun around. "You're taking a lot on yourself, Darling. Feeling ambitious, are we?"

Say who? Jean wondered if once again she'd heard a name incorrectly.

Alasdair extended a hand. "Alasdair Cameron, Northern Constabulary, retired."

"Detective Sergeant Rufus Darling, Berwick," replied the other man.

Oh. Like Hogg, Darling was a Borders name. And setting up an incident room was a sergeant's job. Grinsell had pretty much told him to do so. No surprise the young man's features, even in the uncertain light of the flashlights, seemed to be pinched in a vise. "Jean Fairbairn, *Great Scot,* Edinburgh."

"Good to . . ." Darling began, but was overridden by Grinsell's, "The Lauder woman lives just there, Crawford's telling me. That looks to be her at the gate. Stop wasting time and escort her to this shop of yours. We've got no girls along, have we?"

"We have no female constables with us, no."

"You." Grinsell took such a long step toward Jean she shrank back against the icy side of the Land Rover. "Friend of this Maggie Lauder, are you?"

"We've met." Jean glanced toward Gow House. Yes, Maggie now stood to attention by the front gate. All she needed was a blindfold and a cigarette.

"Come along then," ordered Grinsell. "Sit in on the interview, but no giggling or gossiping, got that?"

Jean's jaw headed south and her brows headed north. "Excuse me?"

"Are you deaf? I'm telling you to keep your gob shut."

"I'll walk her down to the village," said Alasdair, his voice edged as Niamh's song.

"No need. I'll have the local plod see to her. Unless you don't trust her out of your sight." Chuckling, Grinsell strode into the darkness. Darling offered Jean an apologetic nod and hurried off after him.

She pulled herself away from the chill of the car, not that the front of her body felt any warmer. "Holy fricking moly! I know what you said earlier, but I didn't think . . . That guy makes your old sergeant look like a charm school graduate!"

"He does that, aye. I reckon he's been ordered never to interview a female witness on his own, and your being a policeman's wife gives you a reference. Suits you and your curiosity, does it now?"

"Well, yeah. And then I can tell you all about it, right? Unless Grinsell will think you're interfering."

"He'll be thinking that in any event. In for a penny, in for a pound. Have a care." Another beam of light illuminated Alasdair's face. His eyes glinted ice-blue, but still he asked politely of the body-shape in the gloom, "Is that you, Crawford?"

"Aye, that it is," said the local plod's deep voice. "Miss Fairbairn?"

"Sure. Glad to help."

Chapter Nine

Jean walked off beside Crawford and his flashlight, grateful his long legs were taking slow steps, so she wouldn't have to hurry and fall over something. Or into something, although she suspected she'd already fallen into something. And she'd been so worried they wouldn't get here in time for the opening of the grave.

She looked back at Alasdair. He held his cell phone before his face. In its thin, pale light, his features seemed harsh and cold as a glacier, layer after layer of snow compacted into ice. It had been a long time since she'd seen his temperature dip quite so far below zero.

Who was he calling?

She turned her eyes front in time to avoid colliding with Lance Eccleston. He stood alone, in his bulky down jacket, looking like a young troll cast out from his bridge. She dodged around him. He didn't react.

Beyond the glow of the village, past the dark gulf of the sea, the mainland seemed to blend with the now overcast sky. Jean could only tell which was which by the distribution of lights.

The slightest of breezes whispered in the grass beside the flight of steps down to Cuddy's Close. The plants in back of the B&B stood motionless behind their protective wall. The undulating mirror of the harbor shimmered like watered silk. When she stepped through the door Crawford opened for her, the sudden light made her wince.

It came from a fluorescent bulb fixed to the water-stained ceiling of a long, narrow room. Off-white walls were smudged by traces of signs. Torn shag carpet, its original color something between periwinkle and mud, revealed a dirty but otherwise attractive stone floor that continued on through a partly open door at the back. Through it Jean glimpsed little more than darkness, although one anemic beam of light did illuminate a tilting shelf scattered with what looked like old newspapers, cardboard file folders, and several hardcover books without dust jackets.

What had someone once sold here? Books? Clothing? Fishing gear? Had they gone broke, retired, moved on to a shop somewhere else?

The room's musty, stale smell and its aura of better days long gone fitted Grinsell's rancid expression. Jean sat down in the folding plastic chair he indicated, next to a folding plastic table, trying not to look closer into his face now that it was fully illuminated.

His brown, beady eyes held no such compunction. He stared at her. One side of his mouth lifted in distaste. "Mrs. Cameron. Oops, sorry, that's Miss Fairbairn, isn't it? Or Ms." He dragged out the "S" so that the title hissed.

Again she wanted to blurt, *It's not our fault,* if not something considerably stronger. Instead, she said, as evenly as she could, "Either Miss or Ms. works fine." No good adding fuel to his flame by telling him she was also Dr. Fairbairn, thanks to that Ph.D.

Crawford opened the door to admit Maggie, who was almost as tall as Sergeant Darling beside her. The murky light didn't do either of them any favors, although Jean estimated that Darling would clean up nicely—and lose several years—once his square jaw and high forehead released their hunted expression. At least his cap of dark hair seemed to be a natural brown, unlike Maggie's purple and red streaks.

She looked even worse than she had earlier, like death not warmed over but left out in the rain to mildew. As she sat down in a second chair, shooting a curious glance at Jean, Jean caught a whiff of her breath. She'd found at least some of her supper in a bottle. Like daughter, like mother, except Maggie hadn't been drinking anything so mild as Tara's beer. Jean tried an encouraging smile, but it withered on her face.

Grinsell continued to stand, no doubt so he'd be taller and therefore dominant. At five foot three, Jean knew all about occupying as much space as possible in order to be taken seriously, but there was a difference between dignity and hostility.

"Well then." Fishing in his pocket, Grinsell pulled out a cellophane packet enclosing what Alasdair would have called digestive biscuits and Jean would have called a cross between a cracker and a cookie. He tore it open, bit, chewed, and smiled, brown paste matting his long, yellow teeth. "Here we are."

Darling produced a notebook and pen and took a chair to one side. Crawford assumed his parade rest position by the door.

Jean sat back and thought of Alasdair.

Grinsell prompted, "Miss Lauder."

"Dr. Lauder," she informed him.

"Lah-de-dah, aren't we posh, then? You found a body, didn't you, dearie?"

Despite the flash in her eyes, Maggie's voice came from her lips so dull and quiet Darling leaned closer. She told the tale, including the features Jean and Alasdair had figured out for themselves: The preliminary look into the tomb before the press conference. The surprise discovery. The impromptu lecture in the church to deflect the scrutiny of the reporters. The call to Crawford as the tide slipped away.

Grinsell finished his cookies and threw the wrapper down.

He turned to Jean. "You're a reporter."

"More of a journalist. *Great Scot* does history and travel articles, not current events." She waited for him to make some remark about how she'd been participating in current events since her move to Scotland, but either he wasn't up on recent Scottish murder investigations or preferred another angle of attack.

"American, are you?"

"Yes."

He sucked on his teeth. His eyes grew even harder. "Cameron couldn't find himself a wife in the UK? Or would no one have him?"

He didn't want an answer to that. Jean didn't offer one. She dropped her gaze to the hands clasped in her lap and willed her shoulders, tucked defensively up around her ears, to relax. He'd think the lowered eyes meant surrender. Let him. Bullies took a defensive response as encouragement.

With a condescending smirk, Grinsell focused on Maggie. "You've got good reason to be careful of reporters, haven't you now?"

"If you're referring to the old murder trial, yes."

"What else would I be referring to? Don't mess me about!"

Maggie bridled. "I've done nothing wrong, Inspector. I opened a medieval or earlier tomb on my own property is all. I have the proper permits to do so. I've got nothing to do with the recent body. It's been there for a good many years, perhaps since before I was born."

Easy, Jean beamed at her. *Don't put words in his mouth.*

"How do you know that?" murmured Darling from the side of the arena.

"I'm an archaeologist. It's my business to know that."

"All right then, since you're such a clever wee girl," Grinsell said, "who is the body in the tomb?"

For a nanosecond Jean thought he was asking who Maggie theorized had been originally buried there, the intended object of the grand reveal. But no, that wasn't Grinsell's business.

Maggie closed her eyes, perhaps imagining herself somewhere else. Somewhen else. "I don't know."

"For the love of God. Crawley, er Crawford! She identified the body as who?"

The constable said from the door, "Her father, sir."

"Your father." Grinsell leaned across the table, as close as he could get to Maggie's face without actually lying on the plastic surface. "Here's me thinking your father was a man named Walter Lauder, musician. That's never him in the tomb."

"No." Maggie looked up. She sat up. She tilted forward, matching Grinsell stare for stare. "My mother, Elaine Lauder, is suffering from dementia. She's been going on about having a lover, one she calls Lancelot the Fair. We've thought it was the illness speaking. And yet—and yet, there's evidence pointing to her having had a lover, once, years ago. A piper, a member of my father's band, who one day went and disappeared."

Oh. Jean remembered meeting a handsome young piper last year, one who'd spoken of Gallowglass. Some melodies echoed down the years, the refrains to the same old songs. Lancelot. The handsome young knight who tempted Queen Guinevere away from King Arthur. The young knight who fathered Galahad on a woman named Elaine.

"Lancelot? There's a bloke in the village named Lancelot, isn't there, Crawford?"

"Lance Eccleston," replied the constable. "He's in his twenties. Not the same man."

"Don't take the name literally, Inspector. My mother's a scholar and no doubt meant the name symbolically . . ."

"Never you mind what I'm taking, other than you as an uncooperative witness. So your mum's gone doolally, has she? A convenient excuse for avoiding questions. Wants bracing up, most likely."

Whoa, thought Jean.

Maggie snarled, "I assure you . . ."

"This lover of your mum's—runs in the family, eh?—this piper. He had a name, hadn't he?"

"It's all conjecture . . ."

"A name." Grinsell's fists fell onto the table like Norman maces onto the heads of uncooperative Saxon serfs.

If Maggie's gaze had been any sharper, it would have pierced Grinsell's hide from front to back and stuck quivering in the wall behind. "I've heard, I've been told, that his name was Thomas Seaton. He was a piper from Cape Breton, Canada. He played the Great Highland pipes and the Northumbrian small pipes as well. My father, Wat, he wanted to make him a member of Gallowglass."

"Get to the point."

"I am getting to the point. One day Tom was gone. Everyone thought he'd taken the ferry for the mainland. No one heard from him ever again."

"Well then." Straightening, Grinsell reached for another packet of biscuits.

Jean couldn't resist asking, "All this happened before you were born, right? Who told you about it?"

"I told you to keep your gob shut," Grinsell snapped.

Jean sank back in her chair, thinking of happy things like chocolate cake and kittens.

Maggie answered Jean's question. "Pen Fleming, mostly. She was sixteen or so when Mum and, and Wat came here. She helped Mum round the house and looked after me, even after she married. They were great friends. Still are, as much as, well, as much as possible."

"Another Fleming?" asked Darling.

"James does the pub," Crawford explained. "His wife, Penelope, she does the B and B."

His mouth full, Grinsell asked, "Have you any real evidence that this Tom Seaton is your father, other than the chin-wagging of local women?"

"The dates," replied Maggie. "Mum always said I arrived prematurely, and I was quite small, yes. If I was a full-term baby, however, then I was conceived whilst my parents were undergoing a trial separation. Dad was touring Down Under, Mum was researching here on Farnaby. Mind you, I only—I only started looking into this recently, after Mum started going on about the lover."

"Mum's quite the goer, eh?" Again he revealed his crumb-caked teeth, not in a smile but in a leer. "Tell me why, then, you're thinking the chap in the grave is this, this piper. Tom. Tom the piper's son, eh?"

"Because of the chanter in the grave next the body."

"What?"

"A chanter. The part of the bagpipes that makes the music. Rather like a recorder or clarinet."

He crushed the cellophane and threw it onto the floor, where it shifted uneasily in a cold draft. "A chanter, a white elephant, no matter. I told you not to mess me about."

"I'm not . . ."

"There's no chanter in the grave. No flutes, no clarinets, no bleeding bagpipes. You stupid cow, what sort of fool are you thinking I am?"

Jean's brain skidded. *Now what?*

Her face dashed of any expression, Maggie stared up at Grinsell's smirk. The room was so quiet the scratch of Darling's pen and a crunch of tires from outside sounded as loud as a crescendo on Hector's Great Highland pipes.

"We saw the chanter, too," said a woman's voice. Oh, Jean realized. It was hers.

Grinsell turned on her. "Who's *we,* dearie?"

"Alasdair, me, Tara. P.C. Crawford was standing right there." She jerked around to gaze accusingly at Crawford, noting Darling's raised brows on the way. Someone had been looking over her shoulder as they peered into the grave—it might have been Tara, not Crawford—but Tara had been hanging back the whole time.

Crawford gazed into the middle distance.

Grinsell's hiss pulled Jean back around. "You don't follow orders too well, do you Mssss Fairbairn. If I was your husband . . ."

I'd either take poison or put some in your crackers, Jean thought.

"Girls," Grinsell concluded. "They always hang together."

Better than hanging separately. Not that they still hanged murderers in the UK. They might still have been doing so when Rob the Ranter—whether he had been Tom Seaton or someone else—had died and been hidden away. She'd have to look it up.

"Professor Lauder's saying she saw a chanter," Crawford's calm voice allowed, "but me, I'm not so sure what I was seeing. It was dark, there was only the one torch, and the light was jinking about."

Maggie found her voice. "You're saying it's not there now? Edwin, P.C. Crawford, he was watching the place—someone must have taken it."

"Pull the other one." A moist brown blot worked its way into the corner of Grinsell's mouth. "Rufus, Darling"—His whine emphasized the comma—"have Crawford bring in this Elaine, and Tara as well. Tara Hogg, is it? Bacon on the hoof, eh? Must be a right looker. Let's see if she fries up as nicely as her mum and her granny."

"What?"

"You never married. There's a word for women like you, isn't there? More than one for you in particular. Starting with 'murderess.' "

Maggie rose out of her chair, fists clenched, face twisted with rage.

"Your mum, you, your daughter—three generations of goers, eh? Fancy that. Lucky chaps, here on Farnaby. No visiting knocking-shops in the city, then, with all the local talent."

"You'll show my daughter respect, you nasty piece of work, or I'll . . ."

"You'll what, dearie? What makes you think you've got any say in the matter?"

Cursing, Maggie lunged. Jean grabbed her left arm as Darling leapt forward and seized her right. "You're just giving him ammunition," Jean hissed, and Darling muttered, "Steady on. No good making things worse."

"Are you asking to be charged with perverting the course of justice?" Grinsell demanded. He might as well have said, *Make my day.*

"Justice? What do you and your ilk know of justice?" Maggie wrenched herself away.

The door creaked slowly open. Clyde Eccleston stood in the aperture, his cap pulled low, his collar pulled high, so that his face seemed to be only stubble and a bright pair of eyes. Had he been listening in? If so, he displayed not one iota of embarrassment. "The car's down the street a piece. Here's the key. Ignition. No need to be locking it up, not here on Farnaby."

Darling stepped across to take the key. "Thank you."

Clyde stood at ease in the doorway. One beat, two . . . Grinsell snapped, "Off you go, Grandad. Keep from underfoot, eh?"

With a snort of resentment, Clyde vanished back out the door.

Maggie spun around and started across the room. "I'm going now, Inspector. You don't have to warn me about leaving town.

I hope your pea brain has noticed this isn't a town, it's an island. Like Alcatraz."

"You know the drill, don't you now, dearie? None better. Second time's the charm."

"Get out of my way, Edwin."

Receiving a nod from Grinsell, Crawford got out of her way. "I'll drive you home and collect Tara. I know Elaine's poorly . . ."

"Naff off." Maggie shot out into the night.

Jean saw her chance. She achieved a personal best making it through the door, moving so fast her momentum carried her across the sidewalk and over the curb into the street. The abrupt step down and ensuing stumble rattled her from stem to stern, not that she had much left to rattle.

For a minute she simply stood there and breathed deep, cleansing breaths of the cold air.

Chapter Ten

When she looked around, Maggie stood several paces up the street, tapping the glowing screen of her phone. Warning Tara about the ill-tempered detective, the way Tara had warned her earlier about the intrusive journalists?

With a frustrated shrug—no reply?—Maggie jammed her phone into her pocket and stamped away up the street. Jean scurried to join her. "Are you all right?"

"Yeh," Maggie said over her shoulder. "They're all like that, aren't they? Abusive. Insufferable."

Well no, neither male police people nor men in general were all like that, but this was no time to debate gender politics.

The lighted windows along the seafront made smeary rectangles in the thickening mist, and the few street lamps had haloes. Two human shapes walked down to the harbor, where the large police boat was illuminated brightly, its luminescence bleeding off into the haze. A couple more shapes moved around on board, preparing to take the body to Berwick-upon-Tweed for examination.

With a reasonable officer in charge—one like Alasdair, to choose a random example—as soon as the Scene of Crimes team had thoroughly checked over the tomb, Maggie would be cleared to get back to Plan A, the original burial. With Grinsell in charge, who knew when Maggie would be able to get back to her work?

"I'm sorry," Maggie said, not what Jean had been expecting

to hear. "This isn't half what you bargained for when you came here, is it?"

"It's not what you bargained for when you opened the tomb."

"No. I intended to make headlines of an entirely different sort."

"By revealing the burial of Arthur or Merlin? Not Lancelot. I don't care if Bamburgh's just over there." Jean waved vaguely out to sea. "His story is pretty much fantasy, and was added onto the original legends later."

"And came from France at that. Yes. Quite." Maggie brushed irritably at her straggling hair. "You've read my mother's *The Matter of Britannia,* have you?"

"Yes, of course. It's a . . ." Jean stopped before she uttered the truth, that Elaine's *magnum opus* was a mish-mash of half-baked and yet intriguing theories not about Arthur but about his wife. She liked that sort of thing, an amusement park ride careening from historical fact to historical myth and back again, spiced with feminist theory and wry asides. Compared to Elaine's earlier work, however, it was poorly thought-out and awkwardly presented. Rebecca's news that Elaine had claimed to be communicating with the dead came as no surprise. It was while reading *Britannia* that Jean had first suspected the derangement of Elaine's scholarly mind.

Her sentence still dangled in midair. "It's a basic reference," she concluded, and put into words what she'd suspected ever since she'd heard about the press conference. "You think the historical Guinevere was buried at Farnaby Priory, don't you? You think it's her chantry chapel, with the attribution changed between the Romano-British-Celtic period and the Norman one, from Guinevere to Genevieve. The two names do sound alike. You're hoping to prove your mother's theories."

"Well done. Got it in one."

"It's an educated guess."

"That's what I'm making, an educated guess about the origins of the chapel. I've seen Roman lead coffins perforated in similar patterns to the one in the tomb. It might well date back to Romano-British times, even before Aidan came to Lindisfarne. Fifteen hundred years or more."

A guess, Jean asked herself, or a bet, a bet with both Maggie and her mother's academic reputations at stake?

Light and a babble of voices and delectable aromas spilled from The Queen's Arms. So did the music of a fiddle, Hugh playing "Prince of Darkness." The edgy song about working in the coal mines would suit Niamh's voice, but presumably Niamh was caring for Elaine back at Gow House.

Maggie peered through a window, her eyes catching the glow from within, then turned away. Tara must not be inside. "James named the pub for Mum's theory. It was The Percy Arms when I was a child, after the local posh folk in their castle in Alnwick."

"But in *Britannia,*" Jean persisted, "Elaine never makes any claims about Guinevere's burial place. I mean, some legends say she entered a nunnery and died in Amesbury, near Stonehenge. Some say she was buried at Meigle in Perthshire, in Scotland, although her reputation there is hardly saintly."

"Pictish propaganda," said Maggie. "There's good evidence the real Arthur was a Romano-British cavalry leader who lived and fought his battles on the Scottish borders. The Picts never forgot he was their enemy. The Saxons and the Angles did, and claimed him for England."

The Saxons. The Southrons. The Sassenach.

"Merlin was also a historical figure who lived in the Borders. As my mother proved in her reading of Gildas and other writings of the time period and later, he had a sister named Gwendeth. All she did was equate Gwendeth with Arthur's wife. A political marriage—par for the course, then."

"But 'Gwen' just means 'fair,' you see it all the time."

"Mum found other evidence—well, her next book would have moved on from Guinevere's life to her cult after death, which she believed was centered here on Farnaby."

"Are you intending a correspondence between Farnaby and Avalon? Except it's not Arthur carried away by the grieving queens, it's the queen herself."

"Mum thought something of the sort, yes. But these early legends, they're like inkblots."

"Everyone sees something different. Everyone sees what she wants to see. Tell me about it."

But Elaine would never tell anyone about it, would never write that next book, evidence or no evidence. Now Maggie had taken up her mother's torch, only to find her own family's history taking precedence over Arthur's.

Headlights flashed and an engine roared. A small pickup truck in dire need of a tune-up clattered past the corner of Cuddy's Close, Jean glimpsing Crawford's hooked nose behind the windshield. The twin red dots of its tail lamps dwindled down the length of the street and disappeared around the hairpin curve.

"Clyde's old banger," Maggie said. "He sells package deals for wildfowlers and twitchers. Kill the birds or count them, no matter to him." She took a couple of steps up the alley. "Tara. I shan't let that horrid detective rubbish her as well. I'm accustomed to it, more's the pity. She's an innocent bystander, had nothing to do with any of it. As for Mum, well, if Grinsell means to interview her, he can come to the house, and good luck to him." Her laugh sounded more like a cackle, and disintegrated as soon as she released it.

"Good night," Jean said, but her words bounced off Maggie's swiftly retreating back.

A raindrop plunked onto her head. A burst of bagpipe music

sounded from somewhere down the street—the student hostel, probably—a slow piece, a lament for love lost and heroes faded. Someone on the police boat shouted something to someone on shore, words that Jean couldn't decipher, but assumed were not, "Quick, put out to sea and leave Grinsell behind."

Pondering Maggie's reference to Farnaby as Alcatraz—stone walls alone did not a prison make—Jean walked into the B&B. This time she didn't smell baking bread but fabric softener, accompanied by the screeching whir of a British washing machine, like a tiny jet taking off.

"Jean," said Alasdair's velvet-on-steel voice. "In here."

She swerved from the staircase to a door across from it. Ah, a dining table and chairs, and beyond them a lounge provided with overstuffed seating, a flat-screen TV, and shelves of DVDs, books, and boxed games. Hildy, the resident cat, curled on a chair. She raised a languid paw to acknowledge Jean's arrival. Alasdair leaned over the fireplace, switching on the electric fire. "Sit yourself down. You're frozen. There's a whisky for you on the coffee table."

Jean plopped down on the chintz-covered sofa, dumped her mini-backpack, and seized one of two small glasses sitting on a round bar tray. Take-out from the pub. A sip of amber ambrosia filled her mouth with smoke and sunshine and shot tendrils of warmth through the knots in her tendons. When the flare in her senses subsided, she said, "I'm too mad to be frozen. Mad-angry, although mad-crazy is in there too. What a rat bastard that man is. A hyena. A skunk. I see what you mean about his head on a pike."

"That would be an improvement, wouldn't it now?" Sitting down beside her, Alasdair reached for the other glass.

In Jean's present mood, she assessed that glass as half-empty, not half-full. "I understand why Cumbria shipped him off to Northumberland. What I don't understand is why he's still employed, period."

"He's a reasonably good detective, has done effective work despite the abrasive manner. Because of the abrasive manner, in some cases."

"Okay, so he asked the right questions, but really, Alasdair, I don't care if he solved the Jack the Ripper murders, his behavior is indefensible."

Alasdair's cool blue gaze didn't waver. "I'm not defending him, I'm stating the facts. If he was having a go at you, I'll be backing your complaint. Though the sergeant was not recording the interview, was he now?"

"Oh. No, he wasn't. Go figure." Jean sipped again, swallowed, exhaled. "Grinsell wasn't picking on me by comparison to what he was doing to Maggie, harassing her about the old murder case on top of interviewing her about finding the body today. Is her case common knowledge among British cops? You knew about it."

"I looked her up when you told me we were coming here, because I was thinking the name familiar."

"So did Grinsell look her up on the way here? Crawford must have told him who found the body. It's just that . . ."

"Aye?"

"Grinsell knew Maggie never married and that Tara's her daughter."

"Crawford again. Or Grinsell had Darling researching the name. Previous track is important."

"The previous track of a suspect, not the person who finds the body . . ." The background of a witness *was* important. Jean remembered when she'd first met Alasdair her own previous track had been an issue, and Alasdair had proceeded accordingly.

She drank again, cutting her anger loose from its moorings and letting it slip away before she transferred it to Alasdair for also being a cop.

Before she identified too strongly with Maggie.

Chapter Eleven

One corner of Alasdair's mouth tucked in, not quite a smile. Jean wasn't fooling him one bit. She never could. He reached out an arm and she tucked herself into his embrace. Funny how she fit so well against his side. How many years had they each hung stubbornly onto loneliness before fate threw them together? If, as feminists once said, a woman needed a man like a fish needed a bicycle, then Jean would keep right on pedaling away, fins and all.

"I've phoned an acquaintance in the Cumbrian Constabulary," Alasdair said, "one who knew Grinsell at the time of the Borders stramash. He sent me on to a friend of his in the south."

"Looking up his background, huh? There's a nice tasty sauce for the gander. Plus, if he thinks you're interfering then you might as well interfere."

"There's interfering, and there's minding truth and justice and all. Long story short"—his voice went dry and distant—"Cumbria was not the man's first stop on his tour of Britain's police agencies. He came originally from Cambridgeshire."

"Cambridgeshire?" Jean sat up so abruptly Hildy opened an eye. "Maggie's trial was held in Cambridge. Was he one of the cops involved in that?"

"No one in the area could have missed out having an earful about the case and the subsequent trial. Trials. A chap was eventually convicted of the crime."

"Yeah, you said they finally found the murderer . . . Well, being convicted doesn't mean he was the murderer, but the authorities had to have had a good case to convince the jury."

"Exactly. They were after having a good case against Maggie as well. Being found innocent does not mean she was."

"I know."

"Any road, that's why I was thinking her name familiar. Two Cambridgeshire detective constables were threatening to resign the force if she was found not guilty, saying the trial was political correctness and radical feminism run amok."

Jean rolled her eyes. Only twenty years ago, and dinosaurs had still been stomping through the legal swamps. *Being found innocent does not mean she was.* "Grinsell was one of the objectors, right? And they didn't resign."

"Hollow threats, one and all, as you'd be expecting—although Grinsell ended by being transferred to Cumbria. Still, my friend's friend in Cambridgeshire is saying that loads of media, not only the tabloids, were putting it about that Maggie was guilty at the least of conspiring with the chap who was later convicted. That she was found innocent for no more reason than being young and beautiful."

"And pregnant."

"Oh aye. Some decades earlier that would have told against her. But in the nineties, it worked for her. She was no slut, she was a lass poorly treated by the menfolk." His tone made all the social commentary necessary.

Okay, so dinosaurs existed in the eye of the beholder. "The social pendulum swings, huh? And the media overreacts, trying to dumb it all down into an episode of a TV show, with a climax before every commercial." Jean tried to remember Crawford's words beside the tomb, when he'd first mentioned Grinsell's name. It had happened a few hours ago, not last month . . .

Aha. "Crawford said—or implied, to be accurate—Grinsell had volunteered to come out to Farnaby. Otherwise the chief inspector in Berwick, Webber, he would have just sent a sergeant. I mean, it's not exactly a recent death. I bet Grinsell recognized Maggie's name. He may have known her connection to Farnaby all along. I bet he sees himself as some sort of crusader, out to avenge an old miscarriage of justice and set an example for uppity women in the future. Sheesh."

Jean settled back into her nest beside Alasdair, her ears echoing with Maggie's, *Justice? What do you and your ilk know of justice?* There was a concept that cut two ways.

His arm tightened around her. "Good job I left Miranda a message of my own, laying out the situation and asking her to be checking up on the particulars."

"I've got my computer—I could do that—but that's Miranda's area of expertise. If she had any patience with academia and peer review and so forth, she'd make a great social scientist."

"She would that." Alasdair saluted the absent Miranda with his glass, then drained it. He set his cheek against Jean's forehead, lightly, so as not to scratch her skin with what by now was his ten-o'clock shadow.

From the front of the house came the rattling-trash-can noise of an old banger. "Grinsell commandeered a rattletrap of a pickup from Clyde," Jean explained, "and sent Crawford to bring Tara and Elaine back to the incident room. I bet he's coming back all alone."

"Elaine? Is Grinsell not aware of her condition?"

"He's aware, all right. He doesn't care." Jean could see Grinsell dashing himself against Elaine's illness like a boat against a cliff. She could see him ditto against Crawford's stolidity. "Maggie texted Tara the minute she got out of Grinsell's sight—called him 'horrid.' Go figure—probably warned her to lie low."

"Horrid, aye, but even so, you're saying Grinsell was asking all the right questions."

"Oh!" Jean jerked around, Alasdair dodging before her skull

knocked his nose askew. "When Maggie mentioned the chanter, Grinsell said it wasn't there."

"The chanter lying next the dead man?"

No need to reply tartly, *No, the one Hector was playing as we drove by.* Alasdair was being a cop. "Yes. I drew Grenfell's fire by backing Maggie up, saying we saw it, too. But he thinks she was lying."

The telltale crease appeared between Alasdair's eyebrows—cogitation in progress.

"Crawford's claiming he never saw the chanter at all, that the light wasn't right or whatever. What's up with that?"

"Better denying the chanter was there at all than taking stick for letting it go missing on your watch."

"But who knew the chanter was there? Who had the chance to take it? And the biggie: Why?"

"It's a clue. And some villain is hoping to pervert the course of justice by hiding it."

"But it's a clue to a crime that took place decades ago." And whose side was Crawford taking, anyway, now that the situation had devolved into taking sides?

Footsteps in the front hall made them both look around. Hugh, calling it a night at an unusually early hour? No—the outside door hadn't opened. Unless someone else was walking around the B&B, someone they didn't know about, the steps had to be Pen's. Perhaps she was looking for something else to clean.

No one passed the door. In the depths of the house, a telephone bleated, once, twice, three times. Pen's voice, heavier than it had been earlier, answered and carried on an unintelligible conversation.

Dropping her own voice so far Alasdair had to lean into her face to hear it, Jean detailed the story of Elaine's—theoretical, hypothetical, alleged—phantom lover, the piper Thomas Seaton, the Lancelot to Wat's Arthur.

"Well then," Alasdair murmured, "till we've got evidence to the contrary, let's be drawing the simplest conclusion and saying he's aye the chap in the grave."

"Works for me. No way am I speaking for Grinsell." Jean went on, "Maggie said she heard this from Pen, who was—who is—a great friend of Elaine's. Until then, she'd thought the lover was a manifestation of the dementia."

"And now Maggie's doubting her own paternity, thinking the chanter's a clue to that. Is someone else thinking it's a clue to murder?" Alasdair's warm, whisky-scented breath tickled Jean's cheek. Dark lashes edged his cool blue eyes. She wondered what poor Rob the Ranter, Tom, Lancelot, whoever, had looked like in life. She lassoed her brain before it louped off into wondering what Alasdair would look like in death.

"We don't know Tom was murdered," she said. "He could have suffered a heart attack or stroke or at any rate died of natural causes. If that had been the case, there'd have been no reason to hide his body."

"There'd have been reason enough if he died at an inconvenient time, say, whilst having sex."

"Okay, sure, but you don't pick up a body like a sack of groceries and carry it over to the nearest medieval ruin. More than one person had to be involved in getting him into the tomb."

"Unless Tom was in the priory when he died, with or without Elaine."

"That wouldn't be my first or even tenth choice for a tryst."

"Needs must, I'm supposing. Mind you, though, I'm no expert."

Jean had to laugh at that, if dryly. He was no expert in illicit trysts. In, um, trysting itself, he was very accomplished indeed. She thought of a seventeenth-century poem, where the poet woos his reluctant lover by pointing out how the grave was a nicely secluded place but no one ever embraced there.

The lovely room upstairs made a nice, secluded place for the living and their life-affirming activities. She had been anticipating not a cinematic clinch on the beach, exactly, but inspiring moments set to the rhythm of the sea. And now the stimulating weekend jaunt had turned sinister. Too many moments in their lives together turned sinister, as if their happiness was ransomed by other peoples' pain. Perhaps working to balance the scales of justice was payback enough. "What goes around comes around," she said.

"Thinking of Grinsell?"

"Not necessarily. Just thinking. You know, tuppence for my thoughts."

His laugh was more of a soft chuckle.

The orange bars of the electric fire sent a glow over the semi-darkened room and emitted not only warmth but a gentle hum. Overhead marched a row of ceramic pieces, not only the china dogs that sat on every respectable British mantel, but a shepherdess and her male counterpart, a Toby jug in the belligerent image of Winston Churchill, a Mickey Mouse, and a little blue baby Krishna. Photos ranged among the knick-knacks—a teenage girl; the same girl a decade later with two children in front of Bamburgh Castle; the same children, older now, at the music school. One small frame showed a slimmer, smoother Pen and a smiling Elaine of the book-cover era.

Hildy's ears perked up. She stretched, tested a claw by plucking at the fabric of the chair, and then headed for a window on the side of the room facing the garden and the priory. Clearing a lamp and a candy dish with millimeters to spare, she settled down on the sill, a lump behind the lace curtains.

Voices rose and fell in the night. Women's voices, chanting in Latin. A wave of perception rolling forward, inundating everything in its path. Sacred songs persisting long after the throats and tongues that had vocalized them decayed into dust and became one with the sand and soil of Farnaby Island.

CHAPTER TWELVE

No sooner did Jean feel the burden of the supernatural settle on her shoulders, along with the weight of Alasdair's arm as he, too, sensed as much as heard the voices, than the sensation ebbed. For once she hated to see it go. The music was the aural equivalent of the star she'd seen at sunset, a reminder of eternal peace and beauty.

With a sigh, she finished her whisky. Its warmth glistened like quicksilver in her living veins.

"I'm thinking any of Grinsell's folk still watching the priory were not hearing a thing." Alasdair's voice caught in his throat, brushed against the grain.

"I'm wondering whether Elaine really was speaking with a ghost."

He nodded toward the coffee table, where his reading glasses sat next to a booklet. "I found that on the shelf next some books on Farnaby and Lindisfarne and Elaine's *The Matter of Britannia.* Why Britannia, by the by? I was thinking the Arthurian stories the Matter of Britain."

"Elaine focused on Guinevere, though. Britannia, the Roman goddess, the female symbol of Britain. The distaff side."

"So to speak. Britannia's always pictured with weapons and armor. A proper Amazon."

"That was Elaine's point, Guinevere as a strong figure in her own right, a ruler, a priestess, maybe even a warrior. That's not the most novel of concepts—think what Hollywood's done with it—but Elaine's twist is that Guinevere is Gwendeth, Merlin's sister. She intended writing a second book about how Farnaby's chantry chapel is the center of her cult."

"Her evidence being the testimony of a ghost?"

"We don't know that, not for sure." Jean set down her glass and picked up the small book. The shiny cover sported the title, *Hilda, the Enchanted Prioress of Farnaby,* and a rough medieval woodcut of a nun. Her tiny oval face was no more than a sketch of humanity encompassed by wimple and veil. "The magical prioress?"

"You were saying the legends were likely no more than the usual stories of saints and miracles, but this lady was no saint, for all she was a contemporary of Saint Aidan."

"She comes from the era of Saint Hilda of Whitby, too, then, but it sounds as though they have only the name in common."

"I've not finished reading the story. I'm thinking she'll come to a bad end, accused of witchcraft."

"The early Celtic church wasn't nearly as dogmatic about that, and local foundations had a lot more leeway than when the Roman church took over, so maybe not."

On the windowsill, the cat jerked upright, making the curtains billow. Racing steps and urgent voices sounded from outside.

". . . in here," said a male voice, and something thumped.

"Thanks," a woman said breathlessly. "What Mags said—I swear, if that's how your cops treat people . . ."

"Hush."

In a coordinated move worthy of Rogers and Astaire, Jean and Alasdair leaped from the sofa to the window and bumped heads over the cat's alert ears.

Alasdair radiated warmth onto Jean's temple. The glass radiated chill onto her forehead. In the mist-matted darkness beyond the window, nothing moved. She closed her eyes, opened them, and then made out the gravel path between Pen's tidy flower beds, a bench, a bird feeder. A clothesline dripped moisture, each droplet a quick gleam. Beyond the garden wall the priory seemed no more than arched implication.

"I don't . . ." she said, her breath misting the glass, just as Alasdair's hand clamped down on her arm. "There."

Using Hildy's ears as a sighting device, Jean spotted a slender female shape crouching against the wall between the garden and Cuddy's Close, almost concealed by a shrub whose bare branches stitched shadow across the pastel fabric of her jacket. A white bandage glinted on her hand. Tara.

Footsteps moved in stately rhythm down the alley. A burst of light illuminated the broad shoulders and blond hair of Lance Eccleston, his back turned, facing the far end of the wall. Answering—no, from the vantage point of the window Jean could see he only pretended to answer a call of nature.

"Here!" P.C. Crawford's reflective jacket seemed bright as a solar flare.

"Hmm?" Lance's hands moved, but he wasn't actually zipping up. He turned around, his step less steady than it would be strolling across the deck of the ferry in a heavy swell. His words came lazily, a bit slurred. "Oh, it's you, Constable. You're missing a grand session at the pub."

"The pub has loos," Crawford said coldly.

"The gent's was engaged. And I was wanting a breath of air." He clapped Crawford on the shoulder and leaned into his face. From the way Crawford recoiled, Jean deduced that breath was indeed the issue. "I thought you'd be well away home by now. Your shift ended hours ago."

Fending Lance off, Crawford asked, "Have you seen Tara Hogg?"

"Not since eight or thereabouts, round about the time everyone went haring off after the polis. Have you asked at Gow House?"

"Aye, that I have. Maggie's saying Tara's at the music school, but she's not." The beam of the flashlight swooped high and low, over the garden wall and across the back of the house. Behind the shrub, Tara wrapped her arms tightly around her chest and shrank into a ball.

A light flooded the garden and a door slammed open. "Edwin? Lance?" Pen called from the back of the house. "What's all this?"

"Sorry to be bothering you, Pen." Crawford all but knuckled his forehead. "I'm looking out Miss Hogg. D. I. Grinsell wants a word."

Another reflective jacket drifted into the alley behind Crawford, the face above it concealed in shadow. It was either Sergeant Darling, Jean thought, or an official wild card.

Crawford tried again. "Pen, have you seen Tara Hogg?"

Pen had to see Tara crouching in her flower bed. Jean could see the young woman's face as clearly as she could see Alasdair's, drawn and pale against the window.

"Why no," Pen said. "I've not seen the lass for quite some time. It's getting on for half past ten . . . Oh. Hello. I'm Penelope Fleming."

"Detective Sergeant Rufus Darling," he called over the wall. "Sorry for the disturbance, madam." Turning to Crawford, he asked, "No joy with Elaine Lauder either, I assume?"

"Niamh's already put her to bed. Poor old thing's not fit for an interview in any event."

"Well then." Darling made a wagons-ho gesture. "Inspector Grinsell's agreed there's no call chasing wild geese in the darkness. We'll have another go tomorrow. The boat's staying the night—weather's too thick to be out in the shipping lanes unless needs must, but our passenger's in no rush."

"Aye, sir." Crawford fell into step beside Darling and the sound of their shoes on the damp pavement was absorbed into the voices and music from the pub. The light in the garden winked out and the back door shut with a solid thunk.

By the time Jean's eyes adjusted to the sudden darkness, the garden gate had creaked open and clicked shut and both Tara and Lance were gone. To Gow House? There was no better place to hide than one that had already been searched. "What did poor Darling have to do to get Grinsell to give it up for the night? Sacrifice a virgin?"

"I'm hoping he appealed to logic and procedure. No matter. If Grinsell finds Lance was hiding Tara, as was Pen, come to that, he'll be having their guts for garters."

"He'd take a chunk or two out of us for not blowing the whistle."

"Aye, but no one knows we were watching save the cat here."

"True." Jean backed away from the window and realized she still held *Hilda, the Enchanted Prioress of Farnaby,* her fingertips moist against the slick paper. "So was Tara in the pub after all, and didn't hear Maggie's text come in? And then Crawford came looking for her? If so, Lance did some fast thinking. And fast side-choosing. So did Pen."

"Trust Grinsell to set everyone in the village against him. That said," Alasdair went on, "the body's almost sure to be older than Maggie, never mind Tara. She's got nothing to fear from an interview."

The show over, Hildy jumped down and wended her way toward the door.

"You didn't hear how Grinsell treated Maggie," Jean retorted. "You didn't hear what he said about Tara without ever having met her."

"She's making the eventual confrontation even worse, for no good reason."

Jean reminded herself again that Alasdair was a cop. A male cop. "We're only guessing about her reason. What if . . . Whoa!

What if Tara took the chanter out of the grave? I saw someone walking toward the priory right before we went to eat, remember? Maybe she's trying to protect her mother and grandmother."

"Ah." The furrow between Alasdair's eyebrows deepened. "If so, she's making it worse for them as well."

"She is, yes—the missing chanter gave Grinsell another opening to harass Maggie. If only the mist hadn't stranded him . . . Oh, no—where's he staying? Not here, not in Michael and Rebecca's room. Pen will have to fumigate it before Michael and Rebecca can put the baby in there tomorrow."

"Surely this is not the only B and B. There's the hostel as well."

From several rooms away came Pen's voice. "Puss, puss—there you are."

Hildy meowed.

"A bit of cream? I'll warm it for you, shall I?" A door shut.

She who must be obeyed, Jean thought. Surprising herself with a smile, she walked over to the sofa and retrieved her mini-backpack. "Poor Tara. The way she feels about Lance, and then having to take any port in a storm."

Alasdair switched off the electric fire. "Eh?"

"The romantic triangle. I told you earlier."

"When?"

"In the pub, right after Tara broke the glass and Niamh checked her hand."

"Oh aye, James came running with bandages. Seems unlikely, though, with James being so much older and married to boot."

Jean laughed. "Not James. Lance has a crush on Tara, but she doesn't reciprocate. Didn't you hear what they were saying to each other right before we got in the car to drive up to the priory? He called her a proper little bitch and she told him to stuff it where the sun don't shine."

"Ah," Alasdair said. "Hardly a love triangle, then."

"Okay then, it's a frustration polygon. The third angle is Niamh. The way she looks at Lance, I bet she has a crush on him. I bet she called Lance while we were on the ferry, wanting to meet him in the pub. He wasn't thrilled but couldn't avoid it."

Alasdair hadn't blinked.

"Missed the whole thing, didn't you? And you call yourself a detective."

"A detective, not a lonely-hearts columnist. A right weary detective at that, thinking he'd best have himself a good night's sleep before it all starts up again." Alasdair bowed Jean toward the door. "And before you go wasting your breath reminding me, aye, we're never knowing what's evidence and what's not, so your romantic triangle's worth observing."

"It's not *my* triangle," was all Jean replied, without adding that the elusive nature of evidence was Grinsell's justification as well, never mind his nasty remarks about chin-wagging women.

Jean led the way upstairs and plunged into the evening routine, washing the taste of Grinsell out of her mouth with a fierce squeeze of mint toothpaste. By the time she lay down in the bed beside Alasdair he was already asleep, his furrowed brow almost smooth again. She blew him a kiss and picked up the booklet.

The real Hilda of Farnaby had not been clothed in the intricate medieval habit of the cover illustration. She had probably worn a simple wool shift and veil, her wonders to perform. Almost unhinging her jaw with a yawn, Jean flipped quickly through the book, pausing at a sketch of Hilda levitating over the sea to Lindisfarne to visit her opposite number at that priory. Quite the mystic, she had protected her followers from various physical and spiritual dangers and died peacefully in bed surrounded by admirers.

Surely it had occurred to Maggie that the original tomb, later superseded by a Norman chantry, could have been Hilda's. But if Maggie was trying to justify her mother's work . . . Jean promised herself to have another look at the grave slab tomorrow. Who had said something about horsemen? Tara?

Had she taken the chanter? Realistically, anyone on the island could have taken it—assuming the bush telegraph operated as efficiently here as it did in other small communities and word of the body and the chanter had made the rounds before Grinsell's arrival.

You'd have to have a strong motive to poke around in that grave, in the dark, alone. Jean put that image out of her head and considered the booklet's title page: *By Elaine Lauder.* The same name was handwritten below, in a firm, classical script, with the words, *For Pen and James, who know where the bodies are buried.*

Literally? Surely not. Elaine would hardly have autographed the book with those words if so. She only meant that Pen and James were good friends dating back many years.

Poor Elaine. A living ghost haunting Farnaby.

Jean set the book on the bedside table, switched off the light, and settled down against the crisp, fresh pillows. Yawn or no yawn, she knew it would be one of those nights when she was too tired to stay awake but too wired to sleep.

The grave did not belong to Arthur. Even though Arthur's followers had sent him off in a boat. With three queens. Who had welcomed the mortally wounded man to the mystical island of Avalon.

A mystical island. Three queens. Elaine. Maggie. Tara.

Where did Niamh come in?

Jean hadn't realized she'd dozed off until she woke up with a start.

Chapter Thirteen

The bedside clock read one-fifteen a.m. From downstairs, the kitchen, probably, came a murmur of voices. Jean recognized Pen's and James's. The third, a man's lower timbre, she didn't. Unless it was Clyde's. It sure wasn't Grinsell tracking his victims into their domestic sanctuary.

They weren't so much arguing as having an urgent discussion—well, it would have to be urgent to go on so late—and she couldn't make out any words. Maybe one of them had exclaimed and either that or the shushing by the others had awakened her. Maybe one of them had let a door slam.

Whatever. She was awake now, so she threw on her robe and tiptoed in her wool socks into the bathroom. It was only after she flushed that she realized the sound would alert the talkers below that someone was up and about. Not that she had any intention of slipping down the stairs and eavesdropping on them. They had every right to be worried about the events of the, by now, day before.

The house fell into a silence deep and cold as the grave . . . In the daylight she'd have laughed at herself. Now, she turned up the collar of the robe so that it protected the nape of her neck.

She didn't have to make her usual check to see if Alasdair was breathing. She could hear his slow, deep breaths from across the room. Good. He'd need all his strength tomorrow, biting his tongue until Grinsell, Darling, and Crawford gave up and went away—hopefully not without sharing a preliminary pathology report on the body.

If they were able to go away.

Lifting the curtain aside, she looked out at the harbor. The thinning mist shimmered in the few remaining lights of the village. The black shape of the police boat was marked with small lights, too, revealing that it now rode high behind the breakwaters in the company of several smaller craft. She made out the shape of the ferry, farther down the street—it floated at the top of the concrete ramp rather than the bottom. But the Ecclestons had no customers in the middle of the night.

The soft blanket of perception sank onto her shoulders. The hair on her nape lifted like antennae, collar or no collar. Faint but unmistakable women's voices ebbed and flowed. Jean padded across the room to the window overlooking the priory.

The walls and arches seemed to be draped in gauze. She couldn't tell whether those brief flickers of movement were strands of mist wafting through the ruins or the ghosts of the early nuns—whether Hilda's or much later ones—singing the night offices as they had in life. The scene was eerie, yes. Uncanny. And not at all threatening. Father, son, and holy ghost. Mother, daughter, and holy spirit. Profane time, that plodded forward minute by minute, day by day, and sacred time, that circled rather than passed.

The embrace of the sanctified eternal died away, leaving her with the gooseflesh and cold feet of the present. She hurried back to the bed and tucked herself under the weight of the duvet, against Alasdair's warm, living flesh. He stirred, mumbled something, and fell back asleep.

After a while the chanting died away. After a longer while Jean dozed again, and dreamed fitfully of cabbages and kings, of swords and dragons, of ships on the sea and a morning in Texas after an ice storm, the Gallowglass van spinning its wheels on the frozen street but gaining no traction.

I know the feeling, she thought in an instant of lucidity, and then slipped into a deep and blessedly dreamless sleep. She woke up to find the room illuminated by a watery light and Alasdair, fully dressed, sitting on the side of the bed. "It's going on for eight, lass. I've never known you to miss breakfast."

"Good heavens, no." Buoyed by the aromas of coffee and sausages wafting from the kitchen, Jean washed and dressed and was ready to go in record time. On the stairs she told Alasdair about the inscription in the booklet, and about hearing their hosts in conference in the wee hours of the morning.

He nodded. "Saying 'where the bodies are buried' likely means nothing, aye. And yet the Flemings and Clyde were acquainted with Thomas Seaton before he died, weren't they not?"

"Sure, but . . ."

"Pen might could have overheard us talking about the missing chanter."

"That made you sit up and take notice. Why shouldn't it have the same effect on her, especially since, as you said yourself, she knew Tom?"

"If she and James and the other man were simply discussing the matter, why be doing it so late at night?"

"James didn't get home until late. He had to clean up the pub and do the accounts and whatever." Alasdair turned his best—or worst—cool, level, and skeptical gaze on her. She shook her head. "I know, I know, everybody's a suspect, no matter how likeable. I get the message."

He raised his hands. *I come in peace. Back off, already.*

"Sorry," Jean told him, just as Pen herself bustled out of the dining room. "Good morning. Please, come through."

The table was lavishly equipped, from cream pitchers to toast racks to dishes of jelly and marmalade. Before Jean had time to comment to Alasdair how poor Pen looked pale and deflated, the woman herself had returned with plates of steaming eggs, bacon, sausage, grilled tomatoes and baked beans.

James followed, a teapot in one hand and a coffee pot in the other. "Good morning to you," he said through his moustache, which seemed to have wilted since last night.

Hugh walked in the door and sank with a groan into a chair. "So this is morning, eh?"

James poured him a cup of tea. "Thanks for playing so late last night. Didn't think I'd ever get folk to pack up and leave so I could close. Too much to be talking about."

"Thanks for keeping me properly lubricated with the brown ale," Hugh returned. "And that detective, Grinsell. He was knocking back the whisky, kept glowering at me as though I was off-key."

"Seems to be his usual expression," said James.

So, Jean thought, music did not have charms to soothe the savage beast. Or was that breast? She'd have to look it up.

Alasdair passed the toast and the subject. "We've always reckoned you'd rather be playing than sleeping, Hugh."

"Oh aye," Hugh returned. "I'd rather be teaching as well. No rest for the weary, with the concert the night."

Pen produced another plate of food, then covered the teapot with a cozy cleverly knitted in the shape of a cat. "Did you make that?" Jean asked.

"That I did."

"Did you knit the shawl Elaine was wearing last night? That's a beautiful dusky purple color, sort of a heather in the twilight shade."

"Yes, I worked that up as well. The yarn's spun from local sheep's fleece and colored with vegetable dyes, brilliant to work with." Pen's wistful smile bloomed and faded. "Is everything all right for you?"

Jean, Alasdair, and Hugh all managed affirmative mumbles around mouths of food, and waited until James and Pen vanished—him to the kitchen, her down the back hall—before leaning into the center of the table like conspirators in a secret conclave. "What were the townsfolk talking about in the pub?" asked Alasdair. "The discovery of the body and Grinsell's rudeness, aye, but what else?"

"A Canadian chap named Thomas Seaton or Tom was mentioned more than once. Seems he cut quite the dashing figure in the early days of Gallowglass, then up and vanished after rowing with Wat. Is he the dead fellow?"

Revived by several healthy swigs of coffee, Jean detailed the state of the cold case.

"Any idea why Tom—Thomas Seaton—and Wat were arguing?" Alasdair used his knife to mash egg, sausage, and beans onto the back of his fork, a technique Jean had yet to perfect. She still ate like an American, her fork in her right hand.

"Some were saying Wat was jealous of the lad because Elaine was fond of him. Others were saying Wat was jealous of his musical skills—Wat never could work out how to play the pipes, though he was a brilliant fiddler and guitarist, the best going." Hugh's cheeks were rosier now that he'd had two cups of tea. "The chanter's gone missing, has it? I'll have myself a wee keek round the school. Could be it's hidden in plain sight."

"Grand idea," Alasdair told him. "It's in too bad a shape to blend in, though it could be tucked away in a corner, right enough."

"As for Wat and Elaine and this Tom, I'm not at all surprised the way it all happened."

"There's a classic triangle for you," said Jean. "Arthur, Guinevere, and Lancelot."

Pen walked back by the door carrying a load of sheets. That's odd, Jean thought, Pen said yesterday Michael and Rebecca's room was all ready.

"I first met Wat Lauder when I was busking on the streets of Glasgow, hadn't two pennies to rub together. He heard me playing outside a club late one night, found work for me, even offered me the next vacant slot that came up in Gallowglass."

"He appreciated good music."

"And he believed in teaching the young ones, which I was by way of being, once upon a time." Hugh's face went lopsided in a wry smile, probably wondering where the gray hair had come from. *That clock keeps right on ticking* . . . "In the event, I soon had my own band to look after and never did more than fill in with Gallowglass. But I've known Wat and Elaine since the days they had the young musicians in their home here on Farnaby, before they put Wat's royalties into building the school."

Alasdair ever-so-gently directed the witness. "You're not surprised at the romantic triangle?"

"Wat was a grand musician, but a tyrant at home, especially in his cups—and he was more often than not in his cups. Told Elaine his music came first, that she was biding with him only so long as she did her duty by him—and that meant setting aside any thought of having herself a career. He was her career, he'd say. Not that unusual an opinion in the seventies, mind you, but times they were a-changing."

"And thank goodness for that," Jean said.

"He was gentler with Maggie, thought she was by way of being the grandest lass ever spawned—leastways, he did do long as she was Dad's wee girl. Once she was into her teens, though, it all fell apart. She and Wat spent years at sixes and sevens, barely speaking. Ironic, that, if he's not her father at all."

"Where were you hearing that?" Alasdair asked.

Hugh frowned. "Folk were making a meal of it in the pub, but I'm not so sure who first said it."

"Crawford told Grinsell what Maggie said at the grave. If it's true, it might be common knowledge here on Farnaby, at least among people old enough to have known Tom." With a conciliatory smile at Alasdair, Jean paralleled her fork and her knife on the plate. "Ironic that Elaine would fall for another musician, not, say, an accountant. Although I suppose the pool of available men was pretty restricted here on Farnaby. So Wat was an overbearing bully, huh? What a way for Maggie to grow up. No wonder she never married."

"There's more to it than that." Alasdair considered the bottom of his teacup, but apparently could read nothing there.

"Yeah, she was looking for love in all the low places, or whatever the song is."

"Wat," Alasdair said to Hugh. "You were saying he was jealous, and had a row with Tom. Was he by way of being a violent man? Could he have killed Tom if he found he was Elaine's lover?"

"He had a temper, aye, and was not above throwing things about, but whilst he'd bellow and threaten, I never saw him skelping anyone. Elaine, now, she eventually started giving as good as she got, called his bluff a time or two by demanding trial separations and time away at Cambridge for revising and researching and the like. She had her career after all."

"She was no damsel in distress, then."

"No, never mind Wat treating her as one, even encouraging her admirers. They'd be sitting round the kitchen table in the evenings, playing at Arthur and Guinevere with the young folk as the knights paying her court. Wat was after showing her off as a prized possession, offering her for looking but not for touching."

"Very medieval," Jean said. "Courtly love, chivalry, hypocrisy, the whole thing."

"She gave us nicknames—I was Alan a Dale, wandering minstrel. And aye, that's properly from Robin Hood, not Arthur, but it was all a bit of fun, not scholarly work." Hugh buttered another piece of toast. "We'd have lovely sessions, with Elaine on the piano and the rest of us sawing away. Or we'd all go picnicking at Merlin's Tower, on the headland just there, calling it 'Castle Faralot.' "

"Fara—" Alasdair started to ask, then answered his own question. "Ah. Farnaby. Camelot."

Jean didn't need to point out another irony, that the one person who knew the complete, unexpurgated story of Thomas Seaton—and maybe the truth about the forty-year-old murder—was now under a physiological evil spell. She was trapped as irrevocably in her own mind as Merlin had been trapped by his young lover and fellow enchanter in a cave or rock or tree, depending on which legend you liked best. The historical Merlin or Myrddin, the last druid, was another story.

The door creaked and they all jumped, not that they were guilty of doing anything that everyone else on the island wasn't doing. Hildy pushed through, her pink nose checking out the lingering odors of the meal.

Hugh held a crumb of bacon out to her and she nipped it from his fingertip. "Is she not a fine wee moggie?"

"You're a pushover for cats, aren't you, Hugh?" Jean piled her napkin beside her plate and scooted her chair back.

"Oh no," Hugh replied with a twinkle. "Take 'em or leave 'em, that's my motto."

"Right." Alasdair stood up and looked out into the garden, now innocent of last night's dramatic—well, perhaps not a rescue. More of a diversion. "Grinsell's no doubt planning on interviewing Pen. Soon. The body's needing examining in Berwick, and the weather . . ."

Jean peered around his shoulder to see a thin, watery sunlight casting thin, watery shadows. "What about the weather?"

"We're in for a proper sea fret." James walked into the room and plunked a tray onto the table.

"A haar," explained Alasdair.

Hugh added, "Thick fog," and dodged James, who was clashing plates and cups onto the tray.

"Are Clyde and Lance going to be able to get the ferry across to the mainland and back?" Jean asked.

"Hard to say." Clattering like Clyde's old pickup, James whisked his burden across the hall and into the kitchen.

"I don't know whether I'm less enthused about Michael and Rebecca not making it here today or more enthused about a new wave of reporters not making it."

"I'd not like to be staging the concert without Michael's pipes," Hugh said. "I've been singing his praises to Hector and the piping students. We'll see, eh?"

"In the meantime," said Alasdair, "let's be hoping Grinsell's well on his way to Berwick before the island's shut down."

And we're marooned here, Jean concluded. At least they wouldn't be marooned with a murderer. He—or she—was forty years gone.

Chapter Fourteen

In the bedroom, Jean eyed the photo of Merlin's Tower—Faralot, okay—as she switched on her phone. A text message from Rebecca appeared on the screen, sent not ten minutes earlier. *We've crossed the border and are on track to catch the first ferry. Can't wait to hear the latest.*

"Yeah," Jean said aloud, "I can't, either."

Alasdair considered the view out the back window. "Were the nuns chanting last night as well, or was I dreaming that?"

"Yes, they were. I was actually grateful for my paranormal allergy."

"Right before I awoke I was dreaming about driving that one-track road out to Ardnamurchan Lighthouse when the car slipped into a rut and I sat there birling the wheels."

"Funny, I dreamed something similar, the Gallowglass van going up an icy street. Spinning their wheels would have been better than slipping off the road and crashing into a gully."

"I cannot quite see past Pen's garden shed, but there looks to be a car in the priory car park. Maybe the same one that was birling its tires there last night, maybe another."

Jean started toward the window, then did a smart aboutface when the phone in her hand warbled with "Hail to the Chief." Speaking of the latest . . . "Good morning, Miranda."

"Good morning to you, Jean. How are you getting on? Have you identified the mysterious body?" Miranda's smoky tones were annotated by the chime of fine bone china. She no doubt sat in her tastefully appointed boudoir sipping custom-blended tea and nibbling on croissants that had been flown over from France in velvet-lined boxes.

"Well, maybe. So far the police haven't even gotten it to Berwick, though. As for how I personally am getting on, I'm asking questions. What else is new?"

"I'm hoping I've got a few answers for you, as per Alasdair's message from last night. Quite inspiring, how folk are up and about of a Saturday morning."

Alasdair turned away from the window. "Miranda?"

Yep, she mouthed at him. Into the phone she said, "You mean, inspiring how people are willing to answer strange questions on a Saturday morning. I was going to settle down with the Internet and see what I could find, but . . ."

"No need. You're in the field. I'm the rear-echelon support team, eh? And I've already done a fair bit of wandering about the Internet. But the actual folk involved are better at cutting to the chase."

"Who have you talked to? Whom, I guess."

"Maggie Lauder's barrister, who defended her—successfully, as she kept pointing out—in the murder trial."

If in time she arrived at the Pearly Gates, Jean thought, Miranda would be there waiting to introduce her to Saint Peter.

Sitting on the edge of the bed, she waved Alasdair down beside her and tilted the phone so he could hear, too. "All right then, Miranda. We're listening."

"Good morning, Alasdair," Miranda said, and, without waiting for a reply, "Maggie was tried for the murder of her lover, one Oliver Phillips. Quite the handsome young sprig of the landed gentry, judging by his photos—classic features, artfully tousled hair, expression of a man offering noblesse oblige to the local pig farmer."

Jean could see him, nostrils dilated, eyes hooded, his

confidence and refinement like a flower to a bee. So Maggie had been looking for love in high places rather than low. "Oliver Phillips?" she repeated. "Any relationship to the Oliver Montagu Phillips ancient and medieval manuscript library at Cambridge?"

A pause, and the sound of manicured fingertips on a keyboard. "Well done, Jean," Miranda said. "Yes, he was the grandson. No surprise he went up to Cambridge himself, when his family donated such a tidy sum to buy and then house those manuscripts."

"Elaine Lauder's degree is from Cambridge, too. She spent weeks on end studying in the Phillips library. No surprise Maggie went there, too. Nice that getting into a prestigious university here in the UK is a matter of acing the tests, not being independently wealthy."

"Was Maggie not reading archaeology?" asked Alasdair.

"Sure, but historical archaeology requires knowledge of the relevant written materials."

"Furthermore," said Miranda's voice in the phone, "Maggie started out reading literature like her mum, only switched to archaeology in her second year."

"And also in her second year . . ." Jean prompted.

"One lovely autumn day, a group of students went wildfowling—shooting ducks and geese. Before the day was out, Oliver was dead from a shotgun blast to the chest and head. That much for the pretty face, I'm afraid."

Alasdair grimaced. Jean didn't want to know what he remembered. All he said was, "It was no accident, then."

"Maggie claimed it was. However, it was clear that the weapon had been fired within a foot of the lad's anatomy. Aimed directly at him, in other words."

"There was a group of students," Jean said. "I assume no one actually saw the murd—er, accident, but did someone see Maggie threaten Oliver? I mean, why arrest her rather than anyone else?"

"She and Oliver had a terrible row just that morning. According to the others, he was accusing her of having someone else on the side, of playing him for a fool. But she was having none of that, telling him he had no claim on her. She was by way of being a free agent."

She'd learned a few things from her mother, thought Jean. And she'd skipped a few lessons as well, like the one about being doomed to repeat history.

"At the time of Oliver's death, the group had broken up to walk through a belt of woodland. Maggie was alone with him—or so she implied. The barrister made much of Maggie never having held a gun in her life, saying that it was Oliver's fault for handing her a loaded gun, and that no matter how the gun was aimed, the firing was an accident."

"Was it a shotgun with two barrels? Pulling two triggers instead of the one would hardly be an accident." Alasdair was still playing devil's advocate.

"Yes, it had two barrels, but only the one was fired. That helped her case with the jury. They agreed it was an unfortunate accident and since she'd already spent time detained at Her Majesty's pleasure awaiting the trial, she'd paid for her carelessness."

Jean waited for Alasdair to say something about Maggie being young and pretty to boot, but he didn't. She gave Miranda another cue. "There were two local detectives who thought she'd gotten off, if you'll pardon the expression, scot-free."

"That there were. However, they weakened their own argument by making another arrest within the week, an older lad claiming he'd been nowhere near the scene of the crime."

"Was it fingerprint evidence turned the trick?" asked Alasdair.

"There was a muddle of prints on the gun, nothing particularly helpful. No, what finally solved the case was breaking the lad's alibi."

"He was another student?"

"No. He was working as a bar man in the town. Maggie met him busking outside the university. Played a fine set of Irish small pipes, by all accounts. Turned out Oliver's jealousy was well-placed."

"A musician," said Alasdair. "A piper."

"Must be in her DNA," Jean added.

"He was a handsome lad as well—a ginger-haired leprechaun. I expect there was more than a bit of class conflict between him and Oliver, over and beyond the competition for Maggie's favors."

"No kidding. Go on."

"Once he'd been arrested, this fellow, Donal McCarthy, testified he'd followed along behind the shooting party, worried about Oliver's possessiveness. He testified Oliver was cursing at Maggie and pushing her about with the gun. Donal was after taking the gun away and preventing any accidents. In the struggle, it went off. Exit Oliver."

"Did the jury find manslaughter or murder?" Alasdair asked.

"The general feeling seemed to be that if Oliver's death had truly been an accident, Donal should have stepped forward much earlier. If he was by way of defending Maggie in the woods, then why not in court, eh? He was found guilty of the full monty, murder, and the judge sent him down for life."

"A perfect gentle knight would have stepped forward at her arrest," agreed Jean.

"Oh aye. The judge was no doubt thinking Donal was more of a knave."

"Maggie must have parsed her testimony very finely to avoid being charged with perjury," said Alasdair.

"The barrister's saying it was a fine a performance as she'd ever seen, aye."

"Did she testify at Donal's trial at all?"

"No, the Crown had sufficient evidence without her—and was not sure about putting a massively pregnant woman on the stand in any event."

"The pregnancy raised the quality-of-mercy factor in her own trial," Jean said.

Alasdair asked, "Which man was the father?"

"I've got no idea. Oliver, I'm supposing, though Donal's being married makes no difference in the paternity sweepstakes."

"Donal's the father," Jean stated, and to the angle of Alasdair's eyebrow, "Maggie never ratted him out. Grassed him up. She was willing to take the blame and go to prison for him. Maybe she didn't want to break up his marriage, though it was a little late to be worried about that."

His other eyebrow arched up to join the first.

"Okay, so she *believed* Donal was the father." Jean went on, "When the child, a little girl, was born, she gave her up for adoption, and the family who adopted her took her to the U.S. of A."

Miranda laughed. "You've got yourself a crystal ball, have you now, Jean?"

"No more than eyes and ears," explained Alasdair. "The child's here on Farnaby just now, introducing herself to us as Maggie's daughter. Tara Hogg, her name is."

"Aye, that's the lass. Getting a bit more than she bargained for, is she?"

"You don't know the half of it. There's a lot more going on than the stranger in the tomb." Jean quickly summed up the episode of the policeman who barked in the nighttime, how he was one of the Cambridgeshire dissenters still picking bones with Maggie after all these years and showing every intention of hounding her family as well. "There was poor Tara hiding behind the shrub . . ." She stopped dead. *Whoa.*

"What?" asked Alasdair.

"The light caught the bandage on her hand. The one Niamh put on. Miranda, what was Donal's last name? McCarthy?"

"Ah," Alasdair said. "McCarthy, is it?"

"Aye," said Miranda. "Donal McCarthy. Why?"

Alasdair and Jean spoke simultaneously, stopped, made "after you" noises. Finally, Jean managed to babble, "There's a nurse working for Maggie—well, for her mother—suffering from dementia, it's really sad—the nurse is named Niamh McCarthy—has a great voice. She was singing with Hugh last night."

"Well, well, well." That tone in Miranda's voice always indicated plots thickening and headlines generating.

"There are plenty of people named McCarthy in the world," Jean cautioned, even as her thumbs pricked. "Coincidences happen."

"They do that, aye. If I went combing through *Great Scot*'s subscriber list, I'd be turning up who knows how many folk with the same names."

"So you're thinking Niamh working for Elaine's a coincidence?" asked Alasdair.

"No more than you're thinking it. Aye? Half a sec. Jean, Alasdair, Duncan's arrived and is telling me it looks like being a fine day for golf. Nothing like chasing a wee white ball down eighteen rabbit holes."

"The only things we're going to be chasing here on Farnaby are wild geese in the fog." Although a glance at the window showed Jean the same diluted sunlight she'd seen earlier. "Have a good game."

"I shall, thank you. More inquiries later, I'm hoping."

"There's a lot to hope for." Jean switched off the phone and sat slumped over it, her thoughts flapping like wild fowl scattering before a shotgun blast.

Chapter Fifteen

Jean could feel Alasdair's scrutiny on the side of her face. "Yeah. I know. It's Grinsell's case. Oliver's death and Tara and where Niamh comes in—none of that is any of our business. I don't really think it's his business, either, not anymore, but he's in charge. Our business is the original burial and the press conference, and Maggie's been open and aboveboard about that—once we pressed her into being aboveboard."

"Aye."

"But you're not letting that stop you from checking out Grinsell himself. And working up your own file on Maggie. Sort of, anyway."

"No, I'm not letting that stop me."

"You're feeling a disturbance in the police force, aren't you? No pun intended."

With a thin smile and shake of his head, Alasdair got to his feet. He did not bend down to search for conspiracies under the bed, instead sending a searching look through the front window. "The police boat's still there. Grinsell should be out and about harassing the villagers, eager to be getting himself and the body back to Berwick. But all I'm seeing is D.S. Darling on the breakwater, looking at his phone. Let's have us a word."

"Everyone's eager to get Grinsell away." Jean grabbed her backpack and slipped on her jacket. "Surely he doesn't think he'll find some new evidence here about the Phillips case."

"Aye, he's fighting the wrong battle. Even if he's not thinking

Thomas Seaton's case is worth his while, it's the one he's dealing with." Alasdair opened the door and stopped in the opening.

Jean piled up behind him. "What?"

Alasdair pointed to a cloth and a can of polish sitting on the radiator next to the door. "I'm thinking we had us an audience whilst chatting with Miranda."

"None of it was anything Pen didn't already know. The Lauders, and by extension everyone on the island, have to have followed every word of Maggie's trial. We should just *ask* Pen what she knows about Elaine and Tom and everything."

"She'll be biased, Jean, being friends of the family and all. She might even be involved in the murd—the death. Besides, it's no good our interviewing witnesses. It's Grinsell's case."

"But Pen has to expect us to be interested—if we asked a few questions as friends, not as the Spanish Inquisition . . . Oh, never mind."

Supposedly the test of a first-rate intelligence was the ability to hold two opposing concepts in the mind at the same time and still be able to function. She already knew Alasdair had a first-rate, gold-star intelligence. He obviously still functioned.

What she didn't know was whether she and he had chosen opposite sides in a situation that, until Grinsell's arrival, hadn't appeared even to have sides. A situation that would work itself out in spite of their opposition, she told herself—that being one major detail to hope for.

He ushered her down the stairs to the ground floor, where Pen was conspicuous by her absence—although the washing machine in the kitchen was shrieking once again. They stepped from the cool, sausage-scented air of the house to the cold, smoke-scented air of the outside world. White gulls spun across the grayish sky. Several people walked up and down the street, intent on their own errands. A dog trotted along the pebbled beach, ditto.

Here came Sergeant Darling down from the breakwater. His features seemed less pinched, as though his bones relaxed when not carrying the burden of Grinsell. And yet his dark eyes were no less hunted, and his lips were set in such a tight line they were invisible. Prying them apart far enough to speak, he said, "Good morning. Have you seen Inspector Grinsell, by any chance?"

"No, we've not yet been out," said Alasdair. "When were you last seeing him?"

"Before breakfast. He went off at half past six, just at dawn, in a foul temper."

Jean didn't ask, *How could you tell?*

"Had a sore head from last night in the pub, could be. He said nothing to us beyond our finishing up here and getting ourselves back to Berwick. Could be he's having another look at the priory before the media lands like commandos on D-Day."

Or was he having a look in the windows of Gow House? Jean glanced at her watch. Past ten.

Alasdair's nod indicated approval of Darling's choice of words. "You've tried phoning him."

"Oh yes. As per his orders, I've got Clyde Eccleston in the interview room, but he's got his business to be tending to, and with the fret—well, we're all right till the sea breeze starts up." Darling shot a wary glance out to sea, where clouds like dirty rolls of wool massed on the horizon.

One eye shivering in a half-wink toward Jean—*aye, I'm contradicting myself*—Alasdair asked, "You're asking Clyde about Thomas Seaton leaving the island all these years ago?"

"That I—we are, yes. With the time difference in our favor, we were able to have a word with the authorities in Cape Breton, in Canada, last night. They've got no missing persons report on Seaton at all. Likely he had no close family, and his friends there thought he'd stayed here in the UK, but still, that's conjecture, not evidence."

This time Alasdair's nod of commendation was even more emphatic. "You've set the Canadians to work, have you?"

"They'll be sending along what they turn up. Dental records would be helpful, much quicker than DNA—and DNA's only good, in any event, if you've got a relative's to match it with." Darling looked up the street, and down, and across the harbor to where Bamburgh seemed no more than a model photographed in soft focus. "I'll have a look at the priory, see if the inspector slipped into one of those trenches and turned his ankle or the like." He angled toward Cuddy's Close but didn't actually start walking.

Jean would have had a bad feeling about Grinsell wandering around on his own, except she was already up to her armpits in negative vibes.

"Sergeant," said Alasdair, "have you looked out Mr. Eccleston's pickup truck? Perhaps Inspector Grinsell was driving it."

The expanse of Darling's forehead pleated. "I did hear the old banger starting up, now that you mention it."

"Right." Alasdair took off, stepping so briskly up Cuddy's Close that Jean and Darling were sucked into his wake. Between the pub and the B&B, past the garden wall, and they stood in the car park. Maggie's elderly Land Rover and an even older pickup held down different sides.

The pickup's passenger-side rear wheel was stuck deep in a pothole, making the entire vehicle list to the side. "It was a car that ran into the hole last night, wasn't it?" Jean asked.

"That it was, and it ran back out again." replied Darling. "That's Eccleston's truck, right enough, wanting some strong young lads to give it a lift and a push. Lance would do, if he's sobered up, and his mates if he has any."

Alasdair contemplated the car, the tire, and the mud-spattered appearance of both. "I'm seeing Grinsell, not knowing the lay of the land, driving into the pothole. Then, being the impatient sort, he birled the wheel till he'd rammed himself in good and proper. Then he set out on foot. Going where? Why?"

Darling shook his head. "He's been working his mobile phone off and on, but we're all doing that."

"Has P.C. Crawford seen him?" Jean asked.

"Not a hair, no, but then, I sent Crawford home for the night, since the mist wasn't so thick toward Bamburgh. Now he's sitting with Eccleston having a good yarn, near as I can tell."

A recent memory pricked at Jean's mind—Pen, carrying sheets from the first-floor bedroom toward the kitchen. She'd had the room ready for the Campbell-Reids, but someone had spent the night there after all, and, being a conscientious landlady, she was cleaning it all over again.

Had it been Crawford's voice she'd heard last night? And if so, so what? "You may have sent him home, but did he actually go?" she asked, evoking a puzzled frown not only from Darling but from Alasdair.

"He never said," Darling replied. "He came into our B and B this morning freshly turned out is all."

"Ah," said Alasdair. "You're thinking he's the third voice you were hearing in the wee hours. Why?"

Jean explained her theory about the sheets, which, now that she vocalized it, sounded pretty thin. She concluded, "I don't see why it matters that they'd be talking to each other."

"No harm . . ." Alasdair began, then stopped. What was he going to say? No harm in asking Crawford? But it was Grinsell's case, and Grinsell's responsibility to deal with the help, so to speak.

Oblivious to the undercurrents of meaning, Darling turned to consider the silent walls of the priory, the broken arches, the vacant windows. Yeah, Grinsell could have tripped over his own ego and fallen into one of the trenches. A shame, Jean thought, that she was less than enthusiastic about looking for him.

Hector Cruz bounded up from the Close, now dressed in ordinary jeans and a bright yellow sweatshirt emblazoned with the red sunburst flag of his native state. The long case of his bagpipes banged against his thigh. "Good morning."

Jean, Alasdair, and Darling replied in triplicate, with Darling introducing himself and Hector stating name and affiliation.

The courtesies observed, Hector focused not on the tip-tilted pickup but on Merlin's Tower beyond the village. Its stones were a charcoal-gray, probably cut locally, not the red and silver-gray of the priory. Its stolid cylindrical shape seemed to have grown rather than been built. Jean half-expected to see not a sentinel on the alert for Viking raiders but a Neanderthal stroll out from behind the wall, picking his teeth with an antler.

"What is that place, anyway?" Hector asked. "The redhead with the natural pipes, Niamh, she said something about Camelot and Wat Lauder and a castle. But it doesn't look like a castle to me, not like Bamburgh or even that cool mansion house on Lindisfarne."

Jean answered, "Its official name is Merlin's Tower. Why, I don't know, although there are legends of Merlin in the Borders area. Wat and Elaine were thinking of renovating it into a stately home like Lindisfarne Castle—hopefully not designed by the same architect who did the music school. Assuming anyone designed the school and it wasn't assembled from a kit."

"So no one lives there?"

"No, Pen says it's pretty much a ruin."

"Really? Because when I came back from the school about—geez, it must have been almost midnight. I was helping a kid change a reed yesterday and left my own reeds up there, so went back to get them. Anyway, I was walking along right about here and saw a light up there in the tower."

As one, Alasdair and Darling zeroed in. The former asked, "This truck, it was not here just then?" as the latter asked, "It was a misty night and yet you saw a light?"

Hector took a step back from the sudden attention, his obsidian-black eyes widening. "That Land Rover was the only car here, and yeah, the outline of the tower was kind of blurry, but the light was bright. Must have been a high-powered flash-light."

"A torch," Jean translated for Darling.

"Not a torch, a flash—oh, that's what they're called here, isn't it? Call it a tortilla, whatever, it moved around a little while, then went out. Or went behind a wall. Same difference."

"What did you do after you saw it?" Jean asked.

"Went on back to the hostel and went to bed. What should I have done?"

"Not a bleeding thing." Darling turned to Alasdair. "Did the inspector see the light as well? Did he start driving up there? Looks to be a road, mostly ruts, but drivable."

"Unless it was Grinsell showing a light himself," suggested Alasdair.

"No, no, he came in from the pub a bit, well, he was helping me"—Darling winced—"with writing up my notes."

"Is there a problem?" asked Hector.

"We've lost D.I. Grinsell," explained Darling. "We're, ah, worried."

We haven't lost Grinsell, Jean thought. But they were worried, yeah. She could tell by the barometers of Alasdair's brows that worry fought with annoyance for priority.

"Let me run my pipes down to the school and I'll help you look. He may have fallen or something. At home I'm a paramedic. You can't make a living from a pipe band. Be right back." Hector took off across the parking lot and down the road past the church and Gow House.

A flash of red hair in the front garden was Niamh standing with arms crossed, face turned toward the sea. Beside her, Elaine used a small pair of clippers to shape an overgrown shrub, her white hair concealed beneath a floppy canvas hat. So Elaine was the gardener, then. That's why so many plants there and in the cloisters had gone feral.

Hector waved but didn't slacken his pace. Niamh didn't seem to notice. The clippers made a tiny snipping noise.

Murmuring "Might as well have me that look," Darling strode off across the cloister and into the church, peering into corners and trenches as he went. He paused in the door of the chapel, glanced back over his shoulder at Alasdair and Jean, then plunged inside. A moment later he reappeared, running.

They hurried forward to meet him. He held out his hand. In it lay something small and shiny and crinkly. The cellophane wrapper from a packet of snacks. "It was lying inside the police tape round the grave."

"What is it?" Alasdair asked.

"I didn't tell you," said Jean, "Grinsell was eating cookies while he interviewed Maggie. Digestive biscuits. Little rounds of carb and sugar."

"D.C.I. Webber ordered him to give up his pipe-smoking," Darling said. "He wanted something else to fuss about with."

Alasdair's gaze registered skepticism, whether about the propriety of snack-eating or about Jean not telling him something, she couldn't say. Darling thrust the wrapper into his pocket and whipped out his phone. "Crawford. You're wanted at the priory. Bring the lads in from the boat as well."

By the time Hector hotfooted it back from the school, Niamh had ushered Elaine inside and a search party had fanned out across the priory grounds, into the cemetery, over the fences and prickly hawthorne hedges into the surrounding fields.

Darling himself, his chin set, his mouth slitted, led Alasdair, Jean, and Hector up the twin muddy ruts toward the tower. Yes, the path held prints of smooth-soled shoes and scrapes where they had slipped and slid. Darling and Alasdair tried to herd the other two around the prints, onto the verge, through the heather, and over the occasional rock, but Jean couldn't imagine how the churned mud could be turned into evidence. It looked as though a miniature water buffalo had had itself a good wallow.

The hedges closed in, then parted again. Seabirds called. The path wove back and forth up the hill and finally ended at a kissing gate, one that swung back and forth within a half-circle of fencing. Beyond it opened a grassy area, a green moat around the outer wall of the tower. Half a dozen sheep watched curiously from the edge of the headland, explaining why the turf was cropped short as a golf course and promising even more need for careful shoe-cleaning. Later.

Jean was vaguely aware of a fabulous view—not only the priory and the village and harbor below, but also Lindisfarne and the mainland, Bamburgh and the Farne Islands just off the coast, that ominous gray curtain out to sea. She was intensely aware of the grim faces beside her, the muscle jumping in Darling's jaw, Alasdair's cheekbones crusted in ice, Hector frowning with mingled bewilderment and determination.

Up close, the mossy walls and empty arrow-slits of Merlin's Tower seemed romantic rather than forbidding, the stuff of poetry and make-believe, if with a Gothic edge. It would make a great site for a picnic, especially if the picnickers packed more mood elevators than just musical instruments.

Pen said Elaine had poked around the area a bit, supplementing her literary work with some amateur archaeology. It looked as though Maggie, a professional archaeologist, had followed her mother's trail here, too. An exploratory trench cut the ground up to the foundations of the wall, its side caved in like those of the trenches in the priory cloister.

Two black birds croaked from the broken tower. Corbies, the hooded crows of many a Borders ballad. The black bird pacing menacingly across the pasture was a raven, also a bird of myth and legend, a messenger between this world and the next. A carrion-eater.

Jean had second thoughts about that picnic.

Breathing hard, the quartet pushed one by one through the gate and gathered outside the break in the wall that had once been the entrance to the fort. The narrow courtyard between the wall and the keep was clumped with prickly plants, tumbled stones, and lichen-crusted roof slates. Another trench angled across it not far from the black rectangle of the tower door, half exposed by a blotch of hazy sunlight, half concealed by diluted shadow.

A breath of chill wind dispelled the courtyard's miasma of damp and dung. A bit of sparkly cellophane wafted across the grass. Darling swooped down on it. "What the heck?" Hector asked.

"He was here," said Alasdair.

Darling stabbed at his phone. Faintly, like an eerie wail in the corners of the courtyard, a ring tone sounded.

The color drained from Darling's face. He squared his shoulders. He stepped across the threshold and paced to the slumping sides of the trench. He looked down.

The wind died. A sheep baaed. A crow cawed.

Darling's voice was barely audible. "He's here now."

Chapter Sixteen

Jean took two quick steps. She glimpsed the stark white face smeared with red and brown, the hands lying limp, pale starfish. Her heart lurched, then free-fell deep into her abdomen. A wave of sausage-tinged acid splashed into her throat.

Pushing past her, Hector slid rather than climbed down into the black gash of the trench. He bent over, exposing the yellow back of his sweatshirt. It was printed with the words: *New Mexico, Land of Enchantment.*

Jean choked down not only acid but also an insane urge to laugh. Alasdair pulled her back, his hands firm on her arms—*steady on.* His face would have made an iceberg seem warm. "Have a care," he said to Hector. "Those plants alongside the ditch, they're stinging nettles."

Darling dropped onto rather than sat down on a large stone and peered numbly at his phone.

"Crawford?" hinted Alasdair. "Your team from the boat?"

"Ah." Darling thumbed the screen and started muttering directions.

After a brief inspection of—not the body, the man, George Grinsell—Hector said, "He's got a pulse. Not much of one, though. He's shocky. He must have fallen into the hole in the dark and hit his head. Looks like a bad concussion."

With a squeeze of Jean's forearm, Alasdair released her and picked his way to the trench. "Hit his head on what? There are no more than a few cobblestones in the mud at the bottom."

"No, sir." Darling's mutter increased in volume. "We've got folk helping out, yes sir."

Alasdair sent a searching gaze around the courtyard. "He came up here of his own free will. Leastways, he was still eating his biscuits."

"So someone hit him," stated Hector. "Bummer. And that's one heck of a rash on the side of his face."

The nettles beside the trench were broken—someone had stepped on them. Maybe fallen on them. Their wiry stalks and bristly leaves made them look like hostile basil. Any other time, Jean would have thought the plant suited the man. Now she remembered every derogatory remark she'd made about him. Maybe he'd deserved those. Had he deserved this? Who had the right to decide?

Into her mind came the wise words of Tolkien's Gandalf, a literary descendant of Merlin. Some who lived deserved death, and some who were dead deserved life, and mortals should not be so eager to pass judgment.

"Chief Inspector Cameron." Darling held out his phone. "It's Chief Inspector Webber in Berwick-upon-Tweed."

"Eh?" asked Alasdair.

"You're the ranking officer here, sir. In a way."

His features disappearing beneath yet another arctic layer, Alasdair took the phone. "Cameron here. Retired, actually. Northern Constabulary, Inverness. Protect and Survive, aye, that's me." He stepped out of the courtyard and inspected the horizon. The clouds were oozing higher, their upper edges feathering into the hazy bowl of sky. "Aye, there's time for a medical team, if you're moving right-smartish."

Hector stood up. "Yeah. Fast would be good." Mud blotted several of the sun-rays on the front of his sweatshirt like storm clouds blotting the sun—not, Jean thought, following Alasdair's gaze, that the issue was a gathering storm but gathering murk.

Low visibility. Blundering about in a fog.

What else was new?

"Well now," said Alasdair into the phone. "Sergeant Darling's here, he's quite capable."

That was diplomatic. Poor Darling was so pale, Jean wondered if he was shocky, too. His expression was that of a child who'd asked Santa Claus for a turtle and ended up with a T. Rex.

Shouts sounded from down the hill. Crawford scrambled up the path carrying a couple of blankets. The other policemen and several villagers clustered at his heels. Niamh, her hair pulled back in an "open for business" bun, clutched a bag marked by a red cross.

"I knocked up Niamh here," Crawford announced. "You're needing a medic."

Hector's black eyebrows shot up—the first half of Crawford's sentence was a phrase guaranteed to take an American aback. But all he said was, "I'm a medic. I need supplies."

"Here." Without hesitation, Niamh gave Hector the medical kit and clambered into the trench. Crawford passed down the blankets.

Alasdair handed Darling his phone. "Webber's sending a helicopter. He's saying the boat needs launching as soon as may be. He's asking you to bide here, working with me, sorting the situation, till the weather clears and he can be sending another D.I."

"Yes, sir." Darling pulled himself first to his feet, then to attention. He squeezed out the words, "A perimeter. We're wanting a perimeter."

Crawford assumed parade-rest in the entranceway.

"Look at this," said Hector.

Alasdair looked, face grim. Darling looked, face ashen. "Ah," Alasdair said, and to one of the crime-scene guys, "Bag that.

The rest of you, check over the scene inside the wall here."

A fitful breeze lifted Jean's hair and fanned her cheeks. This time the acid that bubbled into her throat was flavored with grilled tomato.

Alasdair looked around at the array of faces. He said, his voice crisp, "Grinsell was thumped on the head with what looks to be an item with a sharp, curving edge."

"How can you tell?" asked a man about James's age.

"There's a bit of metal broken off in the wound," Alasdair answered. "Who owns the sheep?"

Another man, an even more grizzled edition of Clyde, raised a hand. " 'Tis my nephew's hobby flock. You'd like them moved away, would you now?"

"Aye, if it's not too much trouble."

"Ah, no trouble, man. They're sheep."

"Thank you. The rest of you, have a good look round the grassy area. Any villain worth the name will likely have thrown the weapon over the cliff, but . . ."

"A torch," croaked Darling. He stopped, cleared his throat, tried again. "The light seen by Mr. Cruz, here, last night. Had to be a torch. If the inspector came up here at dawn and the chap with the torch was still here—if he hit the inspector with his torch, he'd keep it, wouldn't he? Needing the light and all."

"Well done. That's what that metal bit is, the rim surrounding the lens of the torch." Alasdair moderated his instructions. "If we're not finding the weapon, then could be there'll be something else. Footprints, a scrap of cloth, a bit of paper."

"The light I saw?" asked Hector from the trench. "Aw, geez—I came here to play my pipes, not get involved in an assault and battery or whatever you people call it."

Niamh muttered something about the nettle-rash, drawing his attention back to the patient.

The volunteer sheep wrangler strolled forward waving his

arms and making clucking noises. The sheep, already shifting their weight skittishly, started to move. A woman wearing a bright scarf around her head, a la the Queen on her days off, walked a hundred yards or so along the surrounding fence and heaved open a gate into the next field.

And then, Jean thought, there's me. A bump on a log.

Her arms crossed protectively, she trudged across the turf—no, no clues, just tiny embedded flowers and small black sheep-pellets—to a respectable distance from the cliff edge. She might be dubious about enclosed spaces and the dark, but height held no fears for her. She liked looking out over the world and breathing the free air.

She tried taking several breaths of that fresh, free air, but her chest wouldn't expand. The roil in her stomach eased, though.

Cautiously, Jean *listened.* But she sensed nothing paranormal. People had lived here, and probably died here, and yet the site remained indifferent, never mind the corbies and the ravens and Grinsell's blood leaking out onto the ancient cobblestones beneath the mud.

She didn't know how long she stood, spaced out—or perhaps spaced in, slowing the cyclic hum of her own mind. At last she blinked, and this time managed a deep breath.

Far below, the ferry left the harbor and angled toward the mainland, its wake creasing the water. Clyde and Lance obviously wanted to get in at least one trip before the fog closed in. Supplies for the shops and the pub. The Campbell-Reids. Reporters.

Reporters. *Oh, crap.* An attack on a police officer would generate a lot more headlines than a forty-year-old corpse, even if that corpse had been found in the wrong grave.

Someone walked up beside her. Alasdair, leaving Darling and Crawford to direct the searchers. "So you've been drafted to be detective-in-residence?" she asked, without adding anything about turtles and T. Rexes. It wasn't as though he'd wanted to take over the case.

"Aye. There's no standing on ceremony just now." He faced into the breeze, the sea breeze Darling had warned them about, and closed his eyes, listening less for ghosts than for inspiration, she estimated, and with no better results. When he opened them again, they reflected the gray-tinted blue of sea and sky.

"Is Grinsell going to be all right?"

"He was thumped more than once. I'm guessing his assailant kept hitting him till he was properly laid out, then rolled him into the trench."

He hadn't answered the question. Not in so many words. "Rolled him into the trench thinking he was dead? Or intending for him to die?"

"Seems like wasted effort otherwise. Hardly worth the risk."

"I don't guess it's a robbery."

"Not a bit of it—he's still got his wallet, his watch, and his phone."

"Maybe someone only wanted to injure him, so he'd go away and leave"—she almost said "Maggie"—"leave everyone alone."

"It's possible, aye. But who's so foolish as to think any sort of attack on a policeman would be easing the pressure on Farnaby?"

"Good question. Who. As in, who did it?"

"And how was Grinsell lured up here, come to that? Good thing he's got a thick skull. In the literal sense, mind you."

"I mind, yes. I feel bad about all the ugly things I said about him."

"I'm the one speaking of his head on a pike. I'm the one criticizing his handling of the case, even going behind his back."

"When I said what goes around, comes around, I didn't mean—well, the *why* someone bashed the heck out of him is pretty obvious, isn't it? You said yourself, he set everyone in the village against him."

"To the extent of provoking someone to murder him?"

Jean could only shake her head. "At least you've got a finite pool of suspects here. It's a locked-island mystery."

"Is it then?" Alasdair's thin smile skewed with sardonic humor. "The place is not sealed off by a force field."

"Bloodstains," someone called inside the wall. Someone else ordered, "Bag this."

Jean and Alasdair rotated to see Darling in the entranceway turning from side to side like a conductor in front of an orchestra, trying to direct activity both inside and out. "Is he going to be able to handle it, with or without your help?" she asked.

"I reckon so. He's young is all. Good job Crawford's here as well, as a steadying influence."

"But Crawford seems to have lied about the chanter in the grave. Or is anyone going to care about that and Thomas Seaton and everything, now?"

"There'll be an inquest, still, but quite a lot's depending on whether the attack on Grinsell's related to the body in the chapel." Alasdair scanned the indigo haze that lay like a stroke of paint along the northern horizon. "Maggie, now, Darling's telling me Maggie threatened Grinsell."

"She did? Oh. Well, she told him to treat her daughter with respect or she'd something unspecified. Darling and I grabbed her right then and she never finished her sentence."

"Close enough. She was after keeping him from harassing Tara."

"So was Lance. And Pen. That's hardly a motive for murder."

"I've heard tell of men murdered for a five-pound note."

"Not Maggie, not even for a long-lost daughter—no. Just no." Jean's memory emitted a crystal-clear image of Maggie switching on her industrial-strength flashlight and bending over the open grave. *No.*

Alasdair had to be visualizing the same image. But his profile against the sky communicated as much as the stones of the fort.

Jean realized she heard a faint thrumming sound. Her own heartbeat, still racing?

Several people turned toward the north and pointed. The thrumming became a thumping, growing louder and louder. A black dot appeared in the haze, grew into a yellow-and-black helicopter, and swooped down on Farnaby. Seabirds and land birds alike ricocheted into the air. The sheep galloped away down the field.

The beat of the rotor blades reverberated in Jean's head. She clapped her hands to her ears and braced herself against the blast of wind as the helicopter settled onto the far end of the grassy area.

It had barely landed before a door opened and two flight-suited figures—men, women, Martians, Jean couldn't tell—piled out. Hoisting a stretcher, they ran toward Crawford, the only person in uniform. Alasdair started forward, stopped, recalibrated, and began effecting crowd control. Within what seemed like two minutes the twin flight suits were carrying the stretcher with Grinsell's body . . . Not a body, Jean reminded herself again. A man. A man-shaped bundle of blankets and bandages.

The helicopter's doors slammed shut. The rotors whined and beat a rhythm simultaneously. Like a giant metal bumblebee, the helicopter lifted off and headed toward Berwick-upon-Tweed.

Alasdair had gotten his wish: Grinsell was well on his way to Berwick before the island shut down.

Crawford's cap blew off and rolled away, but he didn't chase it down. He stood watching the dwindling form of the helicopter. And Jean recognized who he reminded her of: A narrow upturned face, a rawboned jaw, a beak of a nose—the statue of

Saint Aidan in the churchyard on Lindisfarne.

What? Was there a certain look in the Northumbrian genetic structure? But hadn't Aidan come from Ireland? Not that it mattered—the statue on Lindisfarne dated from the twentieth century.

Hector emerged from the tower using a moistened wipe to clean the blood from his hands. Niamh walked behind him, closing up the medical kit with fingers still splashed crimson. Niamh McCarthy was an Irish name. So was Donal McCarthy. Did that matter?

A ripple passed through the people gathered on the headland, multiple shoulders slumping, a variety of *What now?* looks passing back and forth. So Grinsell had been whisked efficiently away. That resolved nothing.

Jean retrieved Crawford's cap from where it lay against the wall and handed it back. There. She'd made a contribution, albeit a microscopic one.

"Thank you kindly, madam." Crawford settled his cap so far down his stubble of hair that his eyes looked out from the shadow of the visor like those of the bouncer in a speakeasy through their slot.

Alasdair paced back toward the entranceway. "Thank you," he told Niamh and Hector. His polite but stern nod swept across the sheep-wranglers and the grass-searchers as well. Crawford's subtle shooing motions reinforced the message.

The civilians headed back to the village. Hector opened the gate for Niamh, and she waited for him to pass through it and join her. ". . . multiple-car pile-up on the freeway in a sand storm," he was telling her. "We had to leave the ambulance on the access road and climb up . . ."

He wasn't callous; he was accustomed to dealing with the suffering of strangers. Not that Niamh was listening to him. The thoughts processed behind those delicate features had nothing to do with sand storms and freeways. Jean remembered Tara when they met her waiting at the ferry, gazing toward a point far beyond the island. She thought of Maggie sitting in front of Grinsell and imagining herself somewhere else.

Behind her, Alasdair and Darling conducted a conference with the scene-of-crime technicians. She caught something about footprints and bloodstains, something about trampled nettles. ". . . aye, the investigation's rushed, no help for it—good job finding that wee scraper, now—the question's how to best be keeping gawpers from overrunning the scene."

Standing apart, Crawford gazed out to sea, even as his ears seemed to twitch backwards like a cat's. As the low man on the totem pole, he no doubt awaited orders to pitch a tent and spend the night on guard.

Her own ears simply chilly, Jean looked past the roofs of the village, past the island itself, to see the ash-gray billows of fog inching closer.

Chapter Seventeen

The ferry emerged from the shadow of Lindisfarne, its wake frothing white behind it. Clyde had put the pedal to the metal, Jean told herself.

The deck was crowded with passengers, people planning on attending the concert at the school tonight, no doubt, and reporters onto the story of the unidentified body who would soon discover an even more exciting story underway. Or had they seen the helicopter from the ferry? Were they phoning Berwick to find out what was going on? Any reporter worth the name would have a mobile phone fully supplied with the numbers of sources from law enforcement officials to friendly criminals, if that wasn't a contradiction in terms.

Squinting, Jean could make out a stroller, confirming the presence of little Linda Campbell-Reid and, therefore, her parents. Good. Reinforcements. Friends she could trust. Funny how even Pen's affable face now seemed to be hiding plots. Maybe everyone in Farnaby St. Mary had worked together to dispose of Grinsell, so that the answer to "Whodunit?" was "Everyone." Alasdair and Darling couldn't arrest the entire village.

Well, knowing Alasdair, if he had to, he would.

She looked around to see the technicians taking off down the path, clutching their little bags of evidence, their samples and photos, such as they were. The footprints and scrapes on the path itself would be useless now, after so many people had come and gone.

"P.C. Crawford," said Alasdair.

"Aye, sir?"

"Collect the crime-scene tape from the chantry chapel and bring it up here, then close off the entranceway as best you can, please."

Crawford didn't blink.

Darling weighed in. "I know, a strip of tape won't keep gawpers from messing the scene about. Bring yourself a thermos—anything you think you'll want—and keep an eye out till sunset. Plan on spending the night on the island as well."

"The reporters will be doing a smash and grab, so to speak," Alasdair added. "Here's hoping the haar's clearing and the ferry's running the lot of them back to the mainland before the tide turns. The folk arriving for the concert, well, could be they'll not feel like trekking up here and will be contenting themselves with having a look at the chapel on their way to the school."

"Aye, sir." Crawford turned toward the path.

"Oh, and Crawford . . ."

"Sir?"

"The sergeant here's telling me he sent you home to Bamburgh for the night. Did you go, then?"

Crawford's duty-and-country expression didn't shift in the slightest. "No, sir. Pen kindly offered me an empty bed."

"Very good. Carry on."

Crawford marched off through the gate.

"So he was here the night. Is that significant, sir?" asked Darling.

From the twitch at the corner of Alasdair's mouth, Jean suspected he wanted to reply, *Damned if I know.* But all he said was, "Let's have a care what information we're disclosing round the local folk, and I'm counting Crawford as local folk."

"Yes, sir. Um . . ." Darling grimaced. "Yes, sir."

Crawford's lanky figure diminished down the path. At its far end, two female figures walked just as purposefully through the car park, past the cemetery, and onto the grounds of the priory, each of them holding objects unidentifiable from this distance. Maggie and Tara. Niamh had returned to Gow House, then, and told them they were safe from Grinsell's attentions, if not from those of a greenhorn sergeant and a reluctant Scottish detective.

"Right," said the detective, and held out his hand to Jean. "Off we go."

Off they went, through the gate and toward the village. A chill breeze rustled the hedges. The seabirds had returned to their regularly scheduled program, and coasted around the headland or dived into the sea, depending on the species. A coven of oystercatchers gathered in a nearby field.

Jean, Alasdair, and Darling reached the parking lot in time to hear the rumble of engines that heralded the departure of the police boat. They stood in a row, watching between and over the buildings as it glided out of the harbor, rounded the end of the island, and, skirting the fog bank, sped north.

At the back of the Angle's Rest, a window closed and a shape faded into the shadows of the room. Her and Alasdair's room, Jean realized. The shape moved subtly through the next window over, the one in the sitting area at the top of the stairs. Hildy, holding down the sill with a sphinx-like posture, looked around and then turned back to the scene outside.

It was a B&B, Jean told herself. The owner came into their room and cleaned things up and aired the place out. Nothing even remotely suspicious about that.

Darling eyed Clyde's pickup still leaning drunkenly into the pothole, Clyde having more lucrative matters to deal with. "Why was Grinsell out and about so early? What was he on the go about?"

Neither Jean nor Alasdair had any answers. Alasdair tried another question. "Had he any enemies? Ones motivated to be attacking him, that is. Ones after killing him."

"Any policeman's got enemies, and Grinsell more than most, I reckon, but surely an enemy'd find it easier to attack him in the streets of Berwick." Darling partly shook his head and partly shrugged, so that the gesture came out more of a shudder.

"Does he have any family?" Jean asked.

"A sister in Cambridgeshire's all he's ever mentioned. He's never seemed particularly fond of her, is more than a bit scornful of her and her doings."

"That's a shame. No surprise, but a shame."

Still in a row, like a stunted line of Rockettes, they turned around and faced the priory. Crawford was rolling up the blue-and-white police tape that had been draped from column base to column base. A faint gleam of light shone from inside the chapel, accompanied by the uneven *dink-dink* of metal hitting metal. Had Maggie decided to plunge ahead and open the coffin before anything else happened? Jean took a step forward, then back again. She, too, had more pressing matters, and would have to leave her historical curiosity tip-tilted and stalled. For the moment.

Darling's face was getting its color back, even if it was still set like concrete. "One of the technicians was telling me over breakfast that he whiled away the nighttime hours by inspecting the body. Something long and narrow had been forced up through the roof of the mouth, the soft palate, into the brain stem. Barring a bullet hole or knife wound coming to light during the formal postmortem, that's likely the cause of death."

"Whoa." Great conversation for the breakfast table, although Jean remembered several mealtime discussions of forensics. You got used to it. You got hardened by it. She visualized alternate scenarios—Tom falling onto, say, a garden stake. "That could be an accident."

"Or not," said Alasdair. "Was your technical lad seeing any shreds of wood in the cavity?"

"Why yes, he was. How did you . . ."

Jean and Alasdair exclaimed simultaneously, "The chanter."

"That's why it was stolen from the grave," she went on. "It's the murder weapon. Interesting, that someone would know that, all these years later."

"That it is, aye."

Here came Crawford, the tape draped tidily over his shoulder like a gaudy military braid. He touched his cap but didn't deviate from his track toward Cuddy's Close. Three pairs of eyes watched him disappear down the steps.

At last Darling said, "P.C. Crawford said last night there was no chanter in the grave."

"He said he didn't see it," Jean corrected. "Or that he wasn't sure what it was. Something like that, anyway. He left himself a fudge factor."

"Covering up that it was stolen on his watch," added Alasdair.

Darling's forehead creased in doubt. "A dark night, the mist and all—someone who knew the grounds of the priory could have crept in behind his back."

The quirk of Alasdair's eyebrow acknowledged not only the truth of the statement, but that Darling's crease intensified into another grimace. "Aye. And?"

"Crawford was having himself a cuppa in the kitchen whilst the technician told me of his findings. Likely he overheard. Shouldn't matter to him one way or the other if he never saw the chanter to begin. Might not even have made the connection—I'm thinking the man's a bit, well . . ."

Slow? Jean finished for him. Not too bright? But reticence

could just be reticence.

"Right," Alasdair said.

"Is anyone going to care about Thomas Seaton, now?" Jean asked again.

This time Darling answered. "The reason Inspector Grinsell came here at all was to investigate the body."

Jean looked at Alasdair. He looked at Darling. "Sergeant, we're needing to have us a good chin-wag about, ah, historical matters."

"Yes, sir." The forehead creased even further, going from doubt to puzzlement.

A distant screech was either Hector wrestling with his pipes or the ferry dropping its gangplank. A metallic thud confirmed the latter. So did the murmur of multiple voices and footsteps, along with the roar of a car engine or two.

The back door of the Angle's Rest opened, emitting Crawford. Along with the police tape, he now carried a small insulated bag decorated in a green and yellow paisley pattern. This time he had gone to Pen for sustenance, then, as she'd expected him to do the night he waited at the priory for Grinsell's arrival. Now the woman herself waved from the doorway before abruptly disappearing into the house.

Several human figures surged up Cuddy's Close. By diving out of the garden gate and stepping out briskly with his long legs, Crawford gained the lead and outdistanced the three people who chose the rutted drive to the tower. Good luck getting a statement from P.C. Taciturn.

Two others headed for the chapel. Hadn't they gotten the word yet? Surely Rob the Ranter couldn't be as interesting as a coshed policeman. Whatever, Maggie would deal with them. She'd asked for them to begin with—and her snowflake of a news conference had started an avalanche.

"Are you needing a bite of lunch, Jean?" Alasdair asked.

"Lunch." They needed to put Darling in the picture. They needed to talk to any number of people—Clyde, Lance, James, anyone who might have seen the light Hector saw. But Pen had probably darted back inside because Michael, Rebecca, and Linda had arrived on her doorstep.

That spot beneath her ribs that an hour ago had been a roiling pot of acid was now hollow. Torn in several directions, Jean defaulted to making sure she'd be able to investigate them all. Or at least able to intelligently discuss Alasdair's findings after he and Darling did some investigating. "I saw a tea room near the Co-op. Y'all go on ahead—I'll do something with Rebecca and Michael."

"Come along then, Sergeant," said Alasdair. "A sandwich and a cuppa, eh? My shout."

"That's very kind of you, sir. A cuppa would go down a treat, right enough."

They walked through Cuddy's Close and came out onto Farnaby St. Mary's one street. Across the bay, Bamburgh Castle's towers and battlements rose into the tentative sunlight—and a second later were swallowed whole by the rolling fog bank, leaving not a wrack behind.

The thick mist, the sea fret, the haar seeped inexorably across the bay. Two small boats moored in the harbor winked out. The far end of the street and the hairpin turn went under. The breakwater disappeared. And then the murk smothered the corner of Cuddy's Close, so that Jean and the two men stood in a chill pocket hemmed in by blurry gray walls.

She told herself it was only water vapor, a cloud on the ground, not a suffocating nightmare. Still, she shivered.

They were marooned on Farnaby Island with a very contemporary murderer.

Chapter Eighteen

Jean glanced dubiously from the B&B's dining room out to the garden below the window. The closest plants were visible, including the shrub that had provided an impromptu haven for Tara, but the back wall was blotted out as though by a giant eraser. No matter. There were places to go and investigations to conduct.

She looked around to see Michael stacking the plates and Rebecca corralling the plastic tubs and wrappers. Funny how much the thirty-something couple looked like each other, both sharp of glance and easy of smile. Even Rebecca's long brown hair had adopted a reddish tinge, to closer match Michael's considerably shorter but more auburn cut, even though her intelligent brown eyes were still her own, as his astute blue eyes were his.

Or maybe Rebecca now used a color rinse, the better to look like her ginger-topped child's mother. Jean remembered seeing a performance of *Riverdance* in Dallas some years earlier. She'd never seen so many red-haired people in one place—until she emigrated to Scotland.

Rebecca unstrapped little Linda and eased her out of the plastic seat Pen had produced from a closet. "Did the nice lady bring you crackers?"

Linda gurgled an affirmation, the crumbs from Pen's water crackers still clinging to her mouth. Jean dragged her mind away from images of cracker crumbs, focusing instead on how

Linda's cheery little face had drawn a similarly cheery smile from Pen. Although with Pen's face, the cheer was supplemented by an application of rosy blusher.

"Ta for getting the sandwich makings," Michael told Jean.

Rebecca said, "Sorry you missed eating with Alasdair and Sergeant What's-his-name."

"Sergeant Darling. I wonder if he's related to the famous Grace Darling from down the coast. You know, the lighthouse-keeper's daughter who convinced her father to row out with her and rescue several shipwrecked sailors."

"Sailors who suspended their nineteenth-century opinions about the weakness of women till she got them back on shore, at the least."

Nodding agreement, Jean continued, "Sergeant Darling had enough on his lunch plate without an audience. By the time I walked back with the food and looked into the tea room window—you'd have thought it was a movie screen. They sure know how to light up a room here, must use five-hundred-watt bulbs . . ."

"Go figure." Rebecca shot her own dubious look toward the fog-shrouded window.

". . . he had made room on the table for his notebook and was taking notes. Poor kid—going from working with Grinsell to working with Alasdair has to cause whiplash."

"So Grinsell and Maggie have a history of sorts," Michael said. "That's complicating matters."

"Does Pen know about that?" asked Rebecca.

"I have no idea. Every time I suggested talking to her—not giving her the third degree, just chatting, you know—Alasdair would say no, it's Grinsell's case."

"It's Alasdair's case now." Rebecca set the toddler on the carpet and stood over her as she immediately assumed the all-fours position and crawled off into the living room.

Michael stuffed the waste into one of the plastic Co-op sacks. "He's still expecting you to leave it to him and Darling, I reckon, no matter how brilliantly you've contributed in the past. The polis, they've got their methods."

"Boys," Jean told Rebecca. "They always hang together."

Neither Campbell-Reid replied *Better than hanging separately*, so her joke, weak as it was, evaporated unnoticed.

"The chanter you and Alasdair and all saw in the grave," said Michael. "Was it the sort fixed to the bag of the pipes?"

"Oh, well . . ." Jean thought back. The dark muck. The sightless eyes. The scabrous arm. "It was a black tube with a flattened end. Maggie said it was probably African blackwood."

"My pipes are blackwood, aye, that's the traditional sort—it's a very dense material. If I'd not inherited them I'd have never had the money for them. But a flattened end—sounds to be a practice chanter. An older one, since they're making fine plastic ones the day. Were the holes recessed or flush?"

"It had holes, but I couldn't tell whether they were in a row, let alone recessed or flush. It looked pitted is all."

"No metal keys, then, I'm thinking. Not from a set of small pipes, whether Northumbrian or Irish."

"Seaton played both the small ones and the big ones, Maggie said, for what that's worth. But this chanter had no metal. Or no rust, more likely. It lay in the damp for a long time. I'm surprised anyone could pick it up without it falling apart. A shame the crime scene people didn't get it. They'd have taken care of it."

"And analyzed it as well," said Rebecca from where Linda wobbled precariously around the coffee table, her tiny hands leaving smudges on the polished wood.

Jean thought of Hector's students practicing with their chanters. She thought of a piper she knew back in Texas playing a bombard, a chanter without its bag and drones. It produced an oddly clogged and yet compelling sound, as though pushing a pound of music through a pinhole, an explosion imminent. "Alasdair has to be wondering the same thing I am: if the chanter, of either sort, is the murder weapon, how did the murderer get the victim to hold still while he jammed it up into his skull?"

"He hit him first?"

"The skull didn't look like it was crushed anywhere, and Darling's technical pal didn't say it was, but then, it's hard to tell without a full battery of equipment." This time she articulated her thought. "This is great mealtime conversation, isn't it?"

Michael shrugged with his eyebrows, Rebecca with her shoulders. Linda made a shaky transfer from coffee table to couch and grabbed for an appealing fuzzy pillow.

The pillow sat up with a start, whiskers flared, ears turned back. Hildy leaped to the floor and with a thunder of paws sprinted across the room and dashed up the stairs, moving so fast she only touched every third step.

"Another moggie flees for its life," said Rebecca. "Our Riccio's found himself a spot high in the bedroom cupboard and plans on staying there till Linda's in school, far as I can tell."

Pen walked into the room. "My goodness, I haven't seen her move that fast in years."

"Sorry." Rebecca plucked Linda from causing-harm's way and planted her back at the coffee table.

"Not to worry. She's a lovely little lass, isn't she?" Pen blew a kiss to the baby, whose return grin was mostly pink gum. Then, with an audible inhalation as though steeling herself to a task, Pen went on, "You've come at a difficult time, I'm afraid. Jean, Edwin's telling me your Alasdair's in charge of the case now. Both cases, I expect."

Edwin. P.C. Crawford. The local plod, who was maybe a lot

more taciturn with the outlanders than with the people he'd been protecting and serving for who knows how many years. Since everyone called him by his first name, he wasn't new on the scene. "Alasdair's mainly looking into D.I. Grinsell's, ah, injury, but the earlier case is still relevant." Never mind Alasdair's cautionary torpedoes, she added to herself—he was officially sanctioned now and they were a team. Full speed ahead. "Do you have any idea whose body Maggie found in the tomb?"

Pen's expression revealed nothing but curiosity edged by a worry that the rosy spots on her cheekbones accentuated. "They're saying it's Thomas Seaton. Fine piper Thomas was, a favorite of Wat's till, well—Wat was a bit overprotective of Elaine. She named Tom 'Lancelot the Fair' as a joke, mind, but Wat was not best pleased. One day it all came to a head and Tom found himself on the next ferry. Or so we were thinking. Now, forty years on, who's to say what happened exactly? Not Elaine, poor soul."

Jean drew out the witness with, "Maggie's afraid Tom is her biological father," even though that skirted the line between nosy and insensitive.

Michael nodded supportively. Linda sidled around the table.

"She's not so much afraid as hopeful, sad to say," Pen went on. "She and Wat, they never got on well, especially after her—well, the events in Cambridge. But I can't see it, myself. Elaine speaking of having a lover, that's no more than the illness. Dreadful, even so, thinking of Tom lying there all these years, that close to Gow House."

"Um . . ." Jean went for broke. "Could there have been a fight? Another student? Wat himself, perhaps?"

"Well, as Hugh was saying this morning, Wat had a temper. But murdering a man with his own chanter? Creeping up on him whilst he was playing, perhaps?" Pen frowned. "Wat creeping about, premeditating violence—that wasn't him. He'd shout and glare and sulk is all."

So the walls of the Angle's Rest did have ears, Jean thought. If she and Alasdair or anyone else wanted a private confab, they'd have to go out to the far side of the breakwater and keep an eye open for submersibles.

Linda overbalanced and fell, narrowly missing hitting her chin on the table. Rebecca picked her up. "Can't hold your crackers, can you now?"

Pen turned a wistful smile on the child. "If you'll excuse me—I'm doing a bit of baking—settles the mind as well as the stomach." Collecting the plates and the plastic bags, she headed back to the kitchen.

After a discreet thirty seconds' silence, Michael murmured, "There now. She came talking to *you.*"

"Yes," Jean told him. "That's a relief, in a way. I'd hate to think she was uncomfortable with us around. Or plotting against us, as the case may be. Although she could still be leading us astray."

"Sometimes you're having to grit your teeth and trust," said Rebecca.

Michael asked, "Has anyone questioned the ferryman yet, asking if Tom ever left the island? Or was he biding here then?"

"Darling says Grinsell told him to bring Clyde into the interview room, but no one had actually talked to him before we rushed off looking for Grinsell himself."

Rebecca turned an appreciative gaze on her husband. "I think I first fell in love with Michael when he played his pipes—there's that indefinable air about a musician, catnip in sound. I sympathize with Elaine and Tom."

Michael bowed graciously.

"Wat liked to play at King Arthur, but as you heard yourself, he acted far from chivalrously," Jean said.

"Medieval chivalry was just as thoroughly compartmentalized. Not that the genuine Arthur lived anywhere near the Middle Ages."

"Yes, there's a myth I can shoot down, assuming I get an article out of this weekend after all. Speaking of which, I guess I'll head over to the priory to see whether Maggie's opening the tomb, with or without a journalistic peanut gallery. I don't see why she'd care if y'all came, too. There's even a carved gravestone you can train your fourteenth-century expertise on, Michael, although it's probably older than that."

"Sounds right intriguing," he replied. "But no good taking the wean into the chill and damp."

Rebecca asked, "We'll draw straws, shall we, see who gets to go?"

"No need. My pipes need cleaning and freshening before playing tonight. I'll stay with Linda, see if she's feeling like napping. So long as you're taking photos of the tombstone."

"I promise. Half a tick, Jean?" Clutching a double armful of wriggling child, Rebecca disappeared down the hall, Michael at her heels. Jean slipped upstairs, where she ascertained that Hildy had discorporated.

Both windows in the room showed the same view, a gray smear, although the one in front at least included the glowing top of a lamppost. And two shadowy figures rounding the corner into Cuddy's Close. Trying to see if they were Alasdair and Darling, Jean cracked the corner of her glasses against the window and recoiled. Never mind. If he wanted her, he could call. If she wanted him, she could call.

Well, she always wanted him, she thought as she pulled on a heavier jacket and opened the door . . . Wait a minute. She doubled back to see that, no, *Hilda, the Enchanted Prioress* no longer lay on the bedside table. Pen must have seen it and taken it back downstairs where it belonged.

The scent of baking scones wafted out of the kitchen, boding well. With no Campbell-Reids yet in sight, Jean darted past the dining area into the living room. Alasdair said he'd found *Hilda* on the shelf beside *The Matter of Britannia.*

Prioress, Jean thought as she scanned the shelves. Abbess. Actress. Authoress. Murderess. Modern speakers tended to drop the gender-specific ending—a good thing, in her opinion. Still, she'd recently read an article about an ancient Egyptian priestess with the headline "Tomb of an Egyptian Chantress."

So did a female piper play a chantress? Would it be round rather than long? Aha, there was *Britannia,* next to not only books on Farnaby and Lindisfarne but also to several bound excavation reports—Winchester, Vindolanda, Yeavering a few miles away on the mainland. No *Hilda.*

Her fingers itched to pull out the reports, but she forced them to close around *Britannia* instead. The dust jacket, a lush Pre-Raphaelite image of a red-headed and golden-crowned woman, was worn and frayed. The flyleaf was indeed autographed, if without the provocative words of the autograph in *Hilda.*

For James and Pen. Eternal friendship, Elaine Peveril Lauder.

Eternal, Jean told herself. A word with loaded meanings here on Farnaby.

A thin white rim protruded from the book—an index card marking a chapter titled, "Guinevere the Christian Goddess," one of Elaine's more controversial and, sadly, incoherent themes. In it she theorized that the legends of Guinevere being abducted and rescued indicated an early resurrection scenario, therefore Guinevere hadn't retired to a nunnery; she'd founded one in her own honor. Q.E.D.

The handwriting on the front of the card wasn't Elaine's. Neither was the name. "Athelstan Crawford" was written above the words, "Granite. Classic Roman 2. Letterbox."

Athelstan Crawford. Great name, like that of a Victorian antiquarian—the Saxon king, grandson of King Alfred the Great, hammer of the Celts and Vikings, combined with the down-home "Crawford." Was this man a relative of P.C. Crawford's? And what did the card refer to, anyway?

Jean flipped it over. On the back, written in a smaller, more feminine hand that might be the weekday version of Elaine's Sunday-best signature, was one word, "Merlin."

Rebecca looked through the doorway. "Ready?"

Adding more questions to her ever-expanding list, Jean returned the book to the shelf and herself to the front hall, whence she and Rebecca eased out onto the sidewalk.

Chapter Nineteen

The palisades of fog only seemed impenetrable, Jean discovered. If she and Rebecca kept moving, the pocket of visibility would move along with them. Sort of like navigating through life, now that she thought about it.

Somewhere an engine revved and slowed and men shouted, the sounds reverberating in Cuddy's Close. Trapped in a soft pocket of damp, Jean felt her way between the pub and the B&B and up the flight of steps, Rebecca on her heels. The mist lay chill against her face and her glasses filmed with microscopic droplets, adding to her disorientation. Put one foot in front of the other and follow the voices . . .

The pitted blacktop of the parking area. Moving blurs resolved themselves from the mist. Something large as a dinosaur, with soft glowing eyes, leaped forward. Jean stopped so abruptly Rebecca collided with her. "Sorry."

A group of islanders inspected their muddy pants legs and congratulated themselves on heaving Clyde's pickup out of its pothole. "Thanks, lads. My shout at the pub tonight," said Clyde's voice to a round of cheers. Lance's voice added, "Ah, he'll only be paying for the flavored water, not the good ales, eh?" Multiple footsteps carried an eerily distorted gust of laughter away with them.

So, Jean wondered, did Lance bash Grinsell as a preemptive strike, heading off his potential harassment of Tara? That wouldn't be the first time a young buck thought he could impress the doe with a violent act, but still, even for the young and testosterone-fueled, it seemed like too much.

The clatter of the engine changed timbre, the headlights vanished, tires crunched on the lumpy blacktop. Two red lights faded and vanished along with the noise. If the road lay in that direction, then the priory was just about—there. Jean guided her companion across the parking lot and collided with the wall of the cemetery. Okay—off to the left, then.

Stone arches loomed out of the murk. A smear of luminescence lightened one area of gray. The light grew stronger as they crept toward it, until it took on the shape of an arched doorway. The chapel. The *dink-dink* of metal against metal sounded like water drops falling from a great height.

"Whoa," Rebecca breathed.

Jean turned to see her resting a hand atop a truncated column. "You're getting vibes, aren't you?"

"There's a right interesting fifth dimension to this place, yes. There's a—memory-image, an image-memory, if you can call it that—of people screaming, and the smell of smoke, and Viking raiders running through a church that's not this church—it's got a thatched roof. Even in this climate, a thatched roof burns very quickly."

"That's the original Farnaby Priory. No surprise Vikings would hit here when they hit Lindisfarne, too."

Rebecca lifted her hand from the cold, damp stone and scrubbed it on the front of her coat. After a moment, looking at her own palm as though it belonged to an alien, she said, "Have you picked up a ghost yet?"

"Alasdair and I both sensed something yesterday, when we first arrived. And the nuns are pretty vocal after dark. But you know how it is. A ghost is never there when you want it to provide evidence, but it's always there when you're minding your own business."

"We've heard paranormal plainchant before," Rebecca said. "There's something about those resonances that transcend time and space."

"Yeah, I bet you can still hear the ancient Egyptians chanting in Luxor."

Again Jean deployed her sixth sense, like casting a net out to where strange creatures glided, no more than shadows in deep water. Yes, she caught a faint stirring in the ether—the back of her neck alerted with the tickle she always thought of as the brush of ectoplasm. It wasn't that someone walked over her grave, but over the one in the chapel.

The ghost might not be the disembodied spirit of the man or woman whose body had been hidden in the tomb, though. It could be the intended beneficiary of the cantarist's prayers. Or one of the nuns she'd heard singing. She knew only that it was the lingering emotion of someone who had not resolved his or her life.

Unless the chantry ghost was the mystic Hilda, who had reached for the other side of consciousness and who had found it . . . A woman's face materialized from the wreaths of fog, eyes looking upward, lips parted—it faded out again. A whiff of incense eddied through the murk, followed by one of cooking beans. And the blanket of perception lifted from Jean's shoulders.

Most spirits lingered because of unfinished business, but this one lingered as part of her business, still watching over Farnaby. "I see why Elaine claimed to have a paranormal informant."

"She'd never said anything of the sort before," replied Rebecca. "She'd actually spoken out against ley lines and the like back when folk were criticizing *Britannia*'s excesses and calling her Loony Lauder because of it."

"Was it her imagination then? Or the dementia? Pen thinks her saying she had a lover is the dementia, but maybe she did have a lover—most people keep extramarital affairs secret, after all. Who knows?" Jean continued on toward the chapel. "We've got the questions we can—I hope—answer. And we've got the ones we'll never get answers to. Let's go see which one we've got here."

"Let's," Rebecca said.

Jean stepped through the door to see three photographer's lamps on tall tripods, each connected to a battery pack, ranged around the open grave. The lights shone so brightly the fog was reduced to a softening of the windows and corners, like the effect of a filter over a camera lens. Maggie lay on her stomach at the edge of the tomb, the rectangular excavation, her hands moving slowly inside. *Dink-dink.*

Above her now rose an inverted V-shaped metal structure, like the frame for a child's swing set, dangling a basic block-and-tackle outfit. The coffin lid was definitely coming up, then.

Beside Maggie, Tara leaned in with a brush. The flat tray equipped with trowels, picks, brushes, and other implements, including a clipboard laden with limp papers and a camera, sat nearby. Both women looked sharply up when Jean appeared.

"Hello. I remembered I was supposed to be writing an article for *Great Scot* about your work here."

"So you are." Maggie sat up, laid aside a small hammer and chisel, and considered the mud and ooze caked on her hands.

Jean was reminded of Niamh's and Hector's bloodstained hands. "You didn't have the photographer's lights out here yesterday," was all she said.

"I left them at the house, charging the batteries, meaning to bring them along to the big reveal for the reporters. After the small reveal, well, I thought I'd leave the stage lighting to the police."

The body being a little more close and personal, to say nothing of recent, than she'd expected, Jean concluded.

"Why is a magazine named *Great Scot* interested in England?" asked Tara.

"Northumbria wasn't always England. The kingdom of Bernicia once extended from the Tees to the Forth, straddling today's border. This area's been known as 'South Pict-land.' And don't get me started on the role of the Celtic church based at Melrose and on Iona, both in Scotland."

"Okay," said Tara, dragging out the word.

The sound Maggie made would have been a laugh if it hadn't been quite so strangled. "Tara's telling me she can't ask me to pass the salt without my giving her a historical lecture. My mum was the same way."

Jean introduced her friend. "This is Rebecca Campbell-Reid. She's a historian at Holyrood Palace in Edinburgh. Her husband Michael's a historian, too, and a piper, and is going to play at the concert tonight."

"Maggie Lauder," said Maggie. "My daughter, Tara Hogg."

"Hi," Tara said.

"Nice to meet you," returned Rebecca. "Michael's back at the B and B with our little girl. She's not even a year old yet, so we didn't want to bring her out in the haar."

Maggie looked at Tara, perhaps seeing her as a little girl she never knew. She said, "The more the merrier. The reporters who stopped by earlier skived off to the pub once they found the, ah, associated body was gone. Said they'd come back round when there was something to see."

"What do you want to bet they're hoping for another totally gruesome body?" said Tara.

"Anything you like." Maggie went back to work, tapping the hammer against the chisel so that it cut through the deep gray surface—a much cleaner surface than it had been yesterday, revealing the punched decorations to be straggling loops and lozenges. She now worked on the head end, assuming the occupant of the grave was buried Christian-style, so that when Judgment Day arrived, he or she would sit up and face toward the east, ready for the Resurrection.

The slightly wobbly black gash left by the chisel skipped over four inch-wide strips that Maggie had left intact, holding the lid so it wouldn't plummet onto the contents. The remains. Yes, the lead was very thin. Was it the weight of the man's body that had caused it to buckle and tear in several places? Jean visualized poor Rob, Tom, whoever, being rolled unceremoniously over the edge and falling with a sickening thud onto the coffin.

Rebecca knelt. "Some years ago I worked on the excavation of Rudesburn Priory. Can I help?"

"Please," said Tara. "I'm a web designer. I am so clueless when it comes to this stuff."

"By all means," Maggie told Rebecca. "Although what I'm doing here is no more elegant than opening a tin of sardines. Quite a bit less, actually. Air leaked into the coffin donkey's years ago as the ground shifted and the Norman priory was constructed. There'll not be a great deal preserved, of the body or of any artifacts. Still, it's worth a go. If you'd clear away the metal bits, I'd be obliged."

Tara handed over the brush, and Rebecca started removing tiny scrolls of lead from the track of the chisel.

Fascinated as she was by archaeology, Jean was more experienced in detection. She sidled around the dais the way little Linda had sidled around the coffee table and approached the broken grave slab leaning against the wall. The surfaces of the two pieces definitely had been carved. She could just make out the ghosts of curving lines, rows of lumps, various nubbles. "This looks a bit like one of the so-called pillow-stones from Lindisfarne—eighth century, aren't they? The ones with the incised cross pattern and Day of Judgment motif. But this one's rectangular, not rounded. Could I borrow your flashlight for a minute?" she asked Tara.

Tara shrugged. "That big one? I don't know where it went after Mags gave it to Edwin yesterday."

"He had one with him all evening." Jean tried to remember whether he'd been using Maggie's flashlight all evening or whether he'd picked up a police-issue torch. If he'd changed to the latter, though, he'd have returned the former. She had no idea—it was the light that had been important, not the implement that produced it. Not, at least, until Darling theorized that a large flashlight had been the weapon used to bash in Grinsell's head.

She decided not to mention that to Maggie. Even if she'd had a flashlight to enable a closer look, the stone was more inkblot test than information. "The chapel still has its roof, and yet the stone's badly weathered. Was it brought from somewhere else to serve as a grave marker?"

"Or was the burial so important the chapel was built around and over it?" Maggie replied. "The stone could have spent as long as five centuries outside. Hutchinson mentions it here on the grave in seventeen ninety-four, but says nothing about the actual pattern. It was likely indecipherable even then."

"Granny thought she could make out horsemen," said Tara.

"She also thought the stone was carved with a sheela-na-gig—a woman exposing her sexual organs—which is marginally credible. You do see those occasionally, and having one here might indicate an important female burial with pagan elements. But she also thought she made out the words *uxor draconis,* 'wife of the dragon.' Guinevere, maybe. Maybe not . . ." Her voice died away in the depths of the tomb.

"Seeing is believing, and believing is seeing." Rebecca quoted Jean's oft-repeated motto.

Well, yes. Jean turned back around. "Did you talk to the SOCO or any of the team, Maggie? Did they find anything archaeologically helpful on top of the coffin?"

"SOCO?" Tara repeated.

Maggie and Jean answered as one. "Scene of Crime Officer." After a pause, Maggie's hand started moving again. "No one told me anything. Grinsell's gag order, I expect."

Jean gritted her teeth, loosened them, and cut to the chase. "Someone knocked Grinsell unconscious up at Merlin's Tower early this morning."

Maggie's hand didn't stop. *Dink-dink.* "And your husband's in charge now. Yes, I heard."

Tara glanced sharply up at Jean. "I wasn't sleeping well anyway—I kept hearing voices, but then, Granny talks in her sleep. When I heard tires grinding away in the parking lot around dawn, I didn't even look out of the window. If I'd known it was Inspector Grinsell, I'd have hidden under the bed."

"There not being any shrubs handy?"

Tara's eyes flashed. "Mags warned me about the guy. So did Lance, after Clyde overheard him abusing Mags. Maybe I overreacted, yeah, but I'd had a couple of glasses of beer and would probably have told the jerk what I thought of him. That wouldn't have helped."

"It didn't help me," said Maggie.

Jean said, "It was chivalrous of Lance to help you out."

"I'd say controlling rather than chivalrous. He's okay. He's got a temper and a sense of entitlement. Me big blond Viking guy, me sweep fish out of water off her feet. I mean, fish don't have feet . . ."

"I know what you mean," Jean told her. "He thought because you were new here on Farnaby you'd need—consolation. And he didn't like your telling him thanks but no thanks."

"Funny, isn't it?" asked Rebecca of no one in particular. "You hate machismo, but you hate wimpiness as well."

"No kidding," Tara said. "Niamh just broke up with a guy in

Newcastle and has a thing for Lance. I wish he'd give her the time of day."

"Niamh's saying Grinsell's in a bad way. Good job Tara and I were still at the house when Edwin stopped by, so she could help. She's a grand nurse, Niamh is, never mind her ancestry." Maggie sat back on the stone dais.

"Ancestry?" Rebecca asked, absolving Jean of the need to do it herself.

Maggie didn't ask why Rebecca knew who Niamh was. "Her father was the same sort as my own dad. As Wat Lauder. Handsome, smooth talker, quick-tempered, and possessive."

"Her father, Donal McCarthy," said Jean.

Maggie looked up at her, head tilted to the side, a smile that split the difference between rueful and wistful pulling her lips askew. The light emphasized the subtle bloating of her features. The haze in the air—and on Jean's glasses—softened them into vulnerability. "You're a reporter yourself, aren't you now? Thank you for not pretending you don't know of it all."

"Thank you for understanding why I—we—looked it all up." Jean didn't go into her usual spiel about not *that* kind of reporter. "Do you know Grinsell's one of the Cambridgeshire detective constables who made such a fuss over your acquittal?"

"Is he? Is that why he acted such a pig last night, getting his own back? Damn and blast! They'll be suspecting me of bashing him. I even threatened him, didn't I? But I didn't bash him. I've been through it all once. Why would I look to go through it again?"

"Mags didn't leave the house between the time I heard the pickup stalled in the parking lot and the time Crawford came to get Niamh. Niamh'll testify to that, too," Tara added.

That, Jean told herself, begged the question of whether it was indeed Grinsell spinning the wheels. And of whose testimony was reliable.

Rebecca shrank into herself—*don't mind me.* Maggie contemplated the coffin exposed below her. Tara arranged the items in her tray, lining up the dental picks with the tweezers, her face hidden by her chin-length russet hair.

A lot of redheads around here, Jean thought again—and this time she mentally slapped her forehead with the heel of her hand. Tara and Niamh were half-sisters, weren't they? Donal's daughters, one by his wife, one by his lover.

She said, "There are protocols to be followed when one family member is testifying for another. Or against another. Your giving your mother an alibi doesn't make an open-and-shut case, Tara. And Niamh, well, if she's Donal McCarthy's daughter, too . . ."

The *too* fluttered as slowly to the ground as the dropped handkerchief signaling the start of a duel.

Chapter Twenty

Rebecca shrank another few millimeters, although not without casting a glance up at Jean. Tara froze in place. Maggie shifted restlessly, closed her eyes, opened them again. "Very clever."

"Not particularly."

"Donal is Tara's father, yes. Niamh is the child of his marriage. She was no more than a toddler when it all happened. It was because she was a toddler—stressful little creatures, toddlers . . ."

Rebecca murmured agreement.

". . . that's one reason Donal was on the prowl. The other reason being that it's in the nature of rats to prowl. Sorry, Tara, but it's the truth. I'd say I was a fool for ever giving him the time of day, but he likely saved my life when Oliver thrust that shotgun into my face. Turning the gun back on him and pulling the trigger, now—that's another issue. The gleam in his eye just then will haunt me to my dying day."

"He never had the guts to admit to any of it, not until he was forced to," Tara told her, and to Jean, "My dad is Rick Hogg from Little Rock. I never knew Donal."

A clear voice behind Jean's back said, "Nor I."

She jerked around to see Niamh emerging from the fog the same way the phantom face had emerged earlier. But Niamh's fine, pale features, so much like Tara's, didn't dissolve again.

Maggie started up. "Mum? Is she having another wander? In this fog . . ."

"Not to worry," Niamh told her. "Pen's come with scones and sympathy. I stopped in to tell you I'm away to the school—Hugh wants me to have another go at 'Foggy Dew.' A little too apt at the moment."

Jean abandoned discretion. "Elaine wanders?"

"Reliving her youth, I expect. We're trying to ensure she's never alone, but she slips away. I can't get it straight in my mind that she's a child again." Maggie bit her lip, then said, "In all the confusion last night she went walkabout—Pen found her sitting on the curb outside the pub without so much as a shawl to keep her warm. That wasn't so bad. Last month we found her at Merlin's Tower. Faralot, she calls it. Farnaby's Camelot, although our own kitchen is where the round table sat, with my—with Wat lording it over them all. Over us all, after I came along. It was more Monty Python than Malory or Tennyson. I suppose Tom Seaton would have been Tom the Enchanter."

Maggie may have intended that as a joke, but instead of smiling, she deflated into a slump. Women of her and Jean's age were sometimes called the sandwich generation. Some of them, more aptly, were called the mammogram generation, crushed not only between parents and children, but also between expectations and reality.

Jean saw no need to mention that the character in *Monty Python and the Holy Grail* was Tim the Enchanter, not Tom, and was not an attractive young musician.

"Seems to be you're holding court here yourself," Niamh said to Maggie. "Or are you reliving your own youth?"

She didn't speak waspishly, Jean estimated, but resignedly. Rebecca scooted to the side and kept on brushing. *No, really, I'm not here at all.*

"My youth was more peculiar than most," returned Maggie. "I long ago gave up keeping it all secret. Secrets hurt, even when they're meant to protect. Especially when they're meant to protect. When Tara reached eighteen I sent her a message through the adoption agency, asking if she'd like to meet up. She said yes. Now she's spending a term here. A semester, you lot call it."

"Maybe not my smartest decision." Tara's own smile was much more rueful than wistful.

"I searched out Donal's other daughter, Tara's sister, and found her working as a nurse in a care home in Newcastle. When my mother needed more care than I could provide, I asked her to come to us."

"I didn't know who Maggie was, not till she told me." The resigned tone in Niamh's voice sharpened with bitterness. "My mum divorced my dad when he went to prison—no standing by her man, thank you very much. Still, she sent him my school photos and the like for quite a few years, but he never replied, and she gave it up as a bad job. Never thought of himself as more than the sperm donor, I reckon."

"Times two," Tara said.

"I arranged for a DNA test. Tara and I, we have the same father—no question about it."

"One who should be ashamed of himself," added Tara.

"There's enough shame to go round." Maggie once again leaned into the grave. *Dink-dink.* "I suppose I could ask for a DNA sample from Tom's—from the body that was hidden here, compare it against my own. I'm not sure I want to know whether Mum, well . . ."

"Too much information?" asked Tara, but she grinned as she said it. "Been there, done that, bio-Mom."

Niamh chuckled. Maggie emitted a dry snort.

Oh yeah, Jean thought. Gone were the days when sexual matters had to be ignored at all costs. Now the pendulum had swung so far toward public pubic exposure that she felt nostalgic for fig leaves.

She blinked, and blinked again, as though the damp gauziness hanging before her eyes was in her vision, not in the air itself. The fog pressed against the windows and the door like dirty cotton candy. She wasn't so sure the ceiling hadn't sunk further into the room. But none of the other women seemed oppressed. Physically oppressed, at least.

She imagined Grinsell walking in to see a group of women caring and sharing and exchanging blunt remarks about the opposite sex. He'd go nuts.

Was he still alive? If not, he really could come walking in.

Jean stepped farther away from the door and closer to one of the light stanchions. "There's already evidence for Arthur and Merlin as historical characters. Adding Guinevere to the list would be quite a coup for you, Maggie. You'd have vindicated your mother's work."

"Guinevere?" repeated Rebecca, darting a sharp upward glance at Jean that no doubt meant, *There's a detail you forgot to tell me.* Before Jean could speak, though, she rallied. "Ah, well, of course. Elaine believed Guinevere to be historical, and someone historical needs a grave."

"It all started when Mum went against Wat's wishes and went away to Cambridge to read Dark Age literature in the Oliver Montagu Phillips library," Maggie explained. "It all continued when Mum decided I should be living her life over again, doing it properly this time round. So away to Cambridge I went as well. And then I ended being indirectly responsible for Oliver the third's death. Twist of fate. Irony of ironies."

Tara looked one way, Niamh the other.

"According to the notes at the end of *Britannia,* a Dark Age manuscript is where Elaine found evidence for Guinevere and Merlin's sister Gwendeth being the same woman." Saying "crazed extrapolation" instead of "evidence" would have been more truthful but less diplomatic, Jean reminded herself. "But you said she planned a sequel about Gwen-whosis's cult here on Farnaby. Did she find something in the manuscript library about that, too?"

"Not really, no. She said she heard a woman's voice whilst gardening in the cloister. Hilda. Not Whitby's saint, but the seventh-century prioress—although Mum thinks Farnaby's Hilda is the youthful, magical avatar of Whitby's. Either way, it was Hilda who told her the secret history of the convent, how it had grown up round Queen Guinevere's burial place."

"Told her in contemporary English?"

"Good point. Mum heard a voice, I expect, but it was her own. Especially since she'd written a small book about Hilda, based on her work in the Phillips library."

"Hilda, the original flying nun." Jean said nothing about provocative autographs. *Where the bodies are buried.*

"Flying nun. Isn't that an old TV show?" Tara asked.

"I told Mum more than once she should have the grave slab up and be done with it. But she was squeamish. She was literary, not scientific. She was loony, folk said. Loony Lauder. Now that's what folk will be calling me, especially after all this." She gestured around the chapel. "One of the reporters muttered that yesterday morning, thought I couldn't hear him."

"Someone familiar with Elaine's work," said Rebecca, half to herself.

I bet I know which reporter that was, Jean said, entirely to herself.

"Now I know why Mum didn't want the slab up, don't I? She already had it up, and cracked it, and tried to mend it. She had it up to hide her lover's body. Did Wat kill him? A chanter through the mouth is a crime of passion if ever there was one. Makes Oliver and Donal and the shotgun look right dull."

Jean cautioned, "You don't know Thomas Seaton was her lover. You don't know who killed him, or who put his body here. You don't even know if he really is the body in the grave, for that matter."

"True. Just now I'd settle for learning whose grave this was originally."

"Mother Hilda's, the prioress?"

"Probably, but hope springs eternal. For one thing, why would Hilda be buried in a Roman-era-style coffin?"

"Perhaps it was recycled as a mark of honor." Rebecca put down the brush. "You're about ready for the can opener."

"Yes." Maggie set aside her hammer and chisel. From the shadow at the side of the dais she picked up two cloth bands and attached the end of one to a long, thin, metal rod. She worked first that cloth, then the other one, into the gap around the lid of the coffin and through to the other side. Rebecca seized the ends and pulled them through.

Within moments Maggie and her impromptu apprentice had attached the bands to the block-and-tackle. "All right then," she said to Tara, and Tara took a series of photos.

Then Maggie reached for a pair of metal snips. She angled them toward one of the strips of lead still attaching the lid of the coffin to its sides, then retracted her hand. "I considered trying to lift the entire coffin. I could set myself up a lab in the old book shop—Grinsell's incident room—and do a proper exam. But the body of the coffin's bound to be too heavy, thin or not. So we're dealing with the lid alone."

Elaine, thought Jean, hadn't opened the tomb because she didn't want to be proved wrong. And now Maggie didn't want to prove Elaine wrong. Unopened, it was Schrödinger's grave, both the last resting place of Guinevere and the last resting place of Elaine's Arthurian dream.

Again she reached forward, then again sat back. "Mum said that Farnaby is Avalon. Arthur was carried to Avalon by women. Earlier people would bury their dead on islands, to prevent them from returning to haunt the living, and Farnaby's been associated with women since records began. She etymologized the name as Freya-byrig, the settlement of Freya, the great Norse mother-goddess. But the name is from 'farna', or pilgrim, after St. Cuthbert's hermitage on the Farne Islands, farther out to sea. Farnaby would have had another name in Arthur's day. Mum proposed all sorts derived from Latin, Brythonic, Goidelic. She tried to relate 'Medraut,' Mordred's name in the old chronicles, with an early name for Lindisfarne—Medcaut or Metcaud. But the human mouth can only make so many sounds. Most similarities are no more than coincidence."

Rebecca used her forefinger to remove another curl of lead. Tara considered the tray of tools. Niamh glanced at her watch. Jean waited while Maggie played devil's advocate with herself.

"The Priory of Saint Mary," Maggie went on. "Saint Mary the Virgin? Or Mary Magdalene, appropriate for Guinevere, and Mum, and me, save the Magdalene's story as a cautionary tale of a misbehaving woman is no more than propaganda put about by the church patriarchs. Hilda the mystic, Hilda of Whitby. Saint Genevieve."

"I'm pretty sure," Jean said, "the rumor of Saint Cuthbert being prejudiced against women is just that, rumor, but if it were true, having Farnaby on his doorstep might have colored his opinion. Even if the attribution to Saint Genevieve is much later."

"An island of women, luring men to their doom," said Rebecca. "The Lorelei. The sirens."

"So," Jean concluded, "if Lindisfarne is the Holy Island, is Farnaby the Holier Than Thou Island?"

As though the words had broken a spell, Maggie laughed. So did the others, their laughter seeming to lighten the genuine as well as the metaphorical air.

Something fluttered and flapped in the sanctuary. Niamh

jumped, then laughed again, short and self-conscious. "Crows or ravens. There are always a few about the priory."

"There you are," said Rebecca. "The Irish mother goddess, Morrigan, was attended by crows or ravens. That's in the Gallowglass song, isn't it?"

Maggie nodded. " 'The Ravens of Avalon.' Mum wrote the words and the melody. Dad embellished it and claimed it as his, no surprise there." Her face pale but composed, she leaned into the tomb. *Snip.* She turned at another angle. *Snip.* She scrambled around to the far side of the rectangle. *Snip. Snip.*

Jean took a step closer to the scene of the action, then, with visions of the lid swinging back and forth like Edgar Allan Poe's scything pendulum, stepped back again to stand beside Niamh.

The cloth bands tightened. Quickly Maggie gave Tara the cutting tool. Then she and Rebecca, as cautiously as though they lifted a bucket of nitroglycerin, operated the block-and-tackle.

The ropes creaked, but the lid of the coffin rose silently and hung from the bands. Dust particles drifted downward, each a golden mote.

"Hand me a torch," Maggie ordered.

Tara produced a smaller flashlight, of the sort you'd keep in a kitchen drawer or glove compartment. Heedless of the lid swinging gently overhead, Jean pressed forward, Niamh at her side.

It'll be a skeleton, she told herself. A gruesome one, caked with decay, not a nice tidy medical-school or Halloween-decoration version. It'll be wearing armor and have a long sword rusting at its side—it'll be a man, an Angle, probably—or it'll be enveloped in the remains of a wool habit and its bony fingers will be clutching a rosary—did they have rosaries in Hilda's time? She'd have to look it up.

Five heads bumped over the cavity. The light swept from the upright stones lining the tomb across the uneven vertical planes of the coffin and down, to reveal . . .

Nothing. Absolutely nothing.

Chapter Twenty-One

No one spoke. So far as Jean could tell, no one breathed. She knew she didn't—until her nervous system did its thing and she gasped in the taste and smell of mud and decay.

Surely she looked at an optical illusion. Centuries of accumulated shadow and the mud oozing at the bottom concealed the body . . .

The bottom was black mud and ooze. A worm crawled up from the muck, wriggled around blindly, then dived for cover.

"The grave's been robbed," someone said, her voice echoing in the pit. Rebecca.

"Robbers wouldn't steal the bottom of the coffin and leave the rest," said Tara.

"Perhaps the body's completely decomposed," Niamh suggested.

"The body in the Sutton Hoo burial is completely decomposed," said Jean, "leaving all those marvelous grave goods behind. But most Christian burials don't have grave goods. Or very few."

Maggie groped behind her, found one of her metal rods, and thrust it into the bottom of the tomb. The rod penetrated as far as she could push it without falling face-first into the hole. She summed up the situation in two words. "Holy shit."

"What's all this?" asked a young male voice behind them.

And an older one with a familiar Western Highlands accent replied. "They've opened the grave. Tut's tomb, is it?"

Alasdair. And, Jean saw as she raised up and swiveled around, his temporary Tonto, Sergeant Darling. "Tut's tomb it isn't," she told them. "It's empty."

"Empty?" Darling repeated. "Whyever's it empty?"

No one answered. Each of the other women sat up as well, and one by one clambered to her feet, adjusting hair and jackets and brushing off denim knees on the way. The men stepped forward, glanced into the pit, stepped back again. Darling's gaze rested much longer on the elusive Tara. She tried a tentative smile and a subtle shrug. *Sorry.*

Maggie's eyes gleamed with something that might be stubbornness or might be fanaticism. "The coffin's got no bottom. It's a table tomb, set over a grave in the ground below. I'll keep digging. I'll sort it."

"Right," said Alasdair, and to Jean he said, "I stopped in at the B and B. Michael was telling me you and Rebecca were having yourselves a look at the excavation. Good job you came walking over here together. I never thought to warn you against walking about alone."

"It's easy to get lost in the fog," Jean returned.

"More than that, there's someone violent in the area. I'm hoping the villain had himself a wee grudge against Grinsell, or at the least against policemen, not against anyone crossing his—her—path. But till we've laid the villain by the heels, I'm advising caution."

Jean thought of P.C. Crawford holding a lonely vigil at the crime scene. Well, he had his phone, and his cautious nature—she could see him setting his back against one of the monolithic stones—and probably companionship in the occasional looky-loo hoping for the sight of bloodstains.

Alasdair went on, "Sergeant Darling here spoke with Grinsell's sister in Cambridgeshire. She recognized the name Maggie Lauder, said she'd heard it before. Her brother'd rant about the Phillips murder, a female barrister getting a female defendant acquitted."

"I've heard him talk of it myself," said Darling, "every time we've dealt with a female suspect."

"Has a vendetta against women, has he?" Maggie demanded. "Because of me?"

"I imagine your case reinforced existing prejudices, is all," said Alasdair.

Darling stated, "Ah, he bullies everyone. D.C.I. Webber's sent him for anger management courses and the like, but they've done no good, only made him stroppier."

Testosterone poisoning, Jean thought. But that was too easy an appraisal. "You're using the present tense about Grinsell."

"Webber's telling me he's still alive, if barely. If he survives, he'll be incapable of caring for himself."

Cosmic justice? Jean asked herself. The bully reduced to dependence? Or a fate worse than death?

Maggie eyed her own feet, her jaw tight, her hand banging the small flashlight against her thigh. Tara looked at her, expression unreadable. Alasdair looked at the flashlight. "Where's your large torch?"

"I suppose Edwin's still carrying it about," Maggie said. "Why?"

So Niamh hadn't passed on Darling's guess about the weapon. She stood with her arms crossed, gazing at the ruined window. *Somewhere else . . .*

Alasdair said to her, "Miss McCarthy, P.C. Crawford's telling Sergeant Darling here that he handed the torch in at Gow House last night. That he gave it to you."

Whoa, Jean thought, as every face turned toward Niamh.

Her eyebrows, fine as an angel's feathers, crinkled. "I tidied it away into the cupboard by the door. Wasn't it there this morning, Maggie? Tara?"

"No," said Maggie, just as Tara said, "Nope. Sure wasn't."

"Perhaps Elaine's got it. I'll have a look through her things after the rehearsal, shall I?"

"Please," Alasdair told her. When his gaze released her, she took a long step back and crossed her arms even more tightly, making a protective breastplate. Jean could hardly blame her.

Alasdair asked, "What's in that tray, Rebecca?"

She hoisted the tray of tools, carried it out from behind the grave, and presented it to him. Instead of taking it from her hands, Alasdair merely glanced into it. "How many dental picks are you using, Professor Lauder?"

"I've got no idea. I've been accumulating tools for years now. Why?"

Dental pick, Jean repeated to herself. *The wee scraper from the crime scene.*

Alasdair replied, "The scene-of-crime team found a dental pick in the weeds near Grinsell's bod—near where Grinsell was attacked. It was too shiny to have been lying there long, was not lost when those trenches were being cut into the turf. It might have fallen from the assailant's pocket."

"Well then, Chief Inspector Cameron," Maggie snapped, "my fingerprints are on file."

Jean sent a thought wave toward Maggie—*he's not out to get you, he simply wants the truth*—but telepathy hadn't worked last night and it didn't work now.

Maggie kept on, a flush like a rash mounting on her face. "You're thinking I thumped him? He needed getting out of the way so I could get on with my work, is that it? Or was I after protecting myself and my daughter from his abuse? He may have had some sort of filthy fixation on me, but I'd never heard of the prat before yesterday."

Alasdair's eyes shone the cold blue of a glacier, layer upon layer of compressed snow. "Right."

This time Jean tried beaming thoughts to him: *Cut Maggie some slack already!*

Every face pointed in a different direction. The silence inside the chantry chapel seemed as thick as the fog outside. Jean opened her mouth, closed it, bit her tongue, and then thought of a topic that was no less fraught, but was at least less immediate. "Did you ask Clyde about whether his father ferried Thomas Seaton off the island?"

Alasdair turned his gaze on Darling.

"Oh, ah, yes," the young man said. "Seaton left Farnaby in October of nineteen seventy-one. Mr. Eccleston was a schoolboy at the time, and remembers his father making a meal of it. He remembers as well his father saying Wat had asked him for discretion, so the meal was made only in the Eccleston family. Seaton left under some sort of cloud, made off so quickly he left bits and bobs behind—or so he told Eccleston major—but he did leave the island."

"Wat could be a fearsome old devil," Maggie said faintly. "Makes you think Tom had a guilty conscience . . . Half a tick. You're satisfied that he left?"

"The question's moot," said Alasdair. "Some bright spark up and about in Halifax phoned Berwick a couple of hours since to say that he'd spoken with Thomas Seaton's son. Seaton studied piping in the UK, aye, and returned home in nineteen seventy-one, and was known to the local Highland Games and traditional-music circuit for the rest of his life."

"He died three years ago," Darling added. "Liver cancer. These musicians, they like their drink."

Whisky not as the water of life, Jean thought, but as the water of death.

"I was born in December of seventy-two. Tom wasn't my father." What color Maggie had in her face leached slowly away. Tara set her hand on her mother's arm. Rebecca caught Jean's eye and shrugged. Niamh looked at her feet, pigeon-toed on the flagstones like Tara's had been yesterday. It wasn't her fault either.

No one had to say aloud, *That's not Thomas Seaton in the grave.* Since it wasn't, though, then a whole new can of worms opened up, in addition to the barrel of snakes of the attack on Grinsell. To say nothing of the worm-eaten issue of the bottomless grave—which, okay, wasn't a matter of life and death. Not in this century, anyway.

"The chanter," Maggie said. "I thought it belonged to the victim. Maybe it belonged to the murderer. Maybe Thomas ran off because he killed a man."

Alasdair shifted his weight, relaxing his stance, if still frosty of expression. "The medical examiner in Berwick is thinking the dead man to have been over six feet tall and between thirty and forty years old—a bit old to be one of Wat's young students, but he could have been a musician brushing up his skills."

"The doctor was able to turn out the body's pockets," said Darling. "He found a pre-decimal half crown and a two-penny coin as well as a small pad of paper—little more than pulp now, unreadable—and a propelling pencil."

"A mechanical pencil," Jean translated under her breath.

"Buttons and a trouser zip. No jewelry. Two gold teeth and fillings in several others, which would be right helpful if we had the least inkling of whose dental records to be looking over."

"Funny how often you find coins." Jean offered Alasdair the merest hint of a smile.

"Everyone carries coins," he replied.

"We changed over to decimal currency in nineteen seventy-one." Darling had no need to add, *well before my time.* "I looked it up."

Good lad, Jean thought.

"The half crown was demonetized—no longer legal tender—in nineteen seventy," he went on. "Two-pee coins weren't issued until February fifteenth, nineteen seventy-one, the day of the changeover."

Maggie said, "The chap was keeping the half crown as a memento, then. Or he'd not recently turned out his pockets. Either way, the change to decimal currency in nineteen seventy-one dates the burial."

"That's a strong possibility, aye, if not a dead certainty." No one smiled at Alasdair's unintended pun.

With a shuddering inhalation Maggie went on, "Who is he, then? Whether he meant anything to my mother, how he died, at whose hands, why—I can't remember anything helpful."

Tara tightened her grasp. "No one wants you to remember anything, Mags. You weren't even born then, and the guy in the tomb might have squat to do with your family. The cops won't even know if the chanter's really the murder weapon until they find it."

Alasdair's brows tightened. Jean interpreted this particular furrow as, *How does she know we're thinking the chanter's the murder weapon?*

"Chance would be a fine thing," Maggie told Tara skeptically.

Raising her chin, Niamh turned toward the door. "The concert. Rehearsal. The show must go on."

"Oh." Maggie forced a stiff smile. "Well done, Niamh. I'll bring Mum along. That's one thing not entirely left her, the old songs."

"Sergeant," Alasdair said to Darling, "please walk Miss McCarthy to the school."

"The blind leading the near-sighted?" Darling replied, if with an actual smile at Niamh.

Well, well, well, Jean thought. He *was* a handsome lad when he finally shook off the worried frown and the oppressed crouch.

"I'll get us there," Niamh replied, her wry tone indicating

Darling's charms had not escaped her notice. Side-by-side, the pair faded into the fog, which, Jean swore, had grown thicker and heavier. Even Darling's lime-yellow jacket seemed dull.

Who was protecting whom? If someone with a grudge against policemen roamed around with malice aforethought, then Darling was in danger. But then, that someone would need the equivalent of X-ray vision to find him.

Rebecca said, "I see a tarpaulin folded up in the corner. We can stake it down over the hole. Unless you're planning to keep on digging this afternoon."

Maggie looked around the chapel, shoulders slouched, features sagging, exuding such fatigue, Jean felt weak in the knees. "No good going on, not now. The batteries need recharging. As do I. Let's cover the . . ."

Jean waited for her to complete her sentence. *Grave disappointment?*

". . . dig." She went on, muttering under her breath, thinking aloud. "Why build a chantry over a grave if there's nothing in it? There could be any number of burials here, with this simply the most prominent. It would take years of work to excavate them all. A team. Resources."

Maggie directed Jean, Rebecca, and Tara in pulling the same blue tarpaulin that had yesterday concealed the unexpected body over today's unexpected vacancy. ". . . maybe it's the tomb of an unknown soldier, a cenotaph. There was the battle at Heavenfield. The one at Alnwick—no, that was much later. This area was the first landfall for Vikings and Danes like it was for Angles."

The corner Jean held slipped from her grasp. In the instant she leaned over the cavity to reclaim it she caught a quick sparkle, a glint in the mud where Maggie had inserted her probe. Then the interior of the hole plunged into blue-tinted gloom. A stray neutrino had sparked one of her nerve endings, she told herself. It wasn't worth mentioning. Besides, if she did call Maggie's attention to it, the woman would fling back the tarp and dive in.

Tomorrow, Jean told herself, and instead of Macbeth's pessimistic "Tomorrow and tomorrow and tomorrow creeps in this petty pace from day to day" chose Scarlett O'Hara's optimistic mantra about tomorrow being another day. Hopefully one with light, already, in all its various forms.

Alasdair, who had stood politely back while the women spread out the tarp, accepted Maggie's pointing forefinger with good grace. Finding a hammer in the tool tray, he drove small metal stakes through the grommets at the corners of the tarp and into the interstices between the flagstones.

Tara gathered up the tools while Rebecca used her phone to snap a few photos of the grave slab. When Maggie switched off the lights, the dim gray mist, a palpable thundercloud hugging the ground, closed in around them. Jean could hardly see Maggie collecting the battery packs.

Even if Alasdair had his old reflective jacket, she thought, almost no light was available to reflect from it. She wondered if he missed it. It was, after all, a sort of badge of office.

In a group they picked their way out of the church to the graveyard wall. Wat's headstone was a domed shape in the murk, the words unreadable. Maggie paused to gaze at it. Was she convinced that he was her father after all? Or, now that she'd given in to the child's fantasy of being left in a basket on the doorstep of unsympathetic strangers, would she ever be satisfied?

She stated, "The concert's at half past six," and, with Tara at her side, she followed the low stone wall toward Gow House and disappeared into the fog.

Chapter Twenty-Two

Alasdair, Jean, and Rebecca started slowly across the parking lot toward a looming density, the row of houses that made up Farnaby St. Mary. Somewhere a door slammed. Somewhere else a dog barked, short and sharp. A set of footsteps crunched across the blacktop, seemingly unattached to a human form.

Only when the short stairway down to Cuddy's Close materialized before them did Rebecca speak. "Well. That was interesting. But things are usually interesting when I'm hanging about with the pair of you."

"How," Alasdair asked, "did Tara and Maggie know about the chanter possibly being the murder weapon?"

"Pen knows about it," answered Jean. "Maybe Crawford told her when he picked up his picnic lunch. And he might have told Maggie and Tara when he collected the crime scene tape from the chapel. I guess he's had to give up pretending it was never there at all."

"Local constables," Alasdair said with a sigh. "Being part of the community, they're sources of information for the investigation, but the information's flowing the other way as well. I'd hate to think we've got a bent copper here."

"Crooked? I could buy him being curious over and beyond the call of duty, and a gossip, too, when he's speaking at all, but where's his motive to be crooked? He's been straight as an arrow with the contemporary case. The only doubt we—you—have about him concerns the cold case."

Alasdair's only reply was a mutter about keeping options open.

They groped their way between the pub and the B&B, ignoring the voices and scents of food emanating from the former and stepping into the brightly lit entranceway of the latter. This time the predominant aroma was baking meat and pastry with a whiff of furniture polish.

From down the hall came the sound of Michael's voice. "Chanter. Chan-ter."

Linda replied in a two-syllable gurgle.

"Aye, that's it. Chanter. Drone. Bag."

"The bagpipes are going to be ready," said Rebecca. "As for Linda, if she never took a nap, the evening's going to be as interesting as the afternoon, just a lot noisier. And I don't mean musical noise." With a frown of maternal concern, she started toward the room. "Hugh asked Michael to be at the school at six. See you there, eh?"

"See you there," Jean called, and Alasdair waved.

Jean nipped into the sitting room for the copy of *Britannia* and saw that no, *Hilda* hadn't flown back into place. Upstairs, Hildy the cat was still in hiding, her windowsill vacant.

Tucked safely away in their room, Alasdair and Jean sat down with hot cups of tea and a basket of cellophane-wrapped nibbles. "Too much to be sweeping the place for bugs, I'm supposing, but still . . ." A sip of the sugary, milky tea eased the cogitational crease in his forehead but didn't smooth it out.

Jean opened a package of chocolate-covered digestive biscuits and did not think of Grinsell. Instead, she offered Alasdair the second biscuit and launched into a rough draft of the afternoon's events, from Michael's essay on the missing chanter to Pen's and Maggie's reminiscences, from the disappearance of *Hilda, the Enchanted Prioress* to the state of the half-sisters Niamh and Tara.

"I was thinking the 'McCarthy' no coincidence," Alasdair replied, even as he ate the biscuit. That didn't smooth the crease, either.

"I told you there was no harm in talking to Pen. She volunteered a lot of information about Thomas Seaton."

"That hardly matters now."

"Okay then, she volunteered information about the dynamic at Gow House way back when, like how Maggie's probably hoping Wat *isn't* her father. She called him 'a fearsome old devil' there in the chapel. But then, it's his—artistic? passionate?—temperament that made his music so good."

"Hugh's told us of Wat's temper already."

"So Pen corroborated what he said. Not that Hugh isn't trustworthy, but people's memories do get skewed around." Jean took a swig of her caramel-colored tea, hoping to sweeten her growing irritation with her beloved, and then had to swish the liquid around her mouth before it burned. Swallowing, she went on, "Neither Pen nor Hugh thought Wat was capable of murdering anyone, not in a premeditated fashion, anyway. But as Maggie pointed out before you got there, killing someone with the thrust of a chanter does suggest a crime of passion. An argument gone to extremes."

"Maggie's right about the chanter—it could have belonged to the murderer, not the victim. It's possible Thomas Seaton is our man. Was our man. How'd he do it, though?"

"When Michael and Rebecca and I were talking to Pen right after lunch, she suggested the murderer sneaked up on the victim while he was playing the chanter. That way it would already be in his mouth."

"That would be requiring some strength, enough to stun the victim into not fighting back."

"I've seen photos of Wat," Jean said. "He was a big man. I wonder if Thomas was big, too."

Alasdair said nothing.

"But Wat played Arthur in Farnaby's Camelot," Jean went on. "He proposed and everyone else disposed. Not that he ordered someone to rid him of this troublesome, er, Rob. But a confrontational manner breeds more of the same."

Alasdair opened a package of cheese crackers. "Aye, we're back to the body being your Rob the Ranter. But that's all by way of being secondary just now." He bit and chewed, gazing toward the blank panes of the far window.

From downstairs came a toddler's shriek, whether happy or upset was beyond Jean's ken. A door opened and shut and Pen's voice called something about juice and the concert, to be answered by Rebecca's. So Pen, having delivered her scones and sympathy, was back from Gow House.

"Yes," Jean told Alasdair, "the major issue is who attacked Grinsell. Please don't tell me you think it was Maggie."

"All right then, I'll not be telling you that, if that's not what you're wanting to hear."

Steps came up the stairs and a quiet knock sounded on the door. Jean found Pen still wearing a purple padded jacket, her pin curls wrapped with a flowery scarf. "I'm so sorry—please forgive me for intruding—have you seen Hildy? She's not touched her food and she's not in her basket next the Aga cooker."

"Oh." Jean raked back through her memory. "The last I saw of her was when she ran upstairs while we were eating lunch with the baby."

"Ah. Well then. It's as I feared—I found the back door off its latch. James, likely, carrying supplies across to the pub, didn't quite shut it . . . I'll ask about. I'm sure she'll come back." The lines of her face seemed out of kilter, like a portrait by Picasso, stress warring with her usual sanguine temperament. With a "Cheers," she headed back downstairs.

"We'll watch for her," Jean called, and turned back to Alasdair's chill blue gaze.

"Have a look at the evidence for yourself," he said. "Grinsell was likely thumped with a big torch. Maggie cannot account for hers. There was a wee scraper, a dental pick, at the scene, identical to the ones she's using."

"Careless of the bad guy to drop it, wasn't it?"

"You'd not believe the carelessness of criminals—and a good job they are. Makes our lives easier."

Our. The police. When it came to war stories, she had nothing. Instead, she asked, "That tray of tools had to have been in the chapel when we were there yesterday."

"I did not notice, having other things to be noticing."

"Same here. What I do know is that neither Maggie nor Tara carried it away when we all left. Maybe someone else pocketed a pick?" That didn't sound right. Jean paused to mull over the word "pickpocket"—no, that wasn't what she meant—then plunged on. "Someone sneaked in behind Crawford's back and took the chanter. Maybe that someone also took a pick and planted it at the crime scene to implicate Maggie. Or maybe it was two different people."

"A lot of folk sneaking about, then."

"Even Elaine was out and about last night—Maggie says she slips out. Although that was later on in the evening." *Or was it?* Jean asked herself.

"How many folk with diverging motives are we talking about?"

"We all have agendas." Speaking of which, she had to say it. "Alasdair, I know you're not happy seeing a policeman attacked. I know you're not happy having this case dumped on you. Or maybe you are. Maybe that's it."

"What's 'it'?"

"You're being such a pill with Maggie. You're not as bad as

Grinsell. I'm not saying that."

Frost gathered on Alasdair's cheekbones and his eyes took on the color of arctic ice. When Jean's phone trilled with "Hail to the Chief," she leaped to answer it. Give the man a chance not to cool down, but to warm up.

"Hi, Miranda. How'd the golf game go?"

"Par is still a far and distant goal for me, but it was a lovely outing," Miranda replied. "The sun's shining and the Forth is gleaming."

"Meanwhile we're socked in here. Thank goodness for megawatt light bulbs."

Miranda's sultry voice was accompanied by the chime of cut glass on crystal, probably a cut-glass whisky decanter counting coup on the rim of a crystal glass. "I see you've had a much more recent casualty."

"No kidding," Jean replied, and angled the phone toward Alasdair so he could hear.

"It's no coincidence, I'm supposing," said Miranda, "that the police detective struck down there on Farnaby is the same one involved in Maggie's case. George Grinsell."

Jean's brain whirred like a tire in a pothole. "What do you mean, involved in Maggie's case?"

"He was by way of being the detective who ended by proving someone else was the murderer, not her at all. In a way, he had her acquittal to thank for his promotion from detective constable to sergeant."

"He's never shown her any gratitude." Alasdair's tone was dust-dry.

Jean still had no traction. But he'd said, but she'd said.

"I've had a further look into the details," Miranda went on. "Grinsell's the Cambridgeshire detective who broke Donal McCarthy's alibi by intimidating his wife, Annie, into giving information. She gave evidence that he wasn't with her at the time of Oliver's death, as he'd claimed. As well, he'd come back from his secret outing with muddy wellies and a coat smudged with what she took to be soot, but which on further investigation by the police turned out to be gunpowder residue. Once they had his fingerprints, they were finally able to isolate one on the gun."

"Oh," said Jean, but it came out more as a squeak. During Miranda's original phone call, they had all hared off down the fork in the road of Maggie's reproductive life, hadn't they? That was the problem with these investigations, not just forks in the road but also interchanges of the sort the British called "spaghetti junctions." Go with the flow of traffic, she told herself. "I can see Grinsell intimidating Mrs. McCarthy. Browbeating her. Although her daughter said this afternoon—the nurse, Niamh. We mentioned her—that she wasn't about to stand by her man."

"She's the daughter, is she? Fancy that! Aye, at the end of the day Annie divorced the villain, and she also filed a complaint against Grinsell. Since he broke the case, the Cambridgeshire force had a bit of a balancing act in dealing with him, I reckon, hence the promotion and the transfer at one go."

A disturbance in the police force. Was that what she'd said to Alasdair?

Plopping herself down on the edge of the bed, Jean returned the phone to her ear and walked Miranda through the events of the afternoon. The empty tomb and Maggie's disappointment. The body not being Tom the Canadian Enchanter after all. The coins proving that the body was not Maggie's father, either.

Alasdair offered no corrections, no additions. He gazed evenly at her, jaw set, no longer icy but cool and patient. Like a cat before a mouse hole.

"So the body's been there since nineteen seventy-one, most likely," repeated Miranda. "A time when Wat and Elaine were past being newlyweds and well settled in their musical Camelot. No happenstance I've been talking with David Ogletree at Triskelion Records about that."

"Gallowglass' recording label, right?" Jean asked, angling the phone toward Alasdair again. "Hugh's with them, too. They've been around a while."

"So has Ogletree. He's retired now, but has the memory of an elephant—last time I saw him, at a Battlefield Band concert, he was going on about Gallowglass' early days as though he'd played every note himself."

"You phoned him to ask about Wat's early days. Well done!"

"That's me, always helping the police with their inquiries. Literally, not euphemistically. We had us a lovely chat about traditional music starting with Fairport Convention and the Chieftains and all. When I finally managed to bring him round to Wat and Farnaby, we had us another lovely chat about teaching the young folk." Miranda paused for, Jean assumed, a sip of restorative elixir.

"Somewhere in the midst of the memoir," she continued, "he mentioned that before Gallowglass went on to fame and fortune, Wat was so desperate for money, he went so far as to ask Ogletree for a loan. A sizeable loan."

"Wat needed money," Alasdair repeated.

"Aye, he did that. He told Ogletree he was after making over a medieval fortlet on Farnaby into a school and house for himself and Elaine. Renovating a medieval ruin costing much more than purpose-building a school, aye, but it would be giving the place the proper ambience. Or so Ogletree was saying, and I expect he's quoting Wat."

Jean looked up at the photo of the old castle hanging on the wall by the bathroom door. "We were told here that Wat intended to redo Merlin's Tower into a home like Lindisfarne Castle after he retired, but he never got around to it. Not quite the same story. Close."

Alasdair followed her gaze, one eyebrow quirked, and murmured her own words back to her. "Memories can be skewed."

She nodded agreement.

"Merlin's Tower, is it? How quaint." Miranda went on, "Ogletree lent Wat a goodly sum. He's under the impression Wat went so far as to consult an architect. But that was the end of it. After six months or so, out of the blue, Wat returned the money."

"When was this, exactly?" Alasdair asked.

"Erm, from context I'm thinking it was seventy or seventy-one."

"What did Wat tell Ogletree?" asked Jean.

"No more than that he'd changed his mind, thank you just the same. Ogletree's under the impression Wat couldn't get planning permission—the fortlet's by way of being a listed building—but Wat never said. Some years later, when his ship came in, so to speak, he purpose-built the school after all. And he bought himself the manse after the church set the vicar commuting to Farnaby for once-a-month services."

"Maybe the architect told him a renovation wasn't feasible," said Jean. "Or it cost more money than he thought he could get from Ogletree. And yes, getting permission to redo a listed building can be quite a hassle, if not impossible."

"As I'm knowing only too well," said Miranda, "with the *Great Scot* offices here in Edinburgh. Who knows what masses of red tape need unfurling south of the border?"

Alasdair said, "We've been thinking the nineteen seventy-one death was a crime of sexual passion, but money's as good a motive for murder. Tends to inspire a fair bit of passion itself, especially when it's tied so closely to power. Maybe there's an insurance policy or will involved—although since the renovations were never done, that's a right long shot. Well, I'll set Darling to researching Wat's finances."

Lucky Darling. Although he might welcome a stint with some old tax records or whatever, after the alarms and excursions on Farnaby.

"Surely money's not the motive for whoever attacked Grinsell," returned Miranda.

"No," Alasdair stated. "The motive's revenge, most likely."

"Revenge. You mean Maggie or . . ." Jean forced the name between her teeth. "Niamh."

Alasdair got up and paced across the room. The stiffness in his back and shoulders answered her question without her having to ask. "Miranda," she said into the phone, "speaking of the Gallowglass school, it's almost time for the concert and I'm in a pair of jeans with mud and grit on the knees."

"We're away to a tourist agency dinner," Miranda replied. "I'd rather be listening to loads of grand music than blethering on about airport revenues and the like, but needs must. Ta ta for now."

"Cheers." Jean switched off the phone. For a long moment she sat slumped on the bed, willing her train of thought onto another track. Down another fork in the road. But it wouldn't change course.

Chapter Twenty-Three

Finally, Jean said dully, "You told me last night Grinsell had solved cases because of his abrasiveness. You meant he solved the Phillips case by strong-arming Niamh's mother. You knew that all along."

"Aye, that I did." Alasdair still gazed out the window, not that there was anything to see. He was probably gazing at the reflection of the room and her small figure huddled on the bed. "I did not know any names other than Maggie's, not till Miranda phoned this morning. The chap in Cambridgeshire was going on about Grinsell's particulars, not those of the case."

"Right." Jean turned Alasdair's verbal tic back on him. Unlike him, however, she couldn't stop with the one word. "But when I asked whether Grinsell was involved in Maggie's case you fudged. You flanneled. Why? Because I was already on the warpath about Grinsell and you didn't want to add any more arrows to my quiver by defending him? Please let's not get into an argument about ends justifying means."

"That's not my intention at all."

"I know arguing isn't your intention. What is?"

"Last night my intention was getting at the truth with a minimum of fuss, when you and Maggie and Grinsell were already fussed. Without giving you ammunition to confront Grinsell or defend Maggie or anything of the sort. But then, last night I did not know he'd himself be the case today, did I now? You're identifying yourself with her, never mind you've got no more in common than your academic career and your age—your court case was nothing like hers. You weren't being impartial with Grinsell or Maggie as it was, and you're not being impartial with me now."

"No, I'm not. I'm never really impartial, and this time is worse than most, but dammit, Alasdair, it's hardly fussing to give someone the benefit of the doubt. The presumption of innocence."

He turned around and fixed her with his best—his worst—stern look. She was mildly surprised his words didn't fall and shatter like shards of icicle. "Maggie has a motive for attacking Grinsell. Full stop. Niamh does as well. I'm not arresting either of them. I'm not playing the macho cop harassing the wee inoffensive lassies. They're persons of interest, that is all." He might as well have closed, *over and out.*

"I know that. Don't insult me." Jean waved her hands, but the right words didn't materialize in them. "Niamh. Grinsell cost her parents their marriage, sort of. He sent her father to prison. Okay. Fine. You didn't hear her talking about it in the chapel. She realizes it was Donal himself who's to blame. She may not even know what Grinsell's role was."

"Even if Annie never mentioned the name—and I'm not betting tuppence on that—I cannot believe Maggie's not been going on about the man ever since her interview last night."

Jean saw Maggie, Tara, and Niamh sitting around the table at Gow House, caring and sharing. If Alasdair wasn't right so much of the time, fighting with him would be a lot easier.

"Explain this," he went remorselessly on. "Crawford's saying he left Maggie's big torch with Niamh. Niamh's saying she put it away. Maggie's saying it's not there. Which one's telling the truth?"

"Maybe both of them. Maybe—someone else—Elaine . . ." Jean felt as though the bed was sucking her down like quicksand.

She jumped up and cast one way, then the other, but found nowhere to run.

"Last night you saw someone walking along the road between Gow House and the priory. Niamh could have helped herself to one of Maggie's tools and planted it at Merlin's Tower. You were suggesting something of the sort yourself."

"I suggested some mysterious someone, not Niamh. And why would she take the chanter?"

"I'm not saying she did that. I'm saying she might well have gone pushing or tripping Grinsell into the nettles and bashing him whilst he was down, then keeping her head and working to save his life when Crawford brought her along to the scene. She could hardly be doing otherwise, no slipping him the wrong drug or the like, not with Hector looking out for him as well."

"So if Niamh used the flashlight on Grinsell, where is it now? Did she throw it over the cliff, like you originally thought? Did she keep it because she needed the light, like Darling said? Tara heard the car stuck in the pothole—did she hear Niamh leave the house about the same time? How did Niamh lure Grinsell up to the tower anyway? Tell him she had something new on Maggie's case?"

"All grand questions," Alasdair conceded.

"How about this one: Do you really think she did it?"

Breaking eye contact, he glanced toward the bedside clock, then strode across the room to the closet. From inside he said, "Time I was changing myself into my glad rags for the evening."

"Answer me."

He emerged carrying the customized bag for his kilt and its accessories. "I've worked half my life for the Northern Constabulary. Their motto is *Dion is Cuidich.* Protect and serve. Now I'm head of Protect and Survive. You'll be sensing a theme here."

"Law, order, and protection. Yeah. Funny how Maggie said

that secrets hurt, even when they're meant to protect. It seems to me what you're interested in is protecting yourself from fuss."

With an incoherent growl, Alasdair vanished into the bathroom. He closed the door so quietly she didn't even hear the latch snap shut.

No, she wasn't being fair. The situation when they'd been talking last night wasn't the same as it was now. Instead of worrying about Grinsell's tactics, now he worried about the case itself. If he found her feminist fuming unhelpful, well, she could excuse that. But she wasn't going to let go of her righteous indignation that easily.

Grasping at the incongruity of Niamh either taking the chanter or trying to kill Grinsell or both, clinging to the knowledge that she and Alasdair had clashed over issues of crime and criminality before and come through to the other side, Jean stamped up and down several times. Then she stacked the tea cups on the tray with such solid dings she was afraid for a moment she'd cracked them.

A knock on the front door below reverberated in the floor. Footsteps, and Pen's voice was raised in concern and pleasure. "Hildy! Where've you been, puss?"

A masculine aw-shucks mutter clarified into Lance saying, "I found her outside the pub flirting with one of the day-trippers, a reporter fellow eating a bacon sandwich."

"She was flirting with the sandwich, I expect. Thank you ever so much—come along, Hildy." The door shut and Pen's steps moved back down the hall. One crisis had been averted. Lance had proved himself quite the protector of damsels-in-distress.

Peace fell downstairs. Another round of the room, and Jean spotted her computer sitting on the desk next to *The Matter of Britannia.* She pounced on it, booted it up, opened her word-processing program, and stared at the blank expanse of white encapsulated by blue bars and arcane icons.

"Northumbria, The Doubtful Shore," she typed. "Northumberland belongs to both England and Scotland and to neither. It's a place of lost kingdoms, lost saints, and lost treasures such as the ruins of Farnaby Priory."

She clicked on "Save" and stared again. Most readers would be more interested in her adventures with the body that was in the tomb than the body that, so far, wasn't. But writing about that skirted close to true crime, not *Great Scot*'s demographic. Besides, she'd always avoided revealing anything about the cases she and Alasdair had been involved in and she didn't intend to start now.

She wasn't, she realized with a muffled groan, going to start anything until she had more historical speculation and less true crime staring her in the face.

Internet? Were you there? Yes—whatever passed for wi-fi on Farnaby connected.

Only connect. What was the rest of the quote from E. M. Forster? Something about connection robbing the monk and the beast of the isolation each thrived on. A criminal would be a beast, she got that, but the isolation of monks and nuns produced music, manuscripts, mysticism. Maybe Grinsell was the beast and Hilda the monastic, he isolated by temperament and she isolated by time.

A quick search turned up all the latest headlines, from a few passing mentions of Maggie's revised press conference to several more emphatic mentions of the mysterious body in the chantry chapel. The less sober news agencies offered headlines such as "The Piper's Grave." As far as they knew, the chanter was simply an associated artifact, not a possible murder weapon. They didn't know it had taken on the status of lost treasure, either.

Most of the relevant headlines shrieked about the vicious attack on one of England's finest, George Grinsell, Detective

Inspector based in Berwick-upon-Tweed. Jean clicked on a video of D.C.I. Webber making a statement outside the hospital. He turned out to be a handsome middle-aged man, his close-cropped black hair going gray at the temples. His chocolate complexion seemed dulled and the slight West Indian lilt in his voice weighed down by what she knew to be conflicting emotions: *Grinsell's an obnoxious so-and-so, but he's our obnoxious so-and-so.*

Was Webber's ancestry the reason Grinsell's anger-management courses only made the chip on his shoulder larger? However, one sort of prejudice didn't necessarily imply another.

No other reporter had made the same connection between the name "Maggie Lauder" and "Rob the Ranter"—never mind the hard work of groups like Gallowglass, many of the old songs were sadly moribund. But the name "Maggie Lauder" had produced a different variety of connection.

Under the main banner of *The Daily Dish* opened the headline, "At it again?"

The first photo wasn't Maggie's publicity picture, a flattering studio portrait. It was a snapshot of her standing in front of a church window, no doubt taken during her Plan B press event in the church yesterday. Her expression wasn't that of a deer in the headlights but one already dressed out and searing in a skillet.

Much more space was given to a summary of the Cambridgeshire case, illustrated by a picture of a young Maggie escorted into court by a woman police constable. Her face would have made that of a mannequin in a shop window look animated, although otherwise the resemblance to Tara was unmistakable.

A second picture of young Maggie showed her sitting on a broken column in front of a sunlit Farnaby Priory. Here she smiled, although her posture was only marginally more relaxed than it had been when she'd been waiting on the same column drum yesterday.

Next to her sat an even younger woman, beaming broadly. She looked familiar. According to the caption, her name was Lisa Fleming . . . Oh. Fleming. Pen and James's daughter, Pen's affable smile glowing from her face. Two of the photos on the mantel downstairs were of her, too, now that Jean thought about it, one as a teenager, one as an older woman with two children in front of Bamburgh Castle.

From downstairs echoed Michael's, Rebecca's, and Linda's voices, all talking at once. The front door opened and shut. The voices faded into the fog.

Behind her the bathroom door opened. Alasdair's footsteps paced across the room. Jean didn't look around—she was busy, wasn't she? She had work to do.

Once again she opened *The Matter of Britannia* to "Guinevere the Christian Goddess." The card was still there, and the message written in a firm, rather splashy hand, all sprawling loops and dark slashes. *Athelstan Crawford. Granite. Classic Roman 2. Letterbox.* And on the back the cryptic, "Merlin."

She typed the descriptive words into the box of her search engine and considered the answers: Mailboxes. Roman columns. Stone posts. Gravestones. Inscribed granite gravestones, like Wat and Elaine's double-header.

She sensed Alasdair's presence at her back. "What's this?"

"It was in the book."

"Crawford?"

"Yep." She typed in *Athelstan Crawford + Northumbria.* The first hit brought up the archive of the *Northumberland Gazette,* a newspaper based in Alnwick down the way. "Whoa," she said, and read aloud, "October tenth, nineteen seventy-one. Athelstan Crawford, noted local architect, died last week in a tragic accident on Lindisfarne. A memorial service will be held at the parish church of St. Michael, Alnwick, on Thursday next. Crawford is survived by his wife, Mary, Lucy, aged two, and Edwin, an infant."

"He was P.C. Crawford's father, then."

Jean swung around to see Alasdair's face still cool, rimmed with frost, but set in thought rather than rancor. "Is he the architect Wat consulted?" she asked. "Is that why the tower was never renovated, the guy died? A tragic accident. I wonder what happened? Nineteen seventy-one. Just when we—when you—when the police think Rob the Ranter went into the tomb."

"It's saying he died in a tragic accident on Lindisfarne, not disappeared on Farnaby. It's worth asking for details, though. The corpse had a propelling pencil, for one thing."

"The name Merlin's written on the back of the card—see? That might be Elaine's handwriting. If she called Thomas Seaton Lancelot the Fair, was Merlin her Arthurian name for Athelstan? Maybe something to do with Merlin's Tower."

"Looks to be a fuzzy patch where the name's written."

Jean angled the card back and forth. "Yeah. Something else was written there and erased, pretty forcibly. M. Another M-name. Mordred?" Jean stared at the card as though it would suddenly stand up and explain itself. It didn't.

"Aye, but Mordred's by way of being the villain of the piece." Alasdair walked back across the room to the dresser and picked up his phone. "Time's moving on."

The time on the screen and the time on the bedside clock agreed. Straight up six. Powering down the computer, Jean grabbed her clothing and catapulted into the bathroom. She assembled shoes, skirt, blouse, cardigan, and jewelry while hovering inside the door, listening to Alasdair's side of the conversation.

He hadn't called P.C. Crawford but D.S. Darling, who had apparently survived escort duty. ". . . still at the scene, is he?

Time to be bringing him back to the village, then, long as he's thinking the interest's died down and he can leave the tower be."

Ah. Alasdair wanted to talk to Crawford about his father's death in person. Good call.

". . . Lauder's finances. He was going through a bad patch in seventy-one, needing cash. Aye."

His footsteps tracked across the room.

". . . at the school, half past six. Are you now? Good man. Cheers."

The door opened. His steps walked down the stairs on the other side of the bathroom wall. His voice called, "Mrs. Fleming? A word?"

Jean brushed her hair into submission and slap-dashed some makeup onto her face. No one would look at her, not with the attractions on stage. Still, despite the chill- and anger-induced roses in her cheeks she looked almost as pale and wan—Alasdair would say peelie-wally—as Maggie. There. When it came to inventions, eyeliner and lipstick were almost equal to the internal combustion engine.

She grabbed a coat, turned off the lights, and hurried down the stairs as fast as she could go in her dizzying inch-high heels. She didn't dare wear heels any higher—she knew she was clumsy. A friend who studied tai chi once told her she was top heavy because she carried most of her energy in her head, which made sense. Sometimes she visualized her feet as marble carvings, heavy, steady.

Cornering the landing, she saw Alasdair walking along the hall, and at the full-frontal vision she stopped dead.

Ah, the Scots variant of business-casual: The Argyll jacket, the heathered tie, the red-and-green Cameron tartan kilt, the leather sporran, the tall beige socks with their red flashes. The outfit suited any man, of any shape. On Alasdair's compact, upright body, it was the stuff dreams were made of.

"Ready?" He set his hand on the knob of the front door. Only now did she notice his other hand held an insulated bag like the one Crawford had carried away, this one patterned with orange starbursts.

Instead of falling at Alasdair's feet, she got herself down the stairs in the usual fashion and fell in beside him. Much as she wanted to, she did not lean up to steal a kiss from his sober face and set mouth. She'd wait until the music had warmed him up enough her tongue wouldn't stick to his icy carapace like a daring child's to a flagpole.

"Here's us away, then."

Us, she thought. Husband and wife. Domestic partners. Mutual gadflies. "Yep," she said. "Here's us away."

Chapter Twenty-Four

Outside, the fret had either thinned or taken on the glow of late afternoon. There! For a moment the murk parted and Jean glimpsed a dazzling blue sea below a dazzling blue sky. Then the silvery cotton-candy mist closed in again.

Jean couldn't help but emit a heavy sigh, for the mental claustrophobia as well as the physical. When Alasdair offered her his arm, she took it. Between her shoes and the fog, she'd pass on walking two paces behind him, not in submissiveness but in appreciation of the tartan pleats dancing above the braw Cameron calves.

She sensed his mood as she sensed his arm, solid beneath the cool wool fabric of the jacket. His solicitousness wasn't apology for the sentiments he'd expressed upstairs, it was for the rancor with which he'd expressed them. She pressed herself against his side as they mounted the steps into the parking area, sending her own apology.

From the insulated bag wafted a delicious aroma. "What's in there?" she asked.

"Pen was asking me to carry her pies to the school. The village ladies are putting on a supper after the concert. Two quid apiece for food and a cuppa, all in aid of the music."

"Meat pies," Jean clarified, for her own sake, not his.

"Aye."

She waited, but when he said nothing else, she asked—quietly, who knew how many other people were groping through the fog nearby, "What did you want to ask Pen?"

"I was after showing her the card you found in the book. 'Granite' and so forth."

"Yes?" she prodded.

He was teasing her now, wasn't he? His face in the mist was still stern as the west face of Ben Nevis, but his eyes were no longer icy. "It's Wat's handwriting, likely his note on ordering a gravestone for his friend Athelstan, for the cemetery here on Farnaby. And Elaine's name for him was 'Merlin', aye. Pen's got no clue what the original word was."

"Did Pen explain why a card from seventy-one is stuck in a book published so much later?"

"No, she did not, though she seemed more wistful than surprised at seeing it."

"So Athelstan was buried here on Farnaby? Or his ashes, rather, since the newspaper obituary said 'memorial service' rather than 'funeral.' "

"No, the stone was by way of being a memorial. But Wat never followed through with that, either."

"Even though Athelstan was a friend? A member of the Farnaby round table, even, since Elaine gave him a nickname. Speaking of the cemetery, watch it, there's the wall." As one, they adjusted their course to the right.

"He was no musician, Pen's saying, but fell in with Wat and Elaine over Merlin's Tower. That's why Elaine named him 'Merlin', something about Merlin the Enchanter and a castle in Wales built atop a pair of dragons."

"Oh yeah. The castle kept falling down and the king sent for a lad without a father, nudge, nudge, who turned out to be Merlin. He found two dragons fighting beneath the foundations. But there aren't any dragons on Farnaby, never mind the *uxor draconis* inscription Elaine thought she saw on the tombstone."

"Unless you're counting Wat himself, who sounds to have been a bit of a dragon. Pen's telling me she has photos of Athelstan with both Lauders at the Tower. She has photos of Thomas Seaton as well, even though, she's adding, he's never the body in the tomb."

"She was at Gow House when Maggie and Tara got back there. You didn't tell them not to pass on the news." Jean brushed her fingertips across the sign in front of the church, sending a cold chill up her arm. "The Parish Church of St. Hilda. St. Hilda of Whitby, since Hilda of Farnaby wasn't a saint. Not by the standards of the Roman church, anyway. I wonder if tomorrow is the day the vicar comes to conduct a service? A few prayers and a hymn or two might pull us up onto a higher plane, in a way."

"Prioress Hilda's already booked a flight on that plane—I'm thinking that's her I saw whilst walking into the priory earlier."

"I saw her, too," Jean said with a smile. The man was making jokes. Better and better.

"Never mind the vicar, if this haar stays put, no one's coming and no one's going. I was also asking Pen if Darling could doss down on her sitting room couch—he's telling me the visitors and reporters have filled up the other B and Bs."

"Of course she said yes."

"Not exactly. Crawford's already got the couch, but she's saying there's a second bed in Hugh's room, if he's all right with sharing. If not, she'll be asking the Ecclestons for the use of their spare room."

Two arched gleams in the mist, like surprised eyes, had to be the pointed windows of Gow House. "Maybe we could plant Darling at Maggie's house," said Jean. "Get him to do some eavesdropping. Now that Pen's given it up, it seems. Now that it's your case you're no longer reluctant to ask her questions, are you? You must think her knowledge of Farnaby trumps her participating in any plots."

"Oh aye. It's by way of being my case, for the moment, and I've got no toes to be stepping on. As for plotting, my instincts are telling me Pen's knowing more than she's letting on of the seventy-one case."

"Maybe it's a matter of having suspicions rather than actually knowing anything."

"Either way, she's most likely meaning to protect Elaine."

"Your instincts are more finely honed than mine—go figure—but yeah, I think you're right. She's been sounding out how much we know and weighing whether the attack on Grinsell means she needs to open up those closets and drag out the skeletons, hypothetical or otherwise. So far honey is working better than vinegar with her. You have to wonder whether honey would have worked better than vinegar with Niamh's mother way back when."

"The vinegar worked a treat, that's the problem. Ah. Here we are."

Headlights sent shafts of luminescence toward the glowing windows of the school. Human shapes materialized from the fog. Alasdair and Jean followed them into the brightly lit interior of the building, and followed their noses to a canteen area, complete with small kitchen, tables, and chairs. There another comfortably upholstered lady of the island arranged a variety of baked goods on a crisp checkered tablecloth, accompanied by the enthusiastic if tuneless whistle of a tea kettle.

Leaving Pen's carrier bag and Jean's coat, they moved on down a plain, functional hallway to a plain, functional room at the back of the building. Rows of chairs faced a low stage. Electric cords snaked hither and yon, from the instruments sitting ready to an array of speakers and back to a sophisticated control panel, all its tiny levers manned—or womanned—by a lissome lass wearing a Gallowglass T-shirt and long denim skirt.

Spectators crowded the room, but Jean spotted Rebecca to one side of the back row, Linda's stroller parked on her left, two empty chairs on her right. Jean and Alasdair claimed the chairs and sat down.

Sergeant Darling sat in the front row, working the tiny screen of his phone. He glanced back and sent Alasdair the half-salute due to a half-cop. Alasdair returned an encouraging nod.

Detecting a jangle from her chunky necklace, Jean gave it an experimental waggle. Yes, it was a noisemaker, but not enough to compete with ordinary fiddles or guitars, never mind amplified ones. And, she thought as Michael and Hector walked onto the stage, their inflated bagpipes ready beneath their arms, nothing competed with the Great Highland pipes, whose original purpose had been to direct troop movements on a battlefield. As soon as the program started, Linda could wail to her heart's content.

However, the little girl now reposed in that delightfully boneless sleep only a small child could achieve. "Must be nice," Jean told Rebecca.

"Unconsciousness can be appealing," Rebecca returned.

Alasdair gazed up at the open framework of the ceiling. The patterns of light and shadow made by the rafters were the room's only decoration beyond a few posters and album covers mounted between the windows. Jean whispered, "You have to wonder what the school would have looked like if Wat had followed through with his original plans and renovated Merlin's Tower."

"That tower on top of the cliff, where the helicopter landed, right?" Rebecca replied. "Everyone on the ferry took notice of that, even Linda. She grabbed at it like it was a dragonfly . . . Ah, here we go."

"One two three!" shouted Michael. He and Hector launched into "Johnny Cope," their fingers dancing on their chanters.

Scottish regiments used that fiery tune for reveille. The skirl of the pipes probably roused folk in the cemetery up the road, although little Linda, a piper's daughter, barely stirred.

The school might have no particular architectural ambience, but all you had to do was close your eyes and the music provided plenty of atmosphere. Not that Jean did close her eyes, not with kilted musicians on the stage.

She recognized Michael's blue-and-green Campbell tartan, but the identity of Hector's navy blue, hatched with thin lines of red and yellow, eluded her. McCrimmon, she assumed, after his mother's family. And didn't that name have its origins in a Norse word for "protector"? Fitting for a paramedic. Fitting how his last name, Cruz, was similar to Crozier, yet another Borders name, both based on the Latin for "cross."

The pipers segued into "Hector the Hero," demonstrating how the flip side of Caledonian bravado was Caledonian lament. The Hector of the title had been a Scottish general, but that name, too, fitted both cultures.

Names. Place-names, legend-names. Hector as a Trojan warrior. Arthur as a Dark Age cavalry bloke or an overprotective husband.

Lance Eccleston rose from the audience, seated himself on stage, and with a stubby drumstick began thumping a rhythm on the leather head of a bodhran, creating a heartbeat of grief and regret.

For a long moment Jean enjoyed the contrast of small, dark Hector with big, blond Lance, like a rematch of Roman and Celt. Then she wondered whether the young ladies of Gow House were impressed by the indefinable air about a musician, what Rebecca had called catnip in sound.

They were seated in a row at the far front of the audience. Jean could see only their heads above the crowd, Niamh and Tara's shades of ginger, Maggie's tragicomic streaks, Elaine's shining crown, white as a nun's wimple. If either girl swooned over Lance or even Hector, she couldn't tell, although Niamh was much the twitchier of the two. Nervous about singing in a formal setting, perhaps?

The medley finished, everyone applauded. Hector retired to the wings and Lance back to the audience. Hugh took their place on stage and told a couple of stories about his early days as a roving musician. Then he seated his fiddle beneath his chin and swooped into a series of jigs and reels. His bow moved so fast Jean was surprised it didn't set the strings on fire. The audience clapped along.

Even as his hands kept the rhythm, Alasdair's head swiveled back and forth, inspecting the crowd. Jean knew he was not only picking the visitors out from the islanders by their clothing, more stylish than practical, but subdividing them into families of the students—they leaned forward eagerly, clutching cameras—and stranded reporters, who did neither.

Right behind the ladies of Gow House, for example, a woman in a crimson vinyl jacket and lipstick to match leaned back fussing with the cuticle on a talon of a fingernail. She probably worked for a fairly prestigious paper, while the man beside her, wearing a cheap, frayed coat, scratching idly at his arm . . . Was the reporter from the ferry slip, Jean realized, without his iPad and his attitude. Some men spent a fortune on products designed to make their hair stand on end. This man's thinning strands—not white like Elaine's, just colorless—stuck out from his scalp like flexible pick-up sticks.

Several fiddle students walked out onto the stage to enthusiastic applause and a flicker of flashes from cameras and phones. Hugh led them in a rousing rendition of the "Harvest Home" hornpipe, his own skilled playing smoothing over the odd awkward squeak.

Jean glanced back to see Pen swaying back and forth in the

doorway, her bleached white dish towel signaling surrender to the beat of the music, her brilliant smile all the more cheerful for having been absent the last twenty-four hours. Her flowered dress would have made a dandy bedspread, and on her ample figure resembled one. She eclipsed P.C. Crawford in his dark uniform, who stepped out of the hallway holding a mug between his hands—heat as well as sustenance, no doubt.

The smile dropped from Pen's face. She pulled so urgently at Crawford's arm he had to make a quick, offsetting move with his tea, and started speaking to him even before she'd dragged him back into the hall and out of sight.

Jean shot a glance at Alasdair. Either his instincts or his peripheral vision had drawn his attention to the door. He leaned over so that his lips moved against her ear and his breath stirred her hair. "I've likely made a mistake showing Pen the card, if she's warned Crawford off any questions about his father."

Jean in turn set her lips against Alasdair's ear. "Why wouldn't he answer questions about his father?"

Muttering something about local constables, Alasdair sat back in his chair and sent a truculent glance toward the back of Darling's head—*why did you not sit in the back?* The younger man shifted uneasily but kept right on working his phone.

Hugh and the students launched into two reels, perhaps on the theory that missed notes would be much more easily concealed in speedy tunes. Then, after a round of applause, the students trooped away and Hugh picked up his guitar.

Niamh, back in her off-hours garb of military-style boots, jeans, sweater, and hair like liquid flame, took her place on the stage. Lifting her hands, she opened her mouth and emitted music. This time her remarkable voice was not interrupted, but reverberated in the room as though the building itself was a bodhran.

Vinyl-jacket woman sighed and started playing with her

phone. Darling tucked his away and leaned forward. Bad-haircut guy did, too, no longer scratching but sitting motionless.

Gazing fixedly at Maggie, Niamh sang of defiance and alienation, of hearts sore with grief, of parting with valiant men, of praying for the glorious dead. When the song came to an end and the last vibration died away, the room was so silent that a door shutting in the front of the building sounded like an explosion.

Please, Jean thought, don't let that be Crawford taking off with some vital clue.

Wild applause, from Hugh as well. Niamh blushed prettily and returned to her seat, where she sat with her head bowed. Why direct the song to Maggie? Even if Niamh blamed her for her parents' divorce, hadn't the two women reached a truce over the last months?

Or was Niamh visualizing Grinsell, and a descending flashlight, and a pick placed nearby to implicate the ultimately guilty party? Two birds brought down with one stone.

Three students with Northumbrian small pipes filed onto the stage, collected themselves, and at Hector's signal launched into a sprightly melody. The occasional squeal was almost, if not quite, lost in the general sound, lower in volume and more mellow in tone than that of the Highland pipes—something to do with the keys, Jean supposed, which ranged down the length of the chanters like metallic vertebrae.

On the other side of the room, Elaine stood up, edged past Maggie into the aisle, and started to dance. The pipe tunes ended with a skirl and a flourish and Elaine's cracked voice filled the hush. ". . . and the ravens of Avalon carry the word, the king is gone but the queens live on . . ."

Niamh picked up the song, Hugh stepped forward with his guitar, and within a minute half the people in the room were singing "The Ravens of Avalon." Jean and Rebecca leaned together, so that between them they remembered all the lyrics—blood, revenge, betrayal, and love gone wrong. Even Alasdair hummed. Maggie had said Elaine wrote the song to begin with, and Wat had appropriated it. Now her thin but vital voice led the room . . . And died away, leaving Niamh and Hugh to finish.

Maggie rose, put her arm around her mother, and guided her back to her seat. Behind her bad-haircut looked down into his lap. Vinyl-jacket wriggled uncomfortably.

Hugh herded all the musicians back onto the stage for a finale, the lass at the control panel managed to keep the volume from blowing out the windows, and what with the work of clapping and hooching—the equivalent of a shouted "testify!" at a religious revival—the moment the concert concluded everyone in the room surged toward the food and drink.

Chapter Twenty-Five

Clyde sat at the door of the classroom-cum-café collecting pound coins and making change, while Pen, a smile settled comfortably on her face once again, supervised the food-and-tea table. A searching look around informed Jean that while Crawford might still be in the building, he sure wasn't in the room.

Clutching cups and bits of pastry either savory or sweet, she, Alasdair, and Darling put their heads together in one corner. Jean swore Darling stood at least two inches taller now that he no longer hunkered down like a dog expecting a blow. "I've texted our forensic accountant," he said. "I found her at home on a Saturday night—but then, she's an older lady."

Probably my age, Jean thought.

"She'll look into the Lauders' financial records and get back to us."

"Well done," Alasdair told him, and set out the latest in full outline form, starting with "McCarthy, Niamh, person of interest" and ending with, "Constable, local, possible complications of."

The younger man's eyes occasionally moved from Alasdair's face to Jean's, as though pleading, *Please tell me he's joking.* All Jean could do was smile wanly and unbutton her cardigan in the warmth.

At last Darling stuffed the last portion of a scone into his mouth, washed it down with a swig from his cup, and said thickly, "I'll bring Niamh in to the interview room, shall I? And P.C. Crawford wants questioning as well. Not at the same time."

She was no longer "Miss McCarthy," Jean noted. Another look around ascertained Niamh wasn't in the room, either, even though the three generations of Lauder women were. The king was gone, but the queens lived on.

Alasdair told Darling, "Carry on."

"Yes, sir." Collecting his reflective jacket from the coat corner, Darling went off with his phone raised in front of his face, no doubt trying to get hold of Crawford. Who could have walked right by without Darling seeing him, Jean thought with a smile. Nothing said oblivious like someone consulting his auxiliary brain.

"Oh, and . . ." Alasdair followed Darling from the room.

In the doorway they brushed by the two reporters, who were having a serious discussion with Clyde. ". . . gluten-free bakery products?" vinyl-jacket was asking, in a helium-fueled screech that made Tara's voice seem soft and sweet.

"Gluten? What's that when it's at home?" Clyde returned.

Bad-haircut peered around the room and announced, "There's no proper drinks here." He and his *compadre* retreated into the hall.

Jean followed. "Hello again. I guess you had your fill of Farnaby scones on Friday?"

Bad-haircut stared.

"We were chatting at the ferry slip late yesterday afternoon," Jean reminded him. "You told me about Dr. Lauder's change in plans and her lecture in the church with tea and scones."

"Oh! Yes, yes, the ferry slip on the mainland." His sagging jowls tightened in an attempt at a smile. He started to extend his hand, then withdrew it and used it to scratch his arm instead. "Bill Parkinson, *Daily Dish.* Had to fight a moggie for my bacon sandwich outside the pub. Nothing causes an allergy like a cat."

Ah, this was Lance's reporter fellow at the pub, back for another round on Farnaby. He worked for the tabloid whose website had already tried and condemned Maggie. "Jean Fairbairn, *Great Scot,*" she said, hoping her smile concealed the fact that she was just as happy not shaking hands. What if poor Hildy had broken out in hives at coming into contact with *him*?

Vinyl-jacket noted the man's affiliation and back-story with a supercilious smirk. "This is your second journey here in two days, is it? Oh, bad luck." She leaned conspiratorially toward Jean, engulfing her with a rich perfume that hinted more of sewer gas than flowers. "Rosalie Banks. *News of the North.* Fog makes for strange bedfellows, I'm afraid. I had no intention of staying here this long. I've booked a chap with a boat, effective the moment this filthy weather clears. That blond lad with the silly little drum, wasted out here, could have himself a job at a club in the city—or working extortion rackets, considering what he's charging for the boat."

Parkinson's gaze was that of a dead fish. Jean felt her polite smile grow stiff.

"Soon as I get back to Manchester I'm having a word in the guv'nor's ear—I told him it was no good chasing after a moldy old body—when we saw the helicopter from the ferry I hoped there was something more doing on Farnaby than . . ." Rosalie's downward gesture both took in the scene and dismissed it.

"Lucky for you D.I. Grinsell was attacked, then," Jean murmured, trying not to visualize his stark, pale face smeared with blood. "Makes your trip worthwhile."

"That's as may be," said Rosalie. "I'm away to the pub—the others are already there—if I'd gone along I'd be on my second whisky by now, but no, I thought something for the Arts page. Dead loss, though. I hope *you* were happy with Turnip-ville amateur night, Bill." Without waiting for an answer, she turned and clicked off down the hall in her high-heeled boots, Barbie playing Nazi.

Jean coughed, swapping the odor of the perfume for that of baked goods, damp wool sweaters, and a whiff of sour sweat she suspected came from Parkinson.

"I met up with her on the ferry," he explained. "I advised attending the concert. Farnaby's famous for its music, isn't it?"

"Yes. The Lauders have lived here a long time. Do you know Elaine? Or maybe I should ask, did you know her when she was Elaine?"

Through the doorway, Parkinson considered the still tall if emaciated figure cruising down the table of edibles. Maggie stopped her as she tried to insert one of Pen's pies into the pocket of her sweater. Hugh stepped up, tucked Elaine's arm beneath his own, and, exuding affability, launched into what was no doubt a story about Ye Olden Days. "Alan a Dale!" Elaine exclaimed, remembering his nickname, and stood watching him speak as though expecting a prize to fall from his lips.

Elaine the scholar, Jean thought. Elaine the mother. Elaine the elderly. She caught Maggie's eye as she adjusted Elaine's collar and sent her what she hoped was a sympathetic but not pitying smile. Instead of acknowledging Jean's smile, though, Maggie's face puckered into the part frown, part stare of someone not quite able to put her finger on a memory.

Something close to disgust squirmed across Parkinson's sagging features and died away, replaced with a studied expressionlessness.

Well, well, well. Jean asked, "Or do you know Maggie? When we met at the ferry slip you called her 'Loony Lauder.' "

"They're both loony, aren't they? I don't have the pleasure—ha!—of knowing either of them, thank you just the same. I covered Maggie's trial back in the nineties, she all prim and proper in the dock, and her mum playing the intellectual, too good for the likes of us reporters."

Funny about that. Jean voiced not her thought, but another question. "You know the policeman who was attacked here, then."

"I know of him. Had the guts to stand up and tell the truth, that the trial was rubbish from start to finish."

"Is that why you came out here to Farnaby yesterday, to see how Maggie was getting along after all these years? Or was her archaeological discovery really all that fascinating to your editor?"

Parkinson's washed-out eyes, hard as twin marbles, focused on Jean's. "None of your business, is it, luv?"

"No," she conceded. "It isn't." Alasdair strolled back up the hallway and to her side. Instead of introducing him to Parkinson—no need to sic them on each other—she took his arm and steered him back into the room, toward the corner where Rebecca and Michael were chatting with Hector. From the corner of her eye she saw Parkinson follow Ms. *News of the North* down the corridor and out the front door.

"Who's that chap?" Alasdair asked. "A reporter?"

"Yep. *The Daily Dish.* Actually covered Maggie's trial way back when. He'd get along really well with Grinsell. A shame they missed meeting each other."

"Ah," said Alasdair.

Jean took off her cardigan and draped it over her arm, wondering why, despite the cold climate, British rooms tended toward stuffy. And she answered herself, the Brits saw the enclosing warmth as comfort, whereas she'd been born and raised in a hot climate where a breeze was not a draft to be avoided but a nirvana to be gained.

Hugh strolled toward Jean and Alasdair, his face polished by music and perhaps a wee dram behind the scenes.

"Great concert," Jean told him.

"Thank you kindly," he replied. "I'd have phoned you earlier, but folk coming in were telling me about the inspector being attacked and all. Dreadful, just dreadful."

"That it is." Alasdair's voice-of-doom said it all.

"I was after telling you that I've had a look round the school and the only chanters I've found are new ones. Or newer than the one that's gone missing from the grave. But in this instance I was thinking no news was bad news, so I never rang after all."

"Thanks for looking anyway," Jean told him, and waved him back to the food.

With a smile at Linda, still sacked out in her stroller, Hector headed for a refill. Michael traded his cup to Rebecca for her phone, which he slanted toward Jean. "The inscription in the chapel."

Wrenching her mind around to the new topic, Jean said, "Oh! Yes, Rebecca made some photos right before we left."

"This one here's the best. Though I'm not seeing any horsemen." A sweep of Michael's thumb brought up what looked like a moonscape, craters, rills, and all.

Jean took the phone and peered at it. Rebecca had angled her tiny flash so that it illuminated the inscription from the side. The raking light defined each bump and crack as sharply as they were ever going to be without computer enhancement—Tara had said something about Maggie trying to computer-enhance the inscription. "What do you think?"

Michael's forefinger indicated the top of the stone. "I'm thinking this bit here is *hic jacet.*"

" 'Here lies'. That's no surprise. But the name of whoever is lying there is illegible. How about Elaine's *uxor draconis,* 'wife of the dragon'? Can you see that, too?"

Jean handed the phone to Alasdair, who turned it this way and that, squinting. "Was Guinevere not the daughter-in-law of the dragon?" he asked, and gave Rebecca her phone. "Pendragon was Arthur's father, aye?"

"Aye," said Michael. "And you could be making a case for the Viking raiders as dragons, since they carved dragons on their ships, but they're not known for inscriptions in Latin. This bit here is *uxor,* I reckon, but I'm seeing it as *'uxor domini.'* "

"Wife of the lord," Jean translated. "Meaning the lord of the manor?"

"Usually. But here it might could be meaning . . ."

". . . the bride of Christ," Jean and Rebecca said in one voice. Rebecca added, "Snap!"

"It's a convent," Jean said. "Nuns are considered to be brides of Christ, not a metaphor you want to follow too far. As yet no one's found anything that keeps the grave from being Mother Hilda's. Maggie even admits it's probably hers."

Linda stirred and whimpered and Michael squatted down to check on her—ever mindful to drape his kilt modestly as he did so. "She's digging again the morn, aye? The area's been populated almost two millennia. There's bound to be bits and pieces lost in the soil."

Maggie had made a heavy investment in the identity of the burial, not only wanting to vindicate Elaine's work, but also to justify herself and her mother to Wat. Or his shade, which, thank goodness, didn't seem to be hanging around. As investments went, she might be looking at a spell in debtor's prison. Or not. Jean placed her hopes on that teensy glint in the muck at the bottom of the grave. "Maybe she'll turn up a medieval brooch or something else cool. And photogenic."

"Anything is possible," said Rebecca, without adding, *Little is probable.*

Alasdair made a quick turn and headed back to the door. Ah—Sergeant Darling had returned with Crawford, who got a free pass from Clyde as he entered the room. That was fast. Not that Crawford was either trying to escape the island or hide on it. For one thing, he'd reinstalled his reflective jacket, which made him a sitting duck.

As soon as the fog cleared, Jean thought—not as soon as the sun came out, because it was pushing eight p.m. and the sun had long headed west—but as soon as you could see your neighbor's hand in front of your face, a lot of people would be staging escapes.

Well, no, the tide should have gone out again, invisibly, meaning the ferry was docked for the night, and even a small boat wouldn't be able to reach the mainland past the mud flats next to Lindisfarne.

That's right. As Alasdair had pointed out on the ferry yesterday, small boats could make it to ports in the north or the south, and probably even to the east side of Lindisfarne, independent of the tides. Jean visualized Lance and Rosalie leading a flotilla across to Bamburgh. She was tempted to rush back to the Angle's Rest, pack her suitcase, and join in the exodus.

But no. This was Alasdair's case now, and she'd dug herself in by his side.

Chapter Twenty-Six

Alasdair guided his fellow law-enforcers over to Maggie. Jean gestured and shrugged, and with understanding grins the Campbell-Reids waved her on, so that she arrived at Alasdair's side as he asked, "Have you seen Niamh?"

"Niamh?" repeated Elaine. "The girl with the—squeeze music thing—in the pub in—that city, the big one? Ask Wat—it's time he added a woman to Gallowglass."

"Not the woman with the concertina in Liverpool," Maggie replied. "Our Niamh was in the main room with us. She sang 'Foggy Dew.' "

"She told me she felt a headache coming on," said Tara. "She went back to the house."

Hugh stepped again to Elaine's side. "Was the singing too stressful for her? She seemed nervous, didn't she now, and was staring out at you, Maggie."

"No," Maggie said, "she stared just past me. At Lance, perhaps."

Crawford settled his cap beneath his arm. "Niamh's not at Gow House. I left here when she finished singing and waited for her at the gate of the school."

"Maybe she slipped past in the fog," Darling suggested. "Maybe she's back at the house having a lie-down."

"I'll go check on her." Tara set her mug on the table, grabbed a cookie, and headed out. At Alasdair's gesture, Darling hurried after her.

With a tap of his finger against the side of his nose—*I'm doing my bit, Mr. Cop*—Hugh escorted Elaine and Maggie down the table to where Pen poured more boiling water into a teapot.

Drawing Crawford toward a vacant corner, Alasdair asked, "Why did you go looking up Niamh, then?"

"I found the weapon used to cosh Inspector Grinsell," Crawford replied.

Alasdair's eyebrows shot up approximately the same distance Jean's jaw dropped. "Did you now?" he asked.

"Well, I've found the missing torch. Maggie's big one, that I borrowed yesterday afternoon. There's a bit of the metal rim round the lens broken off, right enough, and what's likely blood caked beneath. I reckon the forensics lads will sort out any fingerprints on the barrel."

"Where was it?" Jean asked.

"Lying alongside the path leading up to Merlin's Tower. I was walking back down, as per Sergeant Darling's instructions. The fog cleared for an instant. The sunlight reflected off something in the trough running between the fence and the path, below several broken weeds. I had me a look, and there was the torch."

You'd almost believe in divine intervention, Jean thought, with the sun coming out the exact instant Crawford walked by.

Alasdair chose a more earthly conclusion. "Chucking the torch down where it would be easily found, if not so quickly as it should have been—we walked right on by it, didn't we? Well it's either making a careless villain or a clever one meaning to put Maggie in the frame. Where's the torch now?"

"On my boat. Thought that would be the safest place. I wrapped it in the plastic sack Pen gave me earlier—not with the sandwiches, mind you. I ate them."

Jean reassessed her original estimate—and Darling's too, now that she thought about it—of Crawford being too slow to have earned any promotions. He wasn't slow. He was deliberate.

He went on, "I knew I'd handed that torch in to Niamh last night, right before I brought Miss Fairbairn here down to the incident room."

"What torch were you carrying then?" Alasdair asked.

"I collected the one from my boat soon as Inspector Grinsell arrived at the priory."

"Niamh's saying she put Maggie's torch away in the cupboard, but Maggie's saying it was not there."

"Maybe Elaine took it," Jean suggested. "Maybe she dropped it beside the path."

Elaine now peered intently into the mug of tea she held between her hands—by tilting it back and forth, she created waves and swirls—while Hugh and Maggie chatted with a couple of the students and Hector. Pen opened another carrier bag and laid out a row of sweet-smelling fruit tarts.

"The poor old dear," said Crawford. "Pen's telling me she found Elaine sitting outside the pub last night, listening to Niamh singing, barely got her home before the balloon went up."

So Pen got Elaine back to Gow House right before the police from Berwick arrived, Niamh returned from the pub, and Crawford collected Maggie from her post by the garden gate. None of that answered the question of who took the flashlight.

It was interesting, though, that Elaine had been wandering around while Crawford stood watch at the priory. During the same time period the chanter went missing. But was she capable of slipping past him, either purposely or by luck? How about digging into the open grave—surely she'd be bewildered by it all . . . The thought stabbed into Jean's mind like a knight's lance through his opponent's armor: no one had a better chance to take the chanter than the man who'd been guarding it.

But while Crawford seemed to have quite a busybody streak,

he had no apparent motive for taking the chanter. He'd been a baby when the body went into the grave. Just because the M.E. had found a mechanical pencil in its pocket didn't mean it was that of an architect. Athelstan hadn't even died on Farnaby, and his remains were accounted for. Weren't they?

Jean glanced again at Pen, whose cheeks were less rosy than crimson in the steam from the kettle and from the closeness of the room. And perhaps from hearing the dry rattle of bones in a closet, or the twitch of dirty linen inching toward open air.

On the way back to eyes-front she intercepted a spark in Alasdair's eye—his thoughts were heading in the same direction, if marching rather than louping. "Elaine was accounted for the rest of the night?" he asked. "And all day the day?"

"So far as I know," said Crawford.

"Well then, she had the chance to pick up the torch, but not to be chucking it away. Or using it on Grinsell, come to that."

"Here, sir, you can't be thinking . . ."

"I'm considering every angle, Constable. It's Niamh I'm wanting to speak with."

"That's what I was thinking, sir. That's why I went knocking on her door."

Jean realized that like Niamh, she hadn't seen Lance since the end of the concert. Presumably he was at the pub fending off Rosalie, girl reporter. Or perhaps not fending her off, but Jean wasn't going to worry herself about his virtue. Niamh, now, Niamh had a thing for Lance that had to be more substantial than Rosalie's passing flash of lust. Had she been distracted while singing because he'd finally arranged an assignation with her? Where had he been sitting while she sang? Somewhere on that side of the audience was all Jean could remember.

Having come full circle in his quasi-interrogation, Alasdair drew Crawford farther into the unoccupied area at the end of the tea table and opened the next item on the agenda. "Your father, Constable. Athelstan Crawford."

Crawford didn't so much as blink. Yes, Pen had warned him to expect the Scottish Inquisition. "My father, sir?"

"Could you be telling me about him, please?"

"I never knew him. He died when I was the age of the wee lass yonder." Crawford's nod indicated little Linda, who now resided in her mother's arms, fed morsels of scone by her father. "He was an architect specializing in historic buildings. Give him an old tower house or a timber bothy and he'd shore it up and add in the mod cons. He's best known for working with the teams renovating Alnwick Castle and Cragside."

"And Wat Lauder asked him to draw up plans for Merlin's Tower?"

"Wat did that, aye—the place is in good nick, considering its age. My father organized a part-time office here on Farnaby, thinking the job was his chance to show what he was capable of doing and set himself up on his own. My mum kept the drawings till the day she died. My sister's got the portfolio now."

"That's all that ever came of it? Drawings?"

"Aye."

"Were there hurt feelings when Wat never went ahead with the project?"

"I don't know, sir."

"Was your mother ever saying just why Wat changed his mind about the renovation?"

Crawford's eyes rolled in Jean's direction. She tried to look as solemn as was possible for a bump on a log.

Alasdair prodded, "Could Wat not get the money to pay for the work? Did he even pay for Athelstan's time drawing up the designs?"

Crawford turned back to Alasdair, sucked on his lower lip, then said, "I heard Mum once say to her sister, my Auntie Lucinda, that all my father earned from Merlin's Tower were some photographs and a lady's glove."

"A glove?" asked Jean. "Like a favor given to a knight?"

"Most likely. Mum said my father had himself some good times here on Farnaby, playing at Camelot whilst she sat home in Alnwick with my sister no more than two and me on the way. She was a wee bit put out, I expect."

Jean heard a faint echo in the back of her mind, Maggie saying how Niamh had been a toddler when she and Donal began their affair. That was the problem, wasn't it? The laying of the baby's keel took only a few moments. The actual launching of the adult ship came years later, on an ocean of accumulated blood, sweat, and tears. Yes, raising a child was hard work. A shame so many men focused on the preliminary *hard* rather than the ensuing *work*.

She saw Michael solicitously wiping Linda's rosy little cheeks and reminded herself that the vast majority of men acquitted their responsibilities with competence and grace.

Crawford was still speaking. ". . . Mum also told Auntie Lucinda my father fancied Elaine more than was good for either of them, what with Wat being the jealous sort and stroppy to boot. Not to speak ill of the dead."

Hmm. Jean noticed another spark in Alasdair's eye. They kept coming back to Wat's possessiveness, reinforced by his temper.

He asked, "How old was your father when he died?"

"Thirty-five."

"What happened to be causing his death?"

"He went wildfowling off Lindisfarne with two of the chaps from his office. A sea fret came up and their boats were separated. The other two chaps and the guide came to shore here on Farnaby, and glad they were to find land, but my father, well—the boat with all his kit was found floating far out to sea several days later. He, himself . . ." Crawford looked down at his shoes, noted their flecks of mud and vegetation, and lifted each one in turn to polish it on the back of a trouser leg.

"His body was never found," Alasdair stated, doing an admirable job of keeping the *aha*! out of his voice. But then, he clutched at a chain of happenstance, not evidence, with wide gaps such as: How did Athelstan part ways from his boat? How did his body end up in the grave in the chapel?

If it had. But every instinct Jean possessed told her they'd finally found the answer to at least one question.

Chapter Twenty-Seven

Finally, Crawford looked up. "No, sir. His body was never found. In time Mum went ahead with the memorial service and all, and in due course he was declared legally dead."

"Wat intended to put up a monument here on Farnaby?"

"Pen once said something of the sort. She found Wat's notes to that effect on a card Elaine was using as a bookmark, if I'm remembering correctly. But, again, I was an infant when my father died. All I know is hearsay from Pen and James and all." Crawford drew himself up. "Begging your pardon, sir, but why are you asking me all this?"

Tara appeared in the doorway, with her features creased in a frown but without Darling in her wake. She beelined for Maggie. Pen sidled around the end of the table, wiping out several mugs and arranging them on the checkered tablecloth.

"What do you know of Berwick's preliminary exam of the body from the chapel?" Alasdair asked.

"I've not heard a word about it."

Without saying, *that's a first, then,* Alasdair went on, "The experts are saying the deceased was over six feet tall, between thirty and forty years old. Coins in his pocket are seeming to date the burial to nineteen seventy-one. He was carrying a wee pad of paper and a propelling pencil."

Crawford's long face contracted and his gaze turned inward.

"The chanter lying beside the body in the grave. You were telling D.I. Grinsell you were not sure that it was really there."

"I wasn't sure what I saw is all I meant."

"What were you thinking you'd seen, then?"

"A bone, a shadow, a strip of cloth. An optical illusion."

"Or a chanter, either one from a set of pipes or a practice chanter?"

Crawford said, "It's possible."

"You've heard Sergeant Darling's account of a long, thin object being the murder weapon?"

Crawford nodded. Jean could almost hear the pieces sliding into place in his brain.

"Constable, last night, whilst waiting for Berwick's arrival, did you take the object—chanter, whatever—from the grave?"

With a start, Crawford focused. "Eh? Whyever would I do that, then?"

"You're Athelstan's son. If that's Athelstan's body in the grave, the means of him getting there would be of concern to you and your family. And your friends here on Farnaby."

"I'd be eager to find out what happened to him, wouldn't I then? I'd hardly be concealing evidence. But I never—yesterday, standing there by the grave—I never thought it could be . . ." His already pale complexion fading to a faint green, he frowned so fiercely Jean expected his face to break. His cap fell from beneath his arm and thudded to the floor.

Again, Jean rescued it. As she stood up she saw Elaine had crept to within earshot, her blue eyes bright as buttons, tea sloshing out of her mug as she let it tilt heedlessly to the side. But it had to be cold by now. "Athelstan. Used to stop in. Haven't seen him for a while. He played at being—the wizard. The enchanter. Merlin. Athelstan was a romantic sort of chap. Gave him my token, my glove, didn't I?"

"Romantic?" repeated Crawford.

Maggie stepped forward, took the cup from Elaine's hand, murmured, "Mum, it's all right." Not that Maggie had any clue what Elaine was talking about, Jean estimated from her puzzled expression.

"No, it wasn't all right." Elaine said. "Athelstan played at Medraut, but Medraut was killed at—it's never Camelot."

Camlann, Jean filled in. She'd always wondered if the similarity in names was more than coincidence.

"Arthur was wounded. No. Arthur's—with the wheels, room in the back—it slipped off the road."

"Medraut?" Alasdair repeated.

"Another version of Mordred," Jean told him, without adding, *that's the name on the back of the card, written in Elaine's handwriting and then erased.*

A short scream and a crash sounded from behind the table. Everyone spun around. Pen gripped her own arm, her face white as her dish towel. The tea kettle lay at her feet. "I—I—I was careless—butter on my fingers, wasn't holding the kettle properly—the hot water splashed on my arm."

Or did one heck of a penny fall when Pen heard first Alasdair and Crawford, then Elaine, talking about Athelstan? Did she just realize she'd known all along who'd been hidden in the grave? Jean started forward, then stepped back as Hector materialized at Pen's side.

He grabbed the cup of cool tea from Maggie's hand, turned it out onto the cloth and pressed it onto Pen's arm. "I need cold water—if you people have anything here, it's cold water. Ice water, straight from the faucet."

Maggie leaped to the sink, seized another cloth, and held it under the tap.

"Where's Niamh?" Hector asked. "She must have some anesthetic ointment."

"Niamh isn't at the house," answered Tara. "I called her phone, but it went to voice mail. I checked at the pub—you can't stir the place with a stick, it's so crowded, but she's not there. Lance says he hasn't seen her. He says he'll help look for her if he doesn't have to take the boat out."

Maggie gave Hector the cold cloth and put her arm around Pen, making soothing sounds. Hector peered beneath the cloth. "It's not too bad a burn." Elaine stood awkwardly, uncertain.

"Damn." Alasdair's mouth tightened into a thin line. Jean knew what he was thinking—not that it was unfortunate poor Pen was relatively unscathed, but that he'd let Grinsell's assailant get away. He'd let the woman he thought was Grinsell's assailant get away, rather. If only he'd assigned Darling to walk with Niamh tonight, too. But she'd stolen away by herself. You'd think she was trying to hide.

Someone slammed down the hall—Jean recognized the volunteer sheep wrangler from Merlin's Tower—and announced to all and sundry, "The fret's breaking up at last. Too late for the sun, more's the pity, but there's a grand moon rising."

Islanders milled around the scene of the accident, while various visitors faded discreetly away. Including the Campbell-Reids, Jean saw. Taking Alasdair's do-not-disturb expression to heart, they set out with baby and bagpipes and a wave indicating a resumption of conversation at the B&B.

Hector and Maggie helped Pen to a chair. Never mind the honey—maybe some aloe vera and sympathy would do the trick. Although what she needed most was time and space and peace to work it all out in her own mind, and then work up the courage to approach Alasdair.

With, Jean reminded herself, information about the body in the grave, Rob the Ranter, Athelstan, whoever. Not the attack on Grinsell. That would never have happened without Maggie opening the grave. That would never have happened if Elaine had gone ahead and opened the grave way back when. Or kept it open, rather.

"Come along then," Alasdair snapped to Crawford. "Let's

have us a look at the torch. On your boat, you're saying?"

"Aye, sir." He collected his cap from Jean and set it on his head, his manner once again laconic to the point of aloof. Or it would have been laconic if not for the faint hum of gears turning and cogs meshing behind the expanse of his forehead.

Claiming her coat, Jean hustled down the hallway. Crawford hoisted a flashlight even bigger than Maggie's—this one was presumably his own—and opened the door. At Alasdair's after-you gesture, Jean stepped out into a faceful of fog. "I thought it had cleared up."

"Clearing up, the chap was saying. There'll be pockets for a while yet." He shut the door and with it cut off the light.

Earlier the sinking sun might have polished the fog into a silver sheen, but now it was simply opaque, dull, dark, scented with sea-salt and engine exhaust. The light from Crawford's torch cast a glare on the vapor and illuminated nothing but the ground at their feet.

He angled right to follow the sequence of fences, gained speed, and became no more than a spectral shape in a moving halo. The echoing thuds of his footsteps faded as he outdistanced their slower gait.

Jean glimpsed the sign in front of the church. She glimpsed the gate to Gow House, but no lights from the neo-Gothic windows. Either Tara had turned them off or the fog was simply too thick.

The mossy stone fence along the cemetery seemed to run on forever, like that path to hell paved with good intentions, or the paths of glory that lead but to the grave, or . . .

She and Alasdair stepped out of the fog like stepping through a theater curtain. "Whoa!" She stopped so abruptly her mini-heels slid on the blacktop.

Beside her Alasdair looked left, across the parking lot and down to the houses of the village, their dark facades broken by the squares of lighted windows. Beyond the battlement-like edge of the roofs an aisle of the sea glimmered between banks of fog. Above it all shone a star-scattered sky, a golden-pale radiance seeping into it from the east.

Jean looked right. They stood at the corner of the cemetery wall. Part of the priory cloister ran up to, and then disappeared beneath, an uneven wall of fog sparkling with water crystals.

More than a sea breeze tickled the back of Jean's neck as the fog retreated further.

By the time she set her hand on his arm, Alasdair had already turned to face the priory. They listed together under the weight of perception, small ships seeking safe harbor—sensations colder than ice trickled down her back—a feeling of doom pushed her down, doom, despair, confusion.

A man didn't emerge from the fog before them, the fog rolled back to reveal him standing there, small and alone. It wasn't Crawford. It was George Grinsell.

The image seemed perfectly solid, clearly defined, illuminated by the lights of the village and yet unreal all at once, like a CGI effect in a film.

His reddish hair now had no color at all. His sour slit of a mouth hung slackly open. His eyes were no longer canted sideways but stared straight ahead, struck wide by confusion—not an expression Jean had ever seen on the living face.

But this face was not alive.

The cold wind freshened, rolling up the fog and pushing it away. For another fraction of a second the ghost stood there, a lost soul if ever there was one. And then it was gone.

The broken walls and arches of the priory seemed to move forward rather than the fog retreating, each stone, each column base emerging in sequence. The glow of the moon draped some in light like thin Lindisfarne mead, others in velvet shadow.

A row of candles glided in disembodied hands toward the

church, the nuns—the spirits of the nuns—on their way to vespers. The weight fell from Jean's shoulders and she straightened, her necklace chiming softly as the memory of bells. Voices began to sing. Women's voices. The queens bearing to Avalon the body not of Arthur but . . .

Elaine had never met Grinsell. She'd never given him a nickname from legend.

Jean tried to inhale but the breath caught like a thistle in her chest. Beside her Alasdair emitted a long sigh that carried words with it, ones that she sensed rather than heard.

"It's by way of being a murder case now."

Chapter Twenty-Eight

"Mr. Cameron? Miss Fairbairn?" Crawford stood several feet away, his massive torch casting a beam of light as bright as a searchlight at a Hollywood premiere.

Alasdair cleared his throat. "Aye, Constable. Just having us a look at the priory in the moonlight."

Jean expected Crawford to say, "Right." But he said nothing, merely turned again toward the village.

Here came another figure across the parking lot, carrying a smaller flashlight, shimmering yellow jacket flapping. "Crawford? Mr. Cameron?"

"We're here, Darling," Alasdair replied.

The sergeant skidded to a halt. "D.C.I. Webber phoned, sir. D.I. Grinsell died ten minutes ago."

"I'm sorry to hear that." Alasdair didn't turn a hair.

Jean turned several hairs as the wind blew cold down the back of her neck. She crossed her arms and said, "I am, too."

"And I," added Crawford.

After a suitable moment of silence, punctuated by voices rising from the waterfront, Darling went on, "I walked Tara from Gow House to the pub, but she insisted on going back to the school on her own, with the fog clearing out and all. I've been asking about the town, the student hostel, the tea room. Niamh—Miss McCarthy—no one's seen her."

Alasdair hadn't told him to search for Niamh, but it wasn't a major leap of inference that he'd be doing so in the immediate future. All he told Darling now was, "We're away to Crawford's boat, to be having us a look at Maggie's torch. At the murder weapon, as it is now."

"You've found it then?"

"Crawford did, aye." Alasdair took off at a brisk pace, finally stretching his limbs after being forced to mince around in the fog.

It was Jean who now minced along in her heels, following the vision of Alasdair's kilt, its colors flashing boldly in the beams of the flashlights. At the top of Cuddy's Close, he brought the parade to a halt and turned back toward her. "Sorry, Jean."

"Tell you what," she replied. "I'm going to dart up to the room and change clothes. I'll meet you at the boat."

"Good idea," said Alasdair, and, as he led the other two men through the close and out onto the main street, "Constable, if you'd be so good as to fill in the sergeant here on our discussion of your father's death?"

"Oh," Darling said faintly. "Ah."

"Well, sir . . ." Crawford's flat voice died away as Jean diverted to the Angle's Rest.

The moment she was inside she dumped her shoes and ran up the stairs in her stockinged feet. She changed into serviceable jeans and walking shoes in record time, and paused in her return trip only long enough to pay respects to Hildy, who stretched out in her spot on the upstairs windowsill.

The cat's fur felt warm and soft to Jean's hand. A quiet purr vibrated in her throat. But her ears were raised like semaphores, signaling something of interest outside. Leaning forward to block out any reflections, Jean registered three people strolling left to right through the parking lot and two ambling toward the now dark and silent priory, none of their shadowy figures revealing any identifying features.

In other words, damned if she could tell if any of them were Niamh.

Several more people appeared from the right—the post-concert greet-and-eat at the school had no doubt reached a conclusion. One stocky figure wore what looked like a skirt but had to be a kilt, since he walked very close to a woman in a dress, a white blotch on her arm that Jean knew to be a dish towel. Hector with Pen, making sure she and her injury made it safely to the Angle's Rest.

She couldn't see Gow House, whether the lights were on or what, but surely Tara and Maggie had escorted Elaine home.

With another stroke of Hildy's soft fur, Jean headed down the stairs. The wail of a fretful child came from the room at the end of the hall, along with the soothing murmur of parental voices. She thought of Crawford's parents, and Niamh's, and all parents having to choose between their own wishes and the needs of the child.

Silence fell. A door opened and shut and Michael appeared in the hallway. "Jean! I was expecting you and Alasdair to be sleuthing at the school yet."

"No, we've moved operations to the harbor. Want to come along, get an update on the case—the cases—in progress?"

"Aye, but . . ." He cast a wary eye behind him. "I promised Rebecca I'd bring us each a wee dram from the pub."

"You can do that, too."

"Temptress. I'll have a word with the womenfolk." He hurried down the hall, whispered something through the doorway, hurried back again. "I've got formal permission to join you, mostly because Rebecca's as curious as I am. I've been told off to mind that wee dram as well."

"We'll all end up in the pub drowning our sorrows," Jean told him.

He opened the door for her, asking, "What's on with

Crawford, then?"

"You're not going to believe this angle." Once again outside—and in the free air, not in the oppressive fog, all right!—Jean brought Michael up to speed. When she finished with Grinsell's ghost appearing from the mirk, he winced. "Poor sod."

"Yeah."

At the harbor, lights blazed and people milled. A tour boat with a seat-lined back deck and an open cabin took on passengers, twelve or fifteen people who flocked forward so eagerly the scene reminded Jean of the famous photograph of the helicopter perched atop the American embassy in Saigon, a line of desperate evacuees snaking up toward it.

Crawford's small, sleek number was moored on the opposite side of the concrete breakwater, next to a fishing boat and well down a slimy wall spattered with shells and weed. But then, if the tide had been in, the Ecclestons would no doubt be running the actual ferry.

Glad she'd changed her shoes, Jean picked her way along a water-worn set of steps, across the deck of the fishing boat, and down onto the police boat. Michael followed. She averted her eyes from his billowing tartan, even though she suspected that like Alasdair, he felt no need to air any gender differences and wore proper undergarments beneath his kilt.

Farnaby's complement of police officers huddled together over a locker at the back of the boat. The two arrivals pretty well filled up the rest of the open area. Darling and Crawford looked around—they'd been expecting Jean to arrive solo—but when Alasdair introduced Michael and drew his attention to the object under discussion, they offered polite greetings. "Any road," Darling said, obviously completing a sentence already begun, "I've got no doubt that rim of metal we found at Merlin's Tower will fit a treat."

With a wary glance over the low side at the black water

spangled with reflections, Jean inched closer to Alasdair. Pen's gaudy carrier bag lay open on a narrow seat. Inside, wrapped in a cut-open plastic sack, rested a massive flashlight. Even though Jean herself had momentarily held Maggie's light over the grave, she'd hardly noticed it. Go figure. But if Alasdair and especially Crawford, who'd also had it in their hands, were sure it was hers, she wasn't going to argue.

As far as she could tell with the crinkled and smudged—probably with butter—plastic in the way, russet-brown stains did indeed edge the remaining metal rim like dirt beneath a fingernail. Even if some of the blood had washed off in the wet gully where Crawford found it, the barrel of the flashlight looked dirty enough to hold dozens of fingerprints, not least Maggie's and Niamh's.

Niamh.

Straightening, Jean peered toward the larger boat on the far side of the harbor. Clyde took his position in the small cabin. Rosalie News-of-the-North stood nearby, legs braced wide apart, arms akimbo in the power-pose. Or in the pose of *Hey, I thought the hunk was going to be the pilot here.*

"That's the Ecclestons' boat?" Alasdair asked.

"Aye," said Crawford. "Usually it's taking day-trippers out to the Farne Islands—Cuthbert's cell, birds, all that lot."

"Yon reporters came over on the ferry with us," Michael pointed out. "I mind the woman in the plastic coat in particular, was havering the whole time about being sent to purgatory or Siberia or the like. Their cars are still in the car park near the causeway."

"I reckon Clyde is aiming to dock in Seahouses south of Bamburgh. There's a taxi service."

"Better than spending the night here on Farnaby. Or so the reporters are thinking." Darling made a deprecatory gesture even though none of the people within earshot were islanders.

"It seems like it'd be easier to take a small boat straight over to the seaward side of Lindisfarne and have someone pick you up there," Jean said. "But it's a better deal for the Ecclestons to move a bunch of people at once."

She felt Alasdair's laser-like gaze on the side of her face. Surely what she'd said wasn't that foolish. She looked askance at him. *Yes?* He raised and lowered his shoulders beneath the epaulettes of his jacket. *Move along, nothing to see here.*

On the pier, Lance untied the tour boat and gave a go-ahead wave. The engine emitted a deep-throated rumble. The smooth black water churned, drowning the reflections in a silvery froth. Jean squinted, searching for Bill Parkinson among the passengers, but she couldn't see all of them clearly. She didn't see a certain head of red hair, either. "Y'all don't suppose Niamh's on that boat?"

"Oh, good thinking!" said Darling.

Not really. She hated to suggest Niamh had made a break for it. Conventional wisdom had it that you didn't run away if you were innocent, but conventional wisdom often came closer to clichéd assumption.

Lance sauntered toward the street, not without an inquisitive glance down to the crowded police boat, which heaved up and down in the wash of the larger vessel. Everyone took a steadying step or two but no one went overboard. No lifeguarding required and questions not likely to be answered, Lance walked on.

Five pairs of eyes watched until the boat cleared the jaws of the breakwater. Finally, Alasdair said. "I'm not seeing Niamh on the boat, no. Could be Clyde is hiding her, like Lance was . . ." *Hiding Tara,* Jean concluded silently when Alasdair stopped dead. The active-duty officers, who had been actively pursuing their duty last night, didn't need to know he and Jean witnessed her escape.

"Crawford," Alasdair said, "have you got the number of

Clyde's mobile?"

Stepping into the cockpit, Crawford pulled out his phone. Darling squatted down to close the insulated bag, tuck it deep into the locker, and slam the lid.

"Niamh's your prime suspect, then?" queried Michael.

"Afraid so," Jean told him, and asked Alasdair, "What if Niamh's only guilty of lying about putting the flashlight, the torch, away in the cupboard? What if she gave it to someone? I don't mean someone at Gow House. Maggie or Tara or even Elaine could have picked it up on her own."

"Who'd she give it to, then?" he challenged. "Why?"

"I don't know. Lance? She likes Lance."

Darling turned a key in the lock and stood up. "Has she got a boyfriend, then? Could be she's away with him."

"No, Tara said she broke up with a guy in Newcastle. There's Lance, yeah, but he's not a big fan of hers and anyway, he's right there in front of us."

Darling nodded, but didn't quite keep the look of vague relief and delicate speculation from his face.

So the romantic triangle had become a chain, Jean noted. Lance had a thing for Tara, Niamh had one for Lance, Darling was working on one for Niamh. Now if Tara developed something for Darling . . .

"Lance hasn't got a motive," Alasdair stated. "Not for bashing Grinsell, not for putting Maggie in the frame with both the torch and the wee pick from the tool tray."

Jean replied, "No motive that we know of." But what she did know was that she was grasping at straws.

"Would a random passerby," Darling said, "go into Gow House and help himself to a torch? Why not take jewelry, silverware, electronics? They've not reported anything stolen."

"No sir," said Crawford, pocketing his phone. "Niamh's not on the sightseeing boat."

"Let's be getting ourselves back on terra firma, then." Alasdair boosted Jean out of the chill damp of the harbor up onto the fishing boat. She walked across it, then hauled herself up onto the pier and climbed the damp steps. Funny, she thought, how sometimes footsteps in the darkness behind you could be downright comforting.

Chapter Twenty-Nine

Jean waited in the dark patch between two streetlights, admiring the shine of the moon on the sea and on the village—the seaside crescent resembled a drawing etched on a silver plate, the shadows inked densely in. Picturesque, neither purgatory nor Siberia. The scene of two murders.

That's why Darling and Crawford were there. Even in their glow-in-the-dark jackets, they seemed ho-hum compared to Alasdair and Michael in kilts. She felt quite posh being escorted by two bekilted men. All she had to do was add Hector and she'd have a trifecta.

He'd probably dropped off Pen and gone on to the pub, which, Jean saw when she looked around, might have been crowded earlier but now bulged at the seams. Never mind that one heavy-drinking contingent was now headed out to sea, the musicians and their families had filled in the gaps. People sat on windowsills both inside and out, and others were gathered on the street corner beside the Angle's Rest. A couple of fiddles lilted above the clamor of voices, playing Hugh's "The Best of the Barley."

Michael passed Jean and kept on going. "I'd best be getting that wee dram for Rebecca whilst there's still whisky in the jar. Be seeing you inside?"

"If you have a shoehorn." Jean admired the sway and swing of his kilt as he walked away. The motion didn't have the same connotations as Alasdair's, though. And the red of the Cameron tartan glowed like embers even in the moonlight, while the blue-shaded Campbell sett seemed muted.

She cast an eye along the street. When Crawford stopped nearby she asked, "You said Athelstan, your father, set up an office here on Farnaby, thinking the job renovating the tower would make his reputation. Where was it, do you know? The office, not the tower."

"Which case are we working just now?" asked Alasdair, more diplomatic than a blunt, *Do the whereabouts of his office matter?* in front of Athelstan's son.

Who replied, "It was yon empty shop, Inspector Grinsell's incident room. It was a book and stationery shop at the time. My father hired a space in the back."

That's right, Maggie had said something about making a lab out of "the old book shop" if she'd been able to lift the entire coffin—not knowing at the time the coffin was as empty as the store front. "It looked as though it'd been vacant a long time."

"Aye, the book shop went bankrupt a good many years since. Then it was a wool and craft shop and . . . Well, nothing took hold."

Alasdair's profile, turned toward the shop, the incident room, seemed etched in steel rather than silver. Darling stood with his hands in his pockets, rolling a pebble back and forth beneath his shoe, his face concealed. Jean wished she'd brought a hat—nothing glamorous, just something to keep her ears warm in the cold and yet soft night air.

Grinsell, she thought. Lying there at the tower, cold, damp, alone. Hopefully unconscious, unaware of his slow, sad death. He hadn't deserved that. No one deserved that. No more than Athelstan deserved a chanter thrust into his brain by an irate husband. Had Wat's offer of a memorial stone been the equivalent of the Anglo-Saxon weregild or blood money?

Jean wondered if D.C.I. Webber would turn up tomorrow

morning—given a lack of any more fog—and take control of the case for himself, relieving her and Alasdair both of any need to stay on. She wondered if Alasdair would insist on staying on and seeing both cases to their ends. She wondered what she would do, presented with a choice between answers and escape.

That was a minor issue compared to whether it was better for Grinsell's murder to have a resolution than for Athelstan's. The statute of emotional limitations never ended, it only wasted away.

Alasdair turned to his two canary-coated minions. "Let's have us a look at the time line. Even if the light Hector Cruz saw at Merlin's Tower had nothing to do with the murder, even if Cruz's light came from another torch entirely, the murderer had to have picked up Maggie's torch late last night or early this morning in order to go bashing Grinsell with it. Niamh was saying earlier she'd have a look for it amongst Elaine's things. We know now she cannot have found it. She's avoiding questioning."

Where's Niamh? Jean thought. The Farnaby edition of *Where's Waldo?*

"If she's scarpered," said Darling, the words slipping out beneath a stiff upper lip, "she might well be taking a small boat across to Lindisfarne, as you were suggesting, Miss Fairbairn."

"Oh." How about that? She'd said something helpful.

Alasdair looked narrowly around the harbor—the same two kayaks were lying on the breakwater, but he could have no better idea than she did what watercraft were normally there. "Are all the island's boats kept here in Farnaby St. Mary?"

"I expect there are a few in coves round the island," Crawford replied.

"Have Lance Eccleston help you make an inventory of the island's boats, then."

Crawford opened his mouth, then shut it again.

"Aye, I'm recognizing that this is better a job for the daylight. I'd be obliged if you'd make a start here in the village, just the same."

Touching his finger to his cap, Crawford trudged away toward the pub, it being reasonable to assume Lance was there. Everyone was there. Jean even saw a black-and-white sheep dog come trotting along the sidewalk and sit down outside, tail wagging.

Alasdair turned back to the breakwater, brows knit. Darling followed his gaze. "Setting aside Niamh's location for the moment, setting aside our suspicions of her, come to that . . ." Jean caught a gleam from the corner of his eye—*see me, I'm being impartial.* "What if the murderer's an outsider who came to Farnaby via a small boat from Lindisfarne or the mainland? Last night was a misty one, good for concealment. Save for Cruz seeing the light."

"I wish we'd see the light," Jean murmured, and, louder, "Someone coming in from outside would have to be pretty motivated to row or paddle or swim or whatever over here after dark."

"Exactly." That's why Alasdair had been eyeing the boat leaving earlier, telling himself the sea ran both ways and the list of suspects was much larger than he was comfortable with. "An inventory of the island's boats should be turning up any extras as well as any missing."

Jean felt somewhat mollified that he at least considered someone besides Niamh as the killer.

"Darling," said Alasdair, "get onto the authorities on Lindisfarne—well, I'm thinking Crawford might well be the authorities there as well as here—any road, find yourself someone there and ask them to have a look round, see if any small watercraft have gone missing. And whilst doing that, phone Berwick and tell them we might have an ID for the body. Athelstan Crawford."

"Yes, sir." Darling walked over to the circle of golden light beneath the street lamp and waved his fingertips over his phone like a magician doing hocus-pocus.

And then there were two. Jean stepped up beside Alasdair, assuming the helpmeet's rather than the subordinate's position. "Go ahead, say it."

"All right, then. You're defending Niamh the way you were defending Maggie, even though with her you've got nothing other than gender in common."

"I don't have to have anything in common with someone in order to be—empathetic is the word, I guess. 'Empathic' sounds like something out of *Star Trek.*"

"If Niamh did not kill Grinsell—and the attacker meant to kill, I've got no doubt—then who did do it?"

"You haven't let Maggie off the hook yet."

"No, I've not."

"What about Crawford? He stayed the night here even though Darling told him to go home."

"Aye, he did that."

"But if you—if we—can't see any motive for Lance, we can't see any for Crawford, either. He's not implicated in the Grinsell case. He's not implicated in the seventy-one case, he's only concerned with it."

"Even so, I should be recommending Webber relieve him of duty, but it's too late now. Besides, he's the only constable I've got."

"Besides, we—you—no one's . . ." Dang it, she hated tiptoeing around with pronouns. ". . . settled once and for all that it's Athelstan's body. I mean, that's the simplest explanation even though the details are still fuzzy. It's not presumption of innocence, it's presumption of identity."

"Right," Alasdair said.

Inside the pub, a set of bagpipes squawked, droned, and then burst out with a cover of "Bad Moon Rising." That was Hector rather than Michael, who'd been on a quest for intoxicating beverages rather than intoxicating music. She wondered if Hector knew "In a Gadda da Vida," too. Funny how few rock 'n roll bands ever envisioned adding bagpipes to their line-ups, and yet bagpipes rocked and rolled with the best.

The windows of the pub seemed to be expanding and contracting to the beat of the music. The door opened, spilling an aroma of sausages and fried potatoes as well as several more people out onto the street. Light glittered from their drinking glasses. The dog whined and slunk away, his tail between his legs. Beneath the lamppost, Darling sketched a couple of dance steps, then, with a glance at Alasdair, froze into an authoritative stance.

Alasdair chuckled beneath his breath, then sobered as he assessed the patrons of the pub. The light in his eyes was as much friction from the fine grinding of his internal thought, Jean estimated, as external reflection. "James Fleming might could make an inventory of the folk on the island."

"Pen certainly could, but I bet she's resting. And considering her options. Airing your own dirty linen's bad enough. Airing that of a good friend is worse."

"Wat and Elaine, you're meaning?"

"Yep."

Hector segued into a more traditional hornpipe. Jean forced her own feet to stay flat on the rough cement. Still, she couldn't keep her hips from swaying in the waves of music. "What you mean is that you'd like to know who belongs here, who's visiting, who may have sneaked in, and where every last soul was this morning when Grinsell went down."

"A tall order, I'm afraid. Even on a wee island."

"It might be easier to mobilize the people we can trust—Michael, Hugh, Hector, Darling—and ransack the place until we find Niamh. But then . . ." Jean abruptly stopped swaying. ". . . we're assuming Niamh's somewhere keeping her head down voluntarily. Because, for whatever reason, she doesn't want to talk to us. To you. To the cops. But you know, Alasdair, it's not all about us."

"Eh?"

"What if she's hiding because she thinks she's in danger from the murderer. Maybe she saw something or someone before the fog came in. Or even while it was in."

"Then why's she not coming to us? Because she's protecting someone? She's been in a grand position to catch Maggie at . . ."

"I'm not trying to throw suspicion back on Maggie!" Jean made a frustrated gesture.

Alasdair chilled a few degrees. "What if Niamh and Maggie have been working together? Have you been thinking of that?"

"Sure. No. I don't know. I mean, yeah, but Niamh's been in a great position the last day or so to see Hugh, too, and the other musicians in the concert. And the people *at* the concert."

"She was having herself a good stare at Maggie whilst she was singing."

Yes. Yes she was.

Dammit, Jean thought, she didn't want Maggie to be guilty this time around. She wanted her to have learned from history and not be doomed to repeat it.

Chapter Thirty

Jean thought back not to the concert but to all the conversations afterward. *Ah, yes.* "I thought Niamh stared at Maggie, too, but don't you remember, when Hugh said something about it she, Maggie, said no, Niamh looked past her. Maybe at Lance. He was on that side of the room."

"Aye, but . . ." The crease between Alasdair's eyebrows deepened so far Jean could have parachuted into it. "He was in the back row, on the far end. He had to get himself up to the stage for his bit with the bodhran without climbing over anyone."

"Then who was—oh!"

If he'd been a cat, his whiskers would have perked up. "What's 'oh'?"

"Those two reporters were sitting right behind Maggie. Rosalie-something from *News of the North,* bored out of her skull, and Bill Parkinson from *The Daily Dish.* Who seemed really interested. No surprise—Niamh's a very pretty girl, no matter he's twice her age."

"The woman wearing the shrink-wrapped jacket? And the chap you were chatting with in the hall?"

"Yeah. They came out together on the ferry today. He was out here yesterday, too—he's the guy on the ferry slip who told me Maggie had changed her plans about opening the grave."

Alasdair stretched out the crease by elevating an eyebrow. "The chap covering her trial, you were saying?"

"That's him. He thought it was rubbish, same as Grinsell."

Jean tried to visualize the scene: Niamh's saw-toothed and yet melodious voice, Parkinson leaning forward as though meeting her eye—she had to have been looking either at him or the couple behind him, who, so far as Jean's visualization was accurate, were islanders. "The people behind Rosalie—Banks, Rosalie Banks—and Parkinson wouldn't have had anything to do with Maggie's trial. But he . . . You know, Maggie saw me talking to him and she frowned as if he looked familiar but she couldn't quite place him."

Alasdair's slightly warmer blue gaze fixed on her face. "This is all as may be, but why was Niamh staring at him? She had nothing doing with Maggie's trial. She was an infant then."

Like Crawford was when his father died, Jean thought, and focused. One thing at a time.

"Was Parkinson away on Clyde's boat just now?" Alasdair asked.

"I didn't see him, but I couldn't see everyone. There's a chance he's still here. He said he was going to the pub. Maybe he got to drinking and missed the boat."

"It's worth having a look." Alasdair took off across the street without bothering to check for traffic, but then, the only cars in sight were parked and dark. "Darling! Come along!"

Darling said something into his phone, thrust it into his pocket, and came along. "Tara says Niamh's still not returned to Gow House," he announced. "Maggie's there, though, with her mum, who's right agitated for some reason."

Poor soul, Jean concluded, repeating Pen's words.

Inside the pub, the bagpipes stopped with a flourish and cheers and applause rattled the windows. The door opened and Michael stepped out, balancing two glasses of gleaming amber liquid on a round tray, maybe even the same tray Alasdair had used last night. "Making my way to the bar took quite a while," he said.

"Were you by any chance getting a good look at the other folk inside?" asked Alasdair.

"The place cleared out a bit when Hector blew up his pipes, but I cannot say—"

Jean interrupted. "You remember the pudgy guy with the odd-looking hair I was talking to in the door of the food room? During the concert he sat right behind Maggie, Tara, and Elaine, next to a woman in a red vinyl jacket."

"Oh aye. Him. One of the reporters, was he?"

"Aye. Name's Bill Parkinson. Have you seen him in the pub?" asked Alasdair.

"No, not unless he's set himself up in the gents."

Alasdair turned to Darling. "Contact the constable in Seahouses. I'm thinking there's one in Seahouses."

"There is, yes." Darling reached into his pocket.

"Have him meet Clyde's boat and detain Rosalie Banks, the woman in the vinyl jacket, and Bill Parkinson. They'll cry harassment, I have no doubt, but it'll be harder on us than on them."

"They're traveling together?" Darling asked.

"By accident," said Jean. "Bill said they met on the ferry earlier today."

"Did he now?" Michael stepped aside for a couple of grizzled islanders, putting his body between them and his tray. "I never laid eyes on the man before the concert. He was not on the ferry. Rebecca and I were walking Linda to and fro, hoping she'd not feel seasick, and we excused ourselves to everyone on board twice over. I mind vinyl-jacket-and-boots woman, right enough, but not Parkinson."

Alasdair drew himself up. Jean could almost see his hair standing on end like antennae. "He lied, did he? Why? What does it matter how he arrived here?"

"Eh?" Darling asked faintly.

"Why was Niamh staring at him?" Alasdair went on. "He's

hardly got a handsome face. She must have recognized him from somewhere. They've both lived in Newcastle, have they?"

From the pub came the sound of Hugh's fiddle playing "Dark Island," a song with a melody that resembled "Foggy Dew," if you plugged one ear and screwed up your face a bit. Jean turned to Michael. "You've sung 'Foggy Dew,' haven't you? It's about young Irish soldiers fighting for the British in faraway places during World War I, when they should have stayed home and fought against the British for their freedom."

"Aye, that's the gist of the song," Michael said.

Niamh had been staring intensely at Parkinson while she sang . . . Jean waved her hands, trying to grasp the thoughts before they scuttled away and hid. Again Michael protected his tray.

She visualized Parkinson's colorless hair, pale skin, sagging jowls. Grinsell's ghost had had colorless hair, bleached by some alchemy of death and memory from the living red.

Red hair. Niamh and Tara had red hair, inherited from their father since Maggie's hair was brown.

Had Niamh stared intently at a man who should not have been fighting, who should have stayed home—one who'd lost his freedom? What would a ginger-haired leprechaun look like if he'd spent umpteen years detained at Her Majesty's pleasure, two decades chewing over what-might-have-beens? Would that leprechaun devolve into a troll?

Jean realized all three men were staring at her, Darling nonplussed, Michael amused, Alasdair verging on patient, but not quite there.

From inside came a gust of laughter. A gust of wind from the opposite direction sent a cold, not at all paranormal, chill down Jean's back. "It's not how he arrived here. It's when. He said he was on the ferry because he needed an alibi."

This time it was Alasdair who asked, "Eh?"

"Who has a whopping big motive to kill Grinsell? Who did Grinsell track down, intimidate, and bring to trial—after Maggie's rubbish trial—and those were Parkinson's exact words. Who knew better than anyone that her trial was rubbish? The third person who was there when Oliver Phillips was killed."

"Donal McCarthy?" Alasdair's eyebrows were working overtime.

"Who?" Michael asked.

"Niamh's father. Tara's father. The man who would have gotten away with murder, except for Grinsell." Jean rushed on—it made sense, it hung together—her words fell over each other and a wave of heat rose up her body so swiftly that surely steam wafted from her head. "Miranda said Donal McCarthy was sent down for life. How long is 'life' here?"

"Often no more than fifteen years, with good conduct." Alasdair backed off a step. "Jean, you're making one hell of a leap."

Michael and Darling shared a wary glance. "She's doing this all the time," Michael told him.

"Is she now?" asked Darling.

"Yes, it's a leap." Jean said. "It's an Olympic-quality broad jump. For one thing, how did Niamh recognize Donal in his current condition? Heck, Maggie didn't recognize him, and she sure knew him better than Niamh ever did—she said earlier she and her mother never heard from him."

Alasdair was always willing to consider what-ifs. "Niamh could have become curious about him the way Maggie became curious about the child she gave up."

"Maybe she looked him up ages ago—he told me he'd come to Farnaby to see Maggie again—he was honest about that. He may not have covered her trial as a reporter, but he had to have hung on every word—what if he came out here to see Niamh, too? He might even have sprung himself on her. Ta-da, it's me, your long-lost daddy!"

"If Donal's the murderer, then looks to be Niamh's helping him out. Starting with giving him the torch."

"If Parkinson, if Donal—whoever, if he deliberately killed Grinsell with Maggie's flashlight then left it where it would be easily found . . ."

". . . he could have gone collecting the wee pick during the night, planting it near the scene, trying to put Maggie in the frame." Alasdair's eyes sparked, the mental friction producing fire.

"He intended to get revenge against Grinsell and against her, too. Two birds with one stone." Hadn't she thought of that already? Jean asked herself. Yes, except then she'd been afraid Niamh was the culprit. No matter. "So is Niamh with him now? Voluntarily or otherwise? What if Park—Donal realizes his scheme to implicate Maggie has backfired? What then?"

Darling whipped out his phone the way an American cop would whip out his gun. "I'll get onto Berwick, see if McCarthy is still inside."

"Even if it's not McCarthy," Alasdair told him, "even if Parkinson's his own man, he needs apprehending soon as may be. Sooner."

"I'll get Miranda to check with *The Daily Dish,* see what his background is there." Jean pulled her bag around and groped for her own phone. "We've got to warn Maggie, too."

Michael took off toward the B&B, holding the tray out in front of him. "I'm after telling Rebecca and Pen what's happening. If I can be helping after that . . ."

"You can be helping, aye." Alasdair's words fell like pellets of hail. "Sergeant, have Banks stopped in Seahouses—the more the merrier when it's coming to breaking alibis. Then collect everyone who's sober enough to not go falling over a cliff. We'll be after finding Niamh McCarthy if we're turning over every stone on the island. Let's be hoping she's still on it."

Chapter Thirty-One

Jean stood in the old book shop, the incident room, now Alasdair's command center. In the sickly light of the fluorescent bulb, the place only looked more appealing this time around because Grinsell wasn't in it.

A little voice in her mind counseled, *Don't speak ill of the dead.* Another voice advised, *Honesty is the best policy.* Rejecting both voices, she leaned over several masculine shoulders, the better to see the map of Farnaby Island spread out on the plastic table.

The discussion sounded like a small symphony with Alasdair as conductor. Crawford was the slow beat of a percussion instrument. Darling was more of a flute, providing bright notes both to Alasdair and to different voices on his phone. James Fleming was a woodwind, his deep voice pointing out different sites and options. Other islanders, musicians, and sundry made helpful entrances and purposeful exits.

Nothing like a damsel in distress to clean out the pub and set every sober man's face in determined lines. Nothing like a woman in jeopardy to make Pen rise from her fainting couch—or so Michael had reported—and start preparing yet more tea and baked goods, this time with Rebecca's help. A search party ran on its stomach.

Funny how in a crisis so many people defaulted to more-or-less traditional gender roles. The men protected, the women supplied . . . Well, more than one local woman had turned up, prepared from head scarf to wellies to wade in with the men.

All they needed was Hector and Michael piping inspirational tunes, Hugh fiddling accompaniment. But Michael had gone off with one set of searchers and Hector with another. Hugh, after first volunteering to go as well, had gracefully agreed to oversee an impromptu canteen in the pub.

The soundtrack consisted of voices, footsteps, the revving of engines, the slow pulse of the wind and the sea. And an electronic "Hail to the Chief," which seemed appropriate to Alasdair's calm, cool, voice—oh! Jean realized her own phone called for attention and dived for her bag, sitting on a chair near the door to the back room. "Hey, Miranda. You got my text after all. It was more of a short story, I'm afraid."

"But fascinating reading. I was pleased to feel my phone giving a shudder, to tell the truth. It's a tourist agency dinner. Half the table's asleep in the brandy snifters, the other half is arguing over the pedicures of angels dancing on heads of pins. I'm skiving off in the cloak room just now—Duncan can go filling me in on what I'm missing, if anything."

"No angels on pins here. It's life and death. I'm hoping Niamh's not in danger."

"You're also hoping she's not gone over to her father's dark side, I expect."

"You think?" A *Star Wars* joke! Miranda was making progress. "The latest is that Crawford heard back from his counterpart in Seahouses. The *News of the North* reporter, Rosalie, met Donal at the pub. She'd never laid eyes on him before then—certainly not on the ferry. She had no idea Parkinson wasn't his real name and does this mean she's missed a proper scoop here on Farnaby?"

"Parkinson is Donal, then?"

"Oh yeah, it's the same guy. Darling's checked out his photo and everything. Good conduct got him out of prison after fifteen years."

"My contact at the *Dish* was a bit hard to hear, with the techno music in the background—no telling where he was having his Saturday night—but I caught the sense of it. He hired Donal McCarthy on three years since."

"He knew Donal's real identity, then." The door in the back of the shop still stood partly open, like it had been last night. Jean peered through the slit into the shadowed room and its lopsided shelf loaded with moldering bits of dead trees. Were the books worth rescuing?

"Oh aye," Miranda said. "He agreed to keep it secret, though, let Donal work under a *nom de keyboard,* so long as he used his contacts with the criminal element in reporting true crime stories."

"Berwick told Darling that Parkinson worked as a snout, a police informant, in prison. A stool-pigeon. There's your good conduct." Jean laughed humorlessly. "He's still a musician, I guess. Still 'singing.' "

A string quartet trilled behind Miranda's sultry voice, flowing and ebbing as the door of the cloak room opened and shut. "How's Maggie getting on?"

"Alasdair phoned her, told her to lock the doors, close the drapes, and keep Tara inside. She's Donal's daughter too, if not the one he knew as a baby. Lance Eccleston . . ." Did Miranda know who Lance was? It was a bit late to add a new character to the narrative. Whatever, Jean plunged on, "And Lance said he'd keep an eye on Gow House."

"That's all to the good, but how's Maggie getting on?"

"Darned if I know. When I asked Alasdair how she sounded he goggled at me as though I'd said something in Martian."

Miranda laughed. "No, you'd said something in Venusian. Female."

A straightforward mobile ring tone made Crawford step away from the map and set his phone to his ear. After a moment's conversation he said, "Thank you kindly. That's right helpful." And, to Alasdair, "A chap on the south side of the island's found a rowboat abandoned on a bit of beach. It matches the description of the one gone missing from the north side of Lindisfarne."

"Where's this again?" Alasdair indicated the map.

Crawford bent over it and pointed. All the heads leaned in for a better look.

Jean exhaled, so loudly Miranda asked, "Was that by way of being a sigh of relief?"

"Sort of. They've found a boat reported stolen on Lindisfarne. That's probably how Donal got back on the island. It looks like he's still here, and Niamh with him." She didn't need to add all the appropriate caveats. Miranda's imagination might run to matter-of-fact rather than fantasy, but she had enough of one to fill in the cautions for herself.

Alasdair said, "Jean here spoke with McCarthy at the ferry slip on the mainland and saw him going off toward a car. Likely he was still in the area last evening, when the balloon went up about the body in the chapel."

And he saw his chance to score points off Maggie, Jean added silently.

Crawford's face seemed less lively than the one of the statue on Lindisfarne. "Did McCarthy know D.I. Grinsell would be the responding officer?"

"He worked the crime beat for *The Daily Dish,*" Jean said. "He had names, ranks, and serial numbers of every cop in Northumberland. In the UK, probably. I bet he has a contact in Berwick who told him exactly who went where and when."

Darling winced, no doubt wondering how many walls back at headquarters had ears and making a mental note to have a word with D.C.I. Webber sooner rather than later.

"Thank you kindly," Alasdair told Jean, with a curt nod that she accepted at face value—high praise.

He'd been doing quite a balancing act, commanding troops who weren't properly his. Weren't Webber's original orders to liaise with Darling, work side-by-side? But then, an intelligent youth like Darling had to be relieved to fall into competent clutches.

"There's a perfect storm for you," said Miranda in her ear. "Donal had himself Grinsell and Maggie and a juicy story, all at once."

"And his long-lost older daughter working in Maggie's home," Jean replied. "I'll bet he congratulated himself up one side and down the other."

"The causeway was open last evening," Alasdair went on, "so McCarthy quick-smart drove across to Lindisfarne. Or he might have already been there, meaning to spend the night. No matter now. He helped himself to the boat and arrived back on Farnaby in good time to get Maggie's torch from Niamh. He likely slept rough at Merlin's Tower. Cruz is saying he saw a light there just before midnight. Someone's had a look at the place?"

"Aye," James replied. "Went over it with a fine-toothed comb, he did. No one's there."

"Time to be having a look at the outlying barns and byres, then."

"With no more than moonlight to be seeing by . . ."

"Well," Alasdair said, "do the best you can."

It was cold out there. And while the light of the full moon would be helpful, it also created very dense shadows. A searcher could pass Donal and Niamh within a few feet and not see them.

Jean thought of Niamh shivering with the chill, with fear, with uncertainty. At least, she wanted to think that's what

Niamh was doing, not that she sat there high-fiving dear old dad for a scheme well carried out—if complicated by the presence of a certain Scottish detective. "Although," she mused aloud, "if Donal and Niamh were collaborating, surely they'd be long gone by now."

"And now?" Miranda asked.

"We're running around considerably better organized than that headless chicken. More cops are on their way from Berwick to help. Alasdair has people going door to door in the village, since that's something we can do in the dark." There was that *we* again. She'd probably be more helpful going back to the Angle's Rest and strapping on an apron.

"I'd best be getting myself back to the bean-feast, then. Try texting me again when there's anything else wants researching."

"Will do. Thanks."

Chapter Thirty-Two

Ending the call, Jean checked the time. Ten o'clock. She could have sworn it was already tomorrow, and well into it. Biting her lip, she tucked her phone back in her bag.

Alasdair said, "No one goes searching on his own. If anyone's catching a glimpse of either McCarthy or Niamh, call for help. Donal's dangerous."

"Is he armed, sir?" Crawford asked.

"I'm hoping not, since he went using a torch as a weapon, but let's not be making assumptions. In any event, he's desperate. Sergeant?"

Darling responded on cue. "Berwick had a look at D.I. Grinsell's phone, with a message from 'Bill Parkinson,' first saying he appreciated Grinsell's work back in Cambridgeshire to get at the truth about Maggie Lauder and her trial. Then he said he'd met Donal McCarthy in prison and learned some bits of evidence against Maggie that never came out, what with feminist prejudice and all. He said Donal and Maggie had worked together to stage the murder but then she'd turned against him."

"Grinsell believed that?" asked Jean, and answered her own question. "He wanted to believe that. Still, isn't there some sort of double jeopardy rule or something that would have kept Grinsell from charging Maggie again?"

"Up till quite recently there was, aye," Alasdair said. "Nowadays, though, here in England, new evidence might could be leading to a new trial. Failing that, he'd be crowing to the media that he was right all along. He could have recreated the scandal just when Maggie was aiming for a major scholarly achievement. Revenge and vindication, all in one go."

Crawford nodded. Jean wondered if he thought what she was thinking, that a man with an ego like Grinsell's was shockingly easy to trap. Donal had probably been brooding for years about the situation. So had Grinsell. She'd thought at the eat-and-greet after the concert that the two men would have gotten along.

They had not missed each other after all. Oh, to have been a raven on the wall at that confrontation, when Grinsell realized who he faced. When he realized he'd been had . . . No, Jean corrected herself. Having seen the results, she was glad she'd skipped the encounter.

"In the event," Alasdair went on, "Donal lured Grinsell to the Tower, hardly meaning to have a friendly blether. He set a trap with an eye to murder. Now he's looking at being sent down again, this time for the rest of his life, which would not be long, not if the other old lags are suspecting he's a snout."

"Is he holding the lass hostage?" asked James.

"We do not know whether she's with him. If she is, we do not know her state of mind."

Jean considered the dark back room. She remembered Hugh looking for the missing chanter among all the chanters at the school, and Tara going back to Gow House after Crawford had already looked for her there. She aimed her forefinger at the half-open door and asked over her shoulder, "Alasdair, has anyone searched this room?"

Alasdair looked around, his expression shading from *Say what?* to *Oh crap.* "Crawford? Darling?"

James answered. "The back door's locked. Leastways, it was the last time I checked."

"When was that?" Jean asked.

"Last year. Maybe the year before. But then, several folk have keys," he conceded. "The lock's the same one it was when your dad had an office there, Edwin."

"Mum kept his key along with the drawings," replied Crawford. "It's an old metal skeleton key. Seems to me Wat was saying he had one as well."

"Then Donal might have had that off Niamh." Darling, chin set, hands curled into fists, took three swift steps toward the half-open door and kicked it open. The crash sent dust wafting down from the ceiling in the front room and the shelf in the back tilted even further. Every eye followed as the stack of old newspapers slumped in slow motion over the edge and fanned out across the floor.

Someone coughed. Alasdair said, "Do not scare me like that, Jean."

"Scare *you*?" She crept toward the open door, pretending not to hear Darling's unmistakable sigh of relief. Still in the penumbra of fluorescent light, she looked inside the door frame for a light switch. Ah—there it was.

A single incandescent bulb in the ceiling lit up, revealing a room empty except for the shelf, a few tatty cardboard boxes, and a broken chair. The back door, an ancient wooden-framed number, was closed. Taking a deep breath of the chill, musty air, Jean made the journey of five steps across the room in four, set her hand on the icy knob, and turned it.

The door was locked. No—Jean reversed her push to a pull and narrowly avoided hitting herself in the face. It opened inward, not outward. And it was emphatically *not* locked.

She gazed out onto a narrow passage between two stone walls, its moist, mossy cement floor littered with indefinable bits of flotsam and jetsam. At the far end, past a gate hanging from one hinge, rose the hillside behind the village. If she leaned out and looked to the right, past the back of the next building—the student hostel, with lots of lighted windows—she could see the priory sketched in quicksilver and ebony on the velveteen grass.

Tiny lights wavered in the church and gleamed through the windows of the chapel. The ghostly nuns were restless tonight—or were they ghostly candles at all, not the flashlights of search parties? Jean considered the hair on the back of her neck, perkier than normal if not exactly at full alert.

Someone stepped up beside her and she jumped.

"Sorry, madam," said Crawford.

"You've searched the priory already, haven't you? Or not you in person—someone."

"Aye, that we have."

"I—ah—I thought I saw lights there a minute ago." She saw them now, and wondered if they counted as corpse-candles.

"A trick of the moonlight. Or the headlamps of a car in the car park. In any event, it's all dark now."

Saying *yes it is* wasn't an outright lie, but still Jean stepped back into the room without speaking and let Crawford inspect the door and then shut it behind them.

"Looks like a fresh scratch or two on the lock," he said. "Someone fumbling with the key in the dark, most likely."

Donal's hand fumbling in the dark, Jean wondered, or Niamh's?

Her moment of inspiration—if you could call it that—had not produced either of the fugitives. Standing there dithering or chewing her nails wouldn't either. She turned to the newspapers spread out on the flagstone floor and gathered them up. Instead of stacking them back on the shelf, she dumped them against the wall beneath it. Their headlines were five years old—they were probably leftover packing material from when the last shop moved out.

The bland spines of the jacketless books were mottled with

damp. Using only her forefinger, Jean angled one away from its mates and saw that it was an accounting textbook. So were the other two. Delicately she opened the one on the end to the flyleaf and saw again Elaine's steady, youthful handwriting: Elaine Lauder. Gow House, Farnaby Island. 1971.

"Nineteen seventy-one," Jean murmured. So Elaine studied accounting as well as literature? Interesting combination. But perhaps Wat needed help with the Gallowglass accounts. If so, though, why were the books here instead of at their home?

Jean moved on to the cardboard file folders. Both were empty. Both bore the same label: Athelstan Crawford.

Athelstan Crawford's son stood by the door into the front room. She asked him, "Have you seen these?"

"Aye, madam, that I have. My wife and I, we had a quick look round when the last shop closed down. Those folders were tucked away in a corner with the books. Nothing in them save a receipt or two and a note from Elaine Lauder thanking Athelstan for the gift of a wee book of poetry. We took those with us, gave them to my sister to add to the portfolio of drawings."

"Crawford!" called Darling.

"Aye, sir." He stepped through the doorway.

Jean brushed peeling bits of paper and binding from her fingers. She didn't blame Crawford and his spousal unit for not taking away either books or folders. They smelled of wet dog.

The only area of the room she hadn't investigated was the corner where three cardboard boxes slouched beside the broken chair. She took the two paces over to them and stirred them with her toe. Something very small shot out of the far side and vanished into a crack in the wall.

She jerked convulsively, then swallowed her heart back into her chest and grimaced at her own nerviness. There were worse things than mice.

Two of the boxes scraped easily across the floor, empty. The third was heavier. Closing her nostrils against the smell of mildew and decay, she leaned over and opened its flaps.

Palpable shadow filled the bottom of the box. No, that was a dusky purple fabric, its ribbed pattern making stripes of light and dark. Good heavens—was that Elaine's shawl bundled into the box? Both Maggie and Crawford had said Pen found Elaine outside the pub last night, listening to Niamh sing. One of them had said she'd been without her shawl.

The smell was more than that of mildew. It evoked a sharp memory of Maggie pulling back a blue tarp. Her heart continuing on down into her stomach, Jean lifted one corner of the shawl.

Nestled inside it lay a baton. A wand. A long, thin, black, pitted, and scabby tubular shape with a flat flared end.

Chapter Thirty-Three

"Alasdair," Jean called.

The masculine voices in the other room didn't falter. Footsteps receded toward the outside door. It opened and shut.

"Alasdair!" she shouted.

A sudden quiet. "Aye?" he replied, giving her the benefit of the doubt by using a tone more cautious than impatient.

"The chanter. The one Maggie found in the grave. The murder weapon from the seventy-one case. It's in here, wrapped in Elaine's shawl."

A pause, and then a stampede. Jean found herself standing three feet away from the box without having taken any actual steps. Alasdair peered down at the shawl and the chanter while Darling held a flashlight over his shoulder. James craned his neck to see.

Only Crawford stood back, his long face almost uncommunicative, but not quite. Jean detected a range of emotions moving subtly beneath the stern facade, from the cringing realization the chanter was no longer an abstract object but the weapon that had killed his father, to a shrinking resignation that its relocation from chapel to shop hovered over his head like a bat homing in on a roost.

Darling handed the flashlight off to James and lifted the chanter, still in its woolen nest, from the box. Alasdair turned to Crawford. "You were standing watch at the priory last night. Then you were telling Inspector Grinsell you were not so sure you'd seen a chanter lying next to the body."

"Aye, sir."

"What were you seeing, then? Or should I be asking, *who* were you seeing at the priory, in the dark?"

"Elaine Lauder, sir."

"And?" Alasdair prodded.

"She has herself a wander from time to time. If I'd seen her walking off into the fields, say, I'd have taken her back home. But she was leaving the priory for the village. I knew someone would be looking after her. No need to abandon my post."

Alasdair said nothing. Darling, clutching the shawl and the chanter to his chest, tilted his head to the side quizzically. James looked down at the floor, frowning—he remembered the real Elaine, not an old, confused woman fumbling at the lock to the back door of the shop.

Crawford remembered the real Elaine, too, Jean told herself.

He braced his shoulders back, but his eyes were focused on a spot beyond Alasdair's dour face, as though the sheer force of his gaze could open up a window in the far wall, one into the past. "I thought she'd come for a look at the grave was all. She worked there, once. Then, when I was showing Inspector Grinsell the scene, I saw the chanter'd gone missing."

"Why were you lying, Constable?" Alasdair's voice was cold as a glacier about to calve several tons of ice.

"I wasn't dead certain Elaine had taken it. When I took Inspector Grinsell's measure—meaning no disrespect, but once I'd seen him badgering Maggie, once I'd heard him threatening the same to Tara and Elaine as well, I—I wasn't sure what to do. Sir."

Darling exhaled through pursed lips, probably finding it hard to fault Crawford's reasoning.

A tautness at the corner of Alasdair's not even remotely pursed lips indicated his thought: Was Crawford trying to frame

Elaine, who couldn't speak up for herself, and cover up for—whom? Himself?

Motive, thought Jean. Always motive. And so many motives right now came down to a wish to protect, not to harm.

"And yet," Alasdair said, "even after Grinsell was, erm, no longer on the case, you lied to me."

"Begging your pardon, sir, but you're not—you're no Inspector Grinsell, but . . ."

He'd better not say anything about holiday cop, Jean told herself.

He finished his sentence, ". . . you told me the body in the grave's my own father. That's a turn-up for the books. D.I. Grinsell was here, putting himself in harm's way, for my family, wasn't he?"

"He didn't know he'd be in danger here," said Darling. "He came along thinking he could settle a score with Maggie."

The ice still overhung Alasdair's expression.

So the whole time Grinsell had been harassing Maggie last night, the chanter had been lying a few feet away. If anyone had found it, would it have changed anything? No, Jean told herself, probably not even the trajectory of Grinsell's abuse. And none of Donal's actions would have altered in the least.

Taking mercy on Crawford, she said, "It must have been Elaine I saw from the window of the B and B, walking along the road toward the priory. You'd think her white hair would have caught the light, though."

"She was wearing her old gardening hat," said Crawford.

James waded in. "Elaine must have used Wat's old key to the shop, leaving the shawl and the chanter here before I opened it for the police. Then she went on to the pub where Pen found her. Hard to say what she was thinking. The poor old soul's got her own reasoning these days." He set a hand on Crawford's arm. "It's all right, lad. You meant to protect Elaine. You had no idea the chanter had meaning for you personally."

Alasdair's thin lips said, *No, it's not all right.* He turned on James. "You and Pen also knew, then, that Elaine had likely nicked the chanter. Is that why the pair of you and Crawford here were having a chin-wag—when was it, Jean? One in the morning?"

"One-fifteen," she said.

"Sorry to wake you," James told them both, with his best hang-dog, whiskers-drooping expression. "I didn't get back from the pub till late. I found Pen sitting up with Edwin. He thought he'd best stay on the island, not quite trusting the inspector."

Alasdair's voice crackled with fissuring ice. "Just how cozy with members of the public are you planning on making yourself, Constable?"

Darling took a step back, as though planning an escape route.

James and Crawford both stared. "The Flemings aren't members of the public," said Crawford. "They're on my patch, aye, but . . ."

James's voice was louder. "Edwin's our son-in-law, Mr. Cameron. He and our daughter Lisa have been married for fifteen years. Two grandchildren, finest lad and lass you've ever seen."

Alasdair's face, already fair, went stark white.

James added, "You didn't know that?"

Oh shit. Jean, too, stepped aside, visualizing the photo of Maggie with Lisa Fleming. Lisa Crawford.

The villain who had perverted the course of justice was the best friend of the local constable's mother-in-law.

Despite being the shortest man present, Alasdair seemed to loom almost to the ceiling. His voice flash-froze the entire room, left patterns of frost on the flagstones, piled snow banks in the corners, strung icicles from the door frames. "No. I did not know that."

"Aye." Crawford tried a smile, but it withered on his lips. "I'd visited Farnaby often enough over the years. Likely I'd passed Lisa on the street or sat in at the same session. Then, when I was assigned Bamburgh and Farnaby, Wat Lauder introduced me round and I met her and Maggie and . . . Well. Here we are. Sir."

"No," stated Alasdair. "Where you are is sitting in your boat guarding the evidence. Soon as Berwick arrives, you're off the case. Are you hearing me?"

Crawford gulped and nodded. His "Aye, sir," came out as a squeak.

"Give him the shawl and the chanter."

Using the most economical, unobtrusive movement possible, Darling handed over the bundle.

"Away you go. Bearing in mind that I've got no stomach for another round of playing who's got the chanter."

"Aye, sir." Crawford scuttled away, his long legs moving like a crab's. His eyes the size of his own plates, James turned to follow.

"Wait there," Alasdair ordered, and James stopped in the doorway. "Sergeant Darling. I'd be obliged if you'd look into the status of the search teams."

Darling whisked out his phone and retreated to the other room, muttering urgently.

"Mr. Fleming," Alasdair went on. "You were after leading one of the teams yourself?"

"Aye, that I was—I'll be getting on then, shall I?"

"Please."

James's exit was less a scuttle than a quick march, through the outer room and away.

Jean realized she stood with her arms crossed, hunched over against the blizzard. Slowly she straightened. *Evidence is like a quantum particle,* she thought. *The act of observing it changes it.*

She decided this wasn't the best time to mention that fact to Alasdair. Neither was it a good time to remind him how he'd prevented her from having a friendly chat with Pen, a chat that would assuredly have touched on family relationships.

Assessing the chill ebbing from his face and the color returning to it, she said, "How about if I go back to the Angle's Rest, see if I can help Pen there and Hugh at the pub?"

He looked around, briefly puzzled, as though surprised to see her.

"Alasdair?"

He seemed to shrink back into himself. He reached up and loosened his tie. He smoothed his kilt. He turned as stiff a smile on Jean as she'd ever seen, but it was a smile nonetheless, rejecting the fierce Ice King—no, that persona had never been an act. "Best be getting yourself back to the B and B. I'm afeart we've got a long night ahead of us."

She leaned quickly in to brush her lips across his cold cheek, prompting the slightest easing of the smile, and she headed back to the B&B.

Moonlight washed away the stars and laid a shimmer on the sea. The towers of Bamburgh were almost invisible against the land behind, except for pinpricks of lighted windows. A boat glided into the harbor. Reinforcements from Berwick? No, that was the Ecclestons' sightseeing boat. It stopped by the pier. A couple of dim figures hurried down from the street and secured the lines.

You'd think the village was deserted, except for the lights blazing in every window and the occasional ultra-serious voice echoing through a doorway or down Cuddy's Close, annotated by bursts of melody from Hugh's guitar. From Hugh's musical security blanket.

Soon the tide would be at its peak, but Clyde and Lance wouldn't be taking the ferry out, not until tomorrow. Until the sun shone again.

The tide flooded and the tide ebbed, people were born, matured, died. Castles rose and either crumbled or became tourist attractions . . . The siren-like screech of Rosalie Banks punctured Jean's reverie. Yes, there she was, clambering off Clyde's boat and onto the breakwater—she'd realized there was a story here after all, and come back. "No one's found Parkinson? And that ginger lass with the flash voice, that's his daughter? Who's in charge then?"

"The Scots fellow, Cameron," someone replied. "He's away with the search parties, though. Stop in the pub. He'll be back."

Jean quickly tried the knob, but the door of the B&B was locked—and a good thing, too. She tapped on its carved wooden panels, hoping Rosalie-the-Reporter wouldn't see her. Or Crawford sitting in his boat in the darkness, well bundled against the chill night air and the frosty remnants of Alasdair's wrath. Talk about being caught between a rock and an icy place. She imagined Crawford not exactly tallying his sins, but certainly re-evaluating his options.

The lock snicked and Rebecca opened the door. "There you are. And before you ask, yes, I had me a look through the peephole before I opened up."

"Good." Jean stepped into what she hoped was—but feared couldn't be—a sanctuary against the perils of the night.

Chapter Thirty-Four

After the cold shop and the colder night, the front hall of the Angle's Rest seemed warm to the point of suffocating. But the aroma of baking breads and steaming coffee made a wonderful contrast to the stench of decay still clinging to Jean's nose hairs.

Locking the door again, Rebecca glanced down the back hall. "Linda's sound asleep. Michael says he's about to go struggling through a field overgrown with heather. You remember that old folk song with a line about 'tripping through the heather'?"

"Yeah," Jean said, peeling off her coat. "That's what you do. You trip over the heather and fall flat on your face."

Pen looked around the corner from the kitchen. She'd changed into her purple sweatsuit, ruffled apron, and green athletic shoes. A floury bandage peeked out from below her pushed-back sleeve. "Jean. James phoned and said—oh, we're so sorry, we had no idea you didn't know Edwin's a relation."

"What?" asked Rebecca, and winced when Jean told her the tale. "Oh. Bad luck, Pen."

"What's done is done."

"How's your arm?" Jean asked.

"It'll be right as rain in no time at all. That Hector, he's a fine lad, isn't he? I'm thinking he and Tara would get on well, with them both being Americans—not that I'd want to see him and Lance battling it out for her hand like knights of old. We've had that sort of argy-bargy on Farnaby already."

An argument over a woman's affection? Jean's ears pricked, but

Pen was already ushering her into the dining area and seating her in front of a thermal carafe and a plate of scones and bacon rolls. She shoved several photo albums to one side and set a cup and plate in front of Jean. "Have all you like—Hugh's taken two carriers full over to the pub—James is saying it's true what Edwin feared, Elaine lifted the chanter from the grave. I hoped he was wrong, but he's a clever lad. Quiet, but clever."

Of course she would defend the father of her grandchildren. No problem. Jean was grateful Pen was taking it all in stride and wasn't throwing her and Alasdair's things out onto the sidewalk.

She had already heard Crawford's version of events. Accepting a cup of coffee—it wasn't as though she was going to get any sleep tonight anyway—she asked, "Why didn't Edwin tell Alasdair he was afraid Elaine had taken the chanter?"

"Well now," Pen said, "Inspector Grinsell was a bit of a tartar, might have caused poor Elaine as much grief as he caused Maggie. And then the inspector himself became the point of the exercise, didn't he? No good distracting the police in the pursuance of their duties with a situation so long gone."

Okay. Jean accepted that as more or less the same answer Crawford had given. She reached for a roll fragrant with the scents of bacon and butter.

Rebecca turned her chair toward the door, the better to hear any childish whimpers from down the hall. Hildy magically appeared and wafted onto a third chair, her ears and eyes showing above the rim of the tabletop like an alligator cruising the surface of the water. Pen scratched her ears and earned a self-satisfied glance.

Jean took too large a bite of the roll and had to wait until she'd chewed and swallowed to say, "Elaine wrapped the chanter in that lovely purple shawl you knitted for her, Pen. I'm afraid it'll be police evidence now."

"I'll make her another." Instead of pulling out her own chair, Pen leaned on its back. Her plump face no longer drooped with worry but was firm with resolve. *Here we are, then. Mustn't complain. Time to launch the boats toward Dunkirk.*

"Elaine had a key to the back room of the bookshop. The room that had been Athelstan's office."

"Aye. Maggie was saying that Wat's old key went missing years ago, but Elaine's likely had it all along. She's got any number of oddments tucked away at Gow House. Souvenirs, in a way. Memories."

"You've spoken with Maggie?" asked Rebecca.

"We've been phoning to and fro all evening. Keeping our spirits up. We're that worried about poor Niamh. Her father murdering Inspector Grinsell, imagine that! Dreadful. Just dreadful. Is the coffee hot enough for you, Jean?"

"It's delicious, thank you." It was just as well the Farnaby jungle telegraph, or mobile network, to be accurate, worked as well as it did. It saved a lot of explanation. Jean gestured with her cup. "It looks as though you have lots of memories in those photo albums."

"I was having myself a wander down memory lane. Fancy having a look at the old days here on Farnaby?"

"I'd love to."

Jean and Rebecca exchanged a significant look beneath Pen's chin while she chose an album from the stack and seated herself. "The other books have photos of Lisa and the grandchildren. You can never have too many photos of the grandchildren, can you now?"

"Not according to my parents and in-laws, no," said Rebecca.

"These are the photos from Camelot. From Wat and Elaine's early years." Pen opened the album to faded snapshots of sunshine and blue skies, the priory and the village, all backdrops to faces, figures, and musical instruments.

Jean recognized Wat in a stocky youth holding a fiddle, his deep-set eyes peering suspiciously out from beneath a sweep of brown hair. There was Elaine, not tall and elegant like a model but like an athlete, her intelligent smile almost mocking the camera. She even caught a glimpse of young Hugh, his beard black and his long dark locks already giving way to a receding hairline. "You can always tell the late sixties and early seventies. All the barbers seem to have gone on strike."

"And we've all added a bit of, well, gravity since then." Pen pointed to a picture of herself and James, their flared-bottom pants and snug shirts making their already willowy bodies seem positively emaciated. She turned a page or two. "There's Thomas Seaton."

Who's pretty much a moot point now. Still Jean took a careful look. Yes, he'd been a handsome young man, his dark hair tousled fetchingly above a sculpted face and movie-star grin. The drones of his pipes lay against his broad shoulder, and he held the chanter almost suggestively in front of his narrow hips. They made them attractive in Cape Breton.

"It's Tom playing the pipe solo on the 'Ravens of Avalon' album. He could stir you to the marrow of your bones. All we lasses were in love with him."

"Maggie thought he might be her biological father," said Jean. "You said that was wishful thinking because she never got along with Wat. She told Grinsell, though, that if she was born a full-term baby she couldn't be Wat's daughter, and since her mother was going on about having a lover . . ." Jean paused delicately.

"Maggie came early. She was a tiny mite of a baby," Pen replied. "The body in the grave's not her father, in any event, since the dates are all wrong."

"Is someone else her father?"

"No, I'm not seeing that at all. By the time Maggie was conceived, the early days—the court of Camelot, the romance—had wasted away into practicality. Wat and Elaine had given up renovating the tower and were planning a purpose-built school."

"Someone dying," said Rebecca, "someone being murdered, will sober you up straightaway."

"Aye, that it will, though we had no idea, mind you, that was what happened." Pen eyed the photo, lost in another time, then turned another page. The tall, lanky man with the beak of a nose and a jaw like a battle axe had to be Athelstan Crawford, even though the look in his eye—part mischief, part arrogance—didn't remind her at all of Edwin, his son.

He stood with his arm around Elaine. Her blond head leaned against his shoulder while her hands were clasped primly in front of her T-shirt, sending contradictory messages. Her smile seemed smug and secretive. Or, Jean asked herself, was she reading too much into a simple snapshot?

Behind the pair, several people lay on blankets spread across green turf. Around them like the spoils of a Viking raid rested a couple of guitars, the remnants of a picnic complete with an array of bottles, and the stubs of cigarettes whose composition was unknowable at this remove. Merlin's Tower rose in the background, lacking only banners floating in the wind to have played a mythical Camelot.

"Athelstan," Jean stated.

"Aye." Pen's frown deepened. "He was artistic, being an architect and all, but no musician. Had a tin ear, if I'm remembering aright. Not the usual sort to be sitting at the round table with Wat. Steady, not unpredictable."

The sort that Elaine might find refreshing. "P.C. Crawford told us that he heard his mother say his father fancied Elaine more than was good for either of them, because Wat was the jealous sort and contentious as well. Did Elaine fancy him back?

Is her talking about a lover dementia at all, or a memory surfacing from below a layer of regret?"

Jean expected Pen to sit up and protest, *You're not the cop, why are you interrogating me?*

Gently, Rebecca pushed their advantage. "You said you'd not like to see Lance and Hector battling for Tara's hand, that you'd seen that sort of argy-bargy before. Can you expand on that?"

Pen's thoughtfulness deepened to outright rumination. Jean reached for another scone and nibbled at it. Giving up on getting any snacks, Hildy jumped down and made her way to the fireplace, where she settled on the hearth rug in front of the glowing bars of the electric fire.

"Oh my, my, my." At last Pen's pin curls bounced in an affirmative nod and her focus returned. "After all these years, to see how it all must have happened . . . Well, you see, Elaine flirted with all of the chaps. She liked the attention, and Wat liked showing her off, even as he also drew a strict line where the flirting had to stop."

"He liked being in control," said Rebecca.

"He did that, aye. They fought over Thomas. They fought over Athelstan as well, though here's me, thinking they were fighting over plans for renovating the Tower, not Athelstan himself, him being married and all. She'd come running here, leaving the house to Wat's stamping and shouting. They all enjoyed a bottle of best, or second best, come to that, but Wat, he'd often take a bit too much. The artistic temperament, I expect."

An easy excuse, Jean thought, but she said nothing. Pushing her empty plate aside, she leaned in. So did Rebecca.

A door slammed open, admitting a cold draft. All three women jumped, Jean completely out of her chair. "Hugh?" called Pen, swiveling toward the hall door.

Maggie stepped into the doorway, her multicolored hair flying, her cheeks red, her eyes glittering as brightly as the butcher knife she held in her hands. "Jean. I hoped you were here. I hoped you were giving poor Pen the third degree. I can't stand it. I've got to know."

Chapter Thirty-Five

Pen found her voice first. "Elaine? Tara?"

"Mum's asleep. Tara's got herself a cricket bat and is walking round the house like a lioness. She's my girl, isn't she?" Maggie's grin flared and died. "Lance is standing sentry on the front porch. He's even got an old shotgun, looks like one should be in a museum."

Pen, standing *in loco maternis,* asked, "Maggie, dear, are you quite certain you're wanting that knife?"

Maggie held it before her—Jean expected her to declaim Lady Macbeth's famous speech—then set it down on the sideboard.

"Um, Pen," asked Rebecca, "isn't your back door locked?"

"I've got a key." Maggie lifted a metal ring dangling several keys, from small lock-box to big metal skeleton, along with a glow-in-the-dark Statue of Liberty. "This is Mum's key to the bookshop, if you want it for evidence. I left the lot of them on the hall table yesterday morning and just found them in her room."

"We never lock our doors here," Pen added. "Not usually, leastways."

Maggie focused on Jean, so intently Jean had to keep herself from making a warding gesture. "So you were chatting with Donal at the school? I thought he looked familiar, but I'd never have guessed it was him. Sad to see him like that. That fine-looking face, and charm to die for, and well, you know why the

Irish pipes have a bellows instead of a mouthpiece to blow up the bag? So the piper can hand you his line of blarney as he plays."

As one, Jean, Rebecca, and Pen turned up the corners of their lips, but taken together all three of them didn't make one decent smile.

"Did I say charm to die for?" Maggie's eyes appealed to the ceiling. "Donal's a murderer. He and Oliver wrestled for the gun and Donal got it, free and clear. He had it in his hands. Then he turned it on Oliver. I'll never forget the look in his eyes as he pulled the trigger."

"You protected him, even so," Jean said softly.

"Yes. He already had a wife and daughter and here I was up the spout and—oh, it was a bloody mess. In more ways than one. I've been thinking about it. My biggest mistake in not grassing him up was giving Grinsell the chance to interfere." As it had at the side of the tomb, her chuckle edged toward hysteria.

This time it was Pen who rose from her chair, took Maggie firmly by the shoulders, and sat her down at the table. "You've probably had nothing to eat all evening. Have a scone."

Rebecca pushed the serving platter and the butter and jam dishes toward her while Pen brought another cup from the sideboard. Jean doubted the wisdom of pouring caffeine into Maggie. Even though she once again smelled of whisky, if so faintly she might as well have dabbed it behind her ears as drunk it, she had that wired look of someone who'd already had three espressos. But, noting that Pen poured almost more cream than coffee into the cup, Jean kept her own counsel and sat back down.

"And now Donal's killed Grinsell. I'd say good riddance, but no, that's not right." Maggie pinched off a corner of the scone but left it on the plate. "Donal fixed the blame for Oliver's death on me—I played him false, didn't I, going with Oliver?

Now he's fixed the blame for his prison term on Grinsell. That's like him. The brooding seemed romantic, once. Now I see that he's always looking to blame someone else."

"What of Niamh?" Pen asked. "Is she helping him, do you think?"

"I don't see why. She never knew him, spoke of him as nothing more than the sperm donor. If he turned up, though . . ." Maggie laughed again, this time ruefully, under her breath. "Ever since Mum started talking about having a lover, I've wondered if I had a sperm donor. Tom Seaton, she kept a photo of him in her dresser drawer. But it's not him in the grave, is it? And the man in the grave's not my father."

"Alasdair's thinking the body is Athelstan Crawford," Jean told her.

"Edwin's dad? Really? Another of Mum's knights. Queen Guinevere and not-so-courtly love."

Pen said, "Edwin's saying he and Lisa once found a note from Elaine thanking Athelstan for giving her a book of poetry."

"He told me about that," said Jean. "The dates match up. The physical characteristics of the body match up. In time they can get a DNA sample and settle the matter."

"Giving the man in the grave a name's more important than finding me another dad. I have one. I had one. He's gone now. Too late." Maggie tore off another bit of scone.

Pen smoothed the tablecloth. "Edwin's mum was telling Lisa how, as a lad, he'd read the stories of Arthur and ask if his dad was coming back some day as well. He liked Malory—is it Malory? How men say in parts of England that King Arthur isn't dead, but by the will of God has gone into another place?"

"That's Malory, yes. More or less."

"But Athelstan wasn't sent into another place by the will of God, was he?"

Jean felt as though she tiptoed across a waterbed, every word making her lean in a slightly different direction, with the possibility of pitching forward in a pratfall an ever-present danger. "The thing is, Athelstan disappeared on a wildfowling trip. A fog came up and separated him from his companions. They washed up on Farnaby, but his boat was found far out to sea. How did he end up in the tomb?"

"The currents," murmured Pen. "If they swept the other boats in to Farnaby, why not Athelstan's as well? You've seen what a sea fret is like. The boats could have landed on the same beach and the men would be none the wiser."

"Athelstan could have come ashore and seen his chance to meet up with Mum in secret," Maggie said. "Maybe they had an assignation. A rendezvous. Fancy words for a dishonorable bit of business."

"If one," Rebecca murmured in turn, "with a very long pedigree."

"Adultery. Takes one—me—to know one, eh?" Maggie managed to get a morsel of scone into her mouth and chew.

Jean asked Pen, "Up until tonight you thought it was Tom in the grave, didn't you?"

"Aye, that I did."

"Did Wat kill Athelstan over Elaine, do you think? Or did Tom kill him, ditto, and Wat had nothing to do with it? We've thought all along it was a crime of passion, but there seems to have been enough passion to go around."

"Yes," said Pen. "It was a crime of passion, so far as I know."

Maggie turned her glittering eye on Pen. "You've been protecting Mum all these years. Well done, Pen. But it's time to tell what you know."

"But I don't *know,* I've only just put together hints. The one thing—I'm sorry, Maggie dear, but the one thing I do know is this: Elaine confessed to me that once, only once, she was unfaithful to Wat."

Maggie nodded stiffly, her jaw set. "When?"

"You and Lisa were going on six or so. James and Wat were preparing a barbecue at the school and Elaine and I were here cutting vegetables and the like."

"Not when did she tell you. When did it happen?"

"Ah. Well. Whilst Wat was on tour in seventy-one, she said. He was on the road more than he was home in the old days, working to pay for building the school and all. She was telling me that if he could he'd have locked her up tight in a chastity belt every time he was away."

Jean caught Rebecca's glance and tossed it back again. Chastity belts were creations of the Victorian obsession with sex, illicit and otherwise, not truly medieval artifacts.

"He always accused her of infidelity," said Maggie. "No more than his usual bluster, I always thought."

"It was that. And as Elaine told me that day, it was all too little, too late. She'd locked herself away years ago, after the one disastrous—adventure was the word she used. Adventure gone wrong." Pen brushed at the snow-white tablecloth and then considered her fingertips, perhaps to see if they were matted with blood rather than crumbs. "I remembered that day, a sea fret in late seventy-one, the day Athelstan went missing. Two days before Tom vanished from the island."

Maggie pushed her scone away. "Athelstan told everyone he was going wildfowling. When he saw the fret coming up he made his way to Farnaby, knowing Dad was away. Is that it?"

"I believe so. You must understand, love, Elaine didn't tell me all this as a coherent narrative, but in bits and pieces, like coals dragged out of a fire."

"Yes. I should think so."

"She said *he* turned up at Gow House—it's only now I'm realizing *he* was Athelstan. Only a few students were living there at the time, and they were all away. She and *he* were alone. They ended up in her bedroom. How, I didn't ask, although I suspect the whisky was involved."

Lots of poor decisions were incited by alcohol, Jean thought. "Did he force himself on her?"

"I'm thinking not, no. Easy for her to say he took her flirting as agreement, but she never said that. Likely she did agree, however briefly."

Maggie's hands on the tabletop closed into fists.

"She said when she saw *him* asleep on Wat's pillow, snoring fit to beat the band, she was overcome with disgust. With guilt. She hated herself. She hated *him.*" Pen made a thrusting motion, barely missing the coffee pot. "She gestured with the knife she was using to cut the carrots, an outward sort of punch that made me think she'd hit him with something whilst he slept, to wake him and send him on his way. Now, though, now I see . . ." Reclaiming her hand, Pen buried her face in it, hiding her eyes.

Maggie leaped from the chair and walked across the room to the bookshelves, where she stood with her back turned. Rebecca eased to her feet and slipped away, whispering, "I'll have a look at the baby."

Jean's center of gravity seemed to have sunk to her feet. She sat immobile, not seeing the coffee pot, the plate, the crumbs. She saw Elaine in a paroxysm of guilt and grief snatch up the first thing that came to hand—Tom's chanter; he lived at Gow House; his pipes were there—she saw Athelstan asleep, snoring, maybe drooling as people sometimes did when sleeping soundly . . . That was why the victim held still. He was asleep.

Elaine's gesture was one of sexual violence. A long object inserted forcibly in an open mouth. The thrust with the distraught woman's full weight behind it. Athelstan waking, gasping, choking, but Elaine unrelenting, leaning in. It was as much her fault as his, but in that moment it was on his head. It was in his head.

No, as Pen had said over lunch, it hadn't been like Wat to creep about and premeditate. No one had crept about and premeditated. It had been very much a crime of passion, in more ways than one.

Jean croaked, cleared her throat, asked, "Do you know how Athelstan's body ended up in the tomb?"

Pen looked up, sniffed, dabbed at her eyes with the corner of her apron. "No. How could I? I didn't know he, the lover, was dead, did I? Not till Maggie opened the grave yesterday."

Maggie said to the bookshelf, her voice barely carrying across the room, "Mum's always been beguiled by that tomb. That was when she levered up the inscribed stone and broke it, I reckon. When she had a body to hide."

"You don't pick up a dead body like a sack of groceries." There was an echo in here. Jean had said the same thing to Alasdair in this very room, last night. Funny how close to the truth he'd come when he'd pointed out the inconvenience of dying during sex. "You don't put clothes on a dead body, not easily."

"Maybe Athelstan didn't remove his clothes," Maggie said. "A quick encounter, there's no real need."

Jean envisioned the wellie boots. There were romantic articles of clothing for you. But yes, he could have died with his boots on. "The bottom line is, she couldn't have hidden the body alone. She had help."

"That old rusted wheelbarrow in the garden. She used it all the time when I was a child."

"Okay, yes, a big wheelbarrow to roll the body across to the priory in the fog. But I meant human help getting the body into the wheelbarrow to begin with . . . Oh."

"Tom," said Pen, taking the name from Jean's lips. "That's Tom's role. He came home and found Elaine with Athelstan's body. He found that his own chanter had been used to kill a man."

"He found his queen was a murderer. A murderess, she'd probably have said herself." Maggie's voice fell into a whisper. "She was only defending herself."

"A little hard to claim self-defense," Jean replied as quietly.

Maggie darted a look like a javelin over her shoulder. "You—your husband—the police—they can't bring her up on charges! Look at her!"

"They can't bring her up on charges," Jean replied, "because this is all supposition. Even if they found Elaine's fingerprints on the chanter, well, she picked it up yesterday, didn't she? Any older prints on there have probably decayed into illegibility anyway. And no. She's not competent."

Maggie turned again to the bookshelf and ran her fingertips lightly down the spines of the books.

Rebecca padded back into the room. "So, in the fall of seventy-one, when did Wat get home?"

"Soon as the fret cleared," Pen said. "The next day. He appeared unexpectedly, saying his gig had been cancelled, as though he meant to catch her at it. All this time I've been thinking he did catch her at—at something. At something with Tom. The next day he'd vanished as though abducted by aliens. He even left his pipes. You don't do that without good motive."

"He had one," added Jean. "Sergeant Darling says Clyde says his father remembers Tom beating such a fast retreat he left 'bits and bobs' behind. A set of pipes is more than bits and bobs."

Maggie pulled one of the excavation reports off the shelf. "I've seen those pipes. They're at the school."

Well then. D.C.I. Webber could have the chanter tested to see if it was part of the set. And if he could prove it was, what then? Pin the crime on Thomas Seaton, deceased? Wat Lauder, deceased? Elaine Lauder, no longer part of this space–time continuum?

Pen slid down in her chair. "Tom must have untied Athelstan's boat, pushed it offshore—if the tide was running, it was long gone by the time the fret cleared. He couldn't defend himself to Wat. He couldn't tell anyone the truth. He'd helped cover up a murder. He'd have been on trial alongside Elaine."

"I suppose," said Rebecca, "they hid the body in the tomb instead of putting it back into the boat, fearing that the boat would be found . . ."

"As it was," Pen said.

". . . and the nature of Athelstan's injury would tell all. Or tell too much, in any event."

The hum of the electric fire and Hildy's quiet breath made the only noise. Then Pen said, "I know why now Elaine was so generous to Lisa and Edwin when they married. Blood money. Edwin growing up without a father. It was on her head."

"If not for me opening the grave, Mum would have gotten away with murder. Edwin would never have known the ugly truth. Inspector Grinsell would still be alive and badgering someone else. And Donal . . ." Maggie turned around, setting her shoulders, eyeing the photos along the mantelpiece, her face grim as granite. She held the book against her chest like a shield. "I meant to validate Mum's work, damn it. That's all I meant."

Pen hauled herself to her feet and plodded across the room as though every step hurt. She put her arm around Maggie. "There, there, lass. You didn't know."

Had I but known, Jean thought. Funny how often she'd heard that.

Pen told Jean, "The card Alasdair was showing me earlier, with Wat's notes for a memorial for Athelstan. I found that in a library book when I was tidying up Elaine's room some months back. I showed it to her, but she—she didn't remember. I brought it along and tucked it away in my copy of *Britannia.* Merlin, that's Athelstan's nickname."

"The name on the card is written over the name 'Mordred' or 'Medraut,' " Jean pointed out. "Her final summation of Athelstan, maybe? A traitor?"

Pen could only shake her head. "This evening, when she said Athelstan was the romantic sort, that she gave him her glove—she'd give out old gloves, yes, part of their play-acting, but this time roundit's a metaphor for, well, you know. Isn't it?"

"Probably," mumbled Maggie.

"That's when I dropped the kettle. I realized I'd had the wrong end of the stick all these years."

"And all your suspicions fell into place," said Jean. "I've been there, although not on such a personal basis. By the way, did you take Elaine's booklet, *Hilda, the Enchanted Prioress,* from our room?"

"Oh. Aye, I did that. Sorry. The inscription in that book, about bodies being buried—when Elaine wrote that some years ago I thought nothing of it, but after Maggie found the body, well, I thought it might be a bit too revealing."

"She's still feeling guilty," said Maggie. "Even now. Even when she's not herself."

Jean wondered if Elaine, given the choice, would have preferred to have her personal tragedy play out in public the way Maggie's had. Or would Maggie, given the choice, prefer to have kept hers hidden? Either way produced a psychic ghost, a mind haunted with a demon that could never be exorcized.

Again silence filled the room, a silence prickling with unease. It should by rights be a dark and stormy night outside. The waves should be crashing on the shore, thunder should be rolling and lightning flashing. There should be a wild-eyed face looking in the window . . .

A fusillade of knocks echoed through the house. All four

women jumped, then ran one after another into the hall.

A haggard face beneath a floppy canvas hat was pressed to the glass of the back door, and the wide eyes staring into the house brimmed with terror.

Chapter Thirty-Six

When Pen jerked open the door, a shivering Elaine fell rather than stepped inside. She wore only pajamas, a bathrobe, and open-toed slippers.

"Mum!" Maggie wrapped her arm around Elaine's frail shoulders. "You're frozen!"

Words came from Elaine's purplish lips. "Wat's in a frightful temper. He's cutting up rough. That pretty girl with the, the hair like that spice—cinnamon, paprika—she's blubbing like a baby."

"Tara? Tara's weeping?" asked Maggie.

A wave of horror made Jean reel with nausea. "Or does she mean Niamh?"

"Who's playing the part of Wat?" Rebecca asked.

"Oh, my God." Maggie almost hurled Elaine into Pen's arms. "It's Donal, he's got into the house—what's he doing with Tara—where's Lance?"

Through the open doorway Jean saw lights like fireflies on the hillside above the priory. The search parties, blundering around in the dark, missing their quarry.

She'd been right about Donal circling back to a place already searched, damn it all anyway. Jean sprinted for her bag and her phone. Alasdair. Call Alasdair.

Maggie whipped her phone out of the pocket of her cardigan. Rebecca slammed the door, then rushed down the back hall. Pen guided Elaine into the dining area, murmuring soothingly.

Her face, turned to Jean past Elaine's bent head, was that of a carnival mask, emotion stripped of all social constraints. *Help her! Help us!*

"Tara's not answering her phone." Maggie's fingertips danced over the tiny screen. "The house phone, no, not that either. Oh shit."

"Jean." Alasdair's calm voice emanated from the phone jammed against her ear. "We've not found—"

"He's at Gow House. Elaine ran across to Pen's saying that Wat's cutting up rough and the pretty girl with the cinnamon hair is crying, and she has to be talking about Donal and maybe Niamh but certainly Tara and Lance are there too."

"Slow down, Jean. Breathe. What are you saying?"

Jean forced a ragged breath into the vise of her lungs and went through it again, more slowly if equally lacking in punctuation.

"Where's he been then?" Alasdair demanded.

"Oh shit," Maggie said again, this time holding up her key ring with its ghostly Statue of Liberty. "The key to the church. It's not on the ring. It was there yesterday morning when I opened up for the press conference. Parkin—Donal was there, wasn't he? He saw me with the key. He had Niamh take it off the ring and bring it to him."

"He's been hiding in the church," Jean told Alasdair. "He was right under our noses. He and Niamh, they've been here all along—you mobilized everyone too fast for him to get off the island."

"That was you and your thinking, connecting Parkinson to McCarthy."

Jean waved her free hand. "Whatever, he's backed into a corner now."

Alasdair's voice issued rapid-fire orders. When it came clearly to her ears again, he said, "Darling had a look at the church.

Both the front and the vestry doors were locked up tight."

"He has a key. He sat there waiting until everyone fanned out over the island and then went after Maggie. Except she's here at the B and B."

"He saw me leaving Gow House—where's my knife?" Maggie disappeared into the dining room. Rebecca reappeared in the hall. "Michael and his group are hurrying back, but they're a good half-mile away."

"Alasdair," Jean asked, "where are you?"

"Just beyond Merlin's Tower. We're running as fast as we can. I've alerted Darling. Stay clear of the scene."

Yeah, right, like anyone would be able to stay clear of the scene.

Alasdair's breath came in short bursts. "Jean, are you hearing me?"

"I'm hearing you. I hope I'm seeing you real soon." And the connection broke. It was only then Jean realized Alasdair had actually complimented her loup of logic. Maybe he owed her three pence for her thoughts, even.

In the living room, Pen had Elaine tucked up on the couch, a small blanket wrapping her legs and feet, Hildy installed on her lap as combination hot water bottle and soft toy. Elaine's blue-veined hands clutched a cup but she stared into it, not drinking.

If Pen had been sixteen, say, when the Lauders came to Farnaby, she was about six years younger than Elaine. Now Elaine looked twenty years older, rocking back and forth, muttering under her breath. "Wat. He's in a frightful temper. Arthur. Lost his—the thing with a point, sharp. Sword. Excrement. That's its name."

"Excalibur," Pen told Elaine, and to Jean, "Like old times, her running down here. Save it's not like old times at all."

"I found it. Not in a stone. Beneath it. In a—the place you bury a man. Buried Lancelot, not Merlin, dead and buried. The queens live on whilst the king's a dreadful mess. Dreadful." Releasing the cup—Pen snatched it before it fell—Elaine produced a small flashlight from the pocket of her robe. "I don't know where I got this. It's a—it's not a candle. It lights up the corners."

"Niamh gave you that," said Maggie from the sideboard. She ran the edge of the knife across her thumbnail, testing its sharpness. "Are they both there at the house, Mum? Niamh and Tara both? With Wat?"

"Arthur." Elaine switched the flashlight on and off. Hildy looked up, intrigued by the moving point of light but too comfortable to leap down and chase it. "Wat's Arthur. Athelstan's Merlin. Medraut. I gave him my glove. Dreadful mess."

Glove, Jean thought. Love with a G-spot.

"What did you do with the sword?" Pen collapsed on the edge of the couch. "Did you take it to Athelstan's office? Is that where it belongs, where, erm, Merlin works?"

Elaine played with the flashlight. "Medraut. He had a sword. They said he killed Arthur. But it was Guinevere, it was the queen of Avalon. Without her, nothing."

Maggie turned to the door. "We'll sort this later, if we can. In the meantime . . ."

"Yeah, I'm coming." Jean spotted a set of fireplace tools at the end of the hearth. Judging by the trace of ash on their tips, they'd only recently been demoted to decorative purposes when Pen and James installed the electric fire. She pulled the poker from the rack and tried bending it. Thick, sturdy, black iron.

What the hell she thought she could do with that, or Maggie with the knife, she had no idea. But there was something very satisfying about that cold iron clasped in her hand.

"Take care," Pen told them. At least, that's what Jean thought she said, with her voice stopped up in her throat.

Silently, her face stern, Rebecca brought Jean her coat and

walked her and Maggie to the back door. She opened it and then shut it behind them. Jean stood beside Maggie in the sudden cold air and listened to the key turn in the lock. She didn't look back into the lighted house. She looked over the garden wall toward Gow House, its gables and chimneys defined by cool moonlight, its windows by warm incandescent light.

Footsteps and voices converged on it from every direction. If the shadowy figures had been carrying burning torches instead of the electric kind, they'd have resembled a mob from a horror movie.

Jean and Maggie slipped through the garden gate into Cuddy's Close and found themselves walking beside Hugh, whose face was even darker than when he sang songs about bigotry and injustice.

On his other side, Rosalie chattered away. ". . . so this McCarthy chap was on trial . . ."

"Haud your wheesht, woman!" he snapped, marginally more polite than "Shut up!" in that she probably didn't understand broad Scots dialect—no doubt why he was using it, as an arcane way of swearing.

Jean's distended perceptions registered moving lights in the harbor, as though a UFO was coming in for a landing. They detected a ripple of unease from the priory, the strong emotions of the gathering crowd vibrating the sheer membrane between everyday and paranormal. Mostly, though, her senses focused on the house behind the low wall, past the wrought-iron gate, over the nodding leaves of Elaine's garden.

Every curl and scallop of the Gothic Revival carving along the eaves of Gow House seemed tense, spines bristling in alarm. No one moved behind the arched windows. The lighted porch was an empty cube.

Almost everyone stopped on the blacktop of the parking lot. Jean and Maggie kept going, edging between the now-silent watchers until they stood between them and the gate. On the right the school loomed like a hard-edged hillock. On the left, beyond the mound of the church, the priory lay like a filigree of stone. Overhead the moon looked like a hole punctured in the darkness, the light of another universe shining through.

Except for the slight shuffle of feet and Maggie's breath ragged beside her, the parking area was so quiet Jean heard the clock strike inside the house. She counted down the deep-throated dongs from one to twelve.

Then a rattle of footsteps became Alasdair running along the face of the throng, holding his phone so that its glowing screen illuminated his cold, keen face. ". . . at the house, aye."

His sideways glance registered Jean standing at the front of the group of people. His mouth tightened. His peremptory gesture to her, to Maggie, to everyone was a clear command: *Get back, dammit!*

Like a giant amoeba, the gathered islanders and visitors oozed back. Jean took a couple of steps after them. Maggie stood her ground.

Darling pushed through from the direction of the village, his own phone in one hand, something small and black in the other. He passed that off to Alasdair.

A gun. Jean hadn't seen Alasdair with a gun in his hand since they'd first met. Where on earth had Darling . . .

Another, bulkier man stepped up between Darling and Alasdair, the glow of the house reflecting off his mahogany complexion. Oh. The lights in the harbor. Not a UFO, the police boat from Berwick, with D.C.I. Webber personally in charge. Good man.

From her peripheral vision Jean saw a dark figure slipping along behind the cemetery wall. Another one picked his way along the hillside behind the house. The moonlight glinted from something long and thin in his hands. More guns, rifles with long barrels. It wasn't exactly the cavalry arriving in a cloud of dust—they were easing onto the scene with cat-footed stealth—this might not be a battle that could be won by force of arms.

". . . cannot storm the house unless we know what's going on inside." Alasdair's breath rose before him but didn't soften his features.

"No one's answering any phone number we've got," returned Webber, "including the one off Grinsell's phone that must be McCarthy's own."

"Your mother sounded the alarm?" Alasdair asked Maggie.

"She was asleep, but she doesn't sleep well—seems to be the voices woke her up and she got herself out the side door. I shouldn't have gone off without her. I should have sent Tara away earlier today." Her face contorted.

"How'd McCarthy get into the house?"

Maggie's voice cracked as she forced out words. "It's normally never locked, but Niamh has a key. She's working with him, isn't she? She'd have had both parents if not for me. She knows that."

Gently Jean reached out and pulled Maggie back. Her entire body trembled so hard the vibrations ran up Jean's arm and made her teeth rattle and the poker in her other hand thrum like the drones of a set of pipes.

Someone stepped up beside them. Hector, his black eyes gleaming. "I've got her." He drew Maggie from Jean's hand and wrapped a strong arm firmly around her quivering shoulders.

Breathing like a threshing machine, Clyde popped out of the crowd and came to a halt on Maggie's other side. "Pen's telling me Lance is in there."

"Yes," she replied, "he turned up with an old shotgun. Says it's one you've had locked in the safe for years. Some chap left it behind after a wildfowling trek."

"Ah. That one. It wasn't loaded, but we've got shells put by for the trippers."

"When I left, he was standing on the porch with it." The rest of her sentence, *but he's not there now,* twisted slowly in the icy breeze from the sea.

The porch light winked out. The front door cracked open, showing a thin strip of illumination.

A murmur ran through the crowd. Several people pressed forward, only to have a couple of uniformed figures push them back again.

The lights in the windows faded to dim glows, as did the stripe beside the door. And in the sudden shadow, the door opened.

Chapter Thirty-Seven

Two human shapes, standing very close together, stepped out onto the porch. Blinking frantically against the darkness, Jean made out Donal's colorless hair and pasty complexion. Tucked in beside his cheek, Tara's chin-length russet hair framed red, swollen eyes now devoid of all expression.

Her wrists were hidden behind her back—he must have tied them. His arms pressed her body tightly against his, his hands holding the shotgun upright and pointed at her chin. An awkward posture, that, requiring him to stand in a half-crouch if he wanted to keep his fingers on the trigger. Triggers, maybe. To fire, he'd have to press them down rather than pull them up. His body was off-balance. But then, he'd always been off-balance, and was all the more dangerous for it.

Maggie rocked back against Hector. The white knuckles of her hand clutching the knife looked like old bone. Beneath her breath she murmured a litany of distress. "Oh my little lass. I'm so sorry. I should never have brought you here. I should have left well alone and never found you, never sucked you into all this. You were free. Without me, you were free."

Clyde's bellow shattered the silence. "Where's Lance?"

"Having himself a bit of a kip," replied Donal. "Niamh's looking after him. Angel of mercy, that's a good girl."

Hector said under his breath, "Dang it, Niamh. Why?"

From the darkness, Darling replied, his tone bleak, "She's his daughter, that's why."

"Seriously? Crap-tastic."

Instead of speculating how the romantic chain seemed to have acquired another link, Jean told herself that Donal's saying Lance was napping meant he was unconscious. Hopefully he was no more than unconscious, although a concussion bad enough to cause unconsciousness tended to be serious.

A shape, an image sketched in shadow on twilight, moved in the window to the left of the door. A slender female shape. Niamh. Yes, she must be helping him. All the years of seeing other girls with fathers but having none, that would build more than curiosity, that would build resentment, maybe even a desire for revenge.

Alasdair looked at Webber. Webber made a slight gesture. *It's all yours.* Tucking the gun into the pocket of his coat, Alasdair stepped forward, hands raised. But before he could speak, a tall, lanky figure pushed through the crowd and stepped in front of him.

Crawford. He'd broken out of detention . . . That's right, Alasdair had said something about relieving him of duty when Berwick arrived. Berwick had duly arrived, but Webber had either been in a forgiving mood or realized the occasion demanded all hands on deck.

"Crawford!" Alasdair hissed, an impressive feat when the name had no sibilants.

Ignoring him, the constable lifted his hands into the air and took several more steps toward the house. A convulsive movement on the porch stopped him an arm's length from the gate. Had Tara tried to pull away and Donal jerked her back? Or had Donal deliberately shaken her as a warning? They were no more than a double bulk against the faintly illuminated rectangle of the doorway.

All Jean could see was Crawford standing solitary as a prehistoric megalith in the moonlight, his uniform the color of ebony, his face shadowed by the bill of his cap. "Best you be releasing the lass now," he said.

"Chance would be a fine thing," Donal replied.

No one seemed to be emitting a steamy breath any longer. Everyone had either stopped breathing or was so chilled their breaths were no longer warm. Alasdair dropped back to stand beside Webber, their faces positive and negative images of the same grim expression.

"What are you wanting, then?" Crawford's voice seemed even deeper than usual, a well of patience.

"What do you think, numpty? Safe passage off the island to the mainland. A fast boat. That little police boat in the harbor, that's yours, eh? That'll do. And a car waiting ashore."

"You're only putting off the inevitable, Donal. Best you be cooperating."

"I shan't be going back to prison. I know what's waiting for me inside."

Crawford shifted his weight. The tiny movement made the insignia on his uniform brighten and darken. "It's not your fault, is it, Donal? If Grinsell had left well alone, Maggie would have been freed and you as well. No fault. No foul. No harm done."

The Phillips family would have another opinion on that, Jean thought.

"Grinsell." Donal spat the name. "He cost me my marriage. He cost me my daughter. Like Oliver Phillips, he deserved what he got. As for Maggie, the bitch—it's on her head, isn't it? Are you there, Maggie? Are you hearing this?"

Maggie's head fell forward on a long sigh, but for once she was wise enough not to respond.

Crawford wisely did not ask who made Donal judge, jury, and executioner. He said, "Tara there, she's your daughter as well."

"Niamh's telling me that. She's saying the pair of them, they have the same father."

"You wouldn't harm your own daughter, would you now?"

"No matter. They were both taken from me. I don't know them at all, do I?"

Jean had thought Alasdair's voice in the old book shop had been cold. Compared to Donal's hard, cold callousness, it had been positively tropical.

Far away, a sheep bleated. The dark shapes in the cemetery crept even closer. The leaves of the herbaceous border at the far side of the garden moved against the wind. "Didn't know I'd be wanting sharpshooters," whispered Webber.

"No one's getting in a good shot," Alasdair whispered back. "Not in the dark, with her held so close."

Again Donal jerked Tara up and back, a dog with a rat in its jaws. Her gasp of terror was loud as a scream. "Enough chin-wagging. You'd best be organizing the boat and the car, Constable Numpty."

"I've got lads seeing to it," Crawford said. "Till then, no harm in us having a chat."

Crawford sure had a glib tongue on him. Who knew?

A movement in the doorway behind Donal. A shape lurching inside the darkened house. A halo atop its head—a mane of blond hair. Lance.

Beside Jean, Maggie inhaled sharply and struggled against Hector's grasp. A quickly suppressed murmur ran through the crowd. Alasdair tensed, Webber clenched his fists, Darling crouched. Crawford's voice grew louder and yet calmer at the same time. "We're moving the boat next the steps, Donal. We've got a car coming to the ferry landing near Beal—the tide's in. You'll be away quicker, going past Lindisfarne."

A human body plunged out of the doorway and collided with the double shape that was Donal and Tara, pushing it a long step across the porch. The watchers swirled—some people leaping forward, some back, some—like Jean—dancing up and down in place.

But no one moved as fast as Crawford. He didn't open the gate. He vaulted over it, landing halfway up the sidewalk, his feet running as they hit the ground.

Alasdair jumped forward. So did Darling. The gate opened. The two men jammed together briefly in the opening, then popped out into the garden and ran.

On the porch the now triple shape staggered to the side. Light glanced off the barrel of the shotgun, angled now . . . Lance fell with a sickening crump against a supporting post and slid down it.

Crawford threw himself onto the porch, making another triple shape, which heaved right, then heaved left. And an explosion lit up the night.

The flash glared off two different faces, mouths gaping, eyes staring. Then it was gone, leaving the shadow darker than before. The report rolled away across the island, echoed off the back of the village houses, disappeared over the sea.

Dogs barked. Seabirds screeched. People seethed across the parking lot. The Berwick cops spilled over the walls and out of the shrubbery and formed a perimeter. Someone switched on the lights in the house and on the porch.

Maggie threw Hector to one side, dropped the knife, and sprinted toward the house screaming. "Tara! Tara!"

Jean ran after her, every pulse in her body palpitating, bracing herself for what she'd see in the glare of the light.

Blood, and more than blood, splattered the porch and the walls, Tara's sweater and jeans and her face. Maggie clutched her close, sobbing, scrabbling at the rope, curtain pull, bathrobe cord—the strip of fabric binding her wrists. Released, Tara clutched Maggie close and sobbed like a lost child.

Crawford held the shotgun up in the air, playing keep-away. Gesturing in victory. Frozen in horror. The red blotches didn't show up as well on the dark fabric of his uniform, except where they obscured the insignia. His dour gaze was fixed on the stock of the gun.

Lance sat propped against the post, fresh blood sprinkled on his clothing, old brown blood matted in his hair. Clyde heaved the wicker basket into the yard and threw himself down beside his son. Hector pushed in. "Look at me, Lance. Try to focus." And, under his breath, "I was so not intending a busman's holiday."

Donal's body lay on the other side of the porch. The mutilated face was, thankfully, draped in shadow.

Niamh stood in the doorway. She swayed in one direction, bounced off the door frame, swayed back again. Her complexion brought new meaning to the word "fair," so white it seemed faintly green, a shade that clashed with her red hair.

Darling waded through the others to take her in a firm embrace. At first she stood stiffly in his arms, then relaxed against his chest. Okay, Jean thought, so she wasn't trying to make a break for it. But . . .

Tara sniffed. "Coming here. Worst. Decision. Ever."

Maggie sniffed. "I'm so sorry. I'm so sorry."

"Okay, Mags. S'okay." The two women rocked each other back and forth on the edge of the porch.

One of the Berwick cops appeared with a thin thermal blanket, which he laid over Donal's body. Webber stood surveying the battleground. Alasdair looked around, saw Jean, reached back for her. "What are you going to do with that?"

"What?" She saw she still grasped the poker. "I don't know. Made me feel better."

"Ah, Bonny Jean." He pried her fingers from the handle and let it fall to the earth, making a dull thud. His hand engulfed hers. It was cold, but seemed warm by comparison to the icy chills trickling through her body. She leaned against his side.

Something poked her rib cage. Oh. What was that old joke? Something about are you glad to see me or are you carrying a gun? She couldn't remember.

She could have sworn she heard Michael's voice, and James's, and Hugh's, and Rosalie Banks's, clashing notes in the distance. Up close, a female voice spoke, tones soft and dull. Niamh, peering out from Darling's chest toward the shrouded corpse. "He saw me when he came here for Maggie's press conference. He recognized me. Guess my mum sending all those photos wasn't wasted at all, was it?" Her laugh was more of a gulping sob.

Darling made soothing noises into the top of her head. Hector glanced up, shrugged, turned his attention back to Lance. "No, don't try to stand up. We've gotta get you to a hospital."

Niamh swallowed and said, "He stopped me in the garden late last night. Scared the living daylights out of me. I gave him some sandwiches and a torch, hoping he'd go away. When I saw Inspector Grinsell this morning, when you were talking about him being bashed with a torch—I didn't want to believe it. I couldn't."

"You saw Donal sitting in the audience at the concert," Alasdair stated.

"Yes. I'd hoped he'd gone away, but with the fret he was stranded here. He stopped me outside the school, insisted I give him the key to the church from Maggie's ring—I'm so sorry, Maggie, if I'd cut and run just then . . ."

"You were curious about him," said Maggie over Tara's head. "You never knew him. You thought it was all right to talk."

"Yes. He almost had me convinced he hadn't bashed Grinsell at all—though he kept saying you'd done it, and I knew that wasn't right. Then I caught sight of the rash on his arm. He had to have gotten it rolling Inspector Grinsell through the nettles into the trench. But when I asked—the proper little nurse, mind you, always caring—he told me a cat had rubbed against him outside the pub and he was allergic to cats."

Dang, Jean thought. If only Parkinson's story at the concert of Hildy and the bacon had tipped off her loup of logic earlier. If only she'd seen the rash on his arm rather than his aimless scratching. But even her Byzantine thought processes only went so far.

If only I had known.

Lance quietly vomited over the edge of the porch, Hector steadying his shoulders.

"By then I was right scared of him," Niamh went on. "I decided better to let him play me for a fool. I spent all evening chatting with him. He said Grinsell had mistreated Mum all these years ago. He was right about that. But why was Mum there for the mistreating? Because of Donal's—he's never Dad—Donal's own bad decisions."

Maggie said dryly—and her voice was probably the only dry thing about her, "He claimed he never stepped forward at my trial to protect you and your mum."

"He said that, yes. He said if not for you, I'd have had a dad."

Alasdair asked, "Did he say anything about Grinsell at all?"

"No. Even though he knew I knew—allergic to a cat, my left foot." She inhaled shakily. "I kept thinking I was making him see reason. I kept thinking I was talking him into turning himself in. I even gave him my word I'd not try to escape, that I'd not work against him, if he'd not hurt Maggie."

"Niamh . . ." Maggie began.

Niamh held up her hand, palm forward. *Don't say it.* "I felt sorry for him. He was pitiful. But then he made me let him into the kitchen door of the house. He opened the door behind

Lance and hit him with a stone dragon from the curio cabinet and took the gun away. He threw Tara down and tied her up. It's as though every time he saw her he saw you, Maggie. He was saying ugly, spiteful, loony things. I hated him then. I had to do something. But unlike him, I keep my word."

"You brought me round," said Lance thickly as he settled back against the post. "You helped me up. You got me to the door."

"And I prayed. I didn't know I knew so many prayers. Blessed Saint Mary. Blessed Saint Hilda. Blessed Saint Genevieve. All the holy women associated with Farnaby."

"They listened," said Hector.

Webber looked over at Crawford, who had by now lowered the gun but hadn't otherwise moved. "Constable, are you all right?"

With a sigh that seemed to come from his toes and a desolate look in his eye, Crawford extended the shotgun toward Alasdair. "Look at this, sir."

Squeezing Jean's hand, Alasdair released it and accepted the shotgun. He held it horizontally between him and Webber, the porch light gleaming equally on his straight blond hair stroked with frost and Webber's curly black hair flecked with snow. "Aye, Constable?"

"On the stock, sir."

As Alasdair tilted the gun, two initials leaped into resolution. A and C. "What?" Jean asked, and then realized they didn't stand for Alasdair Cameron. They stood for Athelstan Crawford.

Clyde pulled himself to his feet and took an unsteady step forward. "I was thinking that was the one Lance took from the safe. Aye, it's been hidden away all these years. We found it in Athelstan's boat, my father and me. Seemed only right we should be finding the boat, when we were guiding the trek that ended so badly. Though someone said now—it was Athelstan

. . ." His voice died away at the look on Crawford's face, mirroring the look on Maggie's. The wheel of fate had rolled over them, crushed them, and moved on, leaving them still standing.

Alasdair extended his hand to Crawford. "Well done."

"Begging your pardon, sir." Crawford looked down at his own hands stained with crimson darkening to rust.

"Ah." Nodding, Alasdair desisted.

Webber considered Hector in his kilt. He looked Alasdair up and down, from epaulettes to kilt to tall stockings. "Mr. Cameron. Are you and your lads always wearing your glad rags whilst on duty?"

Alasdair's glance downward was annotated by an upward lift to his brows and a tilt of his head toward Jean. "I cannot speak for Mr. Cruz, but I only started in the last year or so. I have a bad influence now. Women are like that, you ken."

"Well then," said Darling over Niamh's head. "It's done and dusted."

Jean followed the direction of Maggie's gaze, from the lighted porch past the darkened cemetery to the shadowed walls of the priory, and said, "Not yet. Not quite yet."

Chapter Thirty-Eight

Jean stood at the bedroom window watching the mist curl from the sea into the brilliant blue of the noon sky, each wispy whorl a spirit summoned upward by the grace of God.

The debriefing in the incident room had lasted nearly until a dawn as hazy and bleary as Jean's brain had been. Even when she'd gone back to the Angle's Rest she'd lain awake, replaying each scene of the last—had it been little more than thirty-six?—hours, until Alasdair finally came trudging in.

He'd fallen instantly into a sound sleep. She'd tossed and turned until the chanting of the ghostly nuns in the priory consoled her exfoliated nerves and she slept at last.

Now she felt more like a bit of flotsam cast up on the shore of reality than a graceful spirit, but even that was an improvement. Nothing like Pen's warm, fragrant, and delicious breakfast and Hugh's unwavering if wan face across the table to help the healing process. The restoration of the status quo. For her and Alasdair, anyway.

Below her, the concrete jaws of the harbor seemed oddly empty without the large police boat floating inside them. Even Crawford's speedboat was gone, along with Crawford himself, who'd left his Farnaby family for his family in Bamburgh. There were no policemen at all on the island now—well, except for the once-again retired one, who was unplugging his phone from its charger across the room.

There were no dead bodies on the island, either. Athelstan,

Grinsell, Donal—their mortal shells were scientific displays in Berwick. So was the flashlight. And the chanter, a *memento mori,* a souvenir of death if ever there was one.

"I don't see how anyone can ever play that chanter again," Jean said aloud.

"Best you be asking Michael that," replied Alasdair. "I'm no musician."

"I don't mean whether it can be restored. I mean it has to have too many bad vibes—listen to me. Bad vibes."

Alasdair favored her with a dry chuckle.

"You may not be a musician, but you have your talents," Jean added, shooting a meaningful glance across the crumpled if chaste expanse of the bed, but he was peering at his phone.

She turned back to the window, thinking that music threw a bridge across the gulf between this world and the next, whereas the gulf between the world of Farnaby and that of the mainland was covered by the ferry that was coming around the headland. Jean detected Lance's blond head next to the wheelhouse. Good. He'd gotten in and out of the hospital quickly. Nothing like a thick skull—well, Alasdair had said that of Grinsell, too. But Donal had only hit Lance once.

"Good morning, Sergeant," said Alasdair. "You've left a message . . . Ah, the forensic accountant checking over Wat's finances? Is that so? Well now."

Jean went into the bathroom to brush her teeth, emerging as Alasdair ended the call. "You don't mean," she asked, "there really is something about the Lauders' money issues that contributed to Athelstan's death? Once we figured out what happened to him, that it was Elaine, not Wat . . ."

"We were thinking the financial enquiries a dead end, aye. But Darling had already put it to the accountant. Who's turned up the fact that Elaine's family in Yorkshire, the Peverils, were—still are, come to that—landed gentry. The sort with money, not the sort living on pedigree and tourism. Chances are she and Athelstan first met when he and his team were working on the property."

"Really? She might have known Athelstan before she knew Wat? And she had money of her own? There's a motive not for murder but for Wat's possessiveness. Not that some guys need any more motive than testosterone."

"Plenty of folk teeming with estrogen can imagine themselves threatened." Alasdair threw Jean her coat. "Let's be off. We've got one more chance at a grand opening before going back to town."

"In spite of it all, Maggie's still hoping."

Hildy sat in the window, her nose against the glass, ears pricked forward. As one, Alasdair and Jean diverted to her side and followed her gaze. Cats, too, had the ability to cross dimensions.

Four corporeal women strolled past the cemetery toward the priory. Elaine in her canvas hat, Maggie and Tara carrying the battery packs for the photographer's lights, Niamh bringing up the rear in the manner of a sheep dog. From this distance Jean couldn't see any of their expressions, but in the body language of the youngest three she discerned the solid steps of determination rather than the droop of weariness.

Who, she wondered, had scrubbed the blood off the front porch, the door, the wall, the lovely scalloped trim? Any of the women of Gow House? Or had Pen been out there in the misty morning, setting the world to rights in her guise as domestic goddess and guardian of the hearth?

No way was she going to point out to Alasdair that she'd been right about Maggie and Niamh all along. But she couldn't help saying, "If you'd let me talk to Pen I'd have found out who Crawford was."

"Aye, and then Grinsell or Darling would have had to go taking him off the case. He would not have been there saving Tara's life."

"You're going to sound like a believer in destiny if you're not careful."

"Destiny. Fate. The old Celtic *wyrd,* I'm thinking, leading on to our own *weird.*"

"That's actually Anglo-Saxon. Maybe Norse. Whatever—it works for me."

"Right," he said. Somewhere little Linda giggled happily, a sound that drew Jean's face into a smile. Even Alasdair's expression decompressed. They'd come, they'd seen, they'd hardly conquered. But they'd dealt.

Side by side they stepped down the staircase and emerged from the stone walls of the house into the tender light of an early spring day. Together they paused on the doorstep—a mighty symbol that, a doorstep—admiring the sunlight, the green hills, the blue sea, the spiraling birds. Back in Texas, Jean thought, April tended to be the first month of summer. Here, summer was a couple of months away, depending. Down Under, April was autumn. It was all in the location as well as the perception.

They walked through the tunnel of Cuddy's Close, which still held the chill of the night before, and on up to the priory. Jean glanced toward the Victorian church but saw no one there. So this wasn't the Sunday of the monthly service. Ah well. Today she felt considerably more spiritual out in nature.

No pun intended, she thought, when she and Alasdair skirted the faint paranormal resonance of the priory church.

The sound of earthbound church bells resonated faintly on the wind—St. Mary's on Lindisfarne calling her worshipers, no doubt—as they entered the chantry chapel. Tara was saying, ". . . not my worst decision ever. I didn't mean it, Mags. I'm glad I came."

"I'm glad as well," Maggie replied. "I don't blame you for wondering what family you've connected up with, though. Ah. Jean. Alasdair. Here we are again, eh?"

"Here we are again," stated Alasdair.

Maggie and Tara spaced the lights around the blue tarp still covering the tomb, since the roof cast a shadow even in today's bright sunlight. Jean wasn't sure which of the two women looked worse, eyes swollen, cheeks hollow, faces creased like unmade beds. She decided she'd give that dubious honor to Maggie—Tara at least had youth on her side.

Elaine peered down into one of the trenches, frowning slightly, as though trying to place a familiar face. Niamh hovered nearby, her phone to her ear, her back turned, so that Jean heard only the name "Rufus."

Who? Oh! Sergeant Rufus Darling. How nice!

Jean joined the others at the altar end of the chapel as Alasdair approached Maggie not about the mating potential of Darling but about the information he'd gleaned from the forensic accountant. ". . . any idea of your mother's financial situation? Was it a source of conflict between her and your father?"

Maggie starting pulling out the stakes holding down the blue tarp. No one spoke until she and Tara had rolled it back and revealed that the rectangular cavity was as empty today as it had been yesterday.

Then she said, "Money was a conflict, yes. Mum had her own, and she never let Dad forget it. Pen says she's the one wanted Merlin's Tower renovated into a music school. Dad wouldn't let her pay for it, insisted on borrowing the money. Then, when—well, we know now why she dropped her plans for that—when that fell through, Dad returned the borrowed money and worked himself almost to death to earn enough for the new building. He wouldn't let Mum contribute anything, he was that resentful. He had his school, she had hers—Cambridge and her literary work."

"Jean found a set of accounting books in Athelstan's office, ones marked with Elaine's name. She looked after her own money, separate from Wat's?"

"Yes, although whether that was meant to help matters with him or exacerbate them, I've got no idea." She looked over at Elaine, who now stood gazing up at the beams of the ceiling, her face, caught in a shimmer from the window, looking like that of a saint from an illuminated manuscript. "Usually the longer ago it happened, the more likely it is that Mum remembers it. But Athelstan's death is too confusing for her. It's there, but it's not there as it actually happened—you saw that last night, Jean."

"Yes," was all Jean said, even as she thought, *I saw too damn much last night.*

Niamh thrust her phone into her pocket and approached the dais. Of the three, she seemed the best for wear, even though lines now bracketed her pink lips that hadn't been there earlier and the cornflower blue of her eyes seemed a shade less vivid. "How are you doing?" Jean asked.

"It's like an illness. Time's wanted for a full recovery."

"Oh aye," Alasdair said. "I reckon Berwick's got counselors . . ."

"I've got one, thank you just the same." And the faintest blush rose into Niamh's cheeks. Jean could have counseled Niamh about falling for a policeman, but didn't.

With perfect if oblivious timing, Michael and Rebecca entered the chapel and redirected the conversation. "If there's anything in your grave after all, Maggie," he said, "we'd best be seeing it soon. We've got homes and jobs in the city and the ferry's closing down late this afternoon."

"And it may take us that long to liberate Linda from Pen,"

Rebecca added.

"All right then. If my lovely assistant can sit by . . ." Tara took her place with the tray of implements and the camera. "Ready, steady, go." Maggie stretched out on her stomach, looking like a penitent prostrate before the—well, the altar was no longer there, was it? With a trowel she reached into the grave.

That stone must be cold, hard, and damp against her chest and stomach, Jean thought. But she knew better than most how needs must take second stage when the devil of curiosity drives.

Everyone except for Elaine inched forward. She strolled over to the broken pieces of the inscription and sat down in front of it.

Jean couldn't now remember exactly where she'd caught that quick gleam—more or less in the middle of the dark oozing rectangle, where Maggie had inserted her probe.

Maggie's trowel scraped lightly, soundlessly, at the mud, moving a few dark flecks at a time. A minute passed. Then two. And light flared like a struck match.

A chorus of startled exclamations echoed back from the bare stone walls. Tara, too, stretched out on the flagstone, using the camera from the tool tray to take photo after photo.

Maggie's hand made tiny, delicate movements, no more than kissing the mud, and in the flashes of light the bottom of the grave blazed brighter and brighter.

Jean almost overbalanced trying to see, until Alasdair's strong hand grasped her upper arm. But he, too, strained forward, along with Michael, Rebecca, and Niamh. "Have a care," Maggie snapped, and each pair of feet stopped where it was and shuffled back half a pace or so.

Maggie reached for a small sponge-tipped paintbrush and mopped. "What do you see?" Jean asked, expecting her to reply, as Howard Carter did upon opening Tut's tomb, "Wonderful things."

"Roman solidi. Gold coins. There's more. Curved gold rims and red inlays . . . Oh, my God. I don't believe this." Her voice trembled, with relief, Jean estimated, and with more than a little gratitude.

Maggie sat up. For a long moment she peered into the bottom of the grave, the lines in her face perceptibly lightening, the darkness in her eyes clearing. Then she raised her gaze to her mother sitting cross-legged in front of the inscription, leaning forward, running her forefinger along the carvings. *"Uxor draconis,"* the old woman crooned, as though she herself was cantarist.

"Uxor domini," said Michael. "Either the wife of a temporal lord, or a bride of Christ, a nun."

Rebecca said, "Surely this was Prioress Hilda's grave. But Christians don't bury their dead with grave goods."

"Maybe it was her grave once," said Maggie. "Maybe the reused coffin never had a bottom, so she could lie directly in the earth. Maybe when the Viking raiders came the nuns gathered up her bones, her sacred relics, and carried them to a place of safety the way the monks on Lindisfarne carried away Saint Cuthbert's bones."

"Which are now in Durham Cathedral," said Jean. "He's just about the only English saint still in his shrine."

Maggie nodded. "Where Saint Hilda is now, we don't know."

Other than watching over her priory. Jean took the opportunity to kneel down beside the hole and have a good look at the emerging treasure.

She counted nine gold coins, all or partially exposed. Some were turned up heads, showing the profile of a Roman emperor. The inscriptions were too muddy for her to read, but she thought one of them might be the name of Constantine, the emperor who had legitimized Christianity in the Empire. The coins turned up tails were embossed with statues of gods, including one that was a dead ringer for the classic image of Britannia.

Next to them a scattering of lumps emerged from the muck, gold edges holding insets of—garnet, Jean supposed—a deep red gemstone, anyway. Items so delicate and fine that it seemed impossible they could have been made without modern magnifying glasses and lighting. "Anglo-Saxon rings and clasps and sword decorations? You can make a good case the grave, if not the chapel, dates back to the original Celtic foundation. Plus—wow! It's a real treasure trove!"

"You'll be notifying the authorities," stated Alasdair. "Beyond them, though, I'd be keeping this secret. You're not wanting the island overrun with metal detectorists and amateur diggers."

"Good heavens, no. Rigorous excavation. Everything by the book." A grin lurked in Maggie's lips and cheeks.

Jean considered the vertical flagstones lining the cavity behind the sheets of gray lead. "Was this an ancient site once? A large prehistoric cist grave that was converted, so to speak, when the Christians moved in?"

"It's possible."

"But why is there a treasure here if it was once Saint Hilda's grave?" Tara asked.

"Sometimes churches served as banks," replied Maggie. "People would leave their precious items there to protect them from the raiders, Angles perhaps—they first landed in this area—or, later, when the Anglo-Saxons themselves became the targets of Viking raids."

"You're thinking folk carried away Hilda's remains and left the priory's treasure in what had once been her grave?" asked Michael. "Ah, poor sods, if they could rescue only the one treasure, which one to choose? The spiritual one or the temporal one?"

"There's their choice." Jean pulled back from the brink, her eyes still dazzled by the gold. Incorruptible gold, like the bodies of saints. Unlike the body that had lain here for forty years, in darkness and in secrecy. "There's a clue in the late attribution to Genevieve, who saved—well, Paris is a treasure, I guess—from barbarians."

"It's beautiful now," said Rebecca. "Imagine what it'll look like when it's cleaned and displayed and studied. It's a third kind of treasure: academic. It'll make your reputation, Maggie."

"What I was after all along." Maggie's grin broke free, romped across her face, and then dulled when she turned once again toward her mother.

Jean knew what she was thinking: If Elaine had ever opened the grave, she'd have found, if not exact confirmation of her theories, at least a spot in the history books. But by hiding Athelstan's body there, she'd deprived herself of any such conclusion.

There had to be some sort of metaphor in that.

Jean stood up, meeting Alasdair's slightly amused eyes. Treasure trove. Gold coins—or one gold coin, at least. The case that had first brought them together. *Been there, done that, worn the matching T-shirts for a year now.*

A male voice spoke from behind the group and they all spun around, even Elaine, who greeted Lance with a smile. She bounded to her feet and walked toward him. "Get your bodhran, lad. Let's have us a sing-song!"

"Later, Elaine," he returned politely, and kept on walking toward the altar end of the chapel. Specifically to the spot where Tara lay. "I stopped by to see how Tara's—how all you ladies are getting on."

Accepting his hand, Tara rose from her prone position. "We're getting along pretty good, considering. How's that hard head of yours doing?"

"It's not even cracked, though they're telling me my brain

must have sloshed about a bit. I don't remember what happened, not directly, just you helping me," he said to Niamh.

"It's my job," she told him, and ducked aside to follow Elaine toward the door of the church before anyone could point out the circumstances had been a lot more complex than that.

"They tell me I was a bit of a hero. All I remember is thinking that Tara was in danger. I'm sorry I missed the details."

"I wish we'd all missed the details," said Tara, with feeling. Lance raised his arm, hesitated, and instead of placing it around her shoulders patted her arm. She didn't flinch.

Rebecca and Michael swapped looks, hers a comment on developing relationships, his slightly puzzled. There'd been a perturbation in the orbits of Mars and Venus, but he wasn't picking up quite what had caused it.

Men, Jean thought affectionately. Testosterone did have its points, driving even a semi-conscious man to protect the female of the species. "Lance, right before the ferry landed Friday afternoon, you referred to Maggie as Loony Lauder. Where did you pick that up?"

Lance shook his head and winced. "Did I? Don't remember. And I'm not saying that because I was concussed . . . Oh, yeh, I do remember, it was someone coming back on the ferry that day who called her that. Dad said it was Elaine's nickname once. I thought it was funny, I reckon, and passed it on."

Maggie caught Jean's eye. Alasdair nodded. They knew who Lance had overheard. Donal McCarthy, yet to break out of his Bill Parkinson chrysalis and reveal his true nature as a reptile.

Tara elbowed Lance in the ribs. "Hey, I'm a Lauder too, you know."

His smile was brighter than the lights shining down into the grave. "I shan't be holding that against you," he told her, and then, as if afraid he'd presumed too much, looked down into the pit. "What's on here?"

Maggie, Tara, Michael, and Rebecca all gathered around the grave, pointing and explaining. Niamh stopped several paces behind Elaine, pulled out her phone, and started texting. A heads-up to Darling that Farnaby was a place of treasure as well as of death? Or no more than a casual comment?

Through the empty doorway into the church Jean saw movement. A woman wearing a simple woolen shift and an off-white veil glided among the column bases. A woman who appeared thoroughly corporeal, except that she cast no shadow.

Elaine stepped forward to meet her. To meet the ghost, Jean's neck hairs informed her, of the enchanted prioress. Who exchanged a gracious nod with the woman, saint greeting sinner and back again.

Alasdair's hands grasped Jean's arms, just as they had when they sensed the ghost going into the chapel on Friday. Just as they had when they saw their first mutual ghost almost a year ago. His voice whispered in her ear. "There you are. Elaine's seeing the dead."

"But whether the dead are communicating with her . . ." Jean's whisper died away on a breath. "It doesn't matter, not now."

Elaine and Hilda turned as one. The living woman held out a hand. The discarnate woman raised hers in a gesture of blessing. And, as the chorus of nuns chanted the midday service, the shambling shape of George Grinsell walked toward them. Perhaps he would allow himself to be drawn from profane to sacred time and beyond. Perhaps he would turn his back on the women reaching out to him, and choose purgatory.

Elaine stood there all alone, her hand outstretched. Niamh finished her message, tucked her phone into her pocket, and took Elaine's arm. "Let's go home, shall we?"

Young woman and old walked away into the mingled light and shadow of Farnaby Priory.

"Home," repeated Alasdair. "Time we were packing ourselves up and getting on."

"Our work here is done," Jean replied.

As one, the couple emerged from the shade of the chantry chapel into the sunshine of an Avalon that was more than myth, if less than real, and took the first steps of the journey back to the mainland of their lives.

ABOUT THE AUTHOR

Lillian Stewart Carl has wandered countless British single-track roads, from Orkney to Dover and back again. She has also excavated the Biblical city of Gezer in Israel, worn a pink and mauve sari to a wedding in Hyderabad, India, searched for Middle-earth in New Zealand, and sung "Waltzing Matilda" in a haunted cottage in the Australian outback. No surprise her fiction evokes a mythical past, even in contemporary settings.

The Avalon Chanter is book number seven in the Jean Fairbairn/Alasdair Cameron series—America's exile and Scotland's finest on the trail of all-too-living legends.

Lillian is also the author of twenty-five short stories and a dozen other novels that range from science fiction and heroic fantasy to mystery to paranormal romantic suspense. She is the co-editor of *The Vorkosigan Companion,* which was nominated for a Hugo Award.

Her website is *www.lillianstewartcarl.com.*

DISCARD